MARRIED LIFE

Or The True Romance

MAY EDGINTON

1st WORLD
LIBRARY
Literary Society

Married Life

May Edginton

© 1st World Library, 2007
PO Box 2211
Fairfield, IA 52556
www.1stworldlibrary.com
First Edition

LCCN: 2007927844

Softcover ISBN: 978-1-4218-4560-9
Hardcover ISBN: 978-1-4218-4476-3
eBook ISBN: 978-1-4218-4644-6

Purchase *"Married Life"*
as a traditional bound book at:
www.1stWorldLibrary.com/purchase.asp?ISBN= 978-1-4218-4560-9

1st World Library is a literary, educational organization
dedicated to:

- Creating a free internet library of downloadable ebooks

- Hosting writing competitions and offering book publishing
  scholarships.

Interested in more 1st World Library books? contact:
literacy@1stworldlibrary.com

Check us out at: www.1stworldlibrary.com

1ˢᵗ World Library Literary Society

Giving Back to the World

"If you want to work on the core problem, it's early school literacy."

- James Barksdale, former CEO of Netscape

"No skill is more crucial to the future of a child, or to a democratic and prosperous society, than literacy."

- Los Angeles Times

"Literacy... means far more than learning how to read and write... The aim is to transmit... knowledge and promote social participation."

- UNESCO

"Literacy is not a luxury, it is a right and a responsibility. If our world is to meet the challenges of the twenty-first century we must harness the energy and creativity of all our citizens."

- President Bill Clinton

"Parents should be encouraged to read to their children, and teachers should be equipped with all available techniques for teaching literacy, so the varying needs and capacities of individual kids can be taken into account."

- Hugh Mackay

IN ADMIRATION

TO

A COMPLETELY SUCCESSFUL HUSBAND

CONTENTS

CHAPTER I

ANTICIPATION

"I've been round all the sales," said Marie, "hunting and hunting. My feet are tired! But I've got a lovely lot of things. Look! All this washing ribbon, a penny a yard. And these caps—aren't they the last word? Julia, aren't they ducks? I thought I'd have my little caps all alike, flesh-pink tulle."

"When'll you wear them?" asked Julia hardily.

"When do other people wear them?" retorted Marie, rather confused.

"Have you ever worn things like this?"

"Well," said Marie, "perhaps not. But I've been saving up two years for it, haven't I? And if a girl can't have pretty things in her trousseau, when can she have them?"

Julia sighed and looked. There was a little clutch at her heart, but she went on sturdily:

"All you girls going to be married! I don't know what you expect! I know what you'll get. You seem to think a husband's a cross between Romeo and a fairy godmother.

Well, you'll find it's different. You all imagine, when you say good-bye to your typewriter, or the showroom, or whatever line you're in, to marry on an income not so very much bigger than your own, that you're going to live in a palace and be waited upon ever afterwards. You'll have to get up early and cook Osborn's breakfast, shan't you, before he goes out? And make the beds and sweep and dust? And you're buying pink tulle caps as if you were going to breakfast in bed every day!"

"A little housework's nothing! A girl can wear pretty things when she's married, I suppose?"

"Oh, she *can*."

"She ought to. A man has a right to expect—"

"You'll find a man expects everything he has a right to, and a hundred per cent. more."

"Osborn is very different from most men."

Julia smiled, stood up, and pressed her hands over her hips to settle her skirt smoothly; she had an air of abandoning the talk as useless. Her eyes were tired and her mouth drooped.

"It isn't as though you knew such a great deal about men, dear," Marie added.

"I don't want to," said Julia.

"Surely, you must like Osborn?"

"What does it matter whether I do or don't, since you do?"

"I can't think how anyone can fail to like Osborn."

"Of course you can't."

"Even you must own he's the best-tempered boy living."

"I shan't own anything of the kind till you've been married three months, and he's had some bad dinners, and late breakfasts, and has got a bit sick of the butcher's bill. Then we'll see."

"Little things like these can't matter between people who really love each other. You don't understand."

"It's just these little things that take the edge off."

Marie's mother looked in and smiled to see her girl fingering her pretty things.

"Aren't you two nearly ready to leave the inspection and come to tea?"

"Julia doesn't like my caps, mum."

"Yes, I do," said Julia; "all I'm asking, Mrs. Amber, is, when is she going to wear them?"

Marie's mother came in and sat down and thought.

"Ah," she said, shaking her head and looking pinched about the lips, "I don't know. You modern girls buy all these extraordinary things. You ape rich women; but you'll never be able to pay the everlasting cleaners' bills for those caps."

"She'll soon give up wearing them, Mrs. Amber."

"I'm sure I shan't," Marie denied.

"When I was a girl," said Mrs. Amber, smoothing her lap reminiscently, "I remember I wanted a grand trousseau. But girls lived at home more in those days; they didn't go out typing and what not, earning money for themselves. So I couldn't buy what I wanted and my dear mother had too much sense to buy it for me. I had strong, useful things, twelve of everything, and they've lasted to this day. However, Marie thinks differently and she has earned the money to act differently, so let her be happy in her own way while she can."

"Won't she be happy when she's married?" Julia asked, while Marie angrily hid her treasures away in tissue paper.

"I hope so," said Mrs. Amber; "I'm sure I hope so. But things are all so different when you're married. You girls had better come to tea."

Julia linked her arm strongly in Marie's as they followed the elderly woman out. "Marie, love," she whispered, "I'm a grouser. You know I wish you all the luck in the world and more. You know I do?"

"I have it," said Marie, smiling. "And I hope you'll have it, too, before long."

On the sitting-room table tea was spread; the room was red in the firelight; and the flat was so high up in the block that the street noises scarcely ascended to it. The girls sat down on the hearthrug, and Mrs. Amber seated herself before her tea tray and flicked away a tear.

"A week to-day," she said, "I shall be the loneliest old thing in London. I shall be all by myself in this flat when Marie's gone."

There were five cups and saucers on the tray, and in a moment the door-bell rang, and Marie sprang up to answer it. "That's Osborn!" she cried in a flutter.

She returned demurely between two young men, one of them holding her hand captive.

Osborn had brought his friend Desmond Rokeby to talk over details of the great event next week. He kissed Mrs. Amber on the cheek, and turned to Julia with a certain diffidence. "Miss Winter," he said, with a nervous laugh, "I've brought Rokeby. You've met him? Rokeby, Miss Winter's going to be Marie's bridesmaid, you know, and you're going to be mine, so...."

The little joke was received with laughter by Mrs. Amber, Marie and Desmond; Julia only smiled and Rokeby thought, "What a dour young female! What a cold douche! What a perishing mistake!"

He sat down beside her on the chesterfield; the couch was small and Julia, close beside him, cold and hard as a rock. He turned from a glance at her profile to contemplate the bride-elect, and saw in her all that the modern young man wishes to find in a girl, the sparkle of spirit, yet the feminine softness; a frou-frou of temperament as well as of frills; a face of childlike clarity set with two gay eyes; hair dressed to tempt and cajole; a little figure of thin frailty that gave her a beautiful delicacy of appearance; little, modish, manicured hands.

She had such pretty arts; she fluttered about small domestic duties with a delight dainty to see. She set a man imagining how desirable it would be to build a nest for this delicate dear bird, and take her to it, and live deliciously ever afterwards. This is what Osborn Kerr imagined while—like

Rokeby—he watched her. He had never seen her other than pretty and dainty, than happy and gay; he could not conceive of her otherwise. He had not the faintest doubt of being able to keep her so, in that nest which he had built for two on the other side of town. Whenever it was possible, in the teacup passing, he tried to touch her hand; he longed for her to look at him; he wanted her all to himself.

A week seemed over-long to wait.

Mrs. Amber watched him with a resigned and kindly eye. She was sighing a little, kindly and resignedly, in her mind, and thinking how alike men were in their courting. And presently, while Julia and Desmond conversed with a formal hostility on the chesterfield, and the lovers snatched brief moments for communication in lovers' code, she said:

"Osborn, another present came to-day; it's in the dining-room; Marie ought to show it to you."

"Will you, Marie?" asked the young man, while his heart leapt, and the pulses in his head seemed singing like larks on a summer morning.

"Would you care to see it?" she replied, with a studied sedateness which Osborn found unutterably sweet, and which did not in the least deceive the watching mother.

And in a moment the two were alone, it seemed in another world. This new world was compassed by the walls of the slip of an apartment called the dining-room, but which was kitchen as well, for there were no maids in the flat. The top of the oak dresser had been cleared of its bits of blue china and pewter to make way for the array of wedding gifts, and they were presented bravely. Perhaps among the display was the last received of which Mrs. Amber spoke, but whether it was, or was not, neither Marie nor Osborn cared.

They were alone.

There had pressed upon them, hard and perpetually, during the eighteen months of their engagement, the many difficulties with which opportunity is cautiously guarded by its custodians. They met in restaurants, in parks, and in the homes of either, and seldom could they be alone; and because they were superior people, not of the class which loves unashamedly in the public places if it has nowhere else to love, they restrained themselves. It was a long and hard probation, lightened sometimes, some rare and precious times, by such moments as now occurred. As soon as the kitchen-dining-room door closed behind them like the portals of sanctuary, Osborn held out his arms and Marie went to them. She rested there while Osborn kissed her with hard, devouring kisses which made her murmur little pleased protests.

All the while she was thinking, "A week to-day!" Her eyes travelled to the clock. "At six o'clock, a week this afternoon, I shall be Mrs. Kerr. We shall be at the hotel, unpacking."

"Not very long now," said Osborn between his kisses. "Soon we'll be alone as much as we like. We'll be able to shut our own door on everybody. Won't it be priceless?"

Marie thought it would. She fingered his coat lapels with her modish hands, and smiled with downcast eyelashes. In happy procession her dreams paraded by. She flitted a glance up at Osborn's face for a moment and looked down again. He was good-looking; he was the best-looking man she knew; his clothes were so good; his voice was so charming; he had no mean streak like some men; he was all gold. He was generous. Even while he had been spending all his bank balance, and more, on that nest for her at the other side of town, it had been delightful to be taken out by him to the nicest restaurants, hear chic dinners and good wines ordered with a thrilling lavishness. Many girls must envy her.

"A lot of fellows will envy me," Osborn murmured even while Marie thought her thoughts.

She protested again with soft words and the procession of dreams went by. The little home—how charming it would be! The chintz that matched her two best trousseau frocks, the solidity and polish of her dining-room chairs, the white paint and pale spring colours of her sitting-room, how ravishing it all was! The conveniences of the kitchen, the latest household apparatus, would they not make the keeping of the perfect flat a sort of toy occupation for a pretty girl's few serious moments? In spite of Julia, all would be easy and sweet. In a kimono and one of those pink caps one could cook a breakfast without soiling one's fingers. Osborn would like to see his wife look beautiful behind the coffeepot. She would manage splendidly. The income, of course, would seem small to some women, muddleheads, but she *could* manage. She could make the most darling clothes, bake cakes like a confectioner's. Osborn would be surprised.

She must have a pink pinafore, a smocked one.

What would it be like, the first few days together?

"Come and sit down," Osborn begged, and he drew her to the one big chair, into which they both squeezed. "I love you," he said, "oh, I *do* love you! And we can trust old Rokeby to look after your mother and Julia. What a terror the girl is!"

"She hates men," said Marie, with a pouting mouth.

May Edginton

"Then they will hate her and I don't wonder," the young man replied scornfully.

"Don't let us talk about Julia."

"No, let's talk about us. I bought the clock, darling."

"The clock! Did they knock down the price?"

"No, they didn't," said Osborn, "but you wanted it and that was good enough for me."

Her eyes sparkled. "You shouldn't be extravagant on my account."

"Let me kiss you," said Osborn, "that's all I want. You liked the old clock, and it will look ripping in the hall, won't it?"

"We shall be *all* oak now."

"Say you're pleased, then, you beautiful."

"I am. I did want that clock. A grandfather clock—I don't know—there's something about it."

"As for the price, sweetheart, why bother? It'll only add a few more instalments to the whole bally lump. It will be all right. I'll get a rise soon—married man, you know! Responsibilities, you know! Expenses!"

"Mother's starting us with every kind of saucepan and broom and brush you can think of."

"Bless her!"

"Osborn, it will be an awf'ly *smart* flat."

"It will, with you in it."

"No, but really. Everyone will admire it. I mean everyone to admire. We'll have some little dinner-parties, won't we?"

"Will we, Cook?"

"I shall make the sweets beforehand, and we'll have chafing-dish or casserole things. That sort of dinner. It's quite smart, Osborn. And dessert's easy. Julia's giving us finger bowls, tip-top ones—real cut-glass."

"Bless her!"

"We're starting awf'ly well, Osborn."

"Do you think I don't know that? We love each other; nothing ever goes wrong when people love each other. You'll be glad enough to give up the office, too, won't you?"

"*Won't I!*"

"I know you will. I hate to have you in a City office, with any bounder staring at you. When you're Mrs. Kerr only I can stare."

"I like your confidence!"

"But I shall make up for everyone. I shall stare all the time."

"Shall you want to go to the club every evening?"

"I shan't ever want to go to the club."

Although Marie had known what the answer would be—or she would not have asked the question—it made her very happy. It was delightful to hear only what one wanted to hear; to see only what one wanted to see. Life appeared as a graceful spectacle, a sort of orderly carnival refined to taste. There would, of course, be the big thrill in it—Osborn. It would be wonderful to have him coming home to her successful little dinners every evening. People didn't want a great deal, after all; all the discontented, puling, peevish, wanting people one met must be great fools; they had made their beds and made them wrong; the great thing, the simple secret, was to make them right. A husband and wife must pull together, in everything. Pulling together would be sheer joy.

"Osborn," she said, "how well we understand each other, don't we?"

"I should think we do," whispered the young man.

"Few married people seem really happy."

"They must manage life badly, mustn't they?"

"I remember mother and father; mother likes the idea of my getting married, but they used often to be nagging about something. Expenses, I think."

"All that I have will be yours, you love," said Osborn, with profound tenderness.

"But I shan't ask for it," said Marie, with a flash of intuition. "You don't know how careful I can be. It won't cost you much more than it does now; less, perhaps, because you won't always be dining at the club."

"But you'll come into town and lunch with me very often, shan't you, dearest?"

"Nearly every day."

"Hush!"

Osborn got out of the chair and sat on its arm; Marie remained alone in the cushioned depths, looking flushed and brilliant; and Mrs. Amber came in slowly.

"Marie, I want to show Julia your dress; or would you like to show it yourself?"

"Is it *the* dress?" Osborn asked, looking down on the top of Marie's shining head.

Mrs. Amber sighed and smiled and the bride-elect sat up, sparkling.

"I'll come, mother."

"Let me come, too," said Osborn.

"I'll bring it into the sitting-room and let everyone see it, shall I, Marie?" her mother asked hastily.

She hurried away and Marie followed her to the bedroom, while Osborn stood in the doorway, looking in at the two eager women about their joyous errand. He put his hands in his pockets and smiled. It was pleasant to be involved in the bustle about the precious thing they were unwrapping from swathes of tissue paper. "Be careful, dear," the elder woman kept saying, "there's a pin here." Or "Don't hurry, or you'll have the pleats out of place." And Marie's hands trembled over their task. When all the paper was removed, Mrs. Amber said importantly, "Now just lift it up; give it to me like that; I'll carry it in," but Marie cried: "No, I will," and she threw the gown over her shoulder till her head emerged

May Edginton

as from the froth of sea waves, and ran into the sitting-room with it.

Mrs. Amber's eyes were moist with pride. "It's a beautiful dress," she said to Osborn, who had turned eagerly after his girl; "I want her to look sweet. Here, wouldn't you like to take something? Here's the shoes; I've got the stockings. Wouldn't you like to carry the shoes?"

Marie was spreading out the gown on the chesterfield from which Julia and Desmond had risen to make room for it. Mrs. Amber laid the silk stockings reverently near and Osborn dangled his burden, saying gaily: "And here are Mrs. Kerr's slippers."

Rokeby stood back, observing. "It's all out of my line," he said, "but don't think I'm not respectful; I am. What's more, I'm fairly dazzled. I think I'll have to get married."

"You might do worse, old man," replied Osborn joyfully.

Rokeby lighted another cigarette. He looked around the room and at the people in it. He had been familiar with many such interiors and situations, being the kind of man who officiated at weddings but never in the principal part. "Poor old Osborn!" he thought. "Another good man down and out!" He looked at the girl, decked by Art and Nature for her natural conquest. He did not wonder how long her radiance would endure; he thought he knew. He entertained himself by tracing the likeness to her mother, and the mother's slimness had thickened, and her shoulders rounded; her eyes were tired, a little dour; they looked out without enthusiasm at the world, except when they rested upon her daughter. Then they became rather like the eyes of Marie looking at her wedding gown.

* * * * *

Osborn took Marie's head between his hands, and kissed her eyes and mouth. "That's for good night," he whispered; "Rokeby and I are going home. You are the sweetest thing, and I shall dream of you all night. Promise to dream of me."

"It's a certainty."

"It is?" said the young man rapturously. "I am simply *too* happy, then."

"Let's go and look at the flat to-morrow."

"Have tea with me in town, darling, and I'll take you."

Mrs. Amber and Rokeby came out into the hall. Rokeby wore a very patient air, and Marie's mother beamed with that soft and sorrowful pleasure which women have for such circumstances.

"Now say good night," said she softly, "say good night. Good-bye, Mr. Rokeby, and we shall see you again a week to-day?"

"A week to-day."

The two men went out and down the stairs into the street. Rokeby had his air of good-humoured and invincible patience and Osborn dreamed.

"I'll see you right home," said Rokeby.

"And you'll come in, and have a drink."

"Thanks. Perhaps I will. Haven't *you* got a trousseau to

show me?"

"Get out, you fool!"

"What do chaps feel like, I wonder," said Rokeby, "when the day of judgment is so near?"

"I shan't tell you, you damned scoffer!"

"Well, well," said Rokeby, "I've seen lots of nice fellows go under this same way. It always makes me very sorry. I do all I can in the way of preventive measures, but it's never any good, and there's no cure. Ab-so-lutely none. There's no real luck in the business, either, as far as I've seen, though of course some are luckier than others."

"Did you mention luck?" Osborn exclaimed, from his dream. "Don't you think I'm lucky? I say, Desmond, old thing, don't you think I'm one of the most astonishingly lucky fellows on God's earth?"

"You ought to know."

"Oh, come off that silly pedestal of pretence. Cynicism's rotten. Marriage is the only life."

"'Never for me!'" Rokeby quoted Julia.

"Awful girl!" said Osborn, referring to her briefly. "'Orrid female. What?"

"Very handsome," said Rokeby.

"Handsome! I've never seen it. She's not to be compared to Marie, anyway. You haven't answered my question. Don't you think I'm lucky?"

"Yes, you are," replied Rokeby sincerely, turning to look at him, "for any man to be as happy as you seem to be even for five minutes is a great big slice of luck to be remembered."

"Marie's a wonderful girl. She can do absolutely anything, I believe. It seems incredible that a girl with hands like hers can cook and sew, but she can. Isn't it a wonder?"

"It sounds ripping."

They walked on in silence, Osborn back up in his clouds. At last he awaked to say:

"Well, here we are. You'll come in?"

"Shall I?"

"Do. I shan't have so many more evenings of—"

"Freedom—"

"—Of loneliness, confound you! Come in!"

Rokeby followed him into his rooms, on the second floor. A good fire was burning, but they were just bachelor rooms full of hired—and cheap—furniture. As Osborn cast off his overcoat and took Rokeby's, he glanced around expressively.

"You should see the flat. You *will* see it soon. All Marie's arrangement, and absolutely charming."

"Thanks awfully. I'll be your first caller."

"Well, don't forget it. What'll you have?"

"Whiskey, please."

"So'll I."

Osborn gave Desmond one of the two armchairs by the fire, and took the other himself. Another silence fell, during which Rokeby saw Osborn smiling secretly and involuntarily to himself as he had seen other men smile. The man was uplifted; his mind soared in heaven, while his body dwelt in a hired plush chair in the sitting-room of furnished lodgings. Rokeby took his drink, contented not to interrupt; he watched Osborn, and saw the light play over his face, and the thoughts full of beauty come and go. At length, following the direction of some thought, again it was Osborn who broke the mutual quiet, exclaiming:

"I've never shown you her latest portrait!"

"Let's look. I'd love to."

The lover rose, opened the drawer of a writing-table, and took out a photograph, a very modern affair, of most artistic mounting. He handed it jealously to Desmond and was silent while the other man looked. The girl's face, wondrously young and untroubled, frail, angelic, rose from a slender neck and shoulders swathed in a light gauze cloud. Her gay eyes gazed straight out. Rokeby looked longer than he knew, very thoughtfully, and Osborn put his hand upon the portrait, pulled it away as jealously as he had given it, and said:

"They've almost done her justice for once."

"Top-hole, old man," Rokeby replied sympathetically.

CHAPTER II

IRREVOCABLE

When Osborn dressed for his wedding he felt in what he called first-class form. He thought great things of life; life had been amazingly decent to him throughout. It had never struck him any untoward blow. The death of his parents had been sadness, certainly, but it was a natural calamity, the kind every sane man expected sooner or later and braced himself for. His mother had left him a very little money, and his father had left him a very little money; small as the sum total was, it gave a man the comfortable impression of having private means. He paid the first instalments on the dream-flat's furniture with it, and there was some left still, to take Marie and him away on a fine honey-moon, and to brighten their first year with many jollities. His salary was all right for a fellow of his age. Marie was not far wrong when she said that they were starting "awfully well."

Osborn sang:

> "And—when—I—tell—them,
> And I'm certainly going to tell them,
> That I'm the man whose wife you're one day going to be,
> They'll never believe me—"

That latest thing in revue songs fitted the case to a fraction. He was the luckiest man in the whole great round world.

Osborn was pleased with his reflection in the glass. For his wedding he had bought his first morning-coat and silk hat. He had been as excited as a girl. He had a new dress-suit, too, and a dinner-jacket from the best tailor in town, ready packed for travelling. He had been finicking over his coloured shirts, handkerchiefs, and socks; a set of mauve, a set of blue, a set of grey; the brown set with the striped shirt; they were all awf'ly smart. Marie was so dainty, she liked a man to be smart, too. All he wanted was to please her.

Rokeby came early, as quiet and lacklustre as ever. He sat down in the obvious lodging-house bedroom, lighted a cigarette and looked at Osborn without a smile. He prepared himself to be bored and amazed; weddings, tiresome as they were, always amazed him. And he was prepared, too, for a settled insanity in Osborn until—

"I wonder how long *he'll* be?" Rokeby thought.

"I've finished packing," said Osborn, clapping his old brushes together; the new ones lay among the new suits. "It's time we started, almost, isn't it?"

"Not by an hour," Rokeby answered, consulting a wrist watch. "Have you breakfasted?"

"Not yet."

"You'd better, hadn't you?"

Osborn was concerned with the set of the new coat over his fine shoulders.

"Breakfast was on the table when I came through," added Rokeby.

"Was it?" replied Osborn absently.

Rokeby took his friend's arm, piloted him with patient firmness into the sitting-room, and pulled out a chair.

Osborn ate and drank spasmodically. Between the spasms he hummed under his breath:

"And—when—I—tell—them,
And I'm certainly going to tell them,
That I'm the man whose wife you're one day going to be,
They'll never believe me—"

Rokeby smoked several cigarettes.

"How long'll it take us to get to the church?" Osborn asked presently, with his eye on the clock.

"Ten minutes, about. We'll walk."

"Desmond, I say, I wouldn't like to be late."

"I'll look after that. I've escorted a good many fellows to the tumbril."

"Desmond, that nonsense of yours gets boring."

"All right! Sorry."

"Let's start," said Osborn.

So they started on their short walk. The pale gold sun of a splendid crisp morning hailed them and the streets were bright. Already, though they arrived early at the church, several pews were full of whispering guests who turned and looked and smiled, with nods that beckoned, at the two young men.

"What'll we do?" Osborn whispered.

"Hide," said Rokeby.

They hid in a cold, stony little place which Rokeby said was a vestry, and there they waited while interminable minutes drifted by. Osborn fell into a dream from which he was only fully roused by finding himself paraded side by side at the chancel steps with a dazzling apparition, robed in white clouds, veiled and wreathed. She carried a great bouquet. He stole a look at her entrancing profile and thought that never had she looked so lovely. She had a flush on her cheeks, her gay eyes were serious, and her little bare left hand, when, under whispered instructions, he took it, startled him by being tremulous and cold as ice. He pressed it and felt tremendously protective.

An irrevocable Act had taken place without fuss or difficulty, or any abnormal signs and wonders; the gold circle was on Marie's finger and they were married. For a moment or two, while they knelt and a strange clergyman was addressing them, Osborn was surprised at the ease, the speed and simplicity with which two people gave each other their lives. He did not know what else he had expected, but how simple it all was! This was their day of days; their wedding. He stole another look at Marie and found her rapt, calm.

He began to be annoyed with the presence of the clergyman, of Desmond, and Julia, who waited disapprovingly upon the bride, of Marie's mother and the small horde of friends and relations; he began to think, "If only it was over and I had her to myself! In another hour, surely, we'll be away."

*　*　*　*　*

They had chosen one of the most fashionable seaside resorts as an idyllic honeymoon setting. The journey was not long, only long enough to enjoy the amenities of luxurious travelling. Rokeby had seen to the tea-basket and the foot-warmers, as he had to the magazines. Marie repeated what she had said to Julia:

"Oh, isn't it nice, getting married!"

"Being married is nicer," said Osborn ardently. "I'll come and sit beside you. Let's take off your hat. Now, put your head on my shoulder. Isn't it jolly? I want to tell you how beautiful you looked in church. I was half scared."

"So was I at first."

"But you're not now? You're not scared with me?"

"No—no," said Marie with bated breath.

Osborn smiled. "I'm going to make you very happy. You shall be the happiest girl in town. You're going to have absolutely all you want. But first, before we go back to town, there's our honeymoon, the best holiday of our lives. That's joyful to think of, isn't it, darling?"

"It's lovely!"

"Glad you think so, too, Mrs. Kerr."

"Osborn, now tell me how my frock looked."

"I *couldn't!*" he cried in some awe. He sighed as if at a beautiful memory.

"Ah!" said Marie, satisfied, "you liked it?"

She lay against his shoulder supremely content. The winter landscape, which had lost its morning sun, was rushing by them and it looked cold. But inside the honeymoon carriage all was warm, love-lit and glowing. There was no dusk. Marie reviewed the day in her light, clear mind, and it had been very good. Hers had been a wedding such as she had always wanted. Osborn had looked so fine. She reviewed the details so carefully thought out and arranged for by herself and her mother. With the unthinking selfishness of a young gay girl, she discounted the strain on the mother's purse and heart. The favours had been exactly the right thing; the cake was good; the little rooms hadn't seemed at all bad; Aunt Toppy's new gown was an unexpected concession to the occasion; Mrs. Amber had been really almost distinguished; the country cousins hadn't looked too dreadfully rural. People hadn't been stiff, or awkward, or dull. As for Mr. Rokeby—that was a very graceful speech he made. He was rather a gifted man; worth knowing.

But Osborn had very nice friends.

With the agility of woman, her mind jumped ahead to those little dinner-parties. Soup one prepared well beforehand; a chicken, *en casserole*....

Perhaps Osborn saw the abstraction of her mind and was jealous of it; at the moment she must think of nothing save him, as he could think of nothing but her. He put his hand under her chin, to lift her dreamy face, and he kissed her lips possessively.

"Here," he demanded, against them, "what are you thinking about? We're not going to think of anything or anyone but just ourselves. We're going to live entirely in the next glorious fortnight, for a whole fortnight. Have you any objection to that programme, Mrs. Kerr?"

"No, no," said Marie sighing, "no, no! It's beautiful."

CHAPTER III

BEAUTIFUL

The young Kerrs gave themselves a fine time; an amazing time. A dozen times a day they used to tell each other with a solemn delight how amazing it all was. When they awoke in the mornings, in a sleeping apartment far more splendid than any they could ever sanely hope—not that they were sane— to rent for themselves, when an interested if *blasee* chamber- maid entered with early tea, finding Marie in one of the pink caps and a pink matinee over a miraculously frail nightdress, with Osborn hopelessly surprised and admiring, they used to say to each other, while the bride dispensed the tea:

"Isn't it all *nice*? Did you ever imagine anything *could* be so nice?"

When they descended to breakfast, very fresh and spruce, under the eyes of such servants as they could never expect to hire themselves, they looked at each other across the table for two, and touched each other's foot under it and asked: "Doesn't it seem extraordinary to be breakfasting together like this?"

And when one of the cars from the hotel garage was ordered round to take them for a run, and they snuggled side by side on well-sprung cushions such as they would probably never ride upon again, they held hands and exclaimed under their breath: "This is fine, isn't it? I wish this could last for ever! Some day, when our ship comes in, we'll have this make of car."

And when they walked the length of the pier together, two well-clad and well-looking young people, they would gaze out to sea with the same vision, see the infinite prospects of the horizon and say profoundly: "We're out at last on the big voyage. Didn't our engagement seem endless? But now—we're off!"

For dinner, in the great dining-room, with the orchestra playing dimly in the adjacent Palm Court, Mrs. Osborn Kerr would put on the ineffable wedding gown, and all the other guests and the servants, with experienced eyes, would know it for what it was; and Mr. Osborn Kerr wore the dinner jacket from the best tailor in town, and after they had progressed a little with their wine—they had a half-bottle *every* night; what would the bill be?—they would look into each other's eyes of wonder and murmur: "I always knew we'd have a beautiful honeymoon; but I never imagined it could be so beautiful as this."

Later, much later, when the evening's delights had gone by in soft procession, they went to other delights. Osborn brushed Marie's hair with the tortoise shell-back brushes he had given her for a wedding gift, and compared it with the Golden Fleece, the wealth of Sheba, the dust of stars, till she was arrogant with the homage of man and he was drunk with love of her.

They had their great wild happy moment to which every human being has the right, and no one and nothing robbed them of it. It flowed to its close like a summer's day, and the sun set upon it with great promise of a like to-morrow.

But although the most darling dolly home waited for them in a suburb of the great city where Osborn was to work away his young life like other men, although each saw and recognised the promise of the sunset, they were sad at leaving the palace which, for so short a time, they had made-believe was theirs. A reason was present in the mind of each, though, an irrefutable, hard-and-fast reason, why the stay could not be prolonged, even though Osborn might beg, with success, for another week's holiday. Each knew what the now mutual purse held; each, day by day, had privately been adding the price of the half-bottle, and the hire of the car, to the sum of "everything inclusive." Each had, of necessity, a hard young head.

So they went home very punctually.

The hall-porter at the flats knew how newly married they were. So there was a smile upon the face of the tiger and fires burning in Number Thirty; and he carried up the luggage with a kind alacrity; for newly married people were his prey. They thanked him profusely, touched by his native charm, and they gave him five shillings.

They sat down and looked at each other.

"I think it is lovely to be at home," said Marie.

"There's a comfort about one's own place," Osborn answered, "that you don't get anywhere else."

The hall-porter had even wound up the clocks, which Mrs. Amber and Julia had brought, among other wedding presents, a day or two before, and now four strokes sounded from a silvery-voiced pet of a timepiece on the mantelshelf.

The owners looked at it, arrested and pleased.

"It is really the prettiest clock I have ever seen," said Marie.

"I like the tone," said Osborn, "I can't bear a harsh clock. Darling, that's four. You want tea. I'll get it."

"We'll both get it."

"But you're tired with travelling, pretty cat. You'll just sit there and I'll take your boots off and unpack your slippers; and I'll make your tea."

Marie let Osborn do all this, and he enjoyed his activity for her sake as much as she enjoyed her inactivity. He unpinned her hat, took off her coat as a nurse removes a child's coat, kneeled down to unlace her boots, kissed each slim instep, and carried all the things neatly away to their bedroom. Joyfully he unlocked the suit-case where he knew her slippers reposed, for had he not packed them himself, for her, that morning? He returned to the sitting-room and put them on.

"Mrs. Osborn Kerr at home!" he cried, standing to look down upon her.

"I do want my tea!" said Marie.

"I'll get it now, darling. You sit still. I adore waiting upon you," said Osborn, hurrying away.

It was fine to be in his own place, with his own wife, with the world shut out and snubbed. As Osborn strode along the short and narrow corridor to the kitchen he admired everything he saw. He confirmed his own good taste and Marie's. The cream walls with black and white etchings—

more wedding presents—upon them, and the strip of plain rose felt along the floor, could not be bettered. The kitchen was a spotless little place, up-to-date in the matter of cupboards. Everything was as up-to-date as he and Marie were. There was nothing equal to this fresh and modern comfort.

Osborn looked in a cupboard and there he saw foods, enough to begin on, placed there by the thoughtful Mrs. Amber. Upon the kitchen table was a furnished tea-tray, the one woman knowing by instinct what the other woman would first require after her day's journey. Osborn lighted one of the jets of the gas-stove. What a neat stove! A kettle was handy. What a 'cute kettle! Aluminium, wasn't it? None of those common tin things. He filled the kettle from a tap which was a great improvement on any tap which he had ever seen.

They were all his own.

He cut bread-and-butter.

He lighted the grill of the gas-stove and made toast. They had a handsome hot-toast dish.

He hunted for sugary dainties such as Marie loved. Mrs. Amber had provided them in a tin. He arranged them with thought and care.

Wasn't there any cream for his love? There was a tin of it. He emptied the cream out lavishly.

All the while the petted bride rested by the fire in her little chintz room. Life had petted her, her employers had wanted to, and her mother had petted her, but never had she revelled in such supreme petting as the last fortnight's.

Where did all these fierce, man-hating young women whom one met quite often get their ideas from? If only they knew, if only they could be told, could be forced to open their eyes and see, how perfect the right sort of marriage really was!

Why, a man, poor dear, was abject! A girl had things all her own way. Secretly and sweetly Marie smiled over Osborn's devotion.

As she smiled, looking tender and lovely, in the firelight, the door opened, and Osborn came in, perilously balancing his tray on one hand like a waiter. He meant her to laugh at his dexterity; he felt a first-class drawing-room comedian with his domestic attainments. Over one arm he had slung a brand-new teacloth. He intoned unctuously:

"I think I have all you want, madam."

Marie laughed as Osborn wanted her to do.

"Sit still," he urged, "I'll arrange it all. The toast in the fender; the cloth on the table; the tray on the cloth. I understand everything. See, Mrs. Kerr? You won't be the only know-all in this establishment."

Then he waited upon her; but he let her pour out the tea, because he wanted to see her do it, in her own home, for the first time. The situation thrilled both, after a fortnight of thrills.

"I wish Desmond could see us now!" said Osborn.

"I wish Julia could."

"I think we should convert 'em."

Osborn sat on the hearthrug with shoulders against Marie's knees. One of her hands stole round his neck and he held it there; he knew it was the softest small hand in the world; he had no misgivings about it and its tasks. The hour seemed ineffably rosy.

"And to-morrow," he stated, "I go back to work."

"My poor boy," said Marie, "and I shan't work any more."

"Thank heaven, no." Osborn kissed the hand he held.

"This must always stay as soft as rose-leaves," he said fondly.

"You may count on my doing my best for it," said Marie laughing, "I like nice hands. No woman can look well-dressed without nicely-kept hands. And that reminds me, Osborn, I want some more cream for my nails—cuticle-cream it's called. Any good cuticle-cream will do."

He hastened to jot it down in a notebook. His first little commission for his wife! For Miss Amber there had been many, but this was almost epoch-making as being for Mrs. Osborn Kerr. "I'll get it in the dinner-hour, or on my way home. Can't you think of anything else you want?"

"I have everything else."

"You always shall have."

"What was the kitchen like?" Marie asked. "Was it tidy?"

"It's the smartest little place."

"I'll see it presently, when we wash-up."

"*You're* not going to wash-up."

"But, Osborn, I shall have to, often. Every day, you know."

He looked a trifle unhappy over this, knitting his brows. Of course, they had both known that the moment would come when Marie would handle a dishcloth in the best interests of Number Thirty, but it had seemed somewhat remote in those queer, forgotten unmarried days more than a fortnight ago; more than ever remote during the stay in an hotel palace.

"Yes, yes," he said, "I suppose so. I wish you needn't, though."

"I shan't mind. A little housework is very simple; people make such a fuss about it; mother makes a horrible fuss. I shall always wear gloves."

"That partly solves it," said Osborn nodding eagerly, "rubber gloves for wet work, and housemaid's gloves for dry, eh, dearest? You will always, won't you? You must let me buy you all the gloves you want."

"I have enough to begin with."

"You are a thoughtful little genius."

"We'll have to cook dinner to-night."

"Oh, great work!" cried Osborn.

"I intend to run this flat in a thoroughly up-to-date way," Marie explained; "that's the secret of a comfortable house-hold without help, you know—to be entirely up-to-date."

The husband looked immensely impressed.

"I believe you," he said.

The clock struck five, and six, before they rose reluctantly. It would have been rather nice, of course, just to press a bell and give one's orders, but....

On her way to the kitchen, Marie peeped into the bedroom. She switched up the light and looked it over, well pleased. Soon, when she had unpacked, her dressing-table would be furnished with all her pretty things, tortoiseshell and silver, big glass powder-puff bowl, big glass bowl and spoon with scented salts for her bath, and the manicure set of super-luxury which a girl friend had given her on her marriage. She was really adorably equipped; she was starting so very, very well. Her glance fell upon the two beds, side by side, much-pillowed, pink-quilted.

It would be rather nice if there was a housemaid to whip in every evening and turn down the sheets and lay out the night wear; but....

One can't have everything.

"I think we're quite all right here?" said Osborn over her shoulder, with pride in his voice.

"Isn't it all adorable?" she exclaimed.

"You aren't going to put on The Frock, are you, dear girl, to do the cooking?"

"I'll put it on afterwards, just before we dish up."

"I'll dress, too," said Osborn.

They proceeded to the kitchen and played with all their new

toys there. There was not so much to do, after all, because Mrs. Amber, wise woman, had provided one of those ready-made but expensive little meals from the Stores. You just added this to the soup and heated it; you put that in a casserole dish and shoved it in the oven; you whipped some cream; and you made a savoury out of tinned things. You got out the plated vegetable dish which wasn't to be used except on great occasions—but this was one—and put the potatoes in it. You laid the table with every blessed silver thing you had, till it looked like a wedding-present show, as indeed it was. You lighted four candles and put rose shades over them, almost like those at the hotel palace. You ranged the dessert on the sideboard, for you must have dessert, to use those tiptop finger-bowls. In each finger-bowl you floated a flower to match the table decorations. You placed the coffee apparatus—quite smart to make your own, you know—on the sideboard, too.

Thus you had a swagger little dinner; most delectable.

Then you put on the frock of frocks, and cooled your rather sorched hands with somebody else's gentlest kisses, the healing brand, and with some pinkish powder as smooth as silk. Then somebody else put on his dinner-clothes and looked the finest man in the world. Then you dished up the hot part of the dinner, and the creamy sweet was all ready at the other end of the table—so easy to arrange these things gracefully without a parlourmaid, you know—and absolutely *everything* was accomplished.

You sat down.

Love was about and around you.

What delicious soup by a clever wee cook!

Was there happiness at table? There was not greater happiness in heaven.

CHAPTER IV

DREAMS

"You'll lie still, Mrs. Kerr," said Osborn, when they awoke for the first time in their own flat, "and I shall bring you a cup of tea."

"But," said the drowsy Marie, raising herself on an elbow, with all her shining hair—far prettier than any one of the pinky caps with which she loved to cover it—falling over her childish white shoulders, "I must get up; Osborn, really I must; there's breakfast to cook—and you mustn't be late."

"Lie still, Mrs. Kerr," cried the young husband from the doorway.

It was cold in the kitchen, very cold, when a fellow went out clad only in pyjamas, but Osborn briskly lighted that very superior gas-stove and put the super-kettle on. It was extraordinary how completely they were equipped; there was even an extra little set for morning tea for two. He made toast under the grill, with whose abilities he now felt really familiar, and furnished the tray. He was glad he could have everything so pretty and cosy for Marie. He would never be like some men he knew, utterly careless—to all appearance at least—as to how their wives fared.

May Edginton

He had his cold tub quickly, while the kettle boiled, and lighted the geyser in the bathroom for Marie. What an awfully decent bathroom it was!

It was jolly sitting on the edge of Marie's bed, drinking tea, and admiring her. Fellows who weren't married never really knew how pretty a girl could look. Or at least they ought not. Her nightdress beat any mere suit or frock simply hollow.

"Your bath'll be ready when you are, pretty cat," said Osborn, "and I've left the kettle on and made enough toast for breakfast."

And Julia inferred that husbands were mere brutes!

Before Marie stepped out of bed, Osborn lighted the gas-fire in the bedroom; she mustn't get cold. She went into the bathroom, and he began to shave, in cold water. As he shaved, he remembered—Great Scott!

The dining-room fire. The dining-room grate in ashes.

Wiping the lather hastily from his face, Osborn hastened out once more. It was all right for her to put a match to a gas-fire, but ashes and coals ... he hadn't thought of it.

He did the dining-room grate almost as successfully as a housemaid, cleared the debris, wondering where one put it, coaxed the fire to blaze and hurried back to dress.

Marie dressed, too.

"I'm not going to be a breakfast-wrapper woman," she said, as she slid into her garments. "They're sluts, aren't they? I'm going to look as nice in the mornings as at any other part of the day."

"Bravo, kiddie!" he cried admiringly.

There was still time in hand when both were dressed for the cooking of breakfast, but there seemed quite a lot of things to do yet; and they made rather a rush of them. One couldn't sit down to a meal in a dusty room, so one had to sweep and dust it. And there was, undoubtedly, some trick about eggs and bacon which one had yet to learn.

How easily and quickly one would learn everything, though. Method was the thing.

He asked her many times if she wouldn't come into town and lunch, or have tea, and they would go home together; but she explained convincingly if mysteriously:

"You see, dear, this first day, I'll have to *get straight*," and he went off alone.

Marie fell to work in the greatest spirits. She was armoured with the rubber gloves and the housemaid's gloves and a chic pinafore. As she worked she sang. Of course, a woman must have something to occupy a little of her day. Marie hastened about these tasks cheerfully, and before she was through them her mother came.

Her anxious look at her girl was dispelled by the brightness in the bride's face. The small home was very snug; it maintained a high tone of comfort and elegance. Mrs. Amber sat down by the dining-room fire and drew off her gloves and said:

"Now tell me all about it, duck."

"All about what?" said Marie.

"The honeymoon," said Mrs. Amber.

Marie looked at her mother as if she were mad. She smiled at the fire. "We had a lovely time," she replied evasively.

"And had that man lighted the fires yesterday? I couldn't get round—"

"It was all absolutely ready, thank you, mother."

"I brought the things the day before, except the cream. That I told him to get. And the flowers. I don't see the flowers, love."

"They are mostly in the drawing-room," said Marie.

"I should like to see the drawing-room now it's finished," said Mrs. Amber, rising eagerly.

In the small room of pale hues she stood satisfied, almost entranced. But she had those sad things to say which occur inevitably to elderly women of domestic avocations.

"This white paint! You'll have something to do, my child, keeping it clean. It marks so. I know that. Yes, it's pretty, but this time next year I hope you won't be sorry you had it. But of course, just for the two of you—well, you'll both have to be careful. You'll have to warn Osborn, my dear. Men need reminding so often."

"Osborn is rather different from most men," said Marie. "He is so very thoughtful; he made me some tea early this morning, and did the dining-room grate, and lighted the geyser, and everything."

"That won't last, my dear," replied Mrs. Amber, in a tone of quiet authority, but not lamenting.

"Osborn is not a man who changes, mother," said Marie.

"The chintz is a little light; it will show marks almost as much as the paint, I'm afraid, duck," Mrs. Amber continued. "I don't know if it wouldn't have been better to choose a darker ground. However, you can wash these covers at home. The frills are the only parts which you need to iron. I dare say you know that, dear?"

"Oh, well, I shan't have to think of those things yet, mother. I dare say Osborn would prefer me to send them to the cleaner's, anyway."

"People live more extravagantly now," said Mrs. Amber. "I should have done them at home."

"Things change."

Mrs. Amber thought. "In marriage," she stated presently, "someone has to make sacrifices."

"Why should it be the woman?"

"Because the woman," answered Mrs. Amber quoting someone she had once heard, "is naturally selected for it."

"Mother," said Marie, "don't be tiresome."

Mrs. Amber went away reluctantly at three o'clock. She was a wise woman, and did not want to appear ubiquitous. At four, while Marie was unpacking the trunks they had brought yesterday, Julia came in.

"I begged off an hour earlier," she stated.

She looked quite moved, for Julia; she held Marie at arm's length, stood off and surveyed her. "Well," she asked, "how are you?"

"Very well, and awf'ly happy."

Once more the kettle boiled on the gas-stove; once more toast baked under the grill; and the girls, one eager to tell, the other eager to listen, sat down on the hearthrug in the little dining-room to talk.

"What is marriage really like?" said Julia incredulously. "Haven't you any fault to find? Any fly in your ointment?"

And Marie replied: "Absolutely none."

"It seems wonderful," said Julia thoughtfully.

"It is wonderful," cried Marie fervently; "it is so wonderful that a girl can hardly believe it, Julia. But there it is. Marriage is the only life. I wish you'd believe me. All the old life seems so little and light and trivial and silly—that is, all of it which I can remember, for it seems nearly swept away. Mother came in this morning—if it hadn't been for her I don't think I'd have remembered anything at all of what ever happened to me before I was Osborn's wife. It's beginning all new, you see. It's like starting on the best holiday you ever had in your life, which is going to last for ever. Try to imagine it."

"Ah," said Julia sourly, "a holiday! Holidays *don't* last for ever. You always come back to the day's work and the old round."

"You need a holiday yourself," said Marie severely. "You're so bitter. You want something to sweeten you."

Julia looked at Marie with a yearning softness unexpected in her. "Well, haven't I come to see *you*? You're the sweetest thing I know. And it's fine to see you so happy. As for your toast, it's scrumptious."

"Eat it quickly. I want to show you round before I begin to cook dinner."

"Fancy you cooking dinner!" said Julia, looking at Marie's little, pampered hands.

Marie had the first faint thrill of the heroine.

"I have to. We can't afford a servant, you know, yet, though, when Osborn gets his rise, perhaps we shall."

"When will that be?"

"Oh, I don't know. This year—next year—"

"Sometime—never," said Julia.

"Osborn is very clever. He is so valuable to his firm; they wouldn't lose him for anything, so they'll have to give him a bigger salary. Brains like Osborn's don't go cheap."

"That's awf'ly nice," Julia replied. She looked down, and stroked the furs which she had bought for herself, and thought for a while.

"Show me the flat, there's a dear."

Julia professed raptures over all she saw; kissed Marie, and was gone. Once more the bride, but alone this time, turned earnestly to work.

The work seemed long and arduous and hot and nerve-racking, in spite of the amenities of the gas stove. She was so anxious to have all perfect. Once more the table was decked, the rose shades were placed over the candles, the sitting-room fire was lighted, the coffee apparatus was made ready.

Marie rushed into The Frock, determined to keep up the standard they had set themselves, just two minutes before Osborn arrived home.

He kneeled to kiss her; they embraced rapturously.

"You've had a nice day?" he was anxious to know.

"Lovely. Mother came, and Julia, and I unpacked, and went to market, and did everything by myself—"

"I'm glad you had plenty to amuse you, dear one."

"'Amuse'?" said Marie a trifle blankly. "I've been working ever so hard all day, really, Osborn."

"Work?" he teased, smiling. "You 'working'!" He kissed one little hand after the other. "They couldn't," he mumbled over them. He seemed to take woman's great tasks lightly, as if he did not realise how serious, how enervating they were.

"They're too pretty," he said.

He began to talk, while he carved the chicken.

"It seemed a bit beastly to go back to work to-day after our good time. However, I've all the more reason for going back to work now, haven't I, Mrs. Kerr? You'll keep me up to the scratch, won't you? Look! I'm carving this bird like an old family man already. They were all asking me, down there, how I liked my honeymoon, and where we went and what we saw. A lot of them began talking of the time they'd had. They all said it never lasts. People are fools, aren't they?"

"Not to make it last?" said Marie. "Yes, dear."

"The attitude of the average man towards married life is sickening," said Osborn, "but I'm glad to think *you'll* never know anything about that, little girl."

Marie had a great feeling, as she looked under the candle-shades, at Osborn, that she had found the king of men: lover, protector and knight.

"The attitude of the average woman towards married life is perfectly mean, Osborn. But *you'll* never know anything about that, either."

He knew, as he returned her look across the flowers, that he alone had achieved every man's desire; he had found the perfect mate; she who would never soil, nor age, nor weep, nor wound; the jewel-girl.

CHAPTER V

HOUSEKEEPING

Marie had not thought of money in relation to herself and Osborn. He was known, in the set among which they both moved, and had met and loved and married, as a promising young fellow doing very well indeed, in a steady fashion, for his age. He had a salary, when they set up housekeeping in No. 30, of two hundred a year, with a very good rise indeed, a 25 per cent, rise, at the end of every five years. And he earned this and that now and again in odd channels, vaguely dubbed commission, or expenses. So, as a bachelor, Osborn could be almost splendid in their set, and as a husband he was resolved to be conscientious and careful. He had decided to give up his inexpensive club, and presently he meant to go into the matter of conscience and care, to give it a figure, but not so soon after the honeymoon as Marie drew him into it. It was all very comfortable saying to oneself: "I must make some arrangement; all in good time," but the making of it left one a little cold, a little surprised, inclined to thought.

When the Kerrs had been housekeeping for a week, the butcher and baker and the rest of the clan each dropped through the letter-slit in the front door of No. 30 a very clean, spruce, new book, and the young wife gathered them up with eager trepidation. She had been washing up, when the books arrived, all the dinner things left over from the night before, and the breakfast things of this morning, and from the kitchen she heard and recognised the blunt thump as each record of her housekeeping talents or failings dropped upon the hall floor. She rushed out, collected them, and retired to the dining-room hearthrug to meet her responsibilities.

She knew the sum total was all wrong; her mother's tradesmen's books never reached this figure. Yet people must eat, mustn't they? And wash with soap? And have boot polish, and cleaning things, and candles for their dinner-table?

She asked herself, as so many young wives have done, half-sorrowing, half-injured: "But what have we *had*? I've been awf'ly careful. I couldn't have managed with less. I shall tell Osborn that it simply can't be done for less—"

She shut the books one by one. "But it must," she said to herself. "Our income is—"

She figured out, with pencil and paper and much distaste, their weekly income; she compared it with the sum total of the tradesmen's books, and to that one must add rent, and travel, and holidays and doctor's expenses.

Doctor's expenses? Cut that item out. One must never be ill, that's all.

She was glad she was going to meet Osborn that afternoon, and have tea with him in the West End; he was to beg off early specially for it.

The flat seemed very silent. What a deserted place! It would be nice to go out and see someone, speak to someone.

She went to lie down.

She lay on her pink quilt, and began on that castle again. It was a fine place, a real family seat. While she built, she manicured her finger nails, looking at them critically. She had not begun to spoil them yet, thanks to the rubber gloves and the housemaid's gloves with which Osborn had declared his eternal readiness to provide her. No one would feel it more deeply than Osborn if one of those slim fingers were burned or soiled or roughened ever so little.

She had a few coppers only in her private purse, but they would carry her to Osborn, the legal fount of supply. Out into a fine afternoon she stepped lightly, and the admiring hall porter watched her go. He was not so certain of her, though, for he had seen many young brides pass through his portals, in and out every day, ridden always by some small fretting care till they trembled at the sight of someone who was always looking, through their ageing clothes, at the ill-kept secrets of their pockets. He had entered in his memoranda that the Kerrs rented only a forty-pound flat.

Heedless of the hall porter, Marie was away upon her joyous errand. She was very young, very healthy, and she looked ravishing. These things she knew, and they were enough. She went upon the top of an omnibus to the City street where was her rendezvous, but in her gala suit, her gala hat, and the furs which had nearly broken Mrs. Amber, she felt immensely superior to such humble mode of travel.

Before she alighted from the omnibus she saw, from her altitude, Osborn striding along the street. He was not alone; Desmond Rokeby was with him, listening to something which Osborn was telling him eagerly. Although Marie could not hear the words, she leaned over and looked down with delight upon her man whom she had chosen, so tall and smart, and fine, and young. She loved the turn of his head, the swing of his shoulders, his quick tread and eager look, as if all life were unrolling before him like a map, and he could choose at his lordly will any one of the thousand roads upon it. Osborn was speaking of his wife; he was telling Rokeby about the splendour of the game he had learned to play. He was trying to tell Rokeby something of the wonders and beauties of one woman's mind and heart; and he was telling him, too, of smaller things, of the comforts and attractions of home, of the little kingdom behind a shut front door, of the angel's food an angel cooked, and all her benevolences and graces and mercies.

As he spoke, diffidently but glowingly, of these things, with his words rushing out, or halting over something that was not to be told, his attention was called to the omnibus top on which Marie sat; he did not know what called him, only that he was called, and there she was, leaning over, smiling between the soft rim of her furs and the down-drawn brim of her hat, with her big muff held up against her breast, cuddlingly. Osborn gasped and stood hat in hand, with his face turned upwards.

"Have you seen a vision, man?" asked Rokeby.

"There's Marie," Osborn answered.

Marie descended daintily and crossed the street to the two men. Her hair gleamed and her feet were so light that she seemed to dance like a shaft of sunshine. At the moment she was a queen, as every pretty girl is at moments, with two subjects ready to obey.

Rokeby greeted her smilingly with admiration. "Mrs. Kerr, Osborn talks of no one but you all day. He was in the midst of a song like Solomon's, only modernised, when that chariot of yours bore down upon him and cut it short. How are you? But I needn't ask. And when may I call?"

"Oh, sometime, old man! We'll fix a day," said Osborn, signalling to a taxicab. He jumped in after his wife, and Rokeby went on his way good humouredly. "The perfect deluded ass!" he thought, "and may the dear chap ever remain so!"

Osborn explained to Marie. "He needn't call *yet*. I'm hanged if he's going to come around the loveliest girl in town in the afternoons, when her lawful husband isn't in; and I'm equally hanged if he's going to break in upon one of our very own evenings. So as all the evenings are our very own, there's nothing to be done about it, is there? What do you say, Mrs. Osborn Kerr?"

"We don't want anyone else," said Marie.

"You do look sweet," Osborn cried, "I want all the world to see me with you. So where'll we go? Where's the place where all the world goes?"

They knew it already very well. They drove there. Tea was half a crown a head and one tipped well. What matter? There were soft music, soft lights, pretty women, attentive men. Everyone looked rich, but perhaps everyone was not, any more than were Marie and Osborn. Perhaps everyone was only spending his pockets empty. The stage was well represented. The place had a know-all air blended with a chaste exclusiveness. It was a place where the best people were seen and others wanted and hoped to be seen. Here sat Marie and Osborn, shaded by a great palm group, drinking the choicest blend of tea, eating vague fragments, and looking into each other's eyes. The worries of the morning slipped by; Marie forgot her tradesmen's books, and Osborn the monotony of his daily toil. Life was soft, gracious, easy and elegant. They bought a piece of it, a crumbly piece, with five shillings before they went away.

"Taxi, sir?" asked the commissionaire.

"We'll walk, thanks," said Osborn. Walking was a sort of recreation not too dowdy. They went a little way on foot, then turned into a Tube station and travelled home. When they wormed their way down a crowded tube train compartment to two seats they were faced with the everyday aspect of life again. Tired people were going home; business men had not yet shaken off the pressure of their affairs; business women looked rather driven; here and there women with children worried themselves with their responsibilities. One or two children were cross, and one or two babies cried.

More than one woman looked at Marie jealously.

They read the popular story; the new-married girl, careless in her health and beauty; untouched by time or trouble; the worshipful young man, whose fervour was unworn by toil or fret. Every woman who looked at Marie and Osborn sitting side by side, with shoulders leaning slightly, unconsciously, towards each other, found in her heart some memory, or some empty ache for such fond glory.

The Kerrs alighted at Hampstead and walked briskly, Osborn's hand tucked under Marie's arm, for it was dark, up the road to the flats. On their way they passed rows and tiers of flats, all similar, save that one represented more money, maybe, than another, all holding or remembering sweet stories like theirs. But they did not think of that; they were in haste to reach No. 30 Welham Mansions, the little heaven behind the closed front door.

"We had a jolly old afternoon, hadn't we?" said Osborn after dinner. "I'll take you there again."

"Can we afford it?" said Marie, with a droop to her mouth.

"We will afford it. I'll make lots of money for my Marie. We'll have a dear old time!"

"I've been thinking, Osborn."

"A wretched exercise," he said gaily. "Don't you worry yourself, chicken. Just be happy. That's all I ask." He grew the least degree pathetic. "I can't be here all day to look after you, and see that you're happy; you'll have to see to it yourself. Do that for me, will you? Make my girl awf'ly happy."

"I am happy, Osborn."

"We do ourselves pretty well, don't we, dear?" he said appreciatively. "This is jolly snug. Now I'll make the coffee. You sit still."

Marie watched Osborn. She took her cup from him, and stirred her coffee into a whirlpool, and at last said:

"You see, Osborn, I want some money, please."

"All right, darling," he replied. "I'll give you a bit to go on with any time."

His ready hand jingled in his trousers pocket.

"It's for the tradesmen," said Marie; "I thought we'd pay every week."

"That's it," he enjoined, "be methodical. That's splendid of you."

"And this week it comes to two pounds ten."

Osborn's hand ceased its jingling; he withdrew it and sat still.

"Oh!..." he said in an altered voice, "does it? Well, all right."

"That doesn't include the coal, or—or allow for gas," murmured Marie. "I expect the meter is ready for another half-crown."

Osborn looked at the sitting-room fire.

"Marie love," he said, clearing his throat, "I'm sorry, but—but will it always come to as much?"

"I hope not. No, I'll keep it down as much as I can, Osborn. But this week—"

"Was just a trial trip," said Osborn.

"You see, I told the tradespeople to send in weekly books and—and if I don't pay, they'll wonder."

"Don't fret yourself, kitten. I'll give it to you. But—"

Osborn put down his coffee cup in a final way.

"The fact is, Marie, you see—I don't want you to think me mean—"

"Oh, Osborn!"

"No, but the fact is, it just happens I'm able to give it to you to-day, because I've got a little in the bank. But our honeymoon and the first instalments on the furniture and your engagement ring ran through most of it, and—and so there's only a little left—about twenty pounds or so. My people lived on an annuity, you know; they only left me savings. Well, I thought it seemed snug to keep a balance of twenty pounds or so for emergencies, you know. But I'll draw a cheque on it for you with pleasure. Two pounds ten? All right."

"But, Osborn," said Marie, wide-eyed, "can't you give it to me out of your—"

"My screw doesn't come in till the end of the week," Osborn explained. He flushed and for the first time looked at her a little haughtily.

"I'm sorry," she murmured; "perhaps we ought to make some arrangement and I'll keep to it."

"That's it," he said, still slightly uncomfortable; "now look here, dearie—"

"I'll get my account book and put it down."

"Does she have an account book?" said Osborn more lightly. "How knowing!"

Marie brought a book, and opened it upon her knee, and sat, pencil poised. She was very earnest. "How much ought we to spend?"

"You know what my screw is," said Osborn, as if unwilling to particularise.

Marie wrote at the top of her page, "Two hundred pounds."

"Forty pounds rent," she wrote next.

"And my odd expenses, lunch and clothes, and so on," said Osborn, "have never been less than sixty or seventy pounds, you know."

She wrote slowly. "Sixty to seventy pounds, expenses," when he stopped her.

"I'll have to curtail that!" he exclaimed.

In the ensuing silence both man and wife thought along the same track. It suddenly gave him a nasty jar, to hit up against the necessity of stopping those pleasant little spendings, those odd drinks, those superior smokes, the last word in colourings for shirts and ties. Of course, such stoppage was well worth while. Oh, immensely so!

And she had a lump in her throat. She thought: "He'll find all this a burden. He's had all he wants; and so've I. I wish we were rich."

"Look here, darling," said Osborn. "How much'll food cost us? I don't know a great deal about these things, but if it's any standard to take—well, my old landlady used to give me rooms and breakfasts and dinners for thirty bob a week. Jolly good breakfasts and dinners they were, too!"

Marie murmured very slowly: "I'm not your old landlady." She imaged her, a working drab, saving, pinching, and making the best of all things. Compare Marie with Osborn's old landlady! "Besides," she murmured on, "there's me, too, now."

Osborn nodded. "Well," he said, "how much do you think?"

"Thirty shillings for *both* of us per week," said Marie, inclined to cry. "That's better than your old landlady."

Osborn hastened to soothe her. "Look here," he protested, "don't fuss over it, there's a love. Very well, I'll give you thirty bob a week, but that's seventy-eight pounds a year. My hat! I say, can't you squeeze the gas out of it?"

"I *will* get the gas out of it!" said Marie, with tightened lips.

"Great business!" said Osborn cheering; "put it down, darling."

So under the "Rent, forty pounds," she wrote, "House-keeping, including gas, seventy-eight pounds."

"That's one hundred and eighteen pounds out of my two hundred," said Osborn, knitting his brows and staring into the fire.

"Coal?" whispered Marie, her pencil poised.

Osborn's stare at the fire took on a belligerent nature.

"I say!" he exclaimed, "we can't have two fires every day. It's simply not to be thought of."

"We'll sit in the dining-room in the evenings."

"Put down 'Coal, ten pounds,'" said Osborn grudgingly.

When Marie had put it down, she cast a sorrowing look round her dear little room. She would hardly ever use it, except in summer.

"That's close on a hundred and thirty pounds," said Osborn.

"We'll make allowance for that, but you'll try to do on less, won't you, darling?"

"I'll try."

"That leaves seventy pounds for my life insurance, and for my expenses and yours, Marie. A man ought to insure his life when he's married; it'll cost me fifteen pounds a year."

"Oh, what a greedy world!" cried Marie, despairing tears running down her face.

Osborn kissed them away, but remained much preoccupied.

"It leaves fifty-five pounds between us for my clothes and lunches, and travelling, and your pocket money."

"How about your commission, Osborn? Your 'extras'?"

"With luck they'll pay for a decent holiday once a year or so."

Marie suddenly readjusted her scheme of life while she sat blindly gazing before her into that too-costly fire. "Osborn," she said quietly, "I—I shouldn't think of wanting any of your fifty-five pounds. You'll need it all; you must keep up appearances. I'll squeeze some pocket money out of the housekeeping."

"Oh, my darling!" said Osborn gratefully, "do you really think you could? I expect, though, there'll be a nice bit over, if you're careful, don't you? You won't want to spend ten pounds on coal, for example."

"I intend to manage," Marie replied vigorously.

"And I'll often be able to give you a decent present out of my commission. I shan't let you go short."

"Osborn, I mean to help you. We'll get on splendidly. You do love me, don't you?"

"My darling, I adore you; and I know you're the finest, bravest girl in the world. I would like to load you with everything beautiful under the sun, and some day I will. When I get a rise, you'll be the first to benefit. I'll make you a real pin-money allowance. Don't I long to do it?"

"Osborn, meanwhile, can I have this week's money?"

Osborn wrote out a cheque for two pounds ten very bravely. The discussion had been a weighty one. As he handed it to her, he drew her down on his knee, and, holding her tight, impressed her: "You won't let this happen again, in any circumstances, will you, dear girl?"

"Never!" she promised fervently.

So Marie began housekeeping in the way her mother began, and her grandmother, and those jealous tired women in the Tube; the old way of the labouring souls, the old way scarred with crow's feet and wrinkles, and rained on by tears.

CHAPTER VI

DISCIPLINE

Marie meant always to be trim and neat and lovely, a feast for the eye of man. But when winter had settled upon town in a crescendo of cold, and when you thought twice before lighting that gas-fire which you had meant to dress by every morning, and when, too, Osborn began to resume his normal habit of sleeping till the very last moment, why, you no longer gave yourself—or rather, Osborn no longer gave himself—the trouble of rising to make tea. Marie had much more to do than merely dress, and as soon as she had opened her sleepy eyes she sprang resolutely out into the grim cold that seemed so closely to surround her snug bed, and fell to work. She felt as if the toil of a lifetime lay behind her, by the time she and Osborn sat opposite to one another at their breakfast table, and yet, too, as if the toil of a lifetime lay before her.

Marie took upon her shoulders most of the laundering. Osborn said "Clever kid" when he knew, but it did not impress him much; his feeling about it was vague. Did he not work all day himself? All this fiddling donkey-work with which women occupied themselves at home—he dismissed it. Always, when he returned, by the dining-room fire, in an easy chair and a decent frock, sat Marie, sweet and leisured.

It was evident that her household duties did not overcome her.

And all day the flat was desolately quiet. How queer women's lives were! They grew up, looking infantilely upon men, and reading about them in fairy tales. One day a pretty girl became engaged to one of them. What congratulations! What importance, delight! What prospects! What planning! What roses! The pretty girl then married one of them, the dearest and best of them, and began to wash dishes. Her heart, which had never been perplexed before, grew very perplexed. Her little purse, which had never been so very hungry before, now hungered for things, simple things, matinees, and sweets and blouses. She stayed all day in a flat, desolately quiet, waiting for one moment when the dearest and best came home.

How queer women's lives were!

*   *   *   *   *

When Osborn was going to dine with Rokeby at his club he told Marie about it just as she was stretching a reluctant foot out of her bed into the cold of a grey December morning, and an extraordinary rebellion rose in her with sirocco-like fierceness. She got out of bed without replying, clutched at her dressing-gown and dragged it on, while Osborn's drowsy voice continued, "Desmond asked me, and I thought I would; he wasn't sure if you'd mind—if you'd think it rather often. But I told him you weren't that sort; I told him you were a sport. You'll do something nice this evening, won't you, darling? What'll you do?"

"What is something 'nice'?" said Marie, staring at her face, which looked wan and cold, in the glass.

"I don't know," said Osborn.

"Nor do I!" she cried angrily. "Life's just one slow, beastly grind." She ran out of the room to light the geyser, and tears were streaming down her face, and sobs rising one upon the other in her heart. She sank upon the one bathroom chair, leaned her head against the wall and wept helplessly. Her body was shaken with her crying; never in her life had she so cried before. She felt as if she must collapse under its violence.

She thought: "Osborn's going out to dinner, and I can mope and starve at home."

With the sub-conscious dutifulness of woman she realised that her bath was ready; that she must hurry, that there was breakfast to make, and the dining-room to sweep, and ... and ... what a string of tragic drabnesses! Obeying this instinct of duty in her, she got, still sobbing, into the bath, and her tears fell like rain into the hot water. A man would have cried, "Damn the bath! Damn the breakfast! Damn the brooms and dusters! Scrap 'em all!" And for the while he would straightway have scrapped them and felt better. But Marie went miserably on, as her mother and her grandmother and all those tired women in the Tube had done times out of number, for the sisterhood of woman is a strange thing.

Osborn met her as she was coming from her bath, quiet, subdued and pale. Rather, he had been standing outside the door, waiting and anxious. "Darling," he said scared, "what is it? Tell me! Aren't you well? Has anything upset you? What can I do?"

Marie left her dressing-gown in his detaining hands and, sobbing again, ran along the corridor to her bedroom. She began to put her hair up feverishly with shaking hands.

Osborn followed her quickly with the dressing-gown, beseeching: "Do put it on! Do, Marie, do! You'll get cold. It's freezing."

"M-m-much you'd c-c-care," she sobbed.

"Oh, darling," said Osborn, wrapping the dressing-gown and his arms tightly round her, "tell me! What is the matter? What have I done? Aren't you happy, dearest?"

"Happy!" she gasped. "Why should I be happy?"

"I-I—love you, dearest," said Osborn in a tremulous voice.

"You g-go out, and every d-day it's the same for me. All day I'm alone; and I loathe the work. Everything's always the same."

"I wish I could give you a change, sweetheart," said Osborn, terribly harassed.

She hated herself because she could not be generous, but somehow she could find no generous words to speak.

"Shall I stay with you this evening, Marie?"

"No. You've p-promised. And I'm not that sort; you t-t-told him so!"

"Is that all that's the matter, Marie? Because everything's always the same?"

"I'm so tired. And ragged, somehow."

"Oh, Marie, I wish I could stay at home to-day and look after you. You'll lie down and rest, won't you?"

"When I've finished all my charwoman's work."

Osborn was silent, biting his lips; and presently Marie looked up, and seeing his face, drew it down and kissed him, crying: "Oh, I'm a beast; forgive me! But I'm so tired, and somehow so—so ragged."

"Poor darling!"

"You'd better go and bathe, Osborn. We're late as it is."

"So we are, by Jove! Look, I'll be awf'ly quick this morning, and come and help you. That'll be some good, won't it?"

She assented with sorrowful little sniffs, and he took his perplexities away into the bathroom. He was terribly troubled, not seeing what was to be done. What could a man do? Women's work, women's lives, were the same all the world over—married women's, that is. One couldn't do more than give them the best home one could, and come back to it like a good boy early every evening, and love them very much. If one were only rich! How money helped everything! Osborn cursed his meagre pockets as heartily as Marie had cried over them.

Osborn hastened into his clothes and went to the kitchen. Bacon was sizzling gently over a low flame, coffee and toast were made; nothing remained for him to do, but, very wishful to show his good intentions, he stood over the bacon as if controlling its destinies. Marie found him there, quiet and thoughtful, when she came in.

"It's all ready," she observed in a subdued voice.

"Bravo, kiddie!" said Osborn, "I see it is. You're magnificent."

A little while ago this praise would have made her glow sweetly, but now it tasted sour in her mouth; she did not particularly wish to be a magnificent cook-general, a magnificent charwoman. All her nerves felt stretched as if they must snap and she must scream. Tremblingly she set a tray on the table.

"Don't give me any, please."

"Darling! No breakfast!"

"I'll have some toast. Oh, don't, don't worry me! I've told you I feel simply on edge."

Osborn ate his bacon with a feeling that somehow he ought not; but he was hungry. He ate Marie's portion, too, half apologetically. There was one thing, however, which, very sensibly, he omitted to do; he had the tact not to open the morning paper. There are some things which a woman will not stand, and one is the sight of an abstracted man behind a paper, letting his crumbs fall down his waistcoat, when she feels nervy.

"Lovely morning, dearest," said Osborn; "you ought to go for a brisk walk."

"Perhaps I will."

"You do look awf'ly seedy."

"I feel it."

"I hope your mother will come round this morning. She'd do the marketing for you, or something, wouldn't she?"

"Yes, Osborn, I'm sure she would."

Osborn helped himself to toast and tried to eat it quietly; he had some dumb, blind instinct which comes to men, that crunching would be vexatious. He handed butter and marmalade tenderly to his wife and carried his cup round to her for replenishment, instead of passing it. He did all he knew.

The anticipation of Rokeby and that sanctuary, his club, invaded his mind agreeably. A club was a great institution. If he touched a good commission this year—but no. Certainly not! He put the idea from him.

He put a hand in his trousers pocket and jingled there. A thought had come to him, which comes to all men in moments of trial concerning women, moments calling for prompt treatment and nice judgment.

A present!

He could not afford it, but it must be done. What else could he do? He felt remarkably helpless. He felt about cautiously and intimately in his pocket, knowing with exactitude all that was there. It was not much. On Fridays he now banked half his weekly salary against such demands as rent, furniture instalments and so on. Thirty shillings he gave to Marie; ten he kept. This was Tuesday.

He withdrew his hand with something in it—two half-crowns. He would lunch light for the next three days.

"Darling," he said, with a slight break in his voice, so anxious he was to propitiate the pale, pretty girl who brooded at him from the head of the table, "look here! Do something to please me. When I'm out on the spree to-night let me think of your having a good time too. Why not ring up Miss Winter and get her to go to the theatre with you? Here's two seats."

A slight flush stole into Marie's cheeks.

"Oh, Osborn," she said, "but—"

"What?"

"Can you afford it?"

"Blow 'afford'!" said Osborn largely, placing the half-crowns before her, "we must do absolutely anything to prevent you from getting wretched."

She took the money up, half hesitating. She read the wistfulness in his face, but she felt rather wistful too.

"Thank you, Osborn," she murmured; "it'll be lovely. Julia's sure to come. But, Osborn—"

"What?"

"Some evening you'll take me yourself, won't you?"

"Rather!"

"Shall I save this till to-morrow?"

"No, no!" he cried. "To-day's when you want a tonic, not to-morrow. Go and get your tonic, Mrs. Osborn. Go and enjoy yourself!"

He was restored to content.

"I must go," he said, jumping up. "Let me kiss you. We're friends, aren't we, darling? You'll try not to hate the work so very much? When I get my rise it will make a lot of difference."

Then they clung together, kissing and whispering, and the cream walls and the golden-brown curtains were as beautiful to them as ever.

"Be a happy girl!" he cried, before he shut the front door.

"I am!" she called back, and he was gone.

She went down gaily, in spite of her weariness, and used the hall-porter's telephone to ring up Julia. Miss Winter would come and was very pleased, thank you. Marie went upstairs again, the ascent making her breathless.

The stairs and the landings were grey stone, uncarpeted, for this was the cheapest block of flats in the road. Oh, money, money! Accursed, lovable stuff!

Marie sat down, panting, in her kitchen. A mist rose before her eyes; she shut them and took a long breath; her head was light and dizzy. She began to be afraid.

An angel, in the guise of Mrs. Amber, knocked upon the front door. Marie dragged along the corridor, and could have wept once more for sheer relief at seeing so irreplaceable, so peculiarly comforting a person as her own mother upon the threshold. But she restrained herself with a great effort from the relief.

"Well, duck," said Mrs. Amber cheerfully, with that wise eye upon her girl's face, "I was out and I just thought I'd run in and see how you were. You're not too busy for me, love? Ah, you've overdone it and you look very pale."

She sat in Osborn's easychair in the dining-room. She was stout and solid, a comforting rock upon which the waves of trouble might fret and break in vain, for she had weathered her storms long ago. But Marie refrained from going to her and laying her head in her lap and crying like a little girl. She was twenty-five, married and worldly, with great things upon her shoulders. Instead of going to that true rock of ages, the mother, for shelter she sat down opposite, composedly, in the companion chair, and answered:

"There's a good deal to do in a home."

"Ah, you've found that out?" said Mrs. Amber regretfully. "We all find it out sooner or later. But a little domestic work shouldn't make a girl of your age look so pale and tired as you do. How do you feel, love?"

"Ragged," said Marie, "and—and awf'ly limp."

A great question was crying in Mrs. Amber's heart, but she was too tactful to pursue it. Modern girls were not lightly to be comprehended; she knew well that she did not understand her own daughter, and young people kept their secrets just as long as they thought they would.

"You ought to rest, my dear," she said hesitatingly. "I should lie down on that nice couch of yours every day after lunch, if I were you. A few minutes make all the difference, I assure you."

"I never used to rest," said Marie.

Mrs. Amber continued her matronly diplomacy:

"No, duck; but that was different. It's so different—"

"What is, mother?"

"When you're married, dear. You should rest a bit."

"I don't know what you mean, mother," said Marie.

"Just that, love," Mrs. Amber replied soothingly, "only that you should rest. It's wiser and it will make a great difference to you."

"I can't think what you mean, mother. I don't see why being married should alter one."

Mrs. Amber looked into the fire and said slowly: "Well, duck, it does. Doesn't it?"

Now Marie was conscious of an overpowering irritation. These old wives' tales! These matronly saws! How stupid they were! How meaningless, foundationless and sickening! She did not reply to Mrs. Amber's question, but stirred restlessly in her chair, swinging her foot, and said:

"Well, it's after twelve, and we may as well have some lunch. I'll just run—"

"No, love, you *won't*!" Mrs. Amber exclaimed, showing considerable vivacity. "I'm going to take you straight away to lie down on that nice couch, and I'll find the lunch myself, and we'll have it on a tray together. Now!"

"There isn't a fire in the drawing-room."

"I'll soon put a match to it, dear."

"Then we'll let this fire out," said Marie, after a pause.

May Edginton

Mrs. Amber hesitated, too.

"It's quite right to be careful," she replied.

"After all," said Marie, her irritation breaking out, too rebellious for all bonds, "I don't want it, mother. I'll only have to do the grate to-morrow; two grates instead of one. That's all. Such is life!"

Mrs. Amber looked into the fire.

"I'll tell you what," said she slowly. "You lie down on your bed. I don't know why I didn't think of it before. There's a gas fire there, and we'll have that."

"There are such things as gas bills, too."

"And a time to worry over them," said Mrs. Amber tartly; "but this isn't the time. You're going to be comfortable, and I'm going to make you so. You'll come along with me right now, my duck, and in five minutes you'll say what a wise old woman you've got for a mother."

Suddenly Marie leaned upon her mother and obeyed. She was lying on her bed under the pink quilt, and Mrs. Amber had her hat and coat and walking-shoes off, and the gas fire began to purr, and a heavenly comfort visited her. She knew reluctantly that these matrons were horribly wise women, after all. She looked into her mother's eyes, and saw there the question which cried in her heart, but she could not read it. It was too old for her.

Mrs. Amber said equably:

"Now I'll run into the kitchen and find what I shall find, my dear. You're not to trouble yourself to think and tell me what;

I was housekeeping before you were born. And meanwhile, if I were you, I'd undo my frock and take off my corsets and be really comfortable. You be a good girl, dear, and do as you're told just this once, to please your silly old mother."

Docilely Marie sat up, unhooked her trim skirt-band, and unfastened her corsets. At once she felt lightened. *How* wise these dreadful matrons were! She did more; she cast her skirt and blouse aside with the corsets, and when Mrs. Amber returned she found her lying rest fully under the eiderdown, untrammelled, in thin petticoat and camisole.

"Eggs?" said Marie, craning her neck to look. "They were for Osborn's breakfast—two boiled eggs, mother."

"Well, they're poached now, duck," said Mrs. Amber; "they've gone to glory. Let Osborn have bacon; there's half a dozen rashers in your larder."

"He had bacon this morning."

"Let him have it again," said the comfortable lady.

"Julia's coming to dinner to-night," Marie confided to her mother. "Osborn's dining with Mr. Rokeby, but he's sending us both to the theatre. Isn't it kind of him?"

Mrs. Amber nodded smilingly.

"He hates me to be dull," said Marie.

Again Mrs. Amber nodded smilingly; she thought what a make-believe world these young brides lived in, and then she sighed.

All that afternoon she tended Marie, and gave her tea, and

fulfilled her offer of setting the dinner forward before she went away, with the inquiry still in her heart.

Marie was better.

She rose from her bed about six o'clock, pleased as a cat with the warm room, and set about the business of her toilet. Sitting down to the dressing-table, she looked long and earnestly at her face; the rest she had taken had plumped and coloured it again, but there was a something, a kind of frailty, a blue darkness under the eyes. Perhaps it made her look less pretty? She was inclined to fret over it a trifle. To counteract it she dressed her hair with a fluffy softness unusual to her trim style; she took immense pains over her finger-nails and put on her best high frock. She hurried over her preparations, having been reluctant to leave her bed till the last possible moment. Mrs. Amber had laid the dinner-table, but there were still things to do.

"Some day I shall keep an awf'ly good parlour-maid," Marie promised herself.

She went in to criticise and retouch her mother's painstaking arrangements. She grew flushed and irritated over the cooking.

"*And* a good cook," she added. "What dreams!"

Julia looked a good deal at Marie during dinner in the delusive light of the shaded candles, and at last she said:

"You're thinner. And there's something about you—I don't know what it is. You are almost fragile."

"I manage this flat entirely without help, you know," said Marie, looking round the speckless dining-room proudly.

"*That* ought not to do it," replied Julia, dismissing domestic work with a contemptuous wave of the hand. "Are you worrying?"

"Worrying?" Marie repeated. "What about?"

"Oh, anything."

"I have nothing to worry over."

"Blessed woman!" replied Julia, diving into the freak pocket of an expensive garment bought with her own money. "May I begin to smoke?"

"Let me get cigarettes," said Marie, springing up for Osborn's box, which lay on the mantelpiece behind her.

"Always carry my own, thanks," said Julia, brandishing the cigarette-case she had produced.

The sudden movement she had made gave Marie a curious sensation; Julia and the room and the red fire swam around her; her brain was numb and dizzy; she staggered and caught at her chair-back.

"Oh!" she gasped. "I feel so—so—"

"What?" exclaimed the other girl, springing up.

Marie sank into her chair.

"I was so giddy—and faint, Julia."

Julia drew her chair close to Marie's, put down her yet unlighted cigarette, and looked at her friend shrewdly.

"Look here, kiddy," she began, with a softness Marie had never heard in her voice before. Then she stopped and asked: "Where's the brandy?"

"There isn't any," said Marie in a far-away voice; "there's only Osborn's whisky, and that's horrid. I'll be all right soon. Make the coffee, dear, will you? And make it strong."

Julia not only made the coffee strong, but she made it very quickly; she had a wonderfully quiet, efficient way of accomplishing things. The coffee stimulated Marie and steadied the erratic beating of her heart.

"That's better," she said.

Then Julia was modern enough to ask without preliminary that question which had asked in Mrs. Amber's elderly heart all day.

"Marie, are you going to have a baby?"

Marie could not have been more confused and confounded.

"I!" she stammered. "Have a baby! I never thought of such a thing!"

"It's not an unknown event," said Julia; "it has been done before. Think!"

Marie thought.

"Julia," she whispered, hushed, "perhaps—"

"You must know—or you can make a good guess."

Marie began to tremble. "I've been feeling so simply awful; I couldn't think what was the matter with me, but I—I believe you may be right. I shouldn't be surprised—"

Julia drew at her cigarette savagely; tears were in her eyes; something hurt her and she resented it.

"Shall you be pleased?" she asked.

"Pleased? I—don't—know."

"Will your husband be pleased?"

"I don't know."

"People seem to run about anyhow in the dark," said Julia thoughtfully.

Marie blushed. "Well, we'd never made any sort of plan."

"I think it would be lovely to have a baby," said Julia defiantly.

The challenge called forth an answering thrill in Marie; a force which she had not known she possessed leapt to meet it; she felt warm and glowing, tremulously excited and happy.

"So do I!" she breathed. "Oh, Julia, I wish I knew for certain. I *must* know."

"Go and see a doctor," said Julia; "he'd tell you."

"When?"

"When you like. I know one whose surgery hours are eight till nine-thirty."

"Oh, if I could only know before Osborn comes home to-night!"

"Let's go."

"Now?"

"Now."

Marie's mind flitted to its former anxieties of the purse, which she did not wish to reveal to Julia sitting there so well-dressed in the gown that she so easily had paid for. Theatre or doctor? Doctor or theatre? Which should it be?

She glanced dissemblingly at the clock.

"I don't know if I've time. We ought to be starting to *The Scarlet Pimpernel*."

"Chuck the theatre," said Julia. "I don't mind. This is a far greater business. Come along; I'll take you."

Light and glory flamed in Marie's heart.

"Don't you really mind?"

"My dear kid, I wouldn't let you go to the theatre tonight. You'll come and see that doctor, and then sit here in your easychair and rest quietly."

Marie's feet were no longer leaden as they carried her into her bedroom to fling on coat and hat. She was consumed by a great wonder. Could it be?

She counted all her money hastily into her bag and rejoined Julia. They went out, walked to the end of the road and boarded a car, but it was Julia who paid the fares while Marie sat dreaming beside her. It was not far to the doctor's door.

Marie did not know how to begin, but found the way in which doctors helped one was wonderful. In three minutes he had the story, and was twinkling at her with cheery interest, though as far as he was concerned it was the oldest, ordinariest story in the world, which invariably ended by calling him out of bed in the middle of some wet night, after a day of particular worry.

He asked her all about herself, where she lived, if she got up early, if she was busy, if she frivolled, and arrived at a mental summary of her circumstances. The circumstances were as old and ordinary as the story, but her pretty face and wavy hair, her childish form and dainty clothes, made him wish for a moment that she could have kept out of the struggle.

He could not say to her: "Well, if you feel very tired and faint in the mornings, breakfast in bed; if you feel walking too much for you at the moment, use your car; tempt your appetite; nourish yourself well. And later, when the spring comes, we must tell your husband to give you some nice week-ends at the sea." But, taking her hand and patting it kindly, he substituted this: "Well, Mrs. Kerr, I'm glad to hear that you've plenty to occupy yourself; it's a great thing to keep busy, specially at these times. As a matter of fact, there's no finer exercise than a little normal housework. And you must walk, too; that walk to market in the mornings is just splendid. As for your appetite, you must try not to get faddy; it's a woman's duty to keep up her strength, you know. I congratulate you most heartily on the good news I have just been able to give you."

May Edginton

"Thank you," said Marie, frightened but exultant, "and may I—what is the fee?"

"Five shillings, please," he replied, after a slight pause.

Then Marie was out again in the waiting-room with Julia, to whom she nodded mysteriously, and whose hand she squeezed. The doctor escorted both girls to the door, and looked after them for a moment; but it was an ordinary story, and the world must go round.

Julia and Marie walked all the way home, talking of what was going to happen next September.

They sat for a long while on the hearthrug in the dining-room when they reached home, talking about next September; and when at last Julia left, Marie still sat there hoping and planning, thinking of this perfect flat with a baby in it, and longing for Osborn's return to share the unparalleled news.

She had seen little, intimately, of babies; in the streets and parks she met them, and said: "What sweets! What precious things!" And she had thought more than once how beautiful it would be to own one, sitting in its well-built perambulator with the clean white lacy covers and cushions, and the starched nurse primly wheeling it.

There would be knitting to do, too; endless shawls, swallowing up pounds of the best white wool; and fleecy boots and caps and vests. When the next housekeeping allowance was paid, some of it should be stealthily diverted to this delicious end.

The clock struck eleven; for some while now Marie had ceased to notice how musical was its sound, as compared with other people's clocks, but to-night she noticed it anew.

It was like little silver bells pealing; there ought to be birth-bells as well as wedding-bells.

Osborn was late, but Marie waited up for him, untired. She mended the fire, for he might come in cold, and they were not going to bed yet. No! They must sit and discuss next September. How would Osborn receive the news? What did men really think about these things? It was impossible they could feel the full measure of women's gladness, but in part, surely, they shared it?

At twelve Osborn came in, fresh and pink from the cold outside, with a hilarious eye, and a flavour of good whisky on his breath. He was in great spirits and could have ragged a judge. But as he took off coat and muffler in the hall, displaying himself in dinner clothes, there came creeping out to him from the dining-room, softly as a mouse, but with eyes bright as all the moon and stars, his wife. She had about her an air of lovely mystery, about which Osborn was still too jolly to concern himself. But she looked so beautiful that he caught her to him, and kissed her many times.

"You ripping little kid!" he said fondly, "have you waited up for me? Or have you only just got in?"

"I waited up for you, dear."

"Is there a fire?" asked Osborn.

"A good one."

They went into the dining-room and sat down, Osborn in his chair, she on the hearthrug beside him, and she let him tell his story first, so that afterwards all his attention should be rapt on hers. He said gaily: "I've had a ripping evening. Desmond was in his very best form, and he'd got two more fellows there, and we were a jolly lot, I assure you, my kid. By Jove! don't I wish I belonged to that club! I've half a mind to get Desmond to put me up. He would, like a shot. We had an awf'ly decent dinner; they give you *some* dinner at that club. We drank toasts; you'd like to hear about that, wouldn't you? That old one, you know: 'Our sweethearts and wives; and may they never meet!'"

Osborn laughed.

"I've had a nice evening, too," said Marie, leaning against the caressing hand.

"That's good," said Osborn. "Miss Winter came and you had dinner here, I suppose. What did you see?"

"We didn't go to the theatre."

"Not go!" said Osborn, "how was that? You weren't seedy again, were you, kid?"

"Rather," Marie murmured, "so Julia took me to a doctor instead."

"My dear!" Osborn cried.

"Osborn," said Marie, looking up at him, "we—we're going to have a baby."

"The deuce we are!" Osborn exclaimed abruptly, and he sat back and looked down at her sparkling face incredulously.

"You're glad?" she asked.

Osborn pulled himself sharply together. He said to Rokeby afterwards: "I believe it's the biggest shock of a chap's life.

Awful good news and all that, of course." But now he was concerned only with Marie, that pretty frail thing so joyously taking upon her shoulders what seemed to him so vague and dreadful a burden, and for the moment he was aghast for her.

"Are you?" he stammered.

"I think it's lovely," she murmured.

"Then I'm glad," said Osborn; "if you're glad, I am, you dear, sweet, best girl. But tell me all the doctor said, angel, and just what we're to do and everything."

"We don't do anything till next September."

"Is it to be next September?"

"Yes," said Marie, trembling a little.

CHAPTER VII

DISILLUSION

Osborn had to tell Desmond Rokeby; he simply couldn't help it. They met at a quick lunch counter, an unusual meeting, for Rokeby lunched almost invariably at his club. As Osborn ate his sandwiches and drank his ale he was looking sideways at Rokeby all the time, and feeling, somehow, how futile he was, how worthless bachelors were to the world; and presently, when the space around them had cleared, and the white-capped server had moved away, he almost whispered:

"I say, Desmond, there's great news at my place."

Rokeby looked into Osborn's eager face.

"I wonder," said he, "if I could give a guess."

"I know you couldn't, old chap," said Osborn; "the surprise simply bowled *me* over."

Rokeby had already guessed right, but he had the tact and kindness not to say so; he had known men's pleasure in the telling before.

"Are you going to tell me?" he asked.

"Am I *not*, old man?" said Osborn, looking at the colour of his ale with a kind of smiling remoteness. "Well ... this is it ... how does one put it?... Well, here it is. Next September there'll be three people instead of two at No. 30 Welham Mansions."

"By Jove!" said Rokeby. "You must be awf'ly pleased!"

"Simply off my head! So's Marie."

He did not bank his two pounds that week, but kept them in his pocket. They need not spend both, but one Marie must have. And when he went home that afternoon, having asked permission to leave early, for a family purpose, and when he put the usual 30s. into his wife's hand, he cried:

"You're coming out shopping, Mrs. Kerr. You're coming out to buy yards and yards of whatever it is. And why mayn't we do a little dinner as well? You're to be kept cheerful."

She had been feeling pathetic all day, and she was full of pleasure at this. She hugged Osborn and lavished on him all her peculiar pet endearments, and ran to change into her best suit and furs. They went out together, very happy, and town lay spread before them, as if for their delight. It was scarcely yet full dusk, the sky was like opals and the streets were just becoming grey, the lamps starring them. The cold was crisp, and women in short skirts, trim boots, and big furs stepped briskly, their faces rosy. Osborn had his hand under the arm of a woman as trimly shod, as nicely-furred as any they met, and, as well, as being proud and thrilled with his new significance, he was proud of her. He liked men to glance away from the girls they escorted at Marie's face; and he liked to think: "Yes, you admire her, don't you? That little girl you're with—you're taking her out and spending your money on her and making an ass of yourself, and she don't care tuppence for you. But this beautiful woman I'm taking out is my wife, and she loves me."

Osborn was led, dazzled, into labyrinthine shops; he stood with Marie before long counters, while she inspected fine fabrics and, drawing off her glove, felt them critically with her fine hand. He watched her eagerly and devotedly, as if he read the concentration of her thoughts, and he imagined the thoughts to be these:

"Is this soft enough for him? Is this delicate enough for my baby's body? Nothing harsh shall touch my darling; he must have the best, and the best is not good enough for him. We will buy the most beautiful things in the world for my son."

And she ordered the lengths in a voice which cooed; she bought lawn and flannel, and great skeins of wool, and lace fit for fairies; and she sought, as if trying to remember the persecution of the purse, for bargains in blue ribbon, but by that time Osborn was too exalted to permit bargaining. He, too, was saying within himself:

"Shan't my boy have the best? When he's little and weak shan't I win it for him? And when he's grown and strong, won't he win it for himself, by Jove!"

He bought the blue ribbon.

They had spent one of the two pounds, and there seemed very little for it, of those fine things fit for a baby; but Marie stopped short after the spending of that sum. "It's enough to begin on," she urged; "when I've finished with that I'll get more." And she whispered, when the attendant's back was turned: "I shall squeeze it out of the thirty shillings all right,

Osborn. I shall put by every week."

"Then," Osborn replied in the same *sotto voce*, "if you won't spend more for your baby, you darling, you'll be taken out to dinner, because I love you so; and you're to have a good time and be happy. I'm to keep you cheerful."

They chose one of the smallest West End restaurants, where they spent what Marie called a dream of an evening. Her languors evaporated in that subtle air, her eyes brightened, her cheeks glowed; she could face right into the teeth of the coming storm, and do no more than laugh at it. How good it was to be alive, and how alive she was! She had two lives. She was that most vital of all creatures, the expectant mother. She felt vaguely as if God had granted to her a great and new power.

The next morning the sensation of power had vanished. She was only a tired and nervous girl with a nasty feeling of nausea on her tongue. Once more Osborn brought her tea, and she sipped it leaning back on her pillow; as she stretched out an arm for it she caught sight of her face in the glass and sank back again. It was so tired and fretted, and the freshness of her skin seemed lost. How she wished she need not get up! She dreaded the day with its small and insistent exactions.

She was conscious of a fierce irritation with petty things.

Osborn could hardly eat breakfast himself when he saw how sick and sorry she was; he watched her efforts to eat a piece of dry toast and tried to comfort.

"When I saw the doctor," he said, "he told me this feeling of yours would only last two or three months."

"'Only'!" said Marie despairingly, "'only'!" She recalled Julia to him faintly, when she exclaimed: "I wonder how you men would like to feel sick and faint and ragged-out for 'only' three months!"

He hung his head.

"Well, we can't help it," he pleaded, half guiltily.

"I know," she whispered, with a sob in her throat, "but don't say 'only.'"

Osborn left home somewhat earlier than usual that morning. That sort of half-guilty feeling made him glad to go. It wasn't his fault, was it, that Nature had matters thus arranged? He agreed with his wife that it was bad management, but he couldn't help it. He was glad that, as he left, she asked him to do something for her; glad that he was able to do it.

When he had gone, Marie did a very wise thing, though he would have thought it a foolish one. She lay down and cried. She cried till she could cry no longer. She lay there some while after her tears had ceased, as if their fount had dried, and she adapted her outlook, as well as she was able, to these unforeseen, surprising and dismaying conditions.

She was the victim of the pretty and glossy storybook, the sentimental play, and of a light education. None of these things had prepared her for the realities she was undergoing; the story-book ended glossily with the marriage and happy expectations of a wonder-struck young couple. In book and play the heavenly child simply happened; no one felt miserably sick, ferociously irritable, or despairingly weary because of its coming. There had been no part of her education which had warned her of natural contingencies. She now saw that for her blessing she must pay, and pay heavily maybe, with her body.

She argued with herself a little fractiously on the escape of men. They had children without suffering; marriage without tears. Was it fair? Oh, was it in any sense equal or fair?

*　*　*　*　*

The little clock struck 6.30. Osborn was due, and dinner not yet preparing. Marie ran to the kitchen. "Goodness!" she said to herself, "it's endless! Life's nothing but getting meals. Is eating worth while?" She hurried around the flat till she was tired again, but hasten as she might, Osborn arrived before the cooking was done.

She was changing her gown when he appeared at the door of their room; she had not yet lowered the standard she had set for the ever-dainty wife prepared to charm her lord.

"Hallo, kiddie!" said Osborn, his voice rather tired. "I'm awf'ly hungry. Had a quick lunch. Is dinner ready?"

"No, it isn't," she replied sharply; "and what's more, it won't be for another half-hour."

"Well, you might hurry it."

"I've been hurrying; I'm sick of hurrying, and sick of getting meals."

The door slammed. She swung round with raised eyebrows, hands up to her hair, which she was dressing.

Osborn was gone. She heard him entering the bathroom noisily.

"Temper," she said aloud. "Temper!"

There was a big blank wall, ugly, insurmountable, cutting right across the garden of married life.

CHAPTER VIII

BABY

Marie awoke Osborn very early on a September morning; she leaned upon her elbow, gazing over to his bed, with terror in her eyes.

"Osborn," she gasped, "fetch the doctor! Telephone the nurse! The time's come, and I'm so frightened. You won't leave me long? I can't be left. Come back quickly and help me, Osborn.... I daren't stay alone."

As Osborn ran, roughly dressed, and sick with fear, down the road to the doctor's house, the irritations, the trials and domestic troubles of the past half-year were swept away by comparison with this that loomed infinitely greater. It had seemed to him, though he had borne it more or less silently, very pitiable that a man, the breadwinner, should ever come home weary of evenings to find his dinner not ready; it had seemed to him sometimes, well as he had concealed the feeling for the most part, almost intolerably irksome to bear the strain of the fads and fancies, the nerves and frets of a delicate, child-bearing woman; he had wondered more than once if jolly cynics like Rokeby weren't right after all; the numerous small inroads upon his pocket had been unexpected, pin-pricking sort of shocks. But all this now receded; the hour was upon them, upon him, and the woman he loved; what did a spoiled dinner matter? What did a fretful quarrel matter, if only she won through? He begged the doctor's immediate presence as a man begging life; but he himself hurried ahead, back to Marie. When with trembling lips and trembling hands he had kissed and caressed her, he lighted the fires in the flat, in the dining-room, her bedroom, the bathroom geyser and the kitchen stove; he didn't know what else to do, and he had vague ideas about plenty of hot water for some purpose unknown. He brought Marie tea and she would not let him leave her again; she clung to him as to a saviour, but he felt so helpless.

The doctor arrived before the nurse; the nurse while he was still there. "It won't happen yet," he told them. "You must be a brave girl; nurse'll tell you what to do; and I'll look in again at mid-day."

"You'll stay, doctor?" she cried.

"You won't leave her, doctor," stammered Osborn aghast.

"You'll be all right," said the doctor to Marie; "you've got nurse and I'll be here again long before you want me." Outside in the corridor he faced Osborn's protests.

"My dear fellow, I can't stay. It wouldn't do any good if I could. Remember she isn't the only woman in the world to go through it."

"She's the only woman in the world to me!" cried Osborn in a burst of agony.

The doctor advised Osborn to eat breakfast before he left him, and when he had gone the two terrified young people hung upon the wisdom of the nurse.

Before the doctor came again Osborn was shut out of the chamber of anguish, but the flat was small and from the farthest corner of it he heard Marie's moans and cries and prayers.

He stood with his hands over his ears, praying, too, praying that soon it would be over, that she might not cease to love him. "How can she ever love me again?" he thought over and over.

It seemed to him a dreadful death for love to die.

* * * * *

As September dusk was falling, after a silence like fate through the flat, Osborn heard his child's cry. Half an hour after that the doctor came out of the birth-place. He walked through the open sitting-room door to the spot where Osborn stood as if transfixed and saw how the young man had suffered; but he had seen scores of such young men suffer similarly before. He glanced around the room and saw the dead fire in the grate. He himself looked weary.

"Buck up!" he said, with a hand on Osborn's shoulder. "You've a jolly little boy. You look bad! What have you been doing all this time?"

"Listening," Osborn gasped.

"And you've not done any good at it, have you?" the doctor said, shaking his head. "You might as well have cleared off, you know, on to the Heath—saved yourself a bit. However— Yes, I quite understand how you felt. You'd better have something—a cup of tea, a whisky and soda."

"She?" Osborn uttered.

"She's doing all right; I shall look in again to-night."

"She—she had a—a rough time?"

"Yes," said the doctor, "girls of her type do. We've progressed too far, you know, much too far, for women. She's suffered very much. I'm sorry."

"Can I see her?"

"You may go in now and stay till Nurse sends you away."

While the doctor let himself out quietly, Osborn tiptoed down the corridor between the cream walls whose creaminess mattered so little, and the black-and-white pictures that had lost their values. He tapped with icy finger-tips upon Marie's door and the nurse let him in.

He looked beyond her to the bed where Marie lay, such a slim little outline under the covers, such a little, little girl to suffer tremendously. Her eyes were open, dark and huge and horrified; over her tousled fair hair they had drawn one of the pink tulle caps, now come, indeed, into their own.

"There she is," said the nurse cheerfully. "We've made her look very smart, you see, and she's feeling very well. We shall get on splendidly now, and the baby's bonnie."

But she could fool neither of these young people; they were too modern, too analytic, too disobedient. When the horror-struck eyes of Marie and Osborn met they knew the immensity of what had occurred. No cheerful professional belittlement could avail. Osborn knelt down by his wife.

"Leave her to me a bit, Nurse," he said in a strangled voice. "I'll be very quiet."

"For a few minutes, then," the nurse replied, and she left them.

Osborn put his face down and cried tears that he could not stop. He longed to feel Marie's hand, forgiving him, on his head, but she had no comfort for him. She lay so still, without sound or sign, that soon, checking his grief with an effort nearly too big for him, he looked up and saw that she was crying, too. She was too weak to cry passionately, but her weeping was very bitter. This frightened him, so that he sprang up on tiptoes and called the nurse back. He kept his own shamed, wretched face in shadow.

The nurse sent him away and Marie had not spoken one word.

He crept into the kitchen and made tea, found cold food and ate a scratch sort of meal; he had eaten nothing since early morning, and then not much.

He had received a great big shock.

He did not know that women suffered so. He had sometimes read how after the birth of a baby, the husband went in and found his wife, pale perhaps, tired perhaps, but radiant, joyful, triumphant. He had not known that anguished mothers wept such bitter tears. Nothing was as he had been led to believe.

Could she ever get well?

The nurse came in quickly and softly, and saw the haggard man sitting at a deal table, eating his scraps. She viewed the situation wisely.

"You'll have to get the porter's wife in to look after you a bit," she said. "You can't go on like that. And *my* hands will be full."

"Nurse," said Osborn, "was she very bad? Is that the—the worst?"

"There are worse cases," replied the nurse briskly, "but she has suffered a great deal. What did you expect? She's a delicate, slim girl, and we're not savages now, more's the pity. The first baby is always the hardest, too."

"The first is the last here," said Osborn savagely.

The nurse smiled wisely. "Oh," she said placidly, "no doubt you'll be sending for me again in a couple of years, or less."

"What do you think I'm made of?" Osborn cried.

"The same as most men," said the nurse. "But will you tell me where to find the patent groats, for I've come to make gruel and I haven't time to talk."

"I'm afraid we never keep any groats or things," he exclaimed. "I'm sure we don't."

The nurse answered confidently: "Mrs. Kerr is sure to have bought everything."

Search in the larder revealed the groats, and the nurse began the cooking over the gas-stove. While she made the gruel, Osborn thought of Marie awaiting her trial, preparing for it ... buying groats.

He wished he had known what he knew now, so that he could have helped her more, have thought of the groats for her.

"Nurse," he asked, "do you think she can ever get quite well?"

"Of course she will. Rest and good food will be all she wants."

"Nurse, can I go and say good night to her?"

"Don't make her cry again, Mr. Kerr, and you may come in at eight."

As she went out with the cup of steaming food, she looked back to ask:

"Did you see the baby?"

"Don't mention the damned baby!" said Osborn with deep anger.

"The baby can't help it," answered the nurse, going out.

Osborn sat there thinking. No! The baby couldn't help it. That was very true. Losing his hostility to this fragment of life, he began to feel a faint curiosity. What was it like?

At eight o'clock he would look at the baby.

The nurse looked out of the bedroom door just before eight and signalled to him. This time she did not leave them alone, though she busied herself at the other side of the room, with her back to them, because she knew how shy these young things were. And this time Marie looked at Osborn with the ghost of a smile, barely more than a tremor of the lips. He bent down.

She whispered into his ear: "I don't—think—I could

ever—go—through it—again."

"Never again, my sweetheart," he whispered back.

She made a motion with her lips; he kissed them gently. "Good night," he murmured, "sleep well, poor little angel."

"She'll sleep," said the nurse unexpectedly, from near the fire. She was tending the baby now, and Osborn looked across at it in the subdued light. What a little mottled pink thing! What creases! What insignificance to have brought about all this!

"Look at your bonnie baby, Mr. Kerr," said the nurse, holding the mite aloft.

"Is that a bonnie baby?" said Osborn sourly.

"Osborn," whispered Marie from the bed, "he's a beautiful baby!"

Osborn looked down, startled, and saw in her wan face some glimmer of an unknown thing. She—*she*—was pleased with the baby! *She* admired and loved it!

He went out astonished.

The next morning, still flat on her pillows, she was nursing the baby with a smile on her mouth. Under her pink cap the faintest colour bloomed in her cheek; she asked for a fresh pink ribbon for her nightgown; she had slept peacefully. Some flowers were sent very early, with congratulations. They were from Rokeby and from Julia, and were arranged near her bed as she lay with this wonderful toy, this little new pet, Osborn's son, beside her. She had emerged out of her black darkness into light.

CHAPTER IX

PROBLEMS

Throughout Marie's convalescence there were things to buy; little things, but endless; to a woman who has suffered so greatly for their mutual joy can a man deny anything? The husband of a year cannot. Every day, before he went to his work—he was third salesman to one of the best Light Car Companies in town—Osborn held consultation, over the breakfast table, with the nurse. He used to say, as bravely and carelessly as if he felt no pinch at his pocket, "Is there anything you want to-day, Nurse?" And there was always something, a lotion, or a powder, or a new sponge, or a cake of a particular soap. The nurse had no compunction in adding: "If you *do* see a few nice grapes, or a really tender chicken, Mr. Kerr, I believe she might fancy them."

Osborn's lunches, during that month, grew lighter and lighter; they almost ceased.

Mrs. Ambler proved expensive in the kitchen, breaking for the while through her economical rule, feeling nothing too good for her poor child. She used to remind Osborn every time they met, by word, or look, or expressive sigh, how Marie had suffered. He felt oppressed, overridden and tired; but he was very obedient beneath the rule of the women.

He had to wait upon himself a good deal; sometimes he brought a chop for dinner home in his pocket and grilled it himself.

He slept in the room relegated to him as dressing-room or to a chance visitor, as occasion might arise; it looked forlorn and dusty, and the toilet covers wanted changing.

He longed to have Marie about again, blithe and pretty; and to be rid of this pack. He thought of his mother-in-law and the nurse as a pack.

Several times he succumbed to dining with Rokeby at his club, but he always hurried home in time to say good night to Marie *before* she fell asleep.

When the baby was nearly three weeks old, he was called upon to lift his wife out of bed for the first time, and to put her in an armchair, which had been prepared with pillows and a rug, by the purring gas-fire. She was so eager to be moved, and he so eager to have her to himself for just a little, that he begged permission to take her into another room for awhile, but the nurse would have none of it, and she was right, for Marie was white and tired when she had sat in the chair for only ten minutes. That staggered Osborn afresh. He was speechlessly sorry for her, and sat by her holding her hand, watching her concernedly, until she asked to be put back into bed again. That was on a Sunday.

The Sunday marked his memory. It disappointed him so bitterly to find that Marie was not stronger. After all the chickens and grapes, and doctors' and nurses' fees, she was not strong; and what could he do more for her? He was not a rich man. After the drain of all this they must live more steadily even than before; he could not waft her *and* the baby away to some warm south-coast resort to finish her convalescence; he could not take her for long motoring week-ends.

In a week the nurse would go. Would Marie be ready for her to go? If not, could Osborn keep her longer?

He knew he could not. There was only a sum of twelve or thirteen pounds left from the twenty which had represented the nest-egg which he had when he married; five of those pounds the doctor would take; six of them the nurse would take. He tried to arrange the disposal of his salary afresh, and could do no more than cut down his weekly expenditure of ten shillings to five.

But Marie and the baby were worth it all—if only he could get them alone again.

A week after that the nurse left and Osborn came back to Marie's room.

He looked forward to it; part of the dreadfulness of the past month had been their separation; now they were to be alone again, without that anarchic and despotic pack. On the morning, before he left, he wished the nurse good-bye with a false heartiness and handed her, breezily, a cheque. He would see her no more, God be thanked! When he came home that evening his place would be his own, his wife his own, the baby their own; there would be no stranger intruding upon their snug intimacy.

Osborn's heart was light when, at six o'clock, he put his latchkey into the keyhole and entered; he gave the long, low coo-ee which recalled old glad days, and Marie emerged from the kitchen, finger on mouth.

"Hush, don't wake him!"

"Is he in bed?"

"Nurse stayed to put him to bed before she left."

Osborn embraced her. "We're alone at last, hurrah!"

"Will you help me?" said Marie. "I'm so tired."

"Course I'll help you, little dear," he replied tenderly. "We'll do everything together, just as we used to."

"Osborn," said Marie suddenly, "that's the whole secret of married life, to do everything together, nice things and nasty things."

"Of course, darling. We do, don't we?"

"I suppose we do," she answered doubtfully; "at least there are some things a man doesn't share because he can't."

Her eyes dilated, and he guessed what she was thinking of. "I know, sweetest, I know," he said hastily, "but try not to remember it; it's all over and done with; and, Marie, I suffered, too."

She remembered, then, the tears they had shed together on the night of the baby's birth, and her heart was soft.

The night seemed punctuated to Osborn by the crying of the baby. It woke at regular hours, as if it could read some clock in the darkness; and quickly as, it seemed to him, he must have roused, Marie had wakened quicker, and was hushing the child. He could hear her soft whispers through the darkness, in the subsequent silences during which he guessed, with a thrill of anxious awe, that she was feeding it; frail as she was, she gave of what strength she had to the baby. Never had Marie seemed more wonderful to Osborn.

Very early in the morning she was tending the baby; he wished that he had been able to keep the nurse longer. He left her reluctantly after breakfast, to get through the baby's bath and toilet unaided, before the heavier work of the flat. Women who knew would have understood why Marie trembled and despaired at the tasks before her. When the baby cried as, with hands still weakened, she tried to hold up its slipping little body in the bath, she cried, too. As she cried, she thought how tears seemed to be always near her eyes during these married days. Was something wrong with marriage? Before, in her careless girl-days, she had never wept; she had never so suffered, so wearied and despaired. While she questioned, she dressed the baby in the flannel and lawn things she had made for it a long while ago, and when she had dressed it, she fed it again, and again it slept.

It was astonishing how much heavier a month-old infant could grow during an hour's marketing.

That reminded her that they had something else to buy, a big thing that would swallow up nearly, or quite, a week of Osborn's pay, a perambulator. The baby had luxuries; his toilet set from Rokeby, his christening robe from Julia, his puffed and frilly baby-basket from Grannie Amber, were dreams to delight a mother's heart; but he had no carriage. For a little while she might carry him when she was not too tired; and when she was, he might sleep out on the balcony that jutted from the sitting-room window, and she could stay beside him; but ultimately the question of the perambulator must arise.

As Marie walked home with her baby and her basket, she said to herself: "I won't ask poor Osborn now; not when he's just paid that woman a whole six pounds; not till he's settled the doctor; and there'll be an extra bill for the baby's vaccination soon, and the next furniture instalment's due; but when all that's cleared off, I'll choose the right time and ask him. I shall give him an extra nice dinner, and tell him we'll have to buy one."

In a week, when the doctor called to vaccinate the baby, he ordered the mother to leave off nursing it herself; he put it upon a patent food, not a cheap food; and it formed a pertinacious habit of wearing out best rubber bottle teats quicker than any baby ever known. In the nights Marie did not now reach out in the darkness to her baby and, gathering it to herself, nourish it quietly, without the certainty of waking Osborn; but there had to be a nightlight, there had to be business with a little spirit stove and saucepan, the unlucky jingle of a spoon against the bottle, so that Osborn began to mutter drowsily: "Hang that row!" and she longed to scream at him, "It's *your* baby, isn't it, as well as mine?"

Osborn was unused to and intolerant of domestic discomforts such as these; in the nights his nerves were frayed; at the breakfast-table he showed it: "You look tired to death, and I'm sure I am," he grumbled. "If this is marriage, give me single blessedness every time. Worry and expense! Expense and worry! Such is life!"

In the evenings she was very subdued; she was losing her life and light; he did not know that during the day, after such display of his irritation, she cried herself sick. He asked her to come out to dinner one evening; he said:

"You and I are getting two old mopes. Look here, girlie, put on your best frock, and come and dine at Pagani's; I can't afford it, but we'll do it."

But she could not.

"Baby," she said, hesitating.

Osborn looked at her in silence. "Good heavens!" he exclaimed, after a while, "aren't we ever to have our evenings out, then? Shall you always be tied here now?"

"A baby ties one," she replied.

"So it does, doesn't it?" said Osborn despondently.

Marie looked at him steadily. Just as she wanted to scream at him in the night, so she now longed to cry: "It's harder on me than you! Do you think I don't *want* ever to go out? Do you think I don't often long to go into the West End and look at the shops, or do a matinee with mother or Julia, and come back refreshed?"

But with the prudence of her mother's daughter she restrained herself.

"Day in, day out, are we always to live the life domestic pure and simple?" Osborn demanded.

For answer she shrugged her shoulders. Osborn thought her strangely nonchalant, almost contemptuous.

"Well, I, for one, damned well won't do it," he said, rising from the table.

"But I must," Marie replied in a level voice.

It was Osborn's turn to look at her; he wondered just what she meant by it.

"Well," he asked, "I can't help it, can I?"

"Neither can I," said Marie.

Osborn put on his coat and hat and went out. It was the first time he had ever gone out after dinner at home. For some while after he had left Marie remained alone at the table, staring before her. The small dining-room was still charming in the candlelight, but it took on a new aspect for her. The cream walls and golden-brown curtains enclosed her irrevocably. She would never get away from this place, the prison of home. Day in, day out, as Osborn said, it would be the same. The man might come and go at will, the woman had forged her fetters.

Didn't men ever understand anything? What crass vanity, what selfishness, what intolerance, kept them blind?

Marie was hardening. She did not cry. After a while she rose and cleared the table. As Osborn was not there, wishing for her company, she washed up. That would make it so much easier in the morning.

It left her, though, with an hour now in which to sit down and resume her thinking.

The flat was very quiet, very desolate. The man had gone out to seek amusement. How queer women's lives were!

She knew women whose husbands invariably went out at night, as soon as they had fed. What did these women really think of their men? What did these men really think of their women? How much did each know of the other? At what stage in these varied married lives did the wife become merely a servitor, to serve or order the serving of her husband's dinner, for which he came home before, again, he left her?

Married life!

At nine-thirty Marie prepared the baby's bottle and went to bed. She schooled herself to sleep, knowing that during the night the baby would make his demands, and she fell asleep quickly. She did not hear Osborn come in. He looked about the flat for her before going to his dressing-room, and, not finding her, said to himself wilfully: "Marie's sulking; she wouldn't wait up. Does she always expect a fellow to stay at home?"

By the glim of the nightlight, when he went into their room he saw her sleeping. The child slept, too. Osborn got resentfully into his bed, and thought of Rokeby, with whom he had just parted, and the end of a conversation they had had.

"You could afford to marry, Desmond."

"What's the standard?"

"Being able to keep servants," said Osborn harshly. "You marry the girl you love, a pretty girl you're proud to take about, and she can't come out to dine with you; she can't move from home; babies, they cry all night, burn 'em! And she gets ready to hate you. It's hell!"

CHAPTER X

RECRIMINATION

On a day of January, like spring, Julia went upon a sentimental errand, influenced by she did not know what; but she guessed it was the youth in the air. It made her think of the youngest thing she knew, and that was Marie's baby, and of what she could do for it; and all that she could do, as far as she saw, was to buy it a superfluous woolly lamb. So after her day's work was over, at half-past five, Julia put on her hat and coat with a purpose, and stepped into the toy department of her favourite stores.

Julia was not mean; from out the whole flock of lambs which she found awaiting her selection she chose a beauty. Its white fluffiness and its beady eyes affected her softly; her handsome face grew motherly as she insinuated the stranger into her muff, where her hands stroked it unconsciously. Julia was far more pleased with the lamb than the baby would be, as she boarded an omnibus and rode towards Hampstead.

It was six when she arrived at the door of No. 30 Welham Mansions, and Marie opened it to her with the baby in her arms, huddled up in a rather soiled shawl from which only his incredibly downy head emerged. He looked solemnly at

Julia and emitted an inquiring croak.

"You aren't still carrying that baby out, are you?" Julia asked suddenly.

They entered the sitting-room together.

"What else can I do? If I go out, he's got to go, too."

"You'll get a perambulator?"

"I'm going to ask Osborn soon."

"Why not ask him now?"

"He's had such a lot of expense, poor boy."

"Still," Julia argued, "it's got to be bought, and you ought to be saved. Ask him to-night, after dinner."

"I believe I will," said Marie. "My back ached so."

Julia was more bewildered than angry.

"My goodness!" she said sharply. "What's the matter with life? Why can't a young man and woman have a baby and look healthy over it? I've got to ask someone that, and get an answer."

Julia followed Marie back to the kitchen.

"I'll whip the cream, if he's got to have it," she said grudgingly.

"And I'll go and look nice for once. Then I'll ask him for the perambulator."

Marie came out again in the wedding-frock of chiffons, very tumbled now, looking sweet but with the hectic flush of her exertions still on her cheeks.

"All my clothes are going to glory!" she lamented.

"Tell you what," said Julia, producing frothy mounds of cream round her energetic whisk, "do have my bridesmaid dress. I've never worn it since your wedding—too pictures-que for my style, that frock is. But if you—"

"No, I won't!" Marie protested, tears in her eyes. "I'm not going to take anything from you except your old gloves for the housework. It would be scandalous; you, a girl working for her living, and me, a married woman with a husband to work for me—"

"I know which I'd rather be," Julia remarked.

"So do I," said Marie, with a quick intake of breath.

They looked at each other a little defiantly, but did not proceed to any enlightenment. Then Julia went up to Marie and laid her arms about her neck and her cool lips upon her hot cheek.

"Well, leave it at that," she said. "Good-bye, kiddie; take care of yourself. I can't stay. Send for me any time. I must fly!" And was gone.

Osborn came in hungry before seven, sniffed the dinner cooking, and turned into the dining-room. He took off his boots, fished his carpet slippers from behind the coal-scuttle, and put them on with a sigh of relief. The smell which pervaded the flat was savoury and good; the dinner-table was ready to the last saltspoon; the baby was quiet; all seemed to promise one of those smooth domestic evenings sometimes granted to a man.

He settled down by the fire after dinner to read so much of his evening paper as the Tube journey had not given him time for, while Marie made coffee and handed him his cup.

"Osborn," she said.

"Yes, dear."

"I wanted to ask you about something."

Into Osborn's eyes crept a harassed look, almost of fear; it was a very reluctant look, with repugnance in it and resignation and suspicion.

"About something?" he asked cautiously, "or for something?"

Marie had seen the look and had quite an old acquaintance with it. That ever-ready lump rose to her throat, and she had that passing wonder which she had often felt before—why she should cry so easily now.

"For something," she answered hesitatingly.

There was a silence.

Osborn lifted his paper as if to resume reading. His face flushed and his forehead lined.

"What do you want now?" he asked at last.

Marie flushed, too, till her face burned and tears glittered in her eyes.

"I'm afraid," she said, "that—that we'll have to buy a pram, shan't we?"

"A 'pram'?" said Osborn, as if she had asked for a motor-car.

"All babies have to have one. It's time—he ought to have had after the first month. He's getting so heavy, I can't carry him about much longer."

"Then don't carry him about."

"I've got to, unless I stay in altogether."

Osborn became silent. Because he felt desperately poor he also felt desperately angry; because he felt desperately angry he was angry with the most convenient person—his wife.

"Couldn't we buy one," said Marie, after he had remained mute for some while, "from the furniture people on the instalment plan?"

"Instalment plan!" he barked. "I'm sick of instalments! When am I ever going to be free? When's my money ever going to be my own again? Tell me that!"

"I can't tell you anything," said Marie, beginning to cry.

"Tears again!" he groaned. "Always this blasted tap-turning if you ask a woman a lucid question! Don't you see what you're making life for me? Don't you see the eternal drag you're putting on my wheel? I never drink, I never play cards, I don't do what any other fellow under the sun would expect to do; I give you all I can—every penny's gone in this awful domesticity. Domesticity? Slavery, I call it! What more can I do? What more do you expect? You ask for a perambulator as if it were a sixpenny-ha'penny toy! What would a perambulator cost?"

She retained control enough to reply:

"I—I have a catalogue. The one I've marked—I'd thought of—is—is three pounds ten."

Osborn threw away restraint.

"Three pounds ten!" he cried. "Within ten bob of a week's salary! Do you realise what you're asking? My God, women have a cheek. You bleed a man and bleed him until—until he don't know where to turn. It's ask, ask, ask—"

Then Marie also flung off restraint and gave all her pent-up nerves play. They faced each other like furies, he red and grim, she shaken and shrill.

"Ask, ask, ask! And what has marriage ever given me? Look at me! I was happy till I married you! I never knew what it was to be so poor and—and grudged till I'd married you! I didn't know what marriage was. I didn't know I'd be hungry and worried—yes, hungry!—and made ashamed to ask for every penny that I couldn't get without asking. Why can't I get it? Why, because you took me away from my job and married me! I cook for you, and sew and sweep and dust for you, and you take it all as a matter of course. All I've given up for you you take as a matter of course!

"All I've suffered for you you take as a matter of course ... you *men!*"

"I didn't know what it'd be like to have a baby, or, God knows, I'd never have had one—"

"Be quiet!" shouted Osborn. "Be quiet!"

But she raved on:

"No, I wouldn't! I wouldn't, I tell you! What do you expect of women? You expect us to want babies and bear them in all that—hell, and be pleased to have them; and—and to put up with begging from you for them! And you don't care how weak we are—how our backs ache; you don't care if the baby goes out or stays in—if *I* go out or stay in. It's your child, isn't it? It's not all *my* fault we had it, is it? There's a lucid question for *you*! Answer it!"

"I will do no such thing!" he cried angrily. "You ought to be ashamed of yourself—a woman—a *woman* suggesting she doesn't want a baby!"

"I didn't say it! I suggest I don't want one of yours!"

"My God!" said Osborn, recoiling.

Marie grew ice-cold when she had said a thing that she would have thought impossible to say; but there was a keen triumph in the ice-coldness. She had silenced him.

"Isn't married life ugly?" she asked. "Isn't it little and mean and sordid and stingy and unjust? You create a condition which will tie me to the house; you are angry with the condition because it's expensive; you're angry with me for being house-tied. Can I help it? Can I help anything? Do you think I don't *want* theatres and to go out to dinner with you as I used to? The baby's yours, isn't he, as well as mine?"

"Marie," said Osborn, "Marie—"

He searched for things to say.

"I wish I had never married you—I wish I had never married

at all," said Marie. "Men won't understand; they're impatient, they're brutes! And you haven't answered my question yet."

Osborn went out of the flat.

The inevitable answer of the goaded man—anger, silence and retreat—cried aloud to her.

She was afraid of herself.

What terrible things she had said—she, a little, new, young wife and mother!

She spoke out into the stillness, shocked, appealing, still trembling with her rage.

"Oh, God! Oh, God!... Oh, God, help me!"

CHAPTER XI

THE BANGED DOOR

When Julia had left the Kerrs' flat and was turning out of the building into the windy street, she met Desmond Rokeby about to enter. Her handsome face was grim beneath her veil and her eyes snapped. As she pulled up short and stood in Rokeby's path, she expressed to him the idea of a very determined obstacle.

"How nice to meet you!" he cried goodhumouredly.

"I'm glad I've met you," she replied.

Rokeby surveyed her quizzically. "What an admission," he said, "from an arch-enemy! You *are* the enemy of us all, aren't you? Is there anything I can do for you?"

"Where were you going?" Julia countered.

"To No. 30."

"Then—yes—you can do something for me. You can go away again."

"Are they out?" said Rokeby; "are they ill? What's

the mystery?"

She looked up and down the road; she gave him the impression that she stamped her feet and frowned, though to appearances she did neither. She ordered:

"Don't loiter here. Osborn—Mr. Kerr'll be home directly, and if he sees you he'll take you in, won't he?"

"Probably, I should say."

"Then come away."

"If I may walk a little way with you."

"I don't care where you walk with me," Julia replied vigorously, "if it isn't into Marie's flat."

She set a brisk pace down the opposite side of the road, as if assuming that Osborn might pass them unnoticing on the other, and Rokeby kept step unprotestingly. "It must be after six o'clock," he said presently.

"It is," she replied.

"Which is your way home?"

Julia described her route with a brevity characteristic of her.

He slackened pace, so that she looked round at him, impatiently questioning.

"Look here, Miss Winter," he coaxed, "don't go home. Stay out and dine with me. Of course we're mere strangers, but we're both so emancipated, aren't we? No, emancipated's an out-of-date word. We've passed that, haven't we, long ago?

We're—I dunno what we are; there's no limit to us. Isn't it jolly? So do come into town and dine with me."

"I think I'd like to, thanks," said Julia; "I'm not quite sure."

"Why aren't you quite sure?"

"I might be bored with you. How do I know?"

Rokeby looked at her with an astonished respect and a glim of his saving humour. "So you might; er—I hadn't thought of it; but 'pon my word, I'll do my best. Won't you come if I guarantee that?"

And he wanted her to come, oddly.

"Thanks," said Julia, "I will."

"Queer thing," Rokeby thought in his surprised soul, "when a girl all on her own in this hard world hesitates to come out to a good dinner with not a bad fellow in case she might be bored."

"I know what you're thinking," said Julia calmly; "you're thinking—or you are *almost*—that it was nearly a bit of cheek on my part. I don't blame you. You're spoilt, all of you. The girls you take out earn their dinners and stalls too conscientiously; no matter how dull you are, they take pains to shine. Frankly, if *you* take *me* out, *you've* got to shine. I demand it. And you'd be surprised at the number of invitations an exacting thing like me gets."

"No, I shouldn't," said Rokeby softly, bending his head to look with a new interest at her face. "That's sheer cleverness, that is; that's brilliance. You've seized it. A woman should have confidence to demand and get."

"Women are too humble."

"I never found them so," Rokeby denied respectfully.

"Well, half of them are too humble, and the other half are slave-drivers. If a girl's got to choose one or the other, she'd better drive."

"That's awf'ly sound," said Rokeby.

They neared a taxicab rank, and the first driver watched their approach with inquiring signal. "Cab!" Rokeby sang out, and the man started his engine.

"Where are we going?" Julia asked.

"Where you like," Desmond answered, "only let's start there."

He opened the door, she passed in, and he directed, "Piccadilly; and I'll tell you just where, presently."

He followed Julia in, and they were away, over suburban roads darker than the streets of the West.

Rokeby felt a certain triumph in capturing Julia. Besides her modern fighting quality, to which he was not entirely antagonistic, he realised that she was a pleasure to the eye, a well-tailored, handsome girl, town-bred, town-poised, of the neat, trim type so approved by the male eye. She knew her value too. She made a man think. Cheap attentions she would have handed back as trash, without thanks, to the donor. She conferred a favour, but would never receive one. Her self-assurance was no less than royal, and a word or touch in violation would have been stamped a rank impertinence. Rokeby, who had made the same pleasant uses of taxicabs as most men about town, knew all this with a half-sigh.

"Where would you like to dine?" he asked. "What kind of a place do you like?"

"A quiet place, to-night," said Julia; "it's better for talking, and this evening I've got to talk to someone."

Whereby she flattered Rokeby more than by any degree of easy flirtation which other women might have permitted, as they sped along the ever-brightening streets.

"We'll go to the Pall Mall, if you like, Miss Winter; it's little, it's good, it's quiet; interesting people go there; we'll make two more. How about that?"

"It'll do excellently."

"We shall probably get a balcony table if all those downstairs are booked."

As Rokeby said, they were in time for a balcony table, and he ordered dinner and wine before recurring to his former question.

"What was all the mystery about No. 30?"

"I don't call it a mystery; it was just a very ordinary domestic proposition; I didn't want them to be interrupted this evening, because, you see—you will laugh—"

"No, I swear I won't; do tell me."

"Marie wants to ask for a perambulator."

"'Him'?"

"Yes, him. Who's always 'him' to the household—the husband, the tyrant, the terror. Ugh!"

"Oh, come, Miss Winter. Osborn Kerr—I've known him for years; there's nothing of the tyrant and the terror about him. Why this embroidery of the sad tale?"

"Well, why was Marie afraid to ask him, then?"

"I don't know anything about it. I'm at a disadvantage with you, it seems."

"I'm quite willing to tell you; that's what I'm dining with you for, isn't it?"

"Is it?" said Rokeby, with a very charming smile which but few women knew.

She hurried on: "Yes, it is. You see, I didn't want you to come in and spoil it all, prevent Marie from asking her husband for the perambulator."

"You were awf'ly thoughtful, and I'm sure I didn't want to chip in at the wrong moment; but, I say, would it have mattered so much? Because I'd love to know why; you're interesting me, you know. She could have asked him another time, couldn't she?"

"You see, she was all ready to-night."

"'All ready'?"

"She put on the frock she was married in; and there was the whipped cream he's so fond of, with a cherry pie; and it all seemed so propitious that I thought it would be a pity if you spoilt it."

"You're right. I wouldn't have cut in for the world. But, I say," he cried gleefully, "what guile! What plotfulness! There's no getting even with a woman, is there? Little Mrs. Osborn and you lay your heads together, and she puts on her wedding frock—"

Julia eyed him with a steely disdain.

"Kindly tell me why a woman should trouble herself to make plans to coax her husband?"

"Ask me another. How do I know? She *did* it, didn't she?"

"Yes, because he was one of those beastly 'hims,' to be toadied and cajoled and fussed into a good humour before his wife dare ask for a carriage for the baby that belongs to both of them."

"Oh, I see! I see! I say, I'm stupid, aren't I?"

"I'll forgive you your stupidity if you promise me never to marry and make any woman miserable."

Rokeby became slightly nettled.

"Why shouldn't I marry and make some woman happy?" he demanded.

"Ask *me* another; you men don't seem to, do you?"

"You're not very sympathetic to—"

"Nor you. Look here! Bread and butter, and candles and

bootblacking, and laundering, and expenses for a baby when you've got one, are all everyday things, aren't they? If a woman's got to fuss and plan and cry and worry and fight just every day for the everyday things, is life worth while at all? Isn't a girl like me, in full possession of her health, mistress of her own life, filling her own pocket, better off than a girl like Marie who's married and lost it all?"

"*Are* you?" he demanded, stirred enough to look right into Julia's eyes; and he saw what deep eyes they were, and what sincere trouble and question lay in them.

She fenced doggedly: "I don't see why Marie should be made wretched; she's only twenty-six. Is she to have that kind of fuss every day of her life?"

"She won't want a new perambulator every day, we'll hope."

"Oh ... don't be cheap! You know what I mean. Why can't men meet domestic liabilities fairly and squarely with their wives? Why must they be coaxed to look at a bill which they authorise their wives to incur? Why is a man vexed because he's got to pay the butcher, when he eats meat every day of his life?"

"Since you ask, my dear girl, I'll tell you. People are too selfish to marry nowadays and make a good job of it. Most men always were; but then women used to go to the wall and go unprotestingly. Now something's roused them to jib. They're making the hell of a row. They won't stand it; and nobody else can. So what's to be done?"

"Is this marriage?" Julia asked coldly.

"No," said Rokeby, "it's war."

May Edginton

"It ought not to be."

"What do you suggest?"

"N-nothing."

"Nor does anyone else," Rokeby stated.

They were through the first course, and he replenished her glass with sparkling hock. "Eat, drink, and be merry," he counselled lachrymosely, "for to-morrow we may be married."

"Never for me."

"That's rash. People are caught—oh! it's the very devil to keep out of the net."

"What will be the end of things?"

"What things?"

"Marie's and Osborn's."

"My dear Miss Winter, you exaggerate. They'll shake down, and that's all."

"Will they be happy?"

"You'll have to ask them that, later. But, you see, I know Osborn Kerr, and he'll make the best of it like other people. I wish I could convince you. Don't distress yourself over the normal troubles of normal people."

But Julia still worried on: "She looked so white and tired to-day; she'd been carrying that great baby about round the shops, and she's not strong yet."

"Can't the baby stay peaceably at home?"

"Then she's got to stay too. Where she goes the baby must go. She's given up going out at all except just for her marketing."

"Well," said Rokeby, rubbing his head, "I don't know, I'm sure, what you or I can do. We'd better leave it all alone."

"If I hadn't spent everything I had in the bank only yesterday for a new suit I'd send her a baby-carriage to-morrow. It'll be three weeks before I've put by enough again."

"Don't rob yourself," said Rokeby quickly, with a softening face. "Look here, let me know what happens, will you?"

"About the perambulator?"

"Ah!"

"Will you be fairy godfather, then?"

"If you'd like me to."

"Oh, I would! You—you—"

"What am I?"

"You dear!"

"'Rah! 'Rah!" cried Rokeby, "shake hands on that!" She laid in his frankly a short and capable hand. "I'm not a 'him,' am I? Oh, say I'm not."

"You're not—yet. You're a dear."

"Am now, and ever shall be, world without end. Amen."

"Amen," said Julia, twinkling.

"Here are *peches melba*," said Rokeby, "women always like them. I'm glad they're on our programme to-night."

"I adore them."

"You might try to remember, before we leave the subject," Rokeby suggested, "that the prospects of these 'hims' aren't very rosy either sometimes. You see it comes hard on a man, though doubtless he's a black-hearted scoundrel to admit it, when he marries and has to stretch an income, which was perfectly palmy in the bachelor days, to meet the needs of two, or three, or however many it may ultimately have to meet. He can't help a yelp now and then. It's a horrid sound, but it relieves him. The only remedy I can suggest for the existing state of affairs is that all wives of over a year's standing should pack cotton wool in their ears. Eh? That's brains, isn't it? Kindly applaud."

"'M ..." said Julia, tightening her lips.

"Osborn entered marriage with the most exalted expectations," Rokeby went on.

"So did Marie."

"I assure you I never knew a chap more in love."

"Nor I a girl."

"Oh, chuck it!" begged Rokeby, laughing. "Do chuck it, will

you? Then you'll be a dear too. Look here, wouldn't you like to go on somewhere after this? I can telephone from here for seats."

But she would not. So they lingered on for awhile, talking and smoking over their coffee; and at last, when Julia looked across the room at the clock over the big mirrors, she was astonished and half vexed to find how much time had slipped by. Then she insisted on going, but Rokeby insisted, too, upon his escort all the way home, and she did not gainsay him. As he lifted her furs over her straight shoulders, waving away the waiter who hastened forward for the service, he murmured:

"Were you bored?"

"I've loved it," said Julia graciously, for she could be generous.

They walked home, according to her wishes, for it was a perfect night, and she a robust young creature who loved to give her energy a fling. She walked with a peculiar effect of hope and buoyancy, in spite of her habit of sombre sayings, and Rokeby found a pleasure in noting her. She looked what she was, a woman who had never yet encountered defeat.

This did not rouse in him the hunting desire to run her to earth, or to the dead wall against which she would sturdily plant that fine back of hers, and to vanquish her vainglory; but it made him softer, more protective of her than he had felt before; it made him wish that always she would keep this spirit and courage which burned like a brave candle in the mists of life. As they said good-bye upon the imposing pillar-guarded steps of her boarding-house—called in modern fashion a Ladies' Club—he held her hand longer than he had ever imagined he might want to hold the hand of this dragon of a girl.

"Be happy," he adjured her, "don't take other folks' troubles upon you; let 'em settle their own. Haven't you enough to do?"

"I always feel that there is no end to what I could do," Julia confessed.

"Yes, you generous thing!" Rokeby cried, "but don't abuse yourself. There—you don't want my advice, do you? Forgive me! And thank you so much for an interesting evening. And—and—good night."

He stood at the bottom of the steps watching reluctantly while Julia entered. She had a latchkey which, ordinary possession as it was, seemed a symbol of her freedom. While he would have granted it generously, the freedom somehow piqued Rokeby a little. He stood smiling rather sadly till she shut the door.

A scurrying housemaid paused in her rush upstairs to say:

"Oh, miss! You were rung up on the 'phone just now, and I took the message. From a Mrs. Kerr, miss, and she would be glad if you could go round at once."

Julia stood still for a moment or two, keeping her hands very still in her muff. "I expect ..." she began to think. Then she rushed for the cab-whistle, which hung in the hall, pulled open the door, and whistled until a cab came creeping round the corner, feeling in its blind way for the invisible fare. She ran down the steps, signalling, and it spurted up.

"Number Thirty Welham Mansions, Hampstead," she said as she jumped in.

It was an extravagant method of travel—being some distance to Hampstead—for a young woman earning three pounds ten a week and spending most of it gorgeously, but she did not care. The four shillings were a nothing compared to Marie's need of her. She passed the time in speculations of wrathful trend, until they pulled up in the quiet road from which she had so recently driven away with Desmond Rokeby.

Marie opened the door to her—Marie with a face like white marble and burning eyes. Her dead composure was wonderful and scornful, but Julia would have none of it; as soon as the door was shut upon them and they stood there, between the cream walls and black etchings of the hall, she seized Marie in her arms, exclaiming:

"My poor dear! What's up? Has he—"

For a long while Marie wept on Julia's breast, before the ashes of the dining-room fire, while the clock with the kind voice ticked musically on and on, and the room grew chillier, and herself more tired; but at last she could tell all.

"We—we've had—an awful—quarrel."

"Oh dear!" Julia commented, "oh dear!" She did not know what else to say.

"I asked him—about the pram."

"Yes, yes! As you said you would."

"He is so angry, so unjust."

"My poor old kiddie!"

"And I was so angry, perhaps I was unjust too."

"No, no, you weren't," said Julia viciously. "I'm sure of it. Nothing could be unjust to *him*. He deserves it all."

"No, he doesn't You don't understand. But he wasn't fair tonight; he was so angry, and it wasn't my fault. Do they think we *like* asking, I wonder? And I don't know what I said, Julia, but I know I made him think I didn't want baby."

"Well?"

"But I *do* want him, Julia. I don't know what I'd do without him; I love him so much—they just grow into your life, Julia, babies do. He's so sweet."

"Course you love him. I know that. So does Osborn, so don't cry."

"He said I ought to be ashamed of myself."

"Oh, indeed? *In*deed! And may one ask why?"

"B—because I asked for a pram, I s'pose."

"Really! Indeed! I'd like to—"

"Perhaps it wasn't just that. I don't know—but he got so angry and said he couldn't afford it, and I said, 'P—p—perhaps on the instalment p—p—plan?' and he said he was sick of instalments and when was his money ever going to be his own again? And I can't help it, Julia, can I? I haven't money of my own. And then I got angry and said things; and he said I ought to be ashamed of myself."

"But aren't you going to have the pram?"

"I don't know. I don't expect so. He went out without saying."

"That's like a man. Go out and slam the door if you don't want to give an answer!"

"Julia, I—I'm afraid I hurt his feelings. I made him say, 'My God!'"

"That's nothing. They speak of God like a man in the street. That means nothing."

"Are you sure?"

"Sure, you poor lamb? I'm as sure as sure."

"Do you think you know much about men, Julia?"

"I know too much, thank you."

"I hope you didn't mind coming here again? I didn't know what to do; I was so wretched, and there was no one to speak to; no one to tell; so I thought of you."

"That's right, my dear. Always think of me, if I can do anything. You know I'll always come."

"You *are* a darling, Julia."

The two girls hugged each other strenuously.

Marie said with a break yet in her voice, "It seemed to me I was being quite reasonable."

"There are all sorts of men," said Julia, "kind men and unkind; mean men and generous; good-tempered and bad-tempered; every sort except a reasonable one. There's never been a reasonable man born yet."

When Julia had pronounced this dictum, she stroked Marie's hair, and said: "You know, baby, you ought to go to bed like the other baby. You're tired out and your young man'll be home soon, I've no doubt."

"I don't suppose he'll be later than eleven."

"Well, I'd rather not be still here when he comes, thank you."

"Oh, you wouldn't say I'd told you anything!"

"I won't give myself a chance. I'll put you to bed and then I'll go home."

Julia was like a mother to Marie when she helped her to undress, and tucked her up in the bed beside the infant's cot. And when Marie asked anxiously, with her mind still troubled: "Julia, *you* know that I love baby, don't you?" she was warm in her assurances.

"Would you mind," said Marie, "making up the dining-room fire a little, please, dear, in case Osborn is cold when he comes in?"

Julia stroked on her gloves slowly. "Certainly," she replied, after a pause.

"I should only put on a couple of lumps, dear," said Marie from the bed.

"Righto!" Julia answered at the door. "Good night, babies!"

Very softly she closed the door and left them.

She stood for a few moments in the dining-room trying to persuade herself to make up the fire for Osborn. She hated doing it; she grudged him his fire and his armchair and pipe and the comfort of those carpet slippers she saw behind the coal-box. But at last she took up the tongs, saying to herself sourly:

"It's for Marie, after all, because she asked me; not for him."

She chose her lumps of coal carefully, the two biggest, heavy enough to crush out altogether the tiny glow of the embers which remained; she battened them down and remained to assure herself that they would not burn.

"He won't be able to say the fire wasn't made up," she thought.

She placed Osborn's carpet slippers carefully in front of it.

"He can't say he wasn't made comfortable when he came in."

She went out, with a small sense of satisfaction, and called softly along the corridor, "Good night, babies," before she left the flat. It was very, very cold, and she was more than ready for her own bed.

She travelled homewards upon the Tube.

Before she slept, however, Julia had a letter to write, to Desmond Rokeby; she addressed it to his business address, which she happened to know, and marked it *Very urgent.* The contents were as urgent as the instruction upon the envelope, and once again that night she left the Ladies' Club to post the letter at the pillar-box at the corner. It would be cleared at midnight, and Rokeby should get his news by the first post in the morning.

Then Julia Winter slept; but although her head was full of two babies, a grown-girl one and a tiny weakling one, together in a soiled pink room, it was not of them that she dreamed. She was sitting once more at a balcony table in the quiet red restaurant with the big mirrors, facing an unusual kind of man who cared as little what she thought of him as she cared what he thought of her; the restaurant was warm and rosy, and they drifted upon the flying hours, like two voyagers upon a happy river.

CHAPTER XII

BEHIND THE VEIL

Marie heard Osborn come in and go to the dining-room and hit an unresponsive mass of coal vigorously, but she gave no sign. In the darkness she listened for all the sounds she had learned to know so well; his movements in the dressing-room, his splashing as he washed face and hands in the bathroom, his pat-pat tread in carpet slippers along the corridor to their door. To-night he paused here, as if listening; and it seemed as if her heart paused, too, while she also listened for him. But he spoke no word, and she spoke none, and the baby slept, so presently she heard the cautious turning of the handle and his careful entry.

She feigned sleep.

He knew, by tiny signs he had learnt to discover, that she was not asleep, but he feigned belief that she was.

His bed creaked to tell her that he was getting into it, in the darkness, by her side.

Both Marie and Osborn were still angry, sore, insulted and resentful, and, like other married people in small homes, they must intrude upon each other intimately, sleep side by side, wake side by side, and remain as closely conscious of each other as if they dwelt together, by mutual desire, in a perpetual garden of roses. True, there was a bed in Osborn's dressing-room, but it was an uncomfortable bed of the fold-up family, and when he came in to-night it was folded against the wall, and he did not know exactly where its particular blankets were kept. He looked at it, thinking, "God! If I could only sleep here for a night or two!" But he allowed himself to be daunted by the problem of the blankets, and he went, as usual, to the room he shared with Marie.

But each was too angry to speak, and the presence of each was fuel to the other's anger.

Osborn was wakened in the morning by Marie's attentions to the baby. Though he had gone to sleep turned as completely away from her as possible, in the night he had rolled over, and now he watched her quietly and sulkily in the grey dawn, with just one eye opened upon her above the rim of his bedclothes. If she looked he meant to close his eyes again quickly, pretending sleep.

But there was something about the frailty of her figure as she sat up in bed, turning to the table with the spirit-lamp and saucepan upon it, a quality of wistful charm in her little undressed head, which went towards softening him. She was quiet, too; she spoke no word, nor looked towards him. He watched her patiently waiting for the boiling of the milk; he watched the care with which she mixed the food; and then she got out of bed, not minding the stark cold, and gave the bottle to the drowsy baby. She bent over it for a minute, smoothing its downy head with her light fingers; then she propped the bottle comfortably for the baby, by some ingenious management of its bed-clothing, and looked at the clock by her bedside. After she had looked at the clock she stood hesitating for awhile and he knew what she was deciding.

She wanted five minutes more of that warm bed after a night broken, as usual, by the baby's demands; but it was time to get up and sweep and cook and light fires and lay Osborn's breakfast-table.

After all, it was Osborn who broke the silence between them, sulkily.

"I should give yourself five more minutes; you'll freeze out there."

Marie turned round quickly and looked at his long, comfortable outline under his pink quilt. She hesitated, then spoke in her natural voice, which he was secretly relieved to hear:

"It's half-past six; I'll have to dress."

"Poor old girl!" Osborn mumbled from his pillow. After she had gone quietly out, and he listened to the sounds of running water in the bathroom, and after she had come back, and he watched her again, one eye cocked furtively over the blankets, while she moved about quickly, he thought and considered and argued with himself about her. But, after all, she did as other women do, didn't she? She had a home and a husband and child, and she was bound to look after them, wasn't she? He gave her all he could, and sometimes it seemed to him—though he didn't mean to grouse—that she might have managed better. His mother, for instance, grown grey and quiet in the service of himself and his father, had worked wonders with the limited family money.

Had she been still alive, she might have given Marie a few

wrinkles, perhaps....

There is little doubt that Mrs. Kerr the departed could have given her young daughter-in-law a few wrinkles had she met her—wrinkles of the most unprofitable kind upon her fair face; but as it was, Mrs. Kerr senior lay quietly afar off from No. 30 Welham Mansions, impotent to reform, and Osborn lay thinking his thoughts in silence while Marie, having dressed to petticoat and camisole, wreathed up her long and lustrous hair.

The baby sucked intermittently at his bottle.

When Marie had put on her blouse and skirt, and a pinafore to protect them, she went out without further conversation. Osborn wondered a little whether she sulked, but she was not sulking; she was only occupied much as he was, in thinking and considering and arguing with herself about him. She was modern enough to remain proud and critical and impatient after domestic experiences which would have gone far towards cowing the generation of women before her. Her mother had bowed beneath such experiences without so much as an inquiry or expostulation. As Marie hurried about with brush and duster, with black-lead and fire-fuel, as she stood over the purring stove, and watched toast and eggs and coffee come to their various perfections, each over its ring of flame, she was absorbed in wondering:

"It *is* I who am right? It's I who have the harder time? It's the woman upon whom everything falls? But can't it all be put right somehow? Couldn't I make him see?"

Something definite emerged from her prospecting, at least; the resolve to seek an understanding with Osborn, not now, over breakfast with its time-limit and its haste, but perhaps to-night, after dinner, when he'd come in, and been fed and rested, and had put on his warm slippers. She faced Osborn over the breakfast-table with a brightness which he was relieved to see; but after he had noted it with inward approval, he hid himself behind his newspaper; he wanted to say little; to get away very, very quietly.

He had known many men who had to fly before the domestic sirocco; he had laughed at and despised them in his heart. But—poor beggars! No doubt they had hidden themselves behind newspapers with a child-like faith in the impenetrability of the shield, even as he was hiding.

Poor beggars!

It was no better than the ostrich habit of tucking your head into the sand, to crowd yourself behind your morning paper. You felt awfully nervy behind it, and you kept a scowl handy. There was something in the tension which made you bolt your good food quickly, indifferent as your lunch would be presently, and which made you glad when you were ready to rise, and remark with a forced *bonhomie*:

"Well, so long, girlie! I must be off."

Marie followed Osborn out into the narrow hall, where now faint daubs marked the cream distemper, and helped him on with his coat, and found his gloves and muffler. "It's cold, dear," she said solicitously, "wrap up well."

"Oh, that's all right! Take care of yourself and baby. Good-bye!"

He stooped and kissed her lips quickly, avoiding her eyes, and went out whistling. A forlornness overtook her; she ran back through the dining-room to the window, and, leaning out, watched for him to emerge from the doorway below;

when he came, and started down the street towards the tramcar terminus, she made ready to wave as she used to do should he look up.

But he did not look up, as he strode purposefully away. A few months ago he would have lagged a little, glancing up and waving frequently before he finally disappeared. This morning as she watched the thought smote: "When did he forget to wave to me? When did we leave off—all this?"

She remembered it was when she began to be so really busy, after the baby came. Baby was crying sometimes as they finished breakfast; she must hurry to him; it was time for his bath; he must have his bath, mustn't he? She couldn't help that. But she rather thought that perhaps this was the beginning of the end of all those dear smiles and salutes right down the street back to the girl above. Perhaps Osborn had looked up in vain many mornings, hoping to see her leaning out there, and at last had ceased to mind whether she were there or not.

A surprise came for Marie after lunch. She was making herself ready to carry her baby and her basket to the open-air market a street away, where the thriftier housewives of the neighbourhood shopped, when a delivery carman left at her door the handsome baby-carriage which Julia's note had sent Desmond Rokeby out post-haste to buy. Such a perambulator Marie had never hoped for, nor dreamed of; it boasted every luxury of contrivance, from the umbrella basket, slung to the handles, to its C-springs and its big, smooth-rolling tyres. In colour it was French-grey, extremely dainty; and it came with Desmond's love to his godson and a tactfully expressed hope that his gift had not been forestalled. So Marie put her baby in, and her basket, too; and after she had finished admiring her pink-and-white son among the lavender upholstery, she wheeled him out proudly to the open-air market, where the equipage drew forth delighted comments from the vendors who knew her well. She did not come straight home, as she had to do when carrying the baby; but, her purchases finished, she turned towards the Heath, and wheeled about proudly there for a while, envying no one, not the smart nurses who propelled their smart perambulators, nor the few mothers who strolled beside them. She felt that, with the finest baby in town in a French-grey and lavender chariot, she could meet and beat any turnout of the kind.

Marie sang during the rest of the afternoon when she reached home again. She sang while she made a cup of tea; sang while she put her boy to bed, and set about her preparations for her husband's return; he heard her singing when he fitted his latchkey unobtrusively in the lock, and stepped, still furtively, into the hall. He breathed freely again and told himself that the storm had passed.

He sat down by the fire, before which his wife had set his slippers, but he did not unlace his boots. He was hungry; he cast a short look over the dinner-table to judge, by its arrangement, something of what he might be given to eat. Before he had made a guess, Marie ran in.

"Guess!" she cried, "guess what's happened!"

"Dunno, old girl," said Osborn.

"That dear darling Mr. Rokeby has sent us the *most gorgeous* baby-carriage."

"The devil he has!" said Osborn, with deep feeling, straightening his shoulders as if a burden had been lifted from them.

"It's down in the lobby with the other prams; you must go

down and see it."

"I will after dinner. By Jove, that's good of Rokeby! I wonder what made him think of it."

"I can't imagine; he *is* thoughtful, isn't he?"

"What's it like?"

"It's pale grey, with ball bearings; and C-springs, and an umbrella basket. There's no enamel; it's all nickel. And the upholstery...."

"By Jove, Desmond's done the youngster proud, what?"

"We couldn't *possibly* have bought such a carriage for him, Osborn!"

Osborn began to feel flattered as well as pleased. He had always noticed, of course, the very particular attraction and beauty and the early cleverness of his son, but he had not guessed that the little beggar had so impressed that confirmed bachelor.

"Rokeby thinks no end of the kid, you know," he said, sitting down to the table.

"That's not to be wondered at, is it?" replied the enthusiastic mother.

Osborn caught her hand as she passed by him and kissed it.

"I've been thinking about you—about us—to-day," he confided.

"Have you?" she said timidly.

"We—we were both," Osborn hesitated, "both a bit—mad last night, weren't we?"

He pressed her hand before he relinquished it so that she might proceed to the kitchen to dish up the dinner. And she went with a lighter heart because of his affection.

Opposite him, beneath the candles which she still lighted with pleasure each night, she regarded him with a new earnestness. The quarrel was over, it seemed; but it had opened for her a door through which she had never passed before, the door into the darkness of human hearts, and she felt as if she would never forget that horrific step across the unveiled threshold. She watched Osborn steadily yet unobtrusively while his mind was given to the meal; she saw him eat with a great hunger, and the rather tired look which had marked his face when he first came in disappeared as he ate. Men who perforce eat lunch very frugally look forward keenly to a good meal, and Osborn had no eyes or words for Marie until the edge of his appetite was satisfied. She did not yet understand this very well; she was inclined to a slight resentment in his absorption with his dinner to the exclusion of herself. But she did not interrupt him by chatter; she just sat there quietly observing until he should be ready for more conversation.

Presently she brought his coffee round to his side, and he lighted a cigarette with a sigh of satisfaction. He appreciated, indefinitely, her gift of silence when a man came in sharpset for dinner; he had spent a day among busy men, talking all the time, and he did not wish to talk any more. After all, a man came home for quiet.

Marie had spent the day alone with the baby. There had been no voice save her singing one uplifted in the flat since early morning; she wanted to sit with Osborn by the fire in their dear old way, and to talk and talk; and to hear him talk. After all, was not the companionable evening the time for which the lonely household woman lived through her silent day?

She brought her coffee to a place near him and sat down there.

"Osborn," she said, "I was awf'ly hurt that you were so angry last night. I do want you to see that it isn't my fault."

He looked at her rather appealingly. "Let's chuck it," he suggested.

"If you will only understand! I don't believe men think; but if you *would* think over it for just a few minutes, dear old boy, you'd know that I'm just as careful as a woman can be. You used to give me thirty shillings a week for the housekeeping before we had baby; and I've never asked you for any more since, have I? And his food's awf'ly expensive too. I manage on just the same, Osborn."

"Yes, yes," he said, moving uneasily, "but where's all this leading? I mean—"

"It isn't leading anywhere. I only wanted you to see that I can't help anything."

After a pause, with a little line between his brows, he said:

"No, I know you can't. It's all right. You said some perfectly awful things last night—"

"So did you, Osborn."

He rose slowly. "Well, dear, we won't go over it. We've seen things with the gilt off; and that's that. Anyhow, there's nothing to worry about, is there? We're about straight with the world, though it means every penny earmarked before I earn it. And there's no question of buying a pram now, thank God!"

He turned away and searched on the mantelpiece for matches. "It made me shudder," he said very gravely, "three-pound-ten! Four pounds! After all the expenses I'd had."

"Well...." she said, swallowing hard, "well, come and see Mr. Rokeby's present. It's a ten-guinea carriage, Osborn; nothing less."

He swung round and looked at her, palsied in amazement.

"Ten guineas! *Ten!* Good God! Why ... it takes me the best part of three weeks to earn what that baby of yours just rides about in!"

"Aren't you coming down to see it?"

"I—I shall see it as I go out, thanks."

"When you—go out!"

She looked down quickly and noted that he had not taken off his boots.

She said in a changed voice: "You're going out?"

"I promised a man to look in and see the show at The Happy with him to-night. Just in the prom, you know. We haven't got stalls like giddy bachelors!"

"Osborn, can't you stay in? It—it's lonely all day, and I look forward to your coming home."

"You didn't seem to look forward very kindly last night."

She cried with hot resentment: "I thought you didn't want that mentioned again!"

"Oh, very well! And I shall be in to-morrow night; won't that do? A man can't be always tied up to the kitchen table, you know. Besides, I promised Dicky Vendo I'd go; his wife's away, and he's free."

"Yours isn't away."

"But she's been a damned little shrew, and doesn't deserve me to stay in for her. There! that's what you get by arguing." He laughed a laugh of vexation as much at his own ill-temper as at her pertinacity.

"Very well," she said, drawing back.

The light in the room was subdued, for the candles had not yet given place to the incandescent glare. He cast a glance at her face, but she had withdrawn to the shadow.

"Well," he hesitated, "night-night, in case you don't sit up."

"Good night," she replied. "I shan't sit up."

"You might make up the fire before you go to bed, though, there's a dear girl."

She did not answer, and he went out; she followed him to the doorway, and stood there watching him put on his overcoat and muffler again. His pipe was between his teeth; he removed it for a second to kiss her cheek hastily, then restored it. With a hysterical anger held feverishly in check, she thought that male imperturbability, male selfishness, were incredible.

"Night-night!" he said again, going out. "I'll bring you a programme."

The door shut. She was alone. She advanced passionately upon the strewn dinner-table; it waited there to be cleared by the work of her hands, as imperturbable as he.

She dashed off the candle-shades first.

"What a day!" she gasped.

Early morning and the awakening in the cold, the brushing of grates and the lighting of fires, the sweeping and cooking, to get a man off warmed and comfortable to business; the long, long hours of silence and domestic tasks, waiting for his return; his return to his food; his departure again; a desolate evening of silence and domestic tasks—these were that span of hope and promise called a day.

Married life!

CHAPTER XIII

"THE VERY DEVIL"

When spring had passed, and part of the summer, the Osborn Kerrs did as all their neighbours did; they packed up their best clothes, folded the baby's cot, swathed the ten-guinea perambulator, and with the baby and his cumbersome impedimenta, made an exhausting effort and went to the sea.

They did not go to the sea altogether lightly; it had cost a great deal of thought and arithmetic and discussion as to a stopping-place. Osborn was keen on a boarding-house; he knew a jolly one where he had stayed before, but Marie vetoed that. They wouldn't have babies in boarding-houses; they wouldn't like her keeping the perambulator there, and wheeling it through the hall; likewise they wouldn't like her intruding into the back regions with it. She knew that what one did with a young family was to take rooms, and cater for oneself. So they wrote to engage rooms, and after much correspondence found what would suit their purse, and started for a week by the sea.

The baby fretted a little during its unaccustomed travelling, and, fretting, fretted its parents. Osborn was dimly annoyed with Marie for not being able to keep the baby up to the best standard of infantile behaviour, feeling that the things he was called upon to do, in a public railway carriage, made him look a fool; and Marie was hurt with Osborn that he should show so little sympathy and patience. She wrote, upon arrival, a letter to Mrs. Amber, which brought her down within a couple of days, to stay at a boarding-house within a stone's throw.

Grandmother was very good. She was always nice-tempered and kind and soothing. In the morning she came round early to the rooms in a side street, and took the baby out for his airing upon the promenade, so that Marie and Osborn might bathe together. She it was who persuaded their landlady to take charge of the baby for just one hour, one afternoon, while Marie and Osborn came to take fashionable tea with her at the boarding-house. In the evening, when the pier was lighted and the band played, and the summer life of the place was at its giddiest, she would arrive with her comfortable smile and her knitting to sit within earshot of her sleeping grandson while his parents went out to enjoy themselves.

Marie did not know what she would have done without the wise woman upon this holiday; but when they talked together she was still shy of confidences, and still reluctant to admit any but the most modern interpretation of the married relationship. Mrs. Amber, however, saw all there was to see and felt no resentment about it. Things were so; and they always had been. You might be miserable if you were married, but then you would have been far more miserable if you had not married. She pitied all spinsters profoundly. She was glad her daughter had found a husband and a home; and she would not have dreamed of combating Osborn. He was that strange, wilful despotic thing, a man. She would have handed him without contest that dangerous weapon of complete power over a woman and her children. Mrs. Amber propitiated Osborn; she pleased and flattered him; and her judgment of him was that he was far better than he might have been.

Grannie travelled back with them to town, and she was very useful during the journey. She kept a strict eye upon the hand-luggage and nursed the baby, while Marie and Osborn smiled together over the sketches in a humorous weekly. Their money was all spent, and they were really half-relieved to be going back to the flat, where they need not keep up that air of being so very pleased with every detail of a rather strained holiday. They would meet other people they knew, who had similarly enjoyed themselves, and would cry:

"Have *you* been away? We're just back. We went to Littlehampton and had a gorgeous time! We had such awf'ly comfortable rooms, not actually *on* the front, but within a minute's walk. We *prefer* rooms to an hotel. We enjoyed ourselves tremendously. Where did you go?"

Mrs. Amber was with Marie a great deal during the rest of that hot summer; she had waited for the close intimacy of the honeymoon time, of the first year, to wear away; she had bided her hour very patiently. When the husband began—as he would—to go out for an hour after dinner, just to meet a friend, and would stay two—three, four hours perhaps, then the mother had come into her own again. Sitting with the strangely-quietened Marie by the open windows of the pale sitting-room—which they could use again with perfect economy during the summer weather—Mrs. Amber was well content with the way of things. She knitted placidly for baby George all the while, and Marie, who hated knitting, sewed for him.

They were evenings such as Mrs. Amber the young wife used to spend with her own mother, while young Mr. Amber betook himself to the strange and unexplained haunts of men.

And on one of these evenings, while the weather was still warm enough to sit looking out into the darkness through the opened windows, but when an autumn haze had begun to hang again about the night, Marie had something to tell her mother, which had blanched her cheek and moistened her eyes all day.

"Mother, I don't know *what* you'll think, but—I'm going to have another baby."

"Oh—my—dear!" said Mrs. Amber.

The two women gazed into each other's eyes, and while a half-pleased expression stole through the solicitude in Mrs. Amber's, Marie's were wide with fear.

"Are you sure, duck?" said the elder woman, her knitting dropped in her lap.

"Sure," Marie murmured hoarsely. "I've been afraid—and I waited before I told you. But I'm sure. It—it'll be next summer—in the hot weather, just when we'd have been going away to the sea. We shan't be able to afford to go to Littlehampton next year."

"An only child," said Mrs. Amber comfortingly, "is a mistake. It's almost cruel to have an only child. You'll be much better with two than one."

"How can you say so? All that to go through again—"

"Oh, duck, I know! But it won't be so bad next time; anyone'll tell you that. Ask your doctor."

"I shan't have the doctor till I'm obliged."

"I'm sure Osborn would wish you to—"

"How do you know what Osborn would wish?" And she said as so many rebellious women have said before her: "He promised I should never have another. He was crying. I've never told you before, but he was. He cried; and promised me."

"Cried!" Mrs. Amber echoed aghast. "Poor fellow, oh, poor fellow! Osborn has a very good heart. The dear boy!"

"What about me, mother? Where's your sympathy for me? I cried, too."

"We're different."

"No, we aren't. And he *promised*."

"Oh, my duck," said Mrs. Amber in a voice of confidential bustle, "that's not to be depended on. Men always promise these things; I've known it scores of times. But it doesn't do to depend upon them, love."

"I despise men."

"Oh, don't say that, like Miss Winter. I never did approve of that girl."

"She's wiser than I. She won't marry."

"I guess she hasn't had the chance," said Mrs. Amber, with the disbelief of the old married woman in spinster charms.

"Oh, yes, she has, mother. She's had several chances. But she knows when she's lucky; she's her own mistress, and she has her own money and her own freedom."

"She's missing a great deal; and some day she'll know it."

"She knows it now, thank you. She knows she's missing illness and pain and poverty and worry, and the whims and fancies and bad tempers of a husband."

Mrs. Amber said soothingly: "Now, now, my dear, you're not yourself, or you wouldn't say such things. It's every woman's duty to marry if she can and have children. As to your husband, it's no use expecting anything of men but what you get; and the sooner you realise it, my love, the happier you'll be."

"I'll never realise it!" Marie fired.

"Then you'll never settle down contentedly as you ought to."

"Why ought I, mother?"

"Because there's nothing else to be done," replied Mrs. Amber sensibly.

"You're right there," Marie moaned, with her forehead against the chair back, "there's nothing else to be done."

"What does Osborn say now about a second baby?"

"He doesn't know."

Mrs. Amber paused and thought before she said: "You ought to tell him at once, my dear. It's possible—he might be pleased."

"He'll be anything but pleased. I dread telling him."

"Oh, my duck!" said Mrs. Amber helplessly.

Marie enumerated: "He'll hate the expense, and the worry, and my illness, and the discomforts he'll have while I'm ill. He'll hate everything."

"Men do, of course, poor things," Mrs. Amber commented with sympathy.

"Poor things!" Marie flared. "I'd like to—"

"No, you wouldn't like to do anything unkind, love. And when you've got your dear little new baby you'll love it, and be just as pleased with it as you are with George. You will, my dear; there's no gainsaying it, because we women are made that way."

"I know," said Marie very sorrowfully.

Mrs. Amber regarded her knitting thoughtfully, then she dropped it to regard her daughter thoughtfully. She rose and shut the windows against the now chill night air of October, and drawing the curtains, made the room look cosy. She looked at the fire laid ready in the grate, but unlighted, and puckered her eyebrows doubtfully.

"The dining-room fire isn't lighted either, is it, duck?"

"No mother. When Osborn goes out in the evenings, I don't light one just for myself after these warm days."

"You should, my love. Really you should make yourself more comfortable."

"Now, mother, I'm sure you never lighted fires for yourself when father was out, unless it was to keep all the pipes in the place from freezing solid. I'm sure you screwed and skimped and saved and worried along, as all we other fools of women do."

Mrs. Amber did not deny this, knowing it to be true; she said something remote, however, about the pleasure of women being duty, and their duty sacrifice.

Marie remained limp in her chair.

"The point is, mother, that I don't know how to tell Osborn."

"Well, my love, let me tell him."

"Oh, mother," said Marie, "would you?"

"I'll tell him with pleasure. You go to bed, and I'll wait here to tell him when he comes in."

"Supposing he's very late?"

"He won't be later than the last Tube train. I shall get home comfortably, my love; don't you worry about me. We old women can take care of ourselves, you know. It's ten o'clock, and you go off to bed."

"I don't know that I want to, mother."

"Shoo!" said Mrs. Amber.

When Marie was in bed, her mother went to the dining-room, established herself in an armchair, and put a match to the fire. Her husband being long dead, she regarded her own sacrificial days as over, and she remained tolerably comfortable on what he had left behind him. In the days of his life, the money had taken him away to those vague haunts of men; but now it solaced, every penny of it, his widow. As she sat by the kindled fire, Mrs. Amber resumed her knitting, and as she knitted she wondered fondly what the new baby would be like; whether it would be boy or girl, and just exactly what piece of work she had better get in hand against its arrival.

So Osborn Kerr, arriving home not very late—it was only just after eleven o'clock—found his mother-in-law seated alone upon his hearth, needles flying over one of the pale blue jerseys in which little George was to winter.

She greeted his stare of astonishment placidly, with her propitiating smile and deceitful words:

"I thought you would be cold, Osborn, so I put a match to the fire."

"Oh, thanks," said Osborn, "thanks very much. Where's Marie?"

"She's gone to bed."

"Gone to bed, and left you here by yourself!" Then a thought assailed him: "I say," he asked himself, "is she—is she staying behind to give me a talking-to about anything? What've I done now?"

The question made him antagonistic, and he looked at her keenly.

"Are you—are you staying the night?" he asked; "because, if so, I'll just take my things out of the dressing-room into our room, unless you have done it?"

She lifted her hands. "Oh, my dear boy, I shouldn't dream of putting you so about! It is only that I stayed to tell you a little bit of news which Marie seemed a trifle reluctant to tell you."

She put her head on one side and looked at him smilingly. There was no sign upon her face to tell him how anxious her heart was, nor how she had offered up a prayer as his latchkey clicked in the lock: "Oh, Lord, don't let him be angry; let him be very kind to Marie, for Christ's sake! Amen."

"If there's anything Marie can't tell me herself—"

In her most propitiatory voice she said, smiling up at the young man, "Can't you guess? I expect you do know, don't you, though Marie thinks you don't?"

Osborn sat down.

"I can't possibly guess. Is it a puzzle, at this time of night?"

"It is not a puzzle," said Mrs. Amber, overflowing with feeling so that she had to remove and wipe her glasses; "it is just the most natural and ordinary and beautiful thing in the world."

He sat forward quickly, beginning to have some glimmer of her significance.

"You *can't* mean—"

"You and Marie are going to be blessed with another child."

"'Blessed'?" said Osborn, after a short pause, "'blessed'?"

"Blessed!" repeated Mrs. Amber anxiously.

"Some people," said Osborn, "have rum ideas about blessings."

"Won't you go in and see Marie and tell her you're pleased?"

"Is she awake?"

"I expect she is; most women would be," said Mrs. Amber slowly.

She began with extreme care to roll up her knitting while she awaited his further words; she did not look at him, but glanced about the room, as if seeking some happy idea which she could clothe in the right and most acceptable words.

"Does she expect me to be pleased?" Osborn asked.

"Well," said Mrs. Amber confidentially, "between you and me, she doesn't; and that's why I offered to tell you, Osborn. She didn't like to."

"Poor girl," said Osborn soberly.

He stared in front of him, whistling softly. "Life's queer," he uttered abruptly; "marriage seems so gay at the beginning, and then—all these infernal complications. There's always things nibbling at one; they never seem to stop. When you've weathered one squall another gets up on top of the first...."

"There must be a great deal of give-and-take in marriage," began Mrs. Amber. "I'm as old as both of you put together, and I assure you that everyone has to make sacrifices, and try to do their duty cheerfully, and welcome the children whom God sends them."

A little derision curled Osborn's lips.

"I'm afraid these mere platitudes are no solid help."

Mrs. Amber murmured protestingly, but, not knowing what a platitude was, felt she could not follow up the subject. She rose and picked up her coat from a chair back, and wrapped herself up to face the night.

"Tell Marie you're pleased," she coaxed.

"But she knows I'm not," said Osborn gloomily, "and neither will she be. One child on our income is enough. It would be different if we had plenty of money, but we haven't. Why, a family in this flat! This flat with two bedrooms! Imagine it! When God sends these blessings, as you infer He does, He should build rooms for 'em. *I* can't."

"Oh, don't!" Mrs. Amber implored, "don't! I'm not super-stitious, but—" she looked around her and shuddered—"but you ought not to say such things. It isn't right. People must make sacrifices."

"Don't say it all over again."

She went with her waddling gait, agitatedly, to the door.

"Good night," she said. "Be very, very kind to Marie, won't you?"

"I don't need anyone to tell me how to treat my own wife," he replied stiffly.

"Oh, Osborn, don't be offended."

"I'm not offended," he said shortly. "Good night, and thanks for staying in, and lighting the fire and all that."

He did not remain to watch her slow progress down the stone stairs, but closed the door and went back to the fire. He pulled out his pipe, filled and lighted it. There descended upon him that feeling of hopeless exasperation which many a young man has felt in many such a situation. When one married did one's liabilities never cease? Did they never even remain stationary, allowing a man to settle his course and keep to it, in spite of the boredom involved? Would life be always just a constant ringing of the changes on paying the rent, paying the instalment on the furniture, paying the doctor, paying the nurse, paying to go for one anxious week to Littlehampton? Wasn't there some alternative?

All a man appeared able to do was to escape for furtive minutes from his chains, to steal furtive shillings from his obligations and spend them otherwise.

A lot of men seemed to keep sane under the most unfavourable conditions.

When Osborn had sucked his pipe to the very last draw, he got up with a heavy sigh, stretched himself, took the coal off the fire to effect the minute saving, and went to undress. He wondered whether Marie really was still awake.

She was, and she was lying wide-eyed and watchful for him. As he opened the door cautiously he heard the rustle of her head moving on the pillow, and then the movement of her whole body turning towards him. Her anxiety filled the air with the sense of one poignant question: "Do you know?"

In answer to her unspoken inquiry he went at once to her side, and laid his hand upon her head, where the hair, smoothly parted for the night, looked sleek and innocent like a little girl's.

"Your mother told me," he began; then he bent and kissed her. "I'm awf'ly sorry. I s'pose we've got to make the best of it, old thing. I will if you will. It's the very devil, isn't it?"

"Yes," she sighed.

CHAPTER XIV

DRIFTING

The second baby came in the middle of a blazing summer, unheralded by the hopes, by the buds and blossoms of loving thought, which had opened upon the first child's advent. Marie was remorsefully tender over it, but Osborn continued to be one long uninterrupted sigh. The doctor and nurse seemed to him voracious, greedy creatures seeking for his life-blood. His second child was born at midnight. He came in one day at 6.30 with the fear in his heart men know round and about these agitating times, and found that fear was justified. The nurse had already been sent for, the doctor had looked in once, and the grandmother, fierce and tearful, was putting the first baby to bed. She put it to bed in Osborn's dressing-room, intimating that he would be responsible for it during the night for the next three weeks, anyway.

He could not bear it. He went in and kissed the silent, stone-white Marie, looked resentfully at George, answered his mother-in-law at random, and hurried out again. He was shivering. He remembered too well now that day which, too easily, he had forgotten.

He neither ate nor drank; he walked the Heath madly. He told himself that not for hundreds of precious pounds would he wait in that flat, wait for the sounds of anguish which would inevitably rise and echo about those circumscribed walls. The July sun went down; the moon rose up and found him still walking; still fearing and wondering.

He supposed he was a coward; he could not help it.

It was after twelve o'clock when at last he went home. He went because he suddenly remembered they had left George in his charge, and while there was little he could do for Marie, he could at least be faithful to that trust. He came back shivering as he had gone out; and as he fitted his latchkey with cold fingers into the lock he heard the newborn infant's wail.

The nurse looked out into the corridor at the sound of his entrance; she raised her finger, enjoining silence, and smiled. She was the same nurse who had helped to usher baby George into the world, and who had been so serenely certain that they would send for her again.

She vanished once more into Marie's room.

Osborn crept along the corridor and took off his boots; he was tired out, but still he felt no hunger. Had he been hungry he would have somehow thought it an act of criminal grossness to forage for food. There was none to attend to him, for Mrs. Amber, having waited to reassure herself of her daughter's safety, had been obliged to take the last Tube train home since there was not room for her at the flat. He was about to undress when the nurse came along the corridor and tapped at his door.

He knew what she had come for. Once again, with that air of lase cheerfulness she summoned him to his wife's bedside, and once again he stood there looking down upon Marie as she lay there, quiet and worn. Her quietness was the most striking thing about her. She looked at him steadily and remotely, as if he were a stranger, but with less interest; there was even a little hostility about her regard. It seemed a long while ago since he had fallen beside her bed and wept with her over the catastrophic forces of Nature; they were both ages older; as if a fog had drifted between them, their hearts were obscured from each other. Generations and generations of battle, so old as to be timeless, marked the ground between them.

He spoke hesitatingly, saying:

"How do you feel, dear?"

"I'm—glad it's over."

"So'm I."

"You managed to escape?"

He looked at her hastily, a little red creeping over his pallid face. She spoke almost as to a deserter. "I couldn't have done any good," he said.

She smiled and closed her eyes, as though against him. It was not a natural smile, it drew her lips tight.

"What could I do?" he asked her pleadingly.

She opened her eyes again and looked at him in that remote and quiet regard.

"Men are queer. If you had been suffering, I would never have run away."

He wanted to expostulate, to explain how different such a case would be; how, as a matter of course, a wife's place was beside her husband in good and ill, most particularly ill—but he did not find the heart to do it. She looked so fatigued and was so deadly quiet. He felt at a loss, and looked around vaguely till his eye lighted on the cot. There, beneath the muslin and ribbon which had at last been crisply laundered, lay a burden, now minute, but about to cling and grow like an Old Man of the Sea.

"How's the baby?" he asked, tiptoeing to it.

"It's a girl," said Marie; "I expect you've been told."

He had not been told, having made no inquiry. Here again the story-books which had informed him of romantic life in his very young days had been at fault; they made such an idealised picture of all that had just taken place, and they told about the joy in the heart of a man and the ecstasy in the heart of a woman. Osborn looked down upon a tiny, red and crumpled face.

"I expect she'll grow up as pretty as her mother," he said with an effort, "but now she's—she's curious, isn't she?"

With what relief he hailed the return of the nurse? It was so late that she was stern and cross and cold with him as she shut him out.

Little George awoke at the sounds, cautious though they were, of his father's undressing, and, crying for mummie, could not be consoled until lifted out, and wildly and clumsily petted and lied to, and cajoled. Even then he did not trust this daddy who was such a stranger in the house; who was only jolly by fits and starts when they all woke up in the pink room in the mornings; who hid behind a paper at breakfast, and who, going away in a hurry directly afterwards, only returned after George was asleep, or simulating sleep under threat of a slapping. The baby missed his mother's loving arms and cried miserably, hunched uncomfortably in Osborn's. But at last he must sleep through sheer drowsiness, and they both went to bed. In the morning Osborn dressed him before he went away, and was called upon to make himself generally useful, and made to memorise a string of errands.

The nurse would have no nonsense. She demanded and he complied.

He cursed her within himself. What a pack!

During those days once more Desmond was good to him, sheltering him at his club, inviting him to play golf, or to run out into the country with him in his two-seater. Once they took George because the nurse was so firmly decided that they should do so, and they stayed out past his bedtime, and tired him out, and made him furious.

"It's a gay life!" said Osborn to Rokeby, "a gay life, what?"

Marie sent the nurse away at the end of three weeks, and tackled her increased household alone. She was unable to nurse the baby, and the doctor ordered it to be fed upon the patent food which George used to have, so she was obliged to ask Osborn to increase the housekeeping allowance.

They discussed long and seriously the ways and means to the increase and the amount of it. "Half a crown," was her reiteration; "on half a crown I'd do it somehow."

And he asked: "Yes! But where's the half-crown to come from?"

"You must find it," she said at last.

With compressed lips and lowering brow the young man thought it out. "I give you all I can—"

"And I take as little as I can."

"I'm sick of these discussions about money."

"So'm I."

"It seems as if we were sick of the whole thing, doesn't it?"

Being a woman, she dared not confirm verbally those reckless words; their very recklessness caused her to fear. If they *were* sick of the whole thing—well, what about it? What were they to do? They were in it, weren't they, up to their necks? Of two people who mutually recognised the plight, only one must foam and rage and stutter out unpalatable truths about it; it was for the other to pour on the oil, to deceive and pretend and propitiate and cajole, to try to keep things running and the creaking machinery at work.

Because—what else remained to do?

But when Osborn rapped out: "It seems as if we were sick of the whole thing, doesn't it?" though she would not confirm this in words, her silence confirmed it, her silence and her look. They made him hesitate and catch his breath.

"Well?" he asked.

"I'm not going to say such things."

"But you know they're true, don't you?" he asked in despair.

"You ought to think, as I do, that the babies are worth it all."

"When two people begin telling each other what they *ought* to do, they're reaching the limit."

"You've often told me what I ought to do."

"I don't know what's coming to women."

"A revolution!"

"Rubbish!" said Osborn. "Women have no power to revolt, and no reason either."

"It's true we've no power; that's what keeps most of us quiet."

"I wish it would keep you quiet."

"You see, I can't help it, can I? Keeping quiet doesn't ask you for this other half-crown, and I've got to ask you. I can't help it."

"I daresay not," he admitted reluctantly. "But—"

"Can I have it?" she asked doggedly.

"Oh, take it!" he flared, flung half-a-crown on the table, rose, and went out. She sat for a while looking at the half-crown, then she took it in her hand, and wanted to pitch it into the street for the first beggar to profit by, but, remembering that she was a beggar too, she kept it.

Osborn entered into further discussion of the matter in a reasonable vein.

"Half-a-crown a week's six pound ten a year. Sure you can't

manage without?"

"How do you mean?"

"Well, lots of women have to—to—manage."

"There's a limit even to management."

"I suppose there is. Very well."

"You mean I'm to have it?"

"All right."

"Thank you very much, dear," said Marie very slowly after a while.

"You don't seem in a particular hurry to say it."

"Why should I say it?"

"What! when I've just arranged to give you six pound ten—"

"To feed your daughter."

"Oh, well—"

"Anyway, I *have* said it. I've said 'Thank you very much,' haven't I? Do you want me to show more gratitude?"

"It beats me to think what's come over women."

They sat on either side of their hearth looking at one another in unconcealed bewilderment.

"If you cared to let me make out a budget, Osborn," she said suddenly, "I think we could arrange it all better. So much for everything, you know."

"Oh, yes, I know! I know all about it, thanks! If you want to dole out my pocket-money, my dear, I'm off.... I'm completely off it! No, thank you. I'll keep my hands on my own income."

"I only meant—"

"Women never seem satisfied," said Osborn wrathfully.

As he looked at her sitting there, thin and fair and reserved as she never used to be, with the sheen of her glossy hair almost vanished, and all of her pretty insouciance gone, he saw no more the gay girl, the wifely comrade, whom he had married. In her place sat the immemorial hag, the married man's bane, the blood-sucker, the enemy, the asker.

She had taken from him a sum equivalent to twice his weekly tobacco-money.

The sacrifice of *all* his tobacco would not provide for that red and crumpled baby lying in its fine basket. He took that as a comparison, with no intention of sacrificing his tobacco; but it just gave one the figures involved.

As if feeling through her reserve the gist of his thoughts, she smiled.

"Poor old Osborn!" she said.

"You can stretch an income, and stretch it," said Osborn, "but it isn't eternally elastic, you know."

"*Don't* I know it!"

"Well, all I ask you to do," said Osborn, "is to remember it."

Then life went round as before, except that a great anxiety as to meeting the weekly bills fell upon Marie. Sometimes they were a shilling up and sometimes a shilling down. The day when the greasy books fell through the letter-box into the hall was a day to add a grey hair to the brightest head.

With two babies to dress, she rose earlier; she swept and dusted and cooked quicker; she sent Osborn off to his work as punctually as before; she wheeled two infants instead of one out in the grey perambulator to the open-air market. And there her bargaining became sharp, thin and shrewish. She fought the merchants smartly, and sometimes she won and sometimes they. During the day Grannie Amber usually came in and lent a hand about the babies' bedtime. At 6.30 Osborn came home, a little peevish until after dinner. After dinner he went out again if the new baby cried or if anything went wrong. Once a quarter the demand for the rent came upon him like a fresh blow; once a month he paid the furniture instalment; once a week he gave up, like life-blood, thirty-two and sixpence to her whose palm was always ready.

"It's a gay life!" he often said with a twisted smile, "A gay life, what?"

CHAPTER XV

SURRENDER

Grannie Amber was afraid—she did not know exactly why—that, the year following the second baby's arrival, Osborn would forget Marie's birthday, and she was anxious that it should not be forgotten. Though she herself had, early in her married life, grown tired and quiet, had early learned to bargain shrewishly with the merchants of the cheaper foods and, after the first three years, had always had her birthdays forgotten; though she had been perfectly willing and ready to urge her daughter into the life domestic, upon a small income, yet regrets took her and sighs, all of perfect resignation, when she saw the darkness under Marie's eyes, when she stood by in the market and heard her hard chaffering, when she noted the worried crinkles come to stay in her brow. So that, resolving that Osborn should not forget, natural as it would have been for him, in her judgment, to do so, she trailed his wife's birthday across his path a fortnight before the actual day, wishing in her thoughtfulness to give him the chance to save from two weeks' salary for some gift.

She sewed in his presence and, as she sewed, entered into a full explanation of her work: "This little skirt, Osborn, is for Marie's birthday. I hope I'll get it done in time; there's only a fortnight, as you know."

He did not know; the fact had slipped his memory in the ceaseless dream of other liabilities due; but as he looked at Grannie Amber, and the purple silk petticoat which she was finely sewing, he assumed a perfect memory of the occasion.

He answered: "I was just going to ask Marie what she'd like for it."

"There are a lot of things she'd like," Mrs. Amber began.

That same evening, when Grannie Amber had rolled up the purple petticoat into her workbag and departed, he asked Marie, as they sat together over the fire:

"What would you like for your birthday, my dear?"

A great pleasure shone in her face as she gazed at him.

"Osborn," she stammered, "can you afford to give me a present at all?"

"I should hope so," he replied.

An eagerness, which he had not seen there for a long while, invaded her face; it was an eagerness of pleasure at his remembrance, at his wish to be kind and to give her happiness. About the gift she was not so precious; she hoped it would be small, and she said, almost reverentially:

"I'd rather you chose, dear."

"I'd been thinking," said Osborn, who had thought of it during dinner, "that you might like to be taken out. How would that do for a present? Of course I'd like to do both—to take you out *and* give you a swagger gift—but we know it can't be done, don't we?"

May Edginton

"Of course. Of course, my dear."

"You'd like to go out to dinner? And perhaps we could go somewhere after, too."

"The dinner will be enough, Osborn. Oh! it will be lovely!"

"Righto!" he said. "I—I do wish I could take you out oftener, but you know—"

"Of course I know, Osborn."

She thought with excitement of the charming few hours which they would snatch from routine, together, a fortnight hence. She spoke of it to Mrs. Amber, carelessly, with a high-beating heart and secret, delicious thrills: "We're dining out on my birthday, mother, if you won't mind spending the evening here in case the children wake."

"Oh, duck!" cried Mrs. Amber, "oh, my love! I'll be delighted. Mind you enjoy yourselves very much and don't hurry home. Grandmothers are made to be useful."

Nearly every spare minute of every day during those intervening weeks Marie spent in renovating a frock. She had vast ideas, but no money except a few shillings hoarded only a woman knows how, in spite of the pressing claims of the greasy books. Her wedding frock, four years old, emerged from the tissue paper where it had lain these many months, yellowed and soiled, in dire need of the cleaner's ministrations or the dyer's art. Marie could not afford the cleaner, and did not dare the wash-tub and soap, but she bought one of those fourpenny-ha'penny dyes with which impecunious women achieve amazing results, wherewith she dyed the frock, and the bath, and her own hands a shade of blue satisfactory at least by artificial light. Under it she would wear the purple petticoat, whose flounces would cause the skirt to sway and swing in the present mode, and she would evolve herself a hat. She folded a newspaper round, shaped it to her head, covered it with black velvet, borrowed a great old cameo clasp of her mother's, and had a turban, a saucy thing whose rake brought back for a while the lamp to her eyes and the rose to her cheek. The housemaid's gloves and the rubber gloves had never been renewed, and the supply of Julia's wornout suedes could not cope with the destruction of them at No. 30, so that Marie's fine hands were fine no longer. They were reddened and roughened and thickened like the hands of other household women, but each afternoon in the slow fortnight she sat down to careful manicuring. When the result of these pains was fulfilled; when she stood before the glass in her pink bedroom gasping at her reflection, she could have sung and danced and wept in this glad renewal of her youth.

She had rendezvous with Osborn at the chosen restaurant at seven. Never, it seemed to her, had she felt lighter-footed and lighter-hearted. It was as if the old days were back, the old days when an unlessoned girl met an unlessoned man to dream of heaven together, in some restaurant room full of the lessons and sophistries of love. Westwards she travelled by Tube, emerged at Leicester Square, and walked on flying feet past the Haymarket, across the great stream of traffic at the top, into Shaftesbury Avenue, and into the foyer of a famous restaurant. She sat down on a velvet couch, snuggled her furs around her, and felt a lady of luxury. Osborn kept her waiting some ten minutes, but soon the damper which that put upon her spirits evaporated, leaving her all pure bliss. It was entrancing to sit here once more—where she had often kept Osborn sitting in the old days of her imperious-ness and his humility—and to watch the well-dressed people come in and out, pass to and fro, and enact scenes which suggested the gaudiest stories to her receptive mind. Light

May Edginton

and warmth, rich colour and abundant life flowed there like tides, and many servants stood about the foyer to obey her behests.

The restaurant to Marie was revel and entertainment, and when the slight blankness with which his lateness had oppressed her had been overswayed by her enjoyment, she could have wished to sit here for hours, doing nothing, saying nothing, eating nothing, but just breathing in this atmosphere of wealth and ease.

But Osborn came, hurrying, between seven and seven-fifteen, apology on his lips. A man had come in late to buy a car and they had talked ... never was there such a long-winded customer. He took Marie's arm lightly in his hand, hurried her in, and chose a table, the nearest vacant one. He dropped into his seat and passed his hand over his brow and eyes to brush away the daze of fatigue. He was tired and very, very hungry, too hungry to watch with his old appreciation the dainty movements of his wife, as she shrugged her furs from her shoulders, and drew off her white gloves, and smiled at him radiantly, with the sense of those dear, old, lost, spoiled-girl days returning momentarily to her.

Osborn's brows were knitted over the wine-list and his hand moved restlessly in his pocket. Very carefully he considered and weighed the prices and at last gave his order quickly.

"Half a bottle of '93." Leaning slightly towards his wife, he added: "I'm afraid it can't be a bottle of the one and only these days, kiddie."

"Not now that we're family people!" she cried bravely.

While he leaned back quietly, awaiting the arrival of the first course, and, could she have known it, craving the food with the keen craving of the man who has lunched too lightly, she looked at her hands, from which the white gloves were now removed. A pang, not altogether new, but of renewed sharpness, shot through her, as she looked down at the reddened, hardened fingers with the slight vegetable stains upon them, clasped together on the table edge. Where were the nails trained and kept to an exquisite filbert shape? The oval of the cuticles? The slender softness and coolness of the finger-tips? The backs of the hands were roughened and the palms seamed; there was a tiny crack at a finger-joint; it seemed to her that the spoiling of her beautiful hands had made so insidious a pace through these years that she had, day by day, been almost unaware of the havoc in progress. But looking down upon them in this place of ease and grace, she saw, surprised and sorrowful, the whole of the sad mischief. Her hands were as the hands of a scullery-maid taken out, most unsuitably, to dinner. While Osborn still awaited the first course, she drew her hands down and hid them on her lap. There was time enough to display their effect when they must emerge for the use of the table implements.

Surrounding her were women whose white hands, jewelled and unjewelled, played about their business, lovely as pale and delicate flowers. She cast her glances right and left, seeing them and envying. And she looked at their clothes, their smart and slender shoes, the richness of their cloaks hanging over chair backs, and she saw her own frock as it was, dyed and mended and *demode*.

She knew. "It looked nice when I tried it on at home because there were no comparisons. Here, where there's competition, I—I'm hopeless. I'd better have worn a suit."

Her turban, that thing which had paraded so saucily in the

pink room while the babies slept regardless, was an outsider—a *gamin* among hats.

She was not the first woman who has decked herself at home to her own gratification, to emerge into a wealthier world to her own despair.

While these things were borne in, with the flashlight speed of woman's impressions, upon her brain, the first course arrived and they ate. After it, Osborn roused himself to talk. He asked her several times if she were enjoying herself, and she told him with smiling lips that she was.

"It's not so often that we go out, is it?" he remarked. "We must make the best of the times we get."

"This is *lovely*."

"Poor old girl!" said Osborn, "you don't get out on the loose very much, do you? But I don't suppose you want to, though; women are different from men. A woman's interest centres in her home, and you've quite enough to do to keep your mind occupied, haven't you?"

"And my hands. Look at them!"

She spread them before him.

"Poor old girl!" said Osborn, looking.

A recollection stirred in him, too, of what those hands had been in the days of their romance. "You used to have the prettiest hands I ever saw," he said.

She snatched them petulantly under the table again.

"Don't!"

"Don't what?"

"Don't—say that! I can't bear to think how ugly I'm getting."

Her husband looked at her with a faint, bewildered smile. "Come!" he adjured her, "you mustn't get morbid. You're not ugly, you silly girl. You were one of the prettiest girls I ever saw."

"But *now*?"

"Now?" He looked at her quickly. "You're as pretty as ever you were, of course."

"I'm not," she denied, reading the lie in his eyes.

"Women are bound to change, no doubt," he conceded. "I daresay having the babies aged you a bit. But you needn't get anxious about your looks *yet*."

"I'm not thirty, but I look it."

"No, no, you don't," he said constrainedly.

She smiled, and contented herself with watching him eat the next course while she toyed with it. As a woman, food meant little to her; she was concerned more with the prettiness of its serving; but Osborn was avidly hungry and his enjoyment was palpable.

She thought: "Poor boy! How he likes the good things of life! And how few of them he gets! He oughtn't to have married."

She looked around her again, and saw, a little way across the floor, a gay woman in black. Her hair and eyes were black, her complexion was white, her lips were red. She had with her two men who worshipped. Of her Marie said to herself:

"She's older than I, but she's keeping her looks; her hands are not so nice as mine used to be, but now they're far nicer. She's keeping herself young and gay; she sees to it that she's pampered. But if she had married a poor man, and had two babies, and had been obliged to do all the chores, I wonder...."

"What interests you, my dear?" Osborn asked.

She told him in a fitful, inarticulate way. "I was looking at that woman over there, the one in black, with the diamond comb in her hair. And—and I was wondering—in a way—I can hardly explain—what is really the best thing to do with one's life. She's older than I—a good deal older—but see how smooth her face is. She looks as if she could never do anything other than laugh. And her hands—see, she uses them to show them off—aren't they lovely? But I was wondering, if she was in my shoes, how would she look? What would she do if babies woke her up half a dozen times every night, so that when the morning came she was very tired?

"Tired, and yet she must get up and cook and sweep, and take the children out, and everything. Would her face be smooth and would she laugh then? I was wondering, too, whether she'd take the same trouble over her hair at six o'clock of a cold morning. And, if she had my life, would men admire her so much? Would they look at her as they are looking now?"

Osborn stared at his wife, half-amazed, half-frowning.

"One would think," he said, "to hear you talk, that you weren't happy; that you hadn't all—all—all a woman in your position of life can have."

She flushed quickly. "Don't think that! I was just wondering about her, that's all, as I used to wonder about the people we saw when you took me out to dinner in our engaged days. Do you remember? You used to laugh at me and call me the Eternal Question, and all kinds of silly things."

"I don't remember that."

"No? Well, it was a very long while ago."

"It sounded as if you were envying her."

"I *was* envying her."

"Haven't you all you want?" he said again in resentful surprise.

"I want to be awf'ly young again, and to have a smooth face and manicured hands, and lots of admiration."

"I'll tell you what it is," said Osborn, regaining his good temper with an effort, "this wine has gone to your head."

After he had presented this very satisfactory solution, both laughed; but while he laughed with relief at dismissing the question, she laughed only acquiescently and unconvinced, the laugh which should be called the Laugh of the Wise Wives. It appeased him and it relieved her, as a groan relieves a person in pain. She sipped her unaccustomed wine and looked around her with her wide eyes, which were far, far more widely opened now than in the days of her blind youth.

When a rather tired and preoccupied man takes his wife of four years' standing out to dinner he knows that he need not exert himself to talk, to shine, to please, as with a woman who holds the piquancy of a stranger; so while Osborn spoke spasmodically, or drifted into silence, Marie could look around her and think thoughts which chilled the ardour of her soul. It seemed to her, that evening of her twenty-ninth birthday, that a door was opened to her, revealing nakedly the fears and the trepidations and the minute cares of marriage which have creased many a woman's brow before her time. The restaurant was to her the tide of life, upon which the black-haired woman and her sisters sailed victoriously, but upon which she, and wives like her, trained for the race only in the backwaters of their homes, embarked timidly to their disgrace and peril. What wife of a husband with two hundred a year could row against the black-haired woman and keep pride of place?

As Marie wondered things which all her sisterhood have long ached over, she saw Osborn looking at the black-haired woman too, and in his eyes there was a light of admiration, a keenness, a speculation which drew the tired lines from his face and left it eager once more. It was the male look which once he had looked only for her. With a heart beating sharply she recognised and wanted it again, but she felt strangely impotent. She in her dyed gown, her *gamin* of a hat, with her spoiled hands and thin cheeks—and that tall, rounded beauty with all her life and vivacity, undrained, throbbing in her from toes to finger-tips! What a comparison!

Vain and profitless was the unequal competition. She felt one moment as if, should it come to a struggle, she would relinquish it in sheer despair; the next, as if she would fight, teeth and nails, body and brains, for her inalienable rights over this man. All the while these emotions surged up in her, and ebbed and flowed in again, her intelligence told her the wild absurdity of such supposition. The raven woman was a stranger; and socially, to all appearance, she must always remain so. Yet Marie could not still the passionate unrest of her heart without taking her husband's eyes from the table where two obsequious men adored a goddess.

She drummed her hard finger-tips sharply on the table.

"Osborn, do you know her?"

"Know her? No." He added carelessly: "I wish I did."

Marie said in a voice which she tried hard to keep detached: "Why? Oh, yes.... I—I suppose she's the type men would admire very much."

"Well, *you* were admiring her a few minutes ago."

"In—in a way I was. I mean, she's so smooth, so—so well-kept, and her frock is lovely, with those diamond shoulder-straps and all that black tulle. I thought—you stared as if you knew her."

"I hope I shouldn't stare at any woman because I knew her. As a matter of fact, I believe I know who she is; she's an actress; bound to succeed if she takes the right line, I should think. Just now she's got six lines to speak in that new piece of Mutro's. You know—what's it called?"

"What's her name?"

"Roselle Dates, I think."

Osborn looked at his wife solicitously.

"I'm afraid you're a bit tired, dear; you're getting pale. You had a jolly colour when I met you."

She touched her cheeks mechanically with her fingertips.

"Had I? That was because I was so excited at the prospect of our lovely evening."

"Dear old girl! So it's been a lovely evening?"

"Perfect. I wish it was beginning all over again," she answered hollowly, wishing that she meant what she said.

What was the matter with her? Why did she feel so grey, so plain, so sparkless?

"I ought to rouge a little," she said. "Everyone else does."

He protested quickly and strongly.

"But," she said, "if I'm tired? If I'm a fright? What then?"

"I shouldn't like my wife to make up."

"But, Osborn, I want you to think I'm pretty, well turned out, smart, like all the other women here."

She waved a hand vaguely around, but her look was on the raven woman, on whose face the white cosmetic, exquisitely applied, was like pale rose petals.

"I do think you're pretty. As for your turn-out—" he glanced over it quickly—"it's all right, isn't it? It's what we can afford, anyway. We can't help it, can we?"

She shook her head. "I've had no new clothes since we were married," she murmured suddenly in a voice of yearning.

"Well," said Osborn after a pause, "you had such lots; such a big trousseau, hadn't you? It's supposed to last some while."

"It's lasted!" Her laugh rang out with a curious merriment; her eyes were downcast so that he could not see the tears in them, but something about his wife touched him profoundly.

He exclaimed, with rejuvenated sentiment: "You know I'd always give you everything I could! You know it isn't because I *won't* that I don't give you the most wonderful clothes in town, so that you could beat every other woman hollow."

His sentiment flushed her cheeks and cleared the mist from her eyes. She asked, half shyly and coquettishly:

"Do you think I should?"

"Of course you would, little girl. You're charming; anything more unlike the mother of two great kids I never saw."

"Ah," she said slowly, "but you forget to tell me."

"What?"

"All those—dear little—things."

"Women are rum," he declared. "I believe they're always wanting their husbands to propose to them."

"It would be nice," she said seriously.

Osborn laughed a good deal. "A woman's never tired of love-making."

"A married woman doesn't often get the chance."

"A married man doesn't often get the time."

She looked yet again at the actress across the room, and strange echoes of questions stirred in her. Such a woman, she thought, would always make a man find time. How did they do it? What was the real secret of feminine victory, triumphant and deathless? Was it not to keep burning always, night and day, winter and summer, autumn and spring, throughout the seasons, the clear-flamed lamp of romance?

Behind the wife there stood shades, sturdy, greedy, disagreeable shades, and the two-hundred-pound husband always saw them; they were the butcher, the grocer, the milkman, the doctor, the landlord and the tax-collector.

How could she trim her lamp brightly to burn?

In the restaurant many diners had gone; many, lingering, thought of going; waiters hovered near ready to hand bills, and empty liqueur glasses and coffee cups, and ash trays, and the dead ends of cigarettes lay under the rose lights on all the tables. Osborn had drunk a benedictine and smoked a cigar appreciatively; Marie had begun to think, reluctantly, yet clingingly, maternally, of her babies in the pink room at home. She lifted her furs from the chair back, and a waiter hurried to adjust the stole over her shoulders.

"Sorry," said Osborn, going through the slight motion of attempting to rise from his chair; "I should have done that."

"Never mind, dear," she answered.

Then he paid the bill, got into his own coat, and they walked out. As they went, he asked: "Well, old girl, have you really enjoyed it?"

"It was lovely. Thank you so much!"

"Sure it was the sort of birthday present you wanted?"

"Absolutely the one and only thing, Osborn."

"Happy young woman!" He took her arm and squeezed it.

"Cab, sir?" the commissionaire asked.

"We're walking, thanks."

They walked to the nearest Tube station, took train to Hampstead, and arrived home at eleven, to release the sleepy grandmother on duty.

"Had a lovely time, duck?" asked Mrs. Amber, trotting out into the hall.

"Tophole, Grannie," said Osborn. "Marie's thoroughly enjoyed herself."

"Simply lovely, mother," said Marie. "We went to the Royal Red, and Osborn gave me a scrumptious dinner. Babies been good?"

"Not a sound—the little angels."

Marie kissed her mother good night, waved her out, and went quietly along the corridor to the bedroom; she switched up the light, bent over the cots of the sleeping children, and assured herself of their well-being. They slumbered on, placid and dreamless. Then she went to her dressing-table, and planting her palms flat upon it, leaned forward upon them, and gazed at herself mercilessly. She tore off her hat, rumpled her hair, rubbed her cheeks and gazed again. There were some little fine lines at the corners of her eyes, and as she looked and looked under the strong light, there stood out, silvery around her temples, amid the fairness, the first half-dozen grey hairs. The sight of them petrified her; she had not known she had so many.

"*Oh!*" she breathed.

Her fingers travelled down her neck. It had lost its roundness and, as she turned it this way and that, examining, two muscles stood out; her collar-bones showed faintly. The crude abundance of colour of the dyed dress enhanced her lack of colour.

"Well ..." she began to judge slowly. Then "I suppose there's no help for it."

Two tears dropped down her face. She sobbed and checked herself. She heard her husband moving about quickly in his dressing-room, and she hurried off her own garments, let down her hair, and brushed and plaited it hastily. He came in and kissed her.

"She's had a good time!" he exclaimed, well pleased.

CHAPTER XVI

ISOLATION

Julia was waiting for a guest in that weird institution which she called her club. The weird institution, however, had lost some of its weirdness and gained in comfort and *cachet*. It now boasted many members of distinction, new decorations and enlarged subscriptions. Miss Julia Winter sat in the mauve drawing-room under soft light, in the delicate glow of which her face took on suave and gentle lines, and her eyes held hints of womanly mystery. Before her, one of the many tables of the club drawing-room stood furnished with blue-and-white tea equipage. Behind her back, as she sat settled in the corner of a chesterfield, a fat silk pillow was crushed. For a picture of modern bachelor-womanhood which knew how to do itself thoroughly well, Julia could not, in these moments, have been excelled.

The door opened and a page, after assuring himself of Miss Winter's presence, announced: "Mrs. Kerr!"

A quiet and slender woman, in a shabby suit dated some six years ago, came to meet Julia listlessly. Her listlessness, however, was only bodily, for into her eyes some eager spirit had leapt and her hands went out involuntarily. They were engulfed in Julia's well-shaped large ones, and Marie was drawn down upon the mauve couch and the fat pillow made to transfer its amenities.

Each woman looked at the other with a long, careful look.

"How comfortable this is!" Marie observed.

"Is it, dear?" said Julia. "Lean back and rest. You look tired. Been shopping?"

"Just a few things for the children; I take the opportunity of being in town, you know."

"Did you come up this morning?"

"Yes, before lunch. Mother's staying in the flat with the children."

"How are they all—your big family of three?"

"Awf'ly well, thank you. Baby's got a tooth."

"How splendid! I just must come and see her again. And Georgie?"

"George has grown a lot since you saw him last. I've been hunting about for a little jersey suit for him; they're all so expensive; I'll have to knit one myself."

"My dear girl! When do you get time to knit jersey suits?"

"In the evenings, when dinner is over. There's always an hour or so before bedtime, you know."

After a short silence, Julia asked: "I suppose you *have* lunched, dear? Otherwise I'll order sandwiches."

"I've lunched, thank you."

"Met your husband, I suppose?"

"N—no. I had something, quickly, at Swan and Edgar's. I was in a hurry."

Julia signalled a waitress serving tea at the other end of the vast room. "The usual tea," she ordered, "*and* sandwiches."

Marie leaned back against her cushion restfully. She had the slow glance of a woman much preoccupied, whose mind comes very heavily back to matters not of her immediate concern. She went on for a little while talking of the topics which filled her brain to the exclusion of all else.

"We're thinking of sending George to a day school soon—at least, I am. I've not spoken of it to Osborn yet; there hasn't been a chance."

"How do you mean—no chance? I thought married people lived together."

"Oh, well ... you don't understand. One has to make an opportunity; get a man into the right mood. He won't like the expense, of course, though it's only a guinea and a half a term, if you send them till mid-day only. That would do at first, don't you think? I don't believe in pushing children. Still, a guinea and a half a term is four and a half guineas a year. Well, I can't help it, can I? He'll *have* to go to school soon, there's no doubt of that. He's getting too much for me, and it would be a great help, having him out of the way in the mornings, while I'm doing my work."

"I think it would be a very good plan, darling," Julia replied.

"I know you'd agree with me about it. I shall tell Osborn you think it's a good plan, and I shall get mother to tell him too. We shall persuade him."

"How is your husband?" Julia asked punctiliously.

"Very well, thank you."

"Still delighted with domestic life?"

"Oh, that doesn't last, of course," said Marie, looking away and sighing. "A man always gets to think of his home as just the place where bills are sent. Osborn's out a good deal in the evenings, like other men, of course. There's one thing—it leaves me very free. There's always something to be done, you see, and I can get through a great deal in the evenings if he's out."

"And if he's in?"

"Oh well, a man likes one to sit down and talk to him, naturally."

"How awf'ly obliging wives are!"

"My dear, if you were married, you'd know that the only way is to humour them."

The waitress came in with the tea tray and set the table daintily. To Julia it was a matter of course, but Marie watched the deft girl who handled things so swiftly and quietly; she took in the neatness of her black frock, and the starched whiteness of her laundering; and when the maid had left them, she turned with an envious, smiling sigh to Julia, and said:

"The servants here are so nice. I always used to think, when I had a maid, she'd look like that. We were going to have one, you know, when Osborn got his first rise after we were married, but George came; and now—three of them! It'll always be impossible, of course."

"I daresay you'd rather have the children than the maid."

"Of course I would—the priceless things!" Marie cried, her small pale face warming with maternity.

Julia dispensed tea; and for awhile refused to allow her guest to talk more until she was refreshed. And when she was refreshed and rested among the amenities of the mauve room, that absorption in the affairs around which her whole life moved and had its being grew less keen; her preoccupations lifted; she left the problem which, even here, had begun to worry her, as to whether a pound, or three-quarters of a pound only, of wool would make George a jersey suit, and she turned her eyes with a kind of wondering recollection upon the world outside. She began by looking around the room at the many well-dressed, softly chattering women; at the cut of their gowns and the last thing in hats; then her look wandered to Julia and took in her freshness, the beauty of her tailoring, and the expensiveness of her appearance generally.

"I feel so shabby among you all," she murmured, with a smile which appeared to Julia as a ghost.

"You look very pretty," said Julia, "as you always do, dear."

"When one is first married," Marie said quietly, "one always imagines one will never get old and tired and spoiled, as thousands of other women do; but one does it all the same. One's day is just so full, and with babies one's night is often so full, too, that there simply isn't time to fuss over one's own appearance. With three children and no help, you've got to let something go, and in my case—"

She broke off, to continue: "It's been me."

Julia laid one of her hands over Marie's lying in her lap. Marie's hands produced the effect of toilers glad to rest. They hardly stirred under Julia's, even to give an answering squeeze. And Julia felt, with a burning and angry heart, how rough and tired they were.

"Julia," said Marie, "I've often wanted to ask someone who would be honest with me—and you're the honestest person I knew—do you think I—I've let myself go very badly?"

"My dear kiddie!" Julia cried low, "why, you—you've been brilliant."

"Look at me," said Marie, thrusting forward her face.

Julia looked, to see the lines from nostrils to mouth, the lines at the corners of the eyes, the enervated pallor and the grey hairs among the golden-brown. She was sorry and bitter.

"You look a dear," she said irresolutely.

Marie sank back upon the fat pillow again with a laugh. It was the laugh of a woman who was beat and owned it.

"You can't stand up against it," she said. "I don't care who says you can. Day in, day out; night in, night out; no, you can't stand up against it. I've often thought it out, and something *has* to go. The woman's the only thing who can be let go; the children must be reared and the man must be fed; but the woman must just serve her purpose."

Tears swelled in Julia's eyes. "Don't," she begged huskily, "don't get bitter."

Marie returned her look with the simple and wide-eyed one she remembered so well. "I'm not," she stated; "I was just thinking, and it comes to that. You must feed a man and look after him and make him comfortable, or—or you wouldn't keep him at all."

"What do you mean?"

"Just that. But I sometimes think," she whispered, "if I let myself go, get plain and drab, will I keep him then?"

"It is in his service," said Julia.

Marie said wisely: "That doesn't count. And often—I get frightened when he sometimes takes me out, and we dine at a restaurant. I look round and see the difference between most of the women there and me. In restaurants one always seems to see such wonderful women—women who seem as if *their* purpose was just being taken out to dinner and to be attractive. I compare my clothes with theirs and my hands with theirs; and I think: 'Supposing Osborn is comparing me, too?'"

"He wouldn't."

"Not consciously, perhaps. But he is admiring the other women all the time; I see him doing it. Why shouldn't he? All the women he sees about him in town—the pretty girls in the streets.... He used to admire me so much, when I was very pretty ... the—the things he used to say! But now, I sometimes wonder—"

"What else do you wonder, poor kid?"

"When he goes out alone—sometimes to dinner—in the evenings—"

"Whether he's taking someone—"

Marie nodded. "Someone prettier than I; as I used to be; someone who's not tired with having children; and who hasn't rusted and got dull and stupid from thinking of nothing but grocers' bills, and from staying at home."

"You must try not to think—"

"But I do think. Men are like that; men hate being annoyed and want to be amused. They get to—to—marriage is funny; Osborn seems to get to look upon me as someone who's always going to *ask* for something. I—I know when he had a nice commission the other day, he didn't tell me about it, in case there was something for the children I'd be asking him for."

"Oh!"

"It hurts," said Marie, "always to be considered an asker; but of course men don't think of it like that."

"They ought to think, then."

"Men aren't like women. They set their own lines of conduct."

"What's that in the marriage service," Julia inquired, "about bestowing upon a woman all a man's worldly goods?"

"Ah, well, you think all those things at the time; but they don't work out, really."

"As I always thought," said Julia.

Marie was still away upon her trail. "I don't really let myself go as much as you might think. I'm always dressed for breakfast, if I've been up half the night; I don't allow myself to be slovenly. And however I've had to hurry over putting the children to bed, and cooking dinner and things, I always change my blouse and put on my best slippers before Osborn comes in. I feel—at home I feel as if I look quite nice; but when I come out of it"—she indicated her surroundings—"I realise I'm just a dowd who's fast losing what looks she had. When I come out, and see others, I—I know I can't compete. It makes you almost afraid to come out. And Osborn—while I'm at home, plodding along, you see, he's out, seeing the others all the time. He sees them in the restaurants, and they pass him in the street—girls as I used to be."

"You must leave all these thoughts alone."

"Girls, Julia, as—as I could be again, if I had the chance."

"Would you like a cigarette?" Julia asked abruptly; "if so, we'll go to the smoke-room."

"I'd love it; it's ages since I smoked. But I haven't time. I must be going."

"Already?"

"It'll be the children's bedtime, and mother can't manage them alone."

"Oh, of course, dear," Julia said. "How stupid of me!" She folded very tenderly round Marie's neck the stole which had been star turn in the trousseau six years ago, and very tenderly she pressed her hands.

"Don't make the jersey suit for George; I want to give it to him for Christmas!"

"Oh, Julia, I couldn't!".

"Yes, you could and will."

"You're an old darling."

"That's all right, Mrs. Osborn Kerr. Now I'll take you as far as your Tube or 'bus. Which is it?"

Marie went home the warmer for Julia's companionship and her visit to the most up-to-date women's club in town; she looked almost girlish again when she stepped into No. 30 Welham Mansions, to relieve Grannie Amber of the onerous responsibilities which she undertook so gladly.

"Well, duck," said Mrs. Amber, coming out with her funny walk, which was at once a waddle, because of her weight, and a trip, from the energy of her disposition, "have you had a lovely day?"

"Such a nice time, thank you, mother. Babes been good?"

"Perfect little angels!" Mrs. Amber lied with innocent sincerity.

"I'll begin putting them to bed directly I've laid down these parcels. I've got the cream socks and the flannel for baby's new petticoats, but the jersey suits were too dear. Julia's going to give George one for Christmas."

"That's very kind of her, love. I always think she has a good heart, though I don't like her opinions. The bath water's hot, my duck, and baby's in bed, and the others are undressed, all ready, waiting for you."

"You *are* a good grannie!"

Grannie Amber stayed a while longer to watch the two elder children's bathing; she squeezed her plump form alongside Marie in the tiny bathroom, and from time to time emitted laughs and cries of fond delight. She made herself busy, when the matter was over, in folding towels and wiping up the pools of water which the rampant children had splashed upon the floor. She followed them with her waddling trip along the corridor to see them snugly tucked up in their beds in what had been Osborn's dressing-room, and at last, having murmured, "God bless you all, ducks!" her good work accomplished, she stole away.

The flush of exertion stained Marie's pale cheeks now; it was 6.15, and there was no time for anything but to fly to the kitchen. It was always so, but happily there was seldom time to think about it. If you began to question why, the potatoes boiled dry in immediate protest against your discontent. By the time Marie had set the gas-stove going full blast the very tips of her nose and ears were crimson. Without pause she ran back into her bedroom to put on her best slippers, the only evening toilet she had time to make. She stood a few seconds leaning towards the glass, as she had stood that birthday night after her husband had taken her to dine at the Royal Red, and she fingered her blouse, her hair, her manicure tools passionately, sadly and appealingly, as if she begged them: "Do your best." The underlying anxiety which her confidences to Julia had awakened looked haggardly from her face.

"I am growing very old," she thought, terrified. "I am growing much older than thirty-one. I look older than Osborn."

She was quivering to woman's ageless problem, the problem of the body, the problem of the tired brain and the driven heart; the problem of the great and cruel competition between the woman of pleasure and the woman of toil.

While she still stood there, she heard her husband's key in the lock.

She put up her hands to smooth the worry away from her face and, with the impress of her fingers white on her flushed cheeks, stared at herself again. Surely that was better? She wore a smile, the smile of the Wise Wives, and went out to meet him. He was shedding his overcoat, and as he hung it up he whistled a tune with joy in it. She was struck instantly by something about him, a tiny but material change, which she could not fathom.

"Hallo, old girl!" he turned to say cheerfully.

"Hallo, dear!" she replied.

"Dinner ready?"

"Quite! I'll bring it in."

He went into the dining-room and stood on the hearth in the attitude long appropriate to a master of the house. His eyes were shining, though his brow still wore its habitual creases as if he were thinking very carefully. He stared before him, but without noting anything. They still had a pretty dinner-table, a dinner-table almost, if not quite, up to early-married standards, and the shaded candles were lighted and beneath them there were cut flowers. He never wondered how Marie managed to stretch that weekly thirty-two and sixpence to cover the cost of a third baby, occasional new candle-shades and perpetual flowers. It was better not to inquire. Inquiry raised ideas and suggestions and requests. He could not afford to inquire. It struck him vaguely this evening, as he stood looking out somewhere beyond the dining-room and whistling his happy tune, that everything was very fairly comfortable.

His wife came in with a big tray and arranged the dinner temptingly upon the table. When it was all ready he drew up his chair and sat down with an air of appetite. And he talked; it was as if he exerted himself to interest her and to be interested, himself, in all that she said. He listened and commented upon her day's shopping, asked where she lunched, heard about her visit to Julia at a chic club, and observed lightly how fashionable she was getting.

He said she looked tired to-night, and must take care of herself.

He was going to stay at home this evening, to sit by the fire and talk to her; his manner was almost loverlike, and her heart thrilled to it as she had not thought it could thrill again. She looked at him with eyes in which her wonder showed; and in her quietened body her passion seemed to raise its subdued head again, sweet and strong and young.

"I shan't be two minutes clearing away," she said, when they rose. She felt no more fatigue, but piled all the things on the big tray and carried it out to the kitchen almost like a feather-weight, and in less than the two minutes she had assigned, she was back again with the coffee things, her feet light and her eyes dreaming. She drew her chair nearer his before the hearth, and stretched out her hand to him, hungering across the space. He squeezed and dropped it, and leaned forward, clearing his throat as if he were going to speak words of moment.

He checked himself and obviously said something else.

"Your coffee is good, dear; you do look after me in a simply tophole way."

His words were like the prelude of a song to her. She listened for more, with a smile, a real smile, no more wise, but foolish. It had the foolishness of all love in it, so easily and completely could he give her pain, or pleasure.

He answered the smile with one of constraint.

Feeling in the pocket of his lounge coat, he uttered abruptly:

"I brought you a few sweets, dear; passed a shop on my way; thought—"

He handed over a packet of chocolates and sat back with a sigh expressive of satisfaction, while, with a cry of delight and gratitude, she untied the ribbons.

"You are a dear!" she said tremulously. "I must share them with the children; and this pink ribbon—pink for a girl, blue for a boy! It'll do for baby's bonnet. What lovely ribbon, silk all through!"

"Oh, well, they weren't cheap chocolates," Osborn observed.

"I see that. They're delicious." She broke one slowly between her teeth. Sweets! They brought back those dear old spoiled-girl days to her; precious days which no woman values till she has lost them, and the prize of which no man understands.

"Glad you like them," he said, looking at her with a strange, an almost guilty softness. "I like you to have things that you enjoy. You know that, don't you?"

"Of course I do, dear."

Osborn cleared his throat and leaned forward again, his clasped hands between his knees. He looked down at the hands attentively, appearing to take an undue interest in them.

He began slowly:

"Er—speaking of things you'd enjoy, old girl, we—we've often talked about—wondered when—my ship would be coming in. Grand to see her, wouldn't it be, steaming into harbour, fine as paint, full cargo and all?"

He choked slightly over his words, as with excitement, and that shining in his eyes intensified. She caught it as for a moment he lifted them, and it took her breath away, but in the same instant she knew that this shining was not for her.

"Osborn!" she uttered, and could say no more.

He continued: "I've got something to tell you."

"I felt it when you first came in. Oh, Osborn, darling, don't keep me waiting. What is it?"

"Well—in a way—it's what we've both been thinking of—"

"The ship's—come in!"

As she breathed rather than spoke the words she sank back in her chair; her conviction was so sure that she could have shrieked with ecstasy; yet at the same time it came with such an overpowering relief that she had the sensation of one kept

May Edginton

too long from sleep lying down at last to rest. She would have been content to wait, until after a long dreamful contemplation of the news, for detail and description of the voyage and adventure of the most elusive craft in the world, only that, once off, Osborn plunged on as if he would have her know all as soon as might be.

He started again, with scarcely a pause, after just a nod to confirm her exclamation.

"I'll begin at the beginning. That's the best way, eh, old girl? I see it's staggered you as it staggered me. Woodall—you've heard me speak of Woodall, one of our travellers?—was just about to start for a long trip—New York, Chicago, then Montreal and all over Canada, California, then New Zealand; it was a fine trip, selling our Runaway two-seater. Well, when I got to our place this morning the boss sent for me at once, and told me the news about poor old Woodall— knocked down by a taxi in the street last night, and now in hospital for they don't know how long. The tickets were bought and the tour arranged, and—and—in short, you see, they'd got to pick another man at a moment's notice, to go instead. And so—"

The wife leaned forward, her eyes opened wide and warily on her husband's face. Not looking at her, he rattled on:

"So the boss offered it to me. You don't need telling that I accepted, do you?"

She replied, "No," in a quiet voice.

"I knew you'd think I ought to take it," he said, with a swift glance at her. "Of course, it mayn't be permanent, but I think it's up to me to make it so. I guess I can hold down a job of that kind as well as anyone else, if I've the chance. It's a fine chance! Do you know what it means?"

She uttered a questioning sound.

"Five hundred a year," he said huskily, "with a good commission and all expenses paid. The expenses are—are princely. You see, a fellow selling motors isn't like a fellow selling tea. He's got to do the splendid—get among the right people; among all sorts of people. Oh, it'll be life!"

Passion was subdued again in her; it was old and drowsy and quiet. Knitting her fingers tightly round her knee, she rocked a little, and asked:

"When do you start?"

"Of course it's rather sudden—"

"So I understood from what you said. When will it be, Osborn?"

"To-morrow."

She stared into his face, unbelieving.

"To-morrow?" she whispered.

He got up hurriedly and fumbled about the mantel-piece in a fake search for cigarettes.

"You see, I've got to follow out Woodall's programme exactly; he would have started to-morrow."

"How—how long will you be away?"

"A year."

"A year!" she half screamed. "Oh, no! no! no!"

He looked at her with something of fear and something of sulkiness. He was on the defensive, willing to be very kind, but resolute not to be nagged nor argued with. "Don't," he protested, "don't take it like that."

"I'm sorry, dear," she said more quietly. "It hit me, rather. To-morrow is so soon, and a year is such a long, long time."

"Not so very. A year's nothing. Besides, I've got to go; it's no use making a fuss, is it?"

"I won't make a fuss."

"There'll be a good deal to do. I wanted you to look over my things to-night. I'll help you carry them in here, shall I?"

She rose mechanically and went into the erstwhile dressing-room quietly, so as not to disturb the sleeping children. He waited in the doorway, and she handed out to him pile after pile of his underwear, following the last consignment by carrying out a big armful herself. They returned to the dining-room and laid the garments on the table.

"Sorry to give you so much trouble all at once," he apologised.

He lighted a pipe and sat down again by the fire, while she stood over the heaps on the table, sorting them with neat fingers that had learned a very considerable speed in such tasks, and picking out here and there a shirt or vest which needed further attention. She was white with a kind of grey whiteness like ashes, and in her heart and throat heavy weights of tears lay. She talked automatically to keep herself from exhibition of despair.

"I'll darn that; it's as good as new except for one thin patch. These shirts have lasted very well, haven't they? The colour's hardly faded at all. You ought to have had new vests, but I daresay you'll have ample opportunity for buying them. To-morrow morning I'll sponge your navy suit with ammonia. What time are you going? *T-t-ten o'clock?*...

"I'll sponge it before breakfast. You may want to put it on. I'm going to look for that glove you lost; it was a seven-and-sixpenny pair; we ought to find it." And things like this she continued to say to him, lest, the fantastic fancy of her grief whispered to her, he should hear her heart painfully breaking.

He answered with alacrity, the same alacrity of response which he had shown, at dinner; and he handed to her the packet of chocolates, asking jocularly: "Isn't she going to eat her sweets?"

She broke one slowly between her teeth again; it had an extraordinary bitter taste which remained in the mouth. She hated the packet of sweets for its smug, silly mission of comfort.

Comfort!

How queer women's lives were!

What did men really think regarding their wives? What did Osborn think, sitting there in his accustomed chair, with his accustomed pipe between his teeth and his new and gorgeous plans causing his eyes to shine?

She knew now the wherefore of his eyes shining. He was looking out at a wonderful adventure; at freedom.

Freedom!

What right had he to freedom?

She turned to him with a remark so abrupt that it was exclamatory:

"It will be a good holiday for you."

"Great!" he answered, his satisfaction bursting forth, "great!"

"I wish I could come with you."

"Ah," he said, "ah!..." She watched him with a knifelike keenness while he reflected, and she read the stealthy gratification of the thought he voiced next: "But you can't, old girl There are the kiddies."

"Do you suppose I don't know that?"

"Oh, well; I knew you were only joking."

Joking?

What a joke!

"I shall try to save a bit of money for the first time in my life," he said. "I'll leave you a clear two hundred for yourself and the kids—that's all right, isn't it? Two hundred, and you won't have my enormous appetite to cater for! You'll do very well, won't you, Mrs. Osborn?"

"Thank you. We shall do quite well."

"I'll arrange at the bank, and give you a chequebook."

She said next:

"A whole year! Baby'll forget you."

The remark seemed to him peculiarly womanish and silly. What on earth did it matter, anyway? But he had patience with her, knowing how sorely better men than he were tried by their wives.

"Well," he observed, "kids' memories are very short, aren't they?"

Marie went on sorting the clothes; presently she drew a chair to the table, and began to work with needle and thread, darning, tightening buttons, performing the many jobs which only a wife would find. As she sewed she glanced again and again at her husband; he had sunk deep into his chair in an abandonment of rest, his legs stretched before him, his pipe between his teeth, his shining eyes fixed upon the fire. Now and again his lips twitched to a smile over the pipe stem. He was thinking, imagining, revelling in the freedom of the approaching year. The marriage task had infinitely wearied him. For a year, with a well-lined pocket, and a first-class ticket, he was to travel away from it all. He was deeply allured, and his delight was again young and robust; he looked forward most eagerly, as a school-boy to a promising holiday.

After she had sewed awhile with a methodical tightening of all the buttons, and an unconscious tightening of her lips too, she said:

"Well, you'll come back and find us all the same."

He roused himself slightly.

"I hope so. Take care of yourselves."

She could have screamed at him.

"We shall jog along here," she said.

He looked at her abstractedly. "Take the kids to Littlehampton in the summer; give yourselves a change. Your mother'll go with you, I daresay."

"How jolly!"

He took her seriously. He seemed so densely absorbed in what was coming to him that he only just heard her reply.

He said absently: "I hope it will be; look after yourselves."

She went back, in her busy mind, to the honeymoon adventure on which they had both embarked six and a quarter years ago. Then they had gone out hand-in-hand like children into a big dark and they had found light. Now they had dropped hands; and at the first chance he ran off alone, a boy once more, hungry for thrills. A strong yearning rose in her to run after him, catch his hand again, and set out with him. But there was much in the way; the butcher and baker, speaking through her mouth, had dulled his ears to her voice; he had forgotten how to hold hands; they were out of tune. Nature had sent them, all those years ago, converging together; and married life had sent them apart again.

Married life!

She traced the pattern of it, which she saw in her mind, upon the table with her needle tip—

It was like that.

She saw wet drops falling upon the table; they were her tears. Her husband happened to look up at the moment, and, seeing them too, looked hastily away again. He did not want to see them; there were too many tears in marriage.

But soon he would be away from marriage for a whole year.

He did not want her to cry; it was terribly irritating, and she had cried too much—not lately, but in the first years. Lately she had disciplined herself better, become more cheerful, realised, no doubt, that she was quite as well off as other men's wives, and really had nothing to weep for. But, in case those tears which had fallen should be precursors of one of the old storms, he knocked out his pipe, rose, and said:

"Well, I'll be off to bed. I shall have a lot to do to-morrow."

She answered: "Very well, dear. I shan't be long."

The door shut upon him and she was alone. She listened for the closing of the bedroom door upon him, knowing that then he would not come back, knowing that he had seen and feared her tears. Then she dropped her work, and ran over to the hearthplace, and, kneeling down by his chair still warm from the impress of his body, laid her head upon it, and cried terribly.

When she had married him she gave up her life and took his instead. If he removed it, how should she live? She had become so much a part of him that her suffering was devastating; it was physical. And now, giving rein to herself, her sex side tugged at her pitilessly. Jealousy tore through her like a hot wind. She had a dozen grey hairs, a thin throat, a tired face, rough hands, two spoiled teeth in the front upper row. That was not the worst; the gaiety of her wit had been sapped. She could not have kept two men amused at a dinner table as that raven woman in the Royal Red did had her life depended upon it. Six years ago she could. She could have had them in her white, pretty hands; but not now. Not now! Never any more!

Never had she wept as she wept now before Osborn's chair in the silent dining-room, and when it seemed as if all founts of tears had run dry, so that she was left merely sobbing without weeping, she collected herself to pray.

She prayed:

"O God, teach men! Teach Osborn. Let them know. Let them think and have pity. Make him admire me, God. Make him admire me for the children I've suffered over, even if my face is spoiled. But, God, don't let me be spoiled. Can't I recover? O God, why do You spoil women? It's not fair. Help me! Keep him from the other women—the women who are fresher and prettier than me. Help me to fight. Let me win. Keep him loving me. Keep him thinking of me every day. For Christ's sake."

And after that she prayed on in some formless way till the clock struck half-past eleven, and a rapping came upon the other side of the wall, and with it sounded Osborn's muffled voice.

He somehow guessed that she would cry a little; get things over quietly by herself. It was the best way. But it was now half-past eleven....

She rose, rapped back, and tidied her hair quickly before the round mirror over the mantelpiece. Her face was ravaged. But in the bedroom she would have to undress by a very subdued light lest she awakened the baby, so he would not see, even if he wished to see. She knew, however, that he did not wish it. After making neat piles of the scattered garments again, she raked out the fire, switched off the lights, and went quietly into the bedroom.

His voice was a little testy to conceal his apprehensions.

"I must say you haven't hurried! You haven't been *making* me half a dozen new shirts, have you, old girl?"

She replied in a carefully-steadied tone: "There was a good deal to do, and I wanted to finish it."

He pulled his bedclothes up higher around him. "Well, thanks awfully. Afraid I rushed you. You won't be long now, will you? I want to get to sleep, and I can't with someone moving about."

"I'll be quick. There's baby's bottle to do—it's long past time. She hasn't waked, I suppose?"

"No; hasn't made a sound."

Marie lighted the spirit stove, and put the baby's food on while she undressed. Osborn watched her apprehensively, not knowing that she knew of what he did. But she wasn't going to make a fuss.

He was very thankful for that.

Every time she turned towards him he closed his eyes quickly, fearing conversation which he need not have feared. She could not have talked to him. When the food was ready and the bottle given, she was glad to creep into her own bed, erect a similar barricade of sheet and blankets, and sink into a sort of coma of grief and depression. In a few minutes Osborn slept.

When Marie opened her eyes on the twilight of early winter morning it seemed to her that she could scarcely have had time to close them, but her bedside clock showed her, to her surprise, that she had been sleeping all night. The greatness of the shock had passed, and she had to concern herself imminently with all the bustle of Osborn's departure. As he was not going to business to-day, not going out at all, in fact, until he left gloriously, like a man of leisure, in a taxicab at ten o'clock, he did no more than unclose a sleepy eye when his wife sprang out of her bed and murmur:

"I say, old girl, you will do my packing, won't you?"

"Yes. I'm extra early, on purpose."

So in the grey dawn, Marie went about her business. She packed suit-case and kit-bag and hat-box, and placed the labels ready for Osborn to write; she dressed George and bade him help the three-year-old to dress; she brushed the rooms and lighted the fires; made the morning bottle for the baby; saw that boiling hot shaving water was ready for Osborn; gave the children their breakfast; cooked an unusually lavish one for the traveller; and had accomplished all these things by the time he was dressed and ready at nine o'clock.

He glowed with health and cheer. The creases in his brow were smoothed out; his smile was ready; his voice had its old boyish ring.

Because he was going away from them the metamorphosis occurred which rived the wife's heart afresh. He was so glad to go.

He sat down with a great appetite to breakfast, while she faced him behind the tea tray. The baby, being unable to help herself as yet, was still imprisoned in her cot in the bedroom until such time as her mother could attend to her, and on the dining-room floor George and the three-year-old, ordered to keep extremely quiet and inoffensive, played with their bricks. Now and again an erection of bricks toppled down accidentally with a shattering noise, when Osborn exclaimed: "Shut up, you kids!" and their mother implored: "Do try to keep quiet while Daddy's here."

The parents made conversation at breakfast, but not much. It was kept mainly to material things relevant to the moment, such as:

"You packed *all* my thin shirts, didn't you?"

"Except the striped one, which has gone too far. I'll make it up for George."

"Have you written the labels?"

"No. I didn't know where to."

"All right. I'll do 'em. It's a jolly morning for a start, isn't it?"

"Yes. I'm so glad."

"I'll write and give you an address as soon as I can. I shall be able to find out to-day about mails, I expect. Yesterday I really didn't think of inquiring. 'Sides, I hadn't time. And I can tell you, I was all up a tree with excitement."

"Of course you were. It'll be a lovely holiday for you."

"Wish you could come too. Look after yourselves, won't you?"

"Yes, thanks, dear."

"Did you tell the porter to get a taxi at ten?"

"No! George can run down and do it now. George, run down and tell the porter Daddy wants a taxi at ten sharp."

Marie rose to unlatch the front door for George and returned.

The hour went past like a wheeled thing gathering velocity down an ever steeper and steeper slope. It was extraordinary how quickly it flew, and the moment came for the good-bye. She looked at him, and her heart seemed to beat up in her throat. If only he would have thrown his arms around her and been very sorry to go! She wanted a long good-bye in the flat, where no one could see and pry upon her anguish. But he had been married for six such long years that perhaps he had forgotten the romance and passion of good-byes. He kissed George; he kissed the three-year-old; he kissed her a kiss of mere every day affection; then, taking a hand of each of the children, he said gaily:

"All come down to see Daddy start, won't you?"

The hall porter came up for the bags. Osborn helped the excited children down the long flights of grey stone stairs, and she followed. During the business of stowing the luggage on the cab, she took the children from Osborn, and, heedless of the passers-by, put up her longing face once more.

"Good-bye," she said tremulously.

He kissed her again quickly, turned away, jumped into the cab, and she saw the shining of his eyes through the window. He pulled the strap and let it down. "Be good kids," he exhorted. "Bye-bye, dear! Bye-bye, all of you! Take care of yourselves!"

He was gone.

Marie stood bareheaded in the bleak wind, holding a hand of each of her children, to watch his cab down the street. After it had disappeared she still stood there, gazing blankly at the place of its vanishing, till at last the younger child, shuddering, complained: "Mummy, I's so told."

"Are you, darling?" she said tenderly, lifting the blue mite in her arms. She carried her child up all the grey stone stairs, George following, and they re-entered the flat.

It had an air of missing someone very desolately.

Her face puckered suddenly and she was afraid she was going to cry again, before the children, but George stood in front of her, examining her minutely, and she straightened her lips.

"Mummie," said George, "you hasn't barfed poor baby."

"You come and help Mummie do it," she answered.

The procession of three went together into the bedroom, where the long-suffering baby had begun at last to protest. The rumpled beds were as she and Osborn had left them, and the room looked soiled. She inspected it for a moment before she turned to the business of bathing and dressing the baby.

Osborn's late breakfast had made her late with the house-work, but it didn't matter. There was no one to work for, cook for, keep up the standard for. For a few minutes she thought thus.

George and the three-year-old gave her a great deal of help with the baby. Their little fat, loving faces turned to her in the utmost worship and faith, and they trotted about, vying with each other in bringing her this and that for the infantile toilet. And when it was accomplished, George took charge of the baby in the dining-room while his mother turned to the work which he was accustomed to seeing her do. It was as if a great gift of sympathy for his mother in her hour of need had descended into his small heart.

Marie's first task lay in the bedroom; when she had made her own bed, she turned to Osborn's, and slowly and thought-fully, one by one, she folded up the blankets for storage in the cupboard, dropped the sheets and pillow-case into the linen-basket without replacing them, and then spread the pink quilt over the unmade bed.

It would be a year before Osborn wanted it again. *A year!*

A few things of his lay about the room; only a few, for all that were good enough to pack she had packed. She suddenly advanced upon these few trifles, swept them together, and pushed them out of sight in a drawer. Again she looked around. The room seemed expressive now only of her own entity; she was entirely alone in it.

She advanced to Osborn's bed again, ripped off the quilt and mattress, and bent her strength to taking apart and folding the iron bedstead. It was really a man's task, but she accomp-lished it, and carried it into the dressing-room, where she put it against the wall, in a corner. Again she returned to her own room and looked around. Her bed, her toilet things, every-thing was hers. True, the baby's cot stood there; otherwise it was a virgin room.

Anger had muffled the grief in her heart.

"Well," she said, "I have no husband."

CHAPTER XVII

REVIVAL

She began to tidy the room automatically. Through the partitioning wall she could hear George crooning like a guardian angel to his charge, and she smiled tenderly. "The darling!" she thought. His immature and uncomprehending sympathy warmed her chilled heart as nothing else could have done. She had a great new sensation of leisure; there was all day to potter about in and no one to prepare for in the evening.

Life was now timeless, without the clock of man's habits. Nothing mattered.

She sat down idly before her dressing-table and met again her sallowed face in the mirror. The sight stirred her anger vigorously once more. Wrathfully she wanted to do something—anything—and, to keep her fingers busy, pulled open one of the top drawers of the dressing-table. Confusion met her, for it was the untidy drawer beloved of woman; the drawer where ribbons and lace and scent sachets and waist-belts and flowers and face powder lay pell-mell. For a long while the drawer had not had the periodical setting straight which woman grants it, and its contents were aged, dingy and undesirable—camisole-ribbons like boot-strings, lace collars long out of fashion, a rose or two crumpled into flat and withered blobs, shapeless and faded. She touched things sorrowfully.

"My pretty things!" she thought with regret.

At what precise moment the idea came to her she did not know, but it intruded by degrees. She began to think idly of money, to turn over in her mind the exact allowance with which Osborn had left her, and she knew herself rich. Till yesterday her domestic budget, for herself, the children and Osborn, had been at the rate of about one hundred and forty pounds a year. He had to have the rest. Now she had two hundred and no man to keep. It would have taken a woman to understand why she suddenly sprang up, why her sallowed face took on a hasty colour, and with what an incredulously beating heart she hastened down the grey stone stairs to the hall-porter's box.

"Porter," she said, controlling her voice with difficulty, "I want a charwoman at once; and—and for two or three hours every morning. You could find one for me?"

Like every other block of flats, the place was infested with ladies of the charing profession, and he promised her one within half an hour. Returning to her children, she sat down at ease in the dining-room to await the woman's arrival.

When she came, it was joy to show her round; to say: "I want the bedroom and hall and kitchen done; these things washed up; and these vegetables prepared. And these things of the children's washed out, please. I shall be back before you've finished."

Then she put on the children's outdoor things, established the baby and the three-year-old at either end of the perambulator and, with George walking manfully by her side, set out upon an errand.

She was going to tell her mother of what had befallen; she hardly knew why, but the wisdom of matronly counsel and opinion, irritating as it was, had impressed her forcibly during the past years. So she and George trundled the shabby grey perambulator, Rokeby's gift, across the Heath, and along the intervening streets to Grannie Amber's.

They left the perambulator in the courtyard and made a slow journey up the stairs to her nice flat on the first floor. That flat, which had seemed so small and old-fashioned to the girl Marie, appeared as a haven of refuge and comfort to the woman. It was so warm, so quiet and still. When they arrived there, Grannie Amber was comfortably sewing by her cosy fire, while her charwoman got through the work there was to do. She was surprised and somewhat uneasy to see her daughter so early, but she bustled about to settle them comfortably, taking the baby upon her lap, and bringing out queer old games from cunning hiding-places for the others, as grannies do.

When George and the three-year-old were presumably absorbed, she lifted an anxious, cautionary eyebrow at Marie, and waited to hear the news.

"Osborn's gone away for a year, mother," Marie announced quietly.

Mrs. Amber did not reply for a few moments, but her elderly face flushed with red and her eyes with tears; she was so nonplussed that she hardly knew what to say, but at length she asked:

"What does that mean, duck?"

"He has got a splendid appointment, owing to an accident to one of the firm's travellers," said Marie steadily. "He only knew yesterday, and had to start at ten this morning, so you may guess we've been very busy. It will keep him away for a year and he's going to travel—oh! over nearly half the world, selling the new Runaway two-seater; and the salary is five hundred a year and a good commission and very generous expenses."

She was glad to have got it all out almost at a breath, without a sign of a breakdown; and the eyes of Grannie Amber, who was not meant to understand and knew better than to show she did, kindled at her daughter's courage.

"I am so sorry, duck," she murmured sympathetically. "You'll both have felt the parting very much; but it'll be a splendid holiday for Osborn; and—and I'm not sure whether it won't be a splendid holiday for you, too."

Marie met her mother's eyes with a full look.

"I am not sure, either, mother," she said quietly.

Grannie Amber looked down at the baby's small, meek, round head.

"You need a rest," she murmured, "and this money will help you, won't it, love?"

"I have two hundred a year, clear, for the children and myself."

"He might have halved it!" said Grannie, in a sudden, indignant cry.

Marie replied with a look of steel: "I don't think so at all, mother. And men always think that women ought not to have the handling of too much money, you know."

"*Don't* I know!" said Grannie, with unabated venom.

"Osborn has left me plenty. It's far more than I managed on before."

"I'm glad of that, duck."

"Directly Osborn had gone I suddenly thought—and I got in a charwoman. She's there now. It did seem queer."

"Oh, that's good, my love. I *am* glad of that. Now you'll rest yourself and get your looks back, and I shall be round a great deal to help you with the children."

"I want to ask you to do something for me to-day, mother."

"Certainly, my love. Just name it."

"I—I want a free day. To go into town and lunch and walk about by myself; no household shopping to do; no time to keep; no cooking to hurry back for...."

"What a funny idea, duck!" replied Grannie, still carefully keeping up the attitude of old dunderhead; "but I'm sure I'll be only too delighted to go back home with you, and take the children out on the Heath this afternoon. And I'll put them to bed, too. You'll help me with these very little children, won't you, Georgie?"

"'Ess, G'annie," replied George importantly.

"Mummie needn't hurry back, need she, Georgie?"

"She tan 'tay out all night," replied George, showing a generous breadth of mind.

Grannie and mother both laughed heartily.

"I'll run and put on my things at once," said Mrs. Amber, transferring the baby to Marie's lap, "and I'll go back with you now. I'm an idle old woman with nothing to do, and it will be a delight to me to take the children out."

They trundled the grey baby-carriage back across the Heath, and toiled up the stone staircase of Welham Mansions to Number Thirty. All the windows of the flat were opened; it looked almost fresh and bright once more; and a charwoman of stout build was dealing competently with the few remaining jobs. Marie paid her; instructed her to return to-morrow, and went to make herself ready for town.

She left home again at twelve-thirty, taking with her a replenished purse, and a stock of tremluous emotions. One was of dreadful solitude, a fear of loneliness, spineless and enervating; another of defiance; another of excitement; another of bravado; another almost of shame.

What should she, an old married woman with a family of three, want with a purposeless jaunt to town? Since the birth of George she had never done such a thing. She had never spent money on amusing herself, on passing an agreeable time.

It was almost as if, directly her husband, the master of her life and her children's lives, turned his back, she filled her purse from the store he had left behind him, and went off frivolling.

"I do not care!" she said to herself fearsomely. "I do not care

May Edginton

a damn. I'm off!"

One o'clock found her in the West End, a shabby, thin-faced woman of the suburbs, rubbing shoulders with scores of other women jostling round the shop windows. All that she saw she longed for; but none of it was she foolish enough to buy. Some cold prudence, an offshoot of her curious anger of the morning which still lingered with her, restrained. Unformed, but working in her mind, was the beginning of an impression that during this coming year she had some definite course to follow, plan to make; she felt, almost heroically, as if she were going to salve herself from something she had not, till lately, before her glass, dared to define. She saw that women, caught intricately in the domestic toils, had a dreadful, hard, cunning battle to fight, and she felt as if in some way she was just beginning to fight it, but that it would tax her utmost resources. So she spent none of her money on the fashionable trifles of a moment, which she saw behind the plate-glass, but she gave herself a lunch.

Debating long where to go, she went to the Royal Red and had a little table in an obscure corner behind a pillar, where she could see, but was hardly seen, even if anyone had wanted to look at this woman, apparently just one of a thousand suburban shoppers. She lingered long at her table to get to the full the worth of her three-and-sixpence; to watch the suave, gay women pass in and out, be fed and flattered and entertained. The great furs laid across their slender shoulders, the ephemeral corsages beneath, the hint of pearls on well-massaged necks, the luring cock of a hat, the waft of a perfume that was yet hardly so crude as definite perfume, all roused her hostility, her fighting sense. Not a woman there knew what passed behind the pillar in the breast and brain of the slim, shabby woman with the big eyes and wan face; none knew how she hated and feared; none knew of her prayers; none but would have smiled to hear that she even thought of entering with them the arena of women. And had a man glanced once her way he would not have glanced twice.

All this she knew; she was setting it down definitely in her mind, like writing. When it was written she was willing to read it over and over again till she had learned it by heart.

She had eaten an ice Neapolitaine with voluptuous pleasure and, calling her waiter, ordered coffee and a cigarette.

She was not going yet.

It was a long while since she had smoked, or even thought of it; and though she really did not care very much for smoking, she chose an expensive Egyptian now with the utmost pleasure. What a sensation of leisure it gave, this loitering at will, over a cup of coffee and a cigarette! Besides, it gave her longer to watch her enemies, to learn the modes and tricks of the day.

After lunch she sauntered back into Regent Street and stopped by an American Beauty Parlour. She went in and inquired the price of a manicure. It would be one-and-sixpence. So she entered a warm wee cubicle full of beauty apparatus, sat down, and gave her right hand for the manicurist's ministrations.

The manicurist was a lithe, tall girl, with a small young, wicked face; and meekly demure. Her hair was sleeked down provocatively over her ears, in which emerald drops dangled. She was an Enemy. As she took her client's hand and dabbled the finger-tips in a tiny red bowl of orange-flower water, Marie wondered, without charity, who had given her those earrings of green fire, and why.

The girl talked sweetly, as she was taught to do. She remarked on the coldness of the day and the trials of shopping in such bleak weather; on the bustle of the shops preparing for Christmas; on the smallness of Madame's hands.

They were a charming shape, might she say? But Madame had abused them. Madame had perhaps been gardening? Gardening was becoming so fashionable, with a sweet glance at the client's *ensemble*. Was that the reason for those broken cuticles, those swollen fingertips and brittle nails? It was a thousand pities.

Knowing, as she spoke, the futility, the obviousness of the lie, yet somehow unable to help speaking it, Marie answered in abrupt confusion. Yes, she had been gardening; it—it was a favourite hobby nowadays; all her friends....

With that sleek face before her, those fragile fingertips handling hers, she would not for a fortune have confessed: "I spoil my hands because I spend my days between the stove and the sink; because I've cooked and swept and sewed for a man and three children; because I wash and iron." Secretly the manicurist would laugh and ridicule; in her smooth white face and twinkly eardrops was the story of what she would think of such a domestic fool; of the woman who was the slave of man and home; who had lost her looks and hope in the servitude of married poverty.

Presently the finger-nails were done; they did not look a great deal better even now, but they felt charmingly petted and soothed. Again the manicurist ran her eye over the other from head to heel, letting her glance rest at last upon her face.

"A face massage, madame?" she suggested.

Marie hesitated, and the girl added, smiling: "It would be half a crown."

"I have not time to-day, thank you," Marie said, rising. She paid for the manicure and left the warm and scented place; she had nowhere particular to go, no one to talk to, and yet she did not wish to go home so early. It would have been a tame ending to her day and, besides, she had not seen all yet. She wanted to see the lights rise and twinkle along the streets, to watch the evening life come in like a tide, wave upon wave breaking musically upon the city's shore; and to feel that even then, though six o'clock had passed, and seven, and eight, she was yet her own mistress. She was sampling sensations, not altogether new, but at any rate long forgotten. It occurred to her, as she turned out of the Beauty Shop, to go and call upon someone; but upon whom? She knew, as she asked the question of herself, that, while she had lost a score of light-hearted acquaintances upon her wedding day, she had since been too busy to make more. There were upon her limited horizon, in fact, only Julia and Rokeby. Julia, at this moment still afternoon, would be involved in much business, someone else's business which she could not put aside as if it were her own to do as she pleased with; but Rokeby called no man master.

She hardly knew why she thought of going to tell Rokeby her news, but there was a want in her, a want of a wise someone's comments, a kind someone's sympathy. She boarded a City omnibus and was carried to King William Street.

Here Desmond had his prosperous shipbroking office, and made his enviable thousands and sharpened his innately sharp brain, so well concealed below his lacklustre, almost naive, exterior.

A lift carried her up to the third floor, where she arrived before a door upon the glass panels of which were blazoned his name and profession, and pushing it open, she asked for him uncertainly. A clerk said doubtfully: "Have you come about the typist's situation?" and looked at her in a summary fashion which made her timid.

She hated this timidity which had grown upon her with the married years; a timidity based upon loss of trust in her womanly powers, loss of the natural arrogance of beauty. Holding her head very erect, she replied:

"I am a friend of Mr. Rokeby's. Will you kindly say that Mrs. Osborn Kerr has called?" Second thoughts sent her fumbling in her bag and producing a card.

"You had better send in my card," she said.

Desmond was busy with a client when the card was laid before him, but when he had glanced at it, he took it up and looked again, as if not believing his eyes. "In five minutes," he told the clerk; and, turning to the client, he clinched in that remarkably short while an arrangement which they had been discussing and quarrelling over for half an hour.

He stood up, waiting for Marie to enter. When she came, he was struck, not having seen her since the birth of the third baby, by the further alteration in her. How thin she was! And quiet! With that dullness which, in his judgment, too much domesticity always brought to women. Like most ultra-modern men, while secretly making a fetish of the softer virtues in woman, he wanted them expressed somehow in an up-to-the-minute setting. Yet he understood dimly the struggle of twentieth-century woman in trying to make herself at once as new as to-day and as old as creation.

"Well, this is nice," he said very kindly, taking her hand with deference. "I've a free hour, and lo! you come to fill it. Let me pull the visitor's chair right up to this fire, and give you a cup of tea."

His kindness and attention were all about Marie with the benevolence of a new warm garment on a cold day. She sat down in the great soft chair which he wheeled forwards for her, loosened her out-of-date fur neckwear, and looked around her with feminine interest.

"What a pretty office!" she said. "And you have flowers."

"Ladies sometimes come to tea," he replied smilingly, pressing a bell.

To the clerk he said: "Get tea from Fuller's, right away."

"I ought not to hinder you," said Marie; and, as she said it, there came to her the fragrance of the memory how in her girl days she had, in the course of her business and pleasure, hindered many men like this, and how pleased and flattered they were to be thus hindered. She wished she could feel as sure of herself and her power to charm without the least exertion as she was then. She went on: "I really hardly know why I came, but I was in town; and I thought you'd like to hear the news about Osborn. He's gone, you know; gone."

Rokeby wheeled right round to face her, in his swing chair: "I know," he nodded, "at least I know the bare bones of it. He found time to ring me up yesterday and give me an inkling. So you've really sent him off, have you?"

"Yes; this morning, at ten."

Rokeby felt for his words carefully, in view of what he saw

in her face.

"It must have been a rush for both of you."

"It was. But things are better like that. There isn't so much time to think."

"No," said Rokeby.

"If I'd known he'd told you, I wouldn't have come round to hinder you this afternoon."

"Don't mention that word again, Mrs. Kerr. I'm proud and delighted. And I didn't hear much yesterday, and I want all of it. What's the whole game?"

She sat there telling him; the fire flushed her face so that its wanness disappeared; and in their wonder and bewilderment her eyes were big and solemn like a child's. But the composure to which she had won was complete.

"It will be a splendid holiday for him," she finished. "He hasn't had one since we were married. Of course, we've been nearly every year to the same rooms at Littlehampton, but with children it's different. You can hardly call it a holiday."

"*You* can't, I should think."

She smiled seriously and passed it by. "He was like a schoolboy let out of school," she said with a sudden jerkiness, "he was so pleased. Poor boy! I knew it must mean a lot to him not to have to worry about money any more for a whole year, and—and to get away."

"Yes," said Rokeby gravely, "yes. And how are *you* going to celebrate *your* holiday, Mrs. Kerr?"

She looked at him quickly. A smile broke round her lips. "Do you know," she dared, as if shocked at herself, "last night I was heartbroken; this morning I was bitter; this afternoon I came up to town to try to shake it off—"

"I hope you've shaken it?"

"I—I hardly know. I shall miss him so when I get back. But—but I've got a whole year. *A year!* But why bother you with these things? A woman would understand; Julia would."

"I suppose you're making a day of it? Going to see Miss Winter this evening perhaps, and tell her all about it?"

She scarcely noticed the eager note in his voice.

"That's an idea!" she exclaimed. "I was wondering what I'd do about this evening, and I was determined not to go home till ten o'clock. I don't know why, but if I can make myself stay right away on my own pleasure till then it will be like breaking a spell. But why I'm talking like this to you I don't know. You'll think me mad."

"No, I shan't."

An office-boy staggered in with tea, and for a while the business of it kept them lightly occupied, and talking inconsequently; but presently Rokeby went back to:

"So you *are* going to see Miss Winter this evening? Look here, Mrs. Kerr, Osborn would never forgive me if I let you go alone. I'll take you—yes, please. Do let me! We'll both give her a surprise."

Recovering a spark of the old audacity which her prettiness used to justify, she laughed: "No, you won't. We shall want to talk—and *talk*. You'd be in the way."

"I solemnly swear I won't. I'll wash up and do a lot of the jobs bachelor girls always keep for their men friends to do. I'll sit and smoke in the kitchen. Honest, I will! There, now?"

Her laughter was real and merry. "*You*? What's come to you?"

"I hardly know," said Rokeby quickly, in a low voice.

Marie's hand and eyes were hovering critically over the dish of cakes; youth and delicious silliness had visited her, if but for an hour, and a curious kind of champagne happiness fizzed through her. The earnestness of Desmond's sudden look passed her by; at the moment there was nothing earnest in her; she was, all so suddenly, a holiday woman out for the day. Selecting her cake, she began to eat it.

"It will be awf'ly good of you to take me there," she answered; "it will be something to write and tell Osborn about."

"Do wives have to hunt for topics for letters, as they have to hunt for suitable conversation, when husbands want it?"

"Oh! have you noticed that?"

"I've noticed my married friends seem to have very little of interest to say to each other."

"Why is it?"

"I don't know. I think they give each other all they've got in a great big lump too soon. But I don't know; how should I?"

"I wonder if I could tell you. *I* think it's because a man carefully robs a woman of all power to have any interest outside her home; but at the same time he votes her home interests too dull to talk about."

"Married life!" said Rokeby quizzically.

"But there are beautiful things in it; children, you know. I shouldn't have said what I did."

They let a silence elapse as if to swallow up the memory of the things Marie shouldn't have said, and after it he asked: "What time shall we go?"

At six o'clock they were speeding down Cannon Street, along the Strand, and the gaudier thoroughfares of the West, in a taxicab, to Julia's flat.

Her delight at seeing Marie was obvious, but a veil of reserve seemed to drop over her vivid, strong face when she saw who escorted her.

Rokeby would not take leave of Marie on the threshold, though; he followed her in and sat down, asking if he might stay. There was about him an air of smiling determination, and his eyes obstinately sought Julia's, which as obstinately avoided his. She began to chatter, as if to slur over a momentary confusion.

"I've only been in ten minutes, and I was going to settle down to a lonely evening. I'm awf'ly glad to have you, Marie darling. If Mr. Rokeby's going to stay he'll have to be useful. I'm afraid you find me almost deshabillee, but I'm one of these sloppy bachelors, as you know."

But Julia had a taut way of putting on even a silk kimono,

and she could not have been sloppy had she tried; her lines were too fine and clean.

The two women went away to Julia's bedroom, a little box like a furnisher's model, and there Julia gleaned Marie's news. But far from giving unmitigated sympathy, she was almost crudely congratulatory.

"It's what most wives of your standing want badly. A year off. A year to go to some theatres, to find their own minds again; to look after their wardrobes, and thread all the ribbons in their cammies that they've been too busy to thread for ages. It's no good coming to me for pity. I'm not sorry for you."

"I—I'm not sure that I want you to be. I see what you mean. But—"

"But?"

"Last night, when I knew, I was just heartbroken. I don't know when I've cried as I did. For a while I thought I'd just have to die."

"You won't die. You'll renovate yourself; you'll get new feathers, like a bird in spring."

Marie looked slowly at Julia.

"I know."

Julia began to smile, first a smile of inquiry, then of delight. "'Rah! 'rah!" she screamed softly; "we'll have Marie pretty again."

Marie took off her hat and coat and began to fluff her

crushed hair.

"See my grey hairs, though, Julia?"

"They're nothing."

"My teeth, of course, haven't been touched since I was married. I don't know if I'll be able to afford that, but I'll try."

"Marie," said Julia, at an inexplicable tangent, "for heaven's sake why bring Desmond Rokeby here?"

"Oh, do you mind, dear? He brought me."

"Mind!" said Julia, now inexplicably tart, "I don't mind! Why should I mind anything about him? Only—"

"Only?"

"Oh, well, it doesn't matter! Let's all be jolly, if he's got to stay."

It was one of those gay, rowdy, delightful, laughing evenings which can happen sometimes. They were all three in the minute kitchen together, Desmond taking off his coat and rolling up his sleeves to cook, and excellently he cooked, too. Julia tied an apron around him, and Marie twisted up a cook's cap from grease-proof paper, and they laughed like people who have discovered the finest jokes in the world. There was no care; there was no worry; no time-table. No Jove-like husband, no fretting, asking wife, no shades of grocers and butchers had a place there. It was a great evening. No one was married. Everyone was young. Oh! it was jolly! jolly! jolly! All one wished—if one stopped to wish at all—was that it might never end.

But the end was at 9.30, punctual to the stroke of Marie's conscience. At No. 30 Welham Mansions, Hampstead, were three little sleepers who depended upon her for all they needed in the world, and over them watched a tired old grannie who would fain go home to bed. Marie left the others suddenly, in case the strength of her resolution should fail her, crying, as she ran out:

"Now don't stop me! I'm going to put on my hat—and GO!"

Julia got up to follow her quickly, but quick as she was, Desmond was quicker. He had his back against the closed door, facing her, and he said:

"Julia! we'll stop ragging. We're alone for just two minutes. Let me ask you—"

"No!" she exclaimed rebelliously.

"Yes, I will! You couldn't get the door open if you tried. Julia, ever since I saw you I believe I've wanted you, and every time I've tried to tell you you've checked me or driven me off somehow. Yet won't you think—"

"I don't want to."

"If you'd marry me—"

"You know you don't believe in marriage any more than I do."

"Not for any fools. But we're different. Besides, you've altered me; converted me. You can do absolutely what you like with me. I'm yours. Let's—let's get married to-morrow and set an example to 'em all of what married people should be."

"Are you mad?"

"Yes, about you," Rokeby replied. He had lost his naive and lacklustre bearing, his eyes were alight and quick, and his fire warmed her as she stood before him, mutinous yet afraid.

"I shall never marry," she said defiantly.

"You will, sooner or later," said Rokeby, "and you will marry me. I'll never leave you till you've done it, and then—then I'll never leave you, either, Julia." He advanced upon her, a sudden whirlwind, before whom she cringed back with a helpless sense she had never known before. He opened his arms, enclosed her in them, and kissed her by force, while she struggled and protested furiously under his lips.

"Do you know," he asked, "I came here to-night just to kiss you. Only that! I didn't hope for any more satisfaction, but some day I shall have it. You're not what you think you are. And I'll make you very happy. As a looker-on I've seen a lot of the game called marriage, and I'd know *how* to make you happy. Don't you believe it?"

Released, she retreated to the other side of the room.

"I don't want to believe it; you'd better go; you've behaved disgracefully, and I don't feel in the least like forgiving you."

"Very well," said Rokeby, as Marie's footsteps sounded on the parquetry of the corridor, "I'm going, but I shall come again, and again! You won't get rid of me, I say, till you've married me. And then you'll never be rid of me."

He swung round, laughing, and opened the door for Marie.

"Now, Mrs. Kerr, I'm to see you well on your way home."

She looked from one to the other, at Julia tall and flaming, and Desmond diffusing a kind of electricity.

"I believe you two have been quarrelling; I ought not to have left you alone."

"We have been quarrelling frightfully. Miss Winter is never going to allow me here again."

"Glad you realise *that*," said Julia frostily.

He went out into the hall goodhumouredly to find his coat and hat, and Marie's umbrella, while the two women kissed good-bye. The fold of kimono that covered Julia's bosom heaved rapidly and her eyes were very bright. She would not offer Rokeby her hand, but went to the front door with her arm round Marie's waist.

They looked back to wave at her before they ran downstairs; she looked very tall and brilliant as she stood in her doorway, her head held high, and her mouth tightly set, and when the door had shut upon her, Marie wondered aloud:

"What can have happened to annoy her so?"

"I've done it," said Rokeby, "but don't worry over it. These things adjust themselves, and nothing matters at the moment, anyway, but seeing you safely home."

"You can't come right out to Hampstead."

"I can; and I should certainly like to, if I may. Osborn would never forgive me for leaving you at this time of night."

She thought how kind he was, and how restful. It was attractive to be looked after again, deferred to and considered. Rokeby drove her the whole way out in a taxicab and found the sincerity of her thanks, as they parted, very touching. As for Marie, not for years had she climbed all those cold stairs so buoyantly; and after her long day, as she put her latchkey in the lock, she suddenly sensed the pleasure of coming home. There was nothing to do, in a rush, when she got in; no preparations to make, or food to cook; no setting forward of work for to-morrow, for the charwoman was coming early.

A man was a man certainly, and a quality to miss, but without him there was a great still peace in the flat.

Grannie Amber, blinking drowsily, came out of the dining-room to meet her daughter.

She noted the bright eyes and cheeks, and her heart beat joyfully.

"Had a nice time, duck?"

"Lovely, mother. I lunched by myself at the Royal Red, and watched the people. Then I had my fingers manicured, and went to tell Mr. Rokeby about Osborn, and had such a nice tea in his office; he's got such a pretty office. Then he took me to Julia's flat, and we three had dinner together. Oh! we were jolly. Mr. Rokeby cooked; how we laughed! Julia made him wear one of her aprons, and I made him the sweetest cook-cap you ever saw. I don't know when I've enjoyed myself so much."

"He's a nice man," said Grannie approvingly; "I wonder if he's thinking of marrying Miss Winter?"

"Mother, your head always runs on somebody marrying somebody else."

"Well, duck, I'm an old woman, and in my long life I've noticed that they always do."

"Julia hates men."

"I don't believe it, my love."

Marie went into her dining-room and looked around it with a new sense of authority; she was now a complete law unto that room and all in it.

"I've got a cup of soup for you here, dear," said Grannie Amber, bustling to the fireplace.

"Mother, you shouldn't trouble yourself! But how nice it is!" She drank gratefully, then put the usual question with the usual anxiety:

"Babes been well? And good?"

"They've been lambs," said Grannie warmly.

"What a pity I folded up Osborn's bed, and put it in the children's room! You could have slept here to-night, mother."

"My duck, I'd rather sleep in my own bed," said the old lady, "and I'll be putting my things on, and going there now. You have the woman coming in the morning?"

"Yes—and every morning."

Mrs. Amber nodded approvingly.

"You'll be very comfortable now, love."

Then she muffled herself in her wraps and went out bravely into the cold towards the old-fashioned flat across the Heath; and Marie, undressing, went to her bed, too. How still it was! The tiny breaths of the baby scarce stirred the immediate air.

Where would Osborn be now?

CHAPTER XVIII

INTRIGUE

Osborn passed that first night at the best hotel in Liverpool. The term "expenses" provided for the best, in reason, of everything; and a good man at his job need not be afraid of making claims. Osborn was going to be a very good man at his job and, somehow, without any undue swelling of the head, he knew it. His chance had come, the big chance which had laid poor Woodall low, and sent him up, up, rejoicing. When they carried his rather goodlooking luggage—which he had bought new for his honeymoon—into a palatial bedroom of the Liverpool hotel, he experienced, only with a thousand degrees more conviction, that sense of freedom from care which his wife was even then timidly grasping, far away in London. He was provided for handsomely and agreeably for three hundred and sixty-five days.

All his liabilities were provided for, too. No unexpected call could come to him, no fingers delve into the purse that he might now keep privately to himself. He was going out into a big world where life had never taken him before, and he was going untrammeled; strong, young.

Osborn dressed for dinner that evening; he wore the links his mother-in-law had given him as a wedding present, and a shirt whose laundering had been paid for out of that omnipresent thirty-two-and-sixpence, and the jacket cut by the tailor whom he had never been able to afford since. He looked a very nice young man, fresh, broad and spruce, but not too spruce; open-browed, clear-eyed and keen. He was now at the zenith of his physical strength, in his thirty-second year, untired and still eager. As he dressed, he looked at himself in the glass as a man regards himself upon his wedding day.

He had remembered to find out about mails from Cook's and, before going in to dinner, sat down in a great lounge and scribbled a note to his wife; just this information, love, and a further injunction to take care of herself; and no more. Like other husbands who had been similarly placed domestically, he had no idea how this process of taking care was to be accomplished by a harassed and busy woman, but it was some satisfaction to express a verdant hope that it should be done.

He went in, duty done, to an aldermanic dinner. He passed a very successful evening. Actually, only on the eve of his mission, he sold a Runaway car to a fat merchant prince who dined opposite to him; or at least he went as near to the actual selling as it was possible to go in the circumstances. He recommended him to their Liverpool agent, wrote a personal letter, gave his card and received one in return, and parted from his probable client with a feeling that the transaction was going through.

He was off at daybreak next morning.

A stupendous piece of luck befell him on board. They were only two days out when he found that a well-known theatrical management was taking a play, with the entire London cast, to New York. It was only on the second day, when, looking across the dining saloon, he saw a raven head on the top of a rather full neck and high shoulders, and met the gay and luring glance which he had met once before, to his secret thrill, across the Royal Red, on the night when he dined there with his wife to celebrate her birthday.

Osborn was a free man; he had broken routine and was out adventuring; and he was goodlooking, he looked worth while. She was a rather stupid actress, with no magnetism but her looks, and no possible chance of ever in this world obtaining a bigger part than the minor one she at present had inveigled from the manager; and she liked well-set-up smart men, men who appeared as if they had money to burn. There were no obstacles placed in Osborn's way.

He was highly elated when the end of a week found him calling her familiarly "Roselle," when he could walk the deck with her after breakfast, and join her party for bridge in the afternoons, and withdraw to a warm corner of the saloon with her after dinner, there to become better acquainted. He was at last, he said to himself, loosening those domestic chains which had hobbled him, and was doing more as other men did.

She gulled him into thinking her clever; all she said and did and looked excited him; she was so different from the women whom men of his class married and with whom only they became intimate; a fellow on two hundred a year with a wife and family could not afford the society of the stage. But a fellow with three hundred a year and any commission his smartness could make, all just for mere pocket-money, was in a different boat altogether. The sums he staked at bridge with Roselle and her party on those winter afternoons in mid-Atlantic used to keep the household at No. 30, Welham Mansions for a week. Sometimes he won and sometimes he lost; but either seemed to him immaterial in this new lightness of his heart.

He was to be in New York two months, and she was to be there three months.

She used to say reckless things to him which stirred the blood. Thus: "You and I, Osborn"—he knew, of course, that familiarity with Christian names was a trait of the stage— "have met, and presently we shall part; and what was the good of meeting if this dear little friendship is just to be packed up with our luggage?"

"You can pack up mine, and I'll pack up yours," he said softly.

"That's a sweet way of putting it; you're one of those light-hearted people who don't mind saying goodbyes."

"I say, Roselle, do you?"

"Saying good-bye to fellow-souls is always sad."

On the windy deck she used to wear a dark purple velvet hat slouched down and pinned close against her darker hair. It showed up the whiteness of her face, which even the saltwinds could not whip into colour, under the coating of white cosmetic almost imperceptibly laid on. Osborn loved that hat, as he loved the graceful tilt of her skirt and the fragility of her blouses; and sometimes it occurred to him to question why men's wives couldn't wear things like that. One sunny afternoon they had, when, instead of playing bridge, they sat in a sheltered corner on deck and talked.

"Where are you putting up in New York?" she asked that afternoon.

"At the Waldorf Astoria."

"Are you really?" she said, and she thought in her shallow mind that he must be very well off indeed.

Osborn did not tell her that his firm sent him to an expensive hotel for their own ends; it was pleasant to have her thinking what she did. He asked if he might call upon her in New York; if she'd have supper with him sometimes; come for a run in his two-seater which he was taking over with him. They made a dozen plans which, after all, could not hurt Marie, and the prospects of which were charming to a degree.

They landed just before Christmas.

Osborn had written his Christmas letters to his wife and children on board, and his first errand on landing was to mail hastily-chosen gifts to them. A box of sweets for the kids, a bottle of scent for Marie, these seemed to suit the occasion quite well. He even remembered a picture-postcard view of the Waldorf Astoria Hotel to bear seasonable wishes to Grannie Amber. Then Roselle claimed him.

Osborn had a good deal of odd time to put at her disposal, and she disposed of it with no uncertain hand. His way was not so uphill as he had expected; within a week he was touching big commission, bigger than he had dreamed of, with the prospects of plenty to follow. And driving his electric-blue, silver-fitted Runaway two-seater about New York, or over to Brooklyn, he placed Roselle in her inevitable fur coat and slouched down purple velvet hat, as a splendid business asset, beside him. At least he told his conscience that a smart woman in a car is unparalleled advertisement for it and perhaps he was right; but that was not the reason for her presence there.

When they said good-bye, under the wintry trees of the remotest part of a great park, it hurt him. He set his hands suddenly on her shoulders, and looked into her eyes; and then, it being almost dusk, and no one very near, he slid an arm round her, and held her to him for one swift instant. When she let him kiss her, with a yielding as passionate as response, he was surprised at his own stupidity in not tasting such sweets before.

"I've got to go," he said. "You've been a darling, to me. I'm crazy about you; I suppose you know that?"

Her slow smile drove deep dimples into her white cheeks; she looked at him warmly; and yet, had he not been too excited to note it, with an acute appraisement. "We're to be here another month," she said, not answering his query, "leave me your address; you have mine."

"Will you write?"

"Reams. And who knows? We may meet again some day."

"That's what I feel; that we haven't met just to part. You're wonderful. You're the most wonderful woman I've ever met."

"And you—you've never told me anything about yourself, Osborn."

"There's nothing to tell."

He had Marie's last letter in his breast-pocket at that moment, and as Roselle stirred against him he heard the slight crackling of the paper. It dropped like a trickle of cold water into his excitement and desire. He took Roselle's arm lightly in his hand, and turned about.

"I must take you to tea somewhere," he said; "where shall we go?"

In a shaded tea room, full of screens, rose-lights and china tinkling, he sat looking at her. She *was* wonderful; with the rather high set of her shoulders, her white, full neck, the depth of her hair and eyes, her short and tenderly kept hands, she was romance. You couldn't imagine such a woman sinking into the household drudge whatever her circumstances; she stood for all that was easy and pleasant, scented and soft, in woman. Osborn felt, as many a man has done and will do again, all memories, all fidelity slipping from him, in the lure of the hour. Leaning forward, he said imperatively:

"I'll have to write every day. You'll answer me, won't you?"

"Of course I will, you exacting boy."

In a very low voice he went on:

"I want to have you all to myself till to-morrow—till I've got to leave you. It would be heaven; but—"

Roselle Dates was of that talented community of stupid women who understand and manipulate life through their super-instinct of sex merely; who know how to take all and give nothing; suckers of life and never feeders. She looked at him and sighed and smiled, and shook her head, and touching his hand, whispered:

"But that's impossible. It isn't often a woman makes a friend like you. Let it last a little longer, there's a dear boy."

"I'm sorry," said Osborn. "I suppose we're all beasts."

She sighed again. "Every inch of life is snared, for women. In a profession like mine you watch each step. My goodness, you do! Or you'd fall into one of the traps."

"Isn't it ever worth while falling in?"

She refused to answer. Becoming suddenly capricious with the caprice that is the armour of her kind, she wished to be taken home. After he had left her, he walked the streets moodily for an hour before going in himself.

He had to pack for an early start next morning. In a bedroom where a prince might have slept, he threw himself into an easychair and brooded. Roselle became more than ever desirable, as he imagined her, sitting in that shaded tea room, her fur coat opened and thrown back to show the fragile corsage underneath. She was romance; the fairy tale, which he had read and mislaid, found again. Putting his hand up, he pulled out his wife's letter, and read it again cursorily before casting it into the wastepaper basket.

How dull it was! What a lack of sparkle and spontaneity it showed! Something seemed to happen to women after marriage, making them prosaic; growing little nagging consciences in them; egging them on to a perpetual striving with things that were damned tiresome. And the letter that he would write back would be just as constrained; there would be no joy in the writing of it as there would be writing the letters that would be sent to Roselle.

*　　*　　*　　*　　*

"MY DEAR OSBORN" (Marie wrote), "Thank you for your letter. You are very good to write so regularly every mail. We are so glad to know what a successful trip you are having. We are all very well; and mother gave the children a tree for Christmas, and we hung your box of sweets and my scent on it. They couldn't think how you had managed to put them there! Thank you so much for the scent. I am having the dining-room carpet cleaned. The children send their love and so do I.—Your affectionate wife,

"MARIE."

"P.S.—Baby has cut another tooth."

"My God!" said Osborn resignedly, as he tore the letter across. "Marriage is a big mistake. To tie oneself up for life at twenty-seven...!"

*   *   *   *   *

Osborn was in Chicago, prospering exceedingly, when Roselle's second letter came.

She was in the same city!

He hurried to her without a moment's loss. She was staying at a boarding-house full of noisy young business people, among whom she was a sensation. She received Osborn in a great smudged parlour decorated with much gilt and lace curtains.

"Aren't you surprised?"

"I was never so glad."

"I expect you were. I expect you've been as glad ever so many times." She looked at him shrewdly. "I didn't tell you in New York," she said, letting her hand remain in his. They were alone in the horrible room. "But my contract was for the passage out and three months playing with Sautree; not for the passage home. You see, I wanted to get out here somehow and see what I could do. It does one good to have been in the States."

"And now—"

"I'm at a loose end."

She saw the quick flush on his face and the light in his eyes, and playfully put against his lips two fingers, which he kissed.

"Only temporarily of course. I'm going round the hotels to-day—I shall get plenty of entertaining to do. When I'm tired of this, I shall move on."

"Why not let our moving on coincide?"

It was what, vaguely, in her mind, Roselle meant to do. She wanted experience; but to gain it comfortably would need a certain amount of financing; and she thought she had tested the fairly satisfactory depth of his pockets, although he had told her nothing.

"I don't know," she reserved. "What are your movements and dates?"

He told her eagerly.

"I've always longed to tour Canada," she cried.

"Then tour it on your own. Only can't we be travelling companions? I'll see to your tickets and luggage and so on."

"And I shan't have any hotel expenses," she added, lighting a cigarette; "I shall work them off and see a profit."

Osborn's year now took on for him the aspect of the most magnificent adventure sated married man ever had.

"Fancy us two trotting about the good old earth together!"

"Don't tell your friends," she laughed.

"Trust me."

"But I don't. I don't trust any of you."

"You are a tease. Roselle, it's so tophole to see you again; let me kiss you good morning."

She took the cigarette from her mouth to return his kiss; she was bright-eyed and hilarious. She knew that he was a fool as men were, unless they were brutes; and you had to make the fools whipping-boys for the brutes. As he kissed her, she knew that she was going to use him; to take all and give nothing.

"You're the dearest boy. And how's the car?"

"She's first-rate. Want her this morning?"

"You might run me around in her; job-hunting."

Into the spring sun they drove; she had the inevitable fur coat and the hat he loved, and she looked beautiful. By the time he ranked the car outside one of Chicago's best restaurants for lunch, she had what she called a pocketful of contracts, to sing at this restaurant and that; to dance for her supper and half a guinea at a ruinous night club, for she could do everything a little. But her greatest asset was her beauty.

CHAPTER XIX

ANOTHER WOOING

Osborn's letters told Marie very little of his doings; they almost conveyed the impression, though he would have been uneasy to know it, of careful epistles penned by a bad schoolboy. His letters from Chicago might have been replicas of those from New York; from Montreal he began on the same old note, though, in answer to her request to teach a stay-at-home woman descriptive geography, he once launched forth into an elaborate account of his rail journey on the Canadian Pacific, from Montreal westwards. Marie was not disappointed in the letters; they were what she would have expected. But sometimes, as she read their terse and uninteresting sentences, their stodgy bits of information, she smiled to think how marriage changed a man.

How dull it made him!

How irritating and constrained it made him! How prosaic! How it walled-up passion, as one read how a nun who had loved too much was walled-up, in the old fierce days, with bricks and mortar!

"MY DEAR MARIE," (or sometimes "Dear Wifie"),—

"How are you all getting along? I'm in—now, as you will see by my changed address. Business has been fairly good.... It was rather a pretty journey here; I must send George a book about the wild flowers on the prairies.... I am glad to hear you are all so comfortable. Are you going earlier to Littlehampton this year, or shall you wait till the summer as usual? Of course, when I went with you, we had to go in the summer because my turn for holidays came then; but I should think the rooms would be cheaper earlier in the year. I am rather glad you are having the carpet cleaned....

"With love to you and the children,

"YOUR AFFECTIONATE HUSBAND."

In the spring a sorrow came with a shock into Marie's even life. Grannie Amber died suddenly. In the evening she had played with the children at No. 30, and in the morning she was found in the little old-fashioned flat on the other side of the Heath, sitting in her easychair by a dead fire, with her bonnet and cloak on, just as she had sat down to rest for awhile on her return.

She left her daughter a good deal of old furniture which sold for a fair sum to dealers; and an income of two hundred and twenty pounds a year.

For a while sorrow kept Marie much to the rut in which she had moved since Osborn's departure; but the grief for a parent is so natural and inevitable a grief; it is not as the grief for a husband or a child; and when the first warm days of April came Marie took some very definite steps forward on that road where she had, last December, set her feet. It was Julia who roused her finally to the course.

Julia came and said: "Do you know, my dear, you're years younger? You're your pretty self again. And what are you going to do now that you are such a rich young woman?"

It was a week later that the capable maid was installed in the flat. She slept in a tiny room which had hitherto been relegated to boxes, but which now was furnished with one or two left-over pieces from Mrs. Amber's sale, and the hall-porter, who realised that Mrs. Osborn Kerr had inherited money, was pleased to care for the boxes. The servant brought rest and charm into that flat; and George went half-daily to a near-by school, taking himself to and fro with the utmost manfulness.

Marie paid at last those longed-for visits to the dentist.

* * * * *

Marie was having the first dinner-party for which she had not to cook herself, and the party consisted of Julia and Desmond Rokeby.

Rokeby had leapt at the invitation flatteringly; but Julia had been inscrutable in her demur, until begged in such terms as were hard to refuse.

"You're the only two people I really know intimately," Marie said; "if you refuse, you'll spoil it all. In fact I don't believe I can have a man to dinner alone without exciting Mr. and Mrs. Hall Porter."

When she uttered this little vain thing, she laughed and looked in the glass and patted her hair.

"I'll come," Julia promised.

As Marie Kerr came out of her bedroom and proceeded down the corridor to inspect the table arrangements, she was a pretty picture of all that a well-dressed, happy, healthy young woman should be. She paused by the door of the erstwhile dressing-room to look in on the two elder children, then entered the dining-room. Spotless napery and most of the wedding-present silver equipped the table, as it used to do in the early days of her marriage. Between the candle-sticks were clusters of violets. A bright wood fire burned upon the hearth, but the golden-brown curtains were not yet drawn upon the evening. The golden-brown carpet, newly cleaned, was speckless again. Marie moved about, improving on the table arrangements, and the hands which touched this or that into better design were little, slim and white. The finger nails had regained their tapering prettiness. And as she smiled with pleasure, between her lips an unblemished row of teeth showed. She wore black, to her mother's memory, but her gown was the last word in cut and contour; it opened in a long V to show her plump white neck; underneath the filmy bodice a hint of mauve ribbons gleamed. In her ears slender earrings twinkled. They were amethyst, and had been her mother's. She had put them on for the first time that evening as she dressed, because, regarding herself earnestly in the glass, there had risen up over her shoulder, for no reason whatever, the sleek pale face of the manicure girl, who wore emeralds in her ears. And when she had clipped them on she was thrilled; they gave her a distinctive, a resolute charm. She could smile at herself again in that glass, at the colour and light and verve which had come back to her. The face pictured there had all the roundness, the softness and pinkiness of the face of the bride Marie, who had waked and looked therein on wonderful mornings, but it held more than the face of Marie the bride. It was strong; it had firmness and judgment and humour. It was no fool of a face. Yet, as the wisest and strongest of women can delight in vanities, so Marie delighted in the earrings which she wore to-night, as an inspiration, for the first time.

From her dining-room Marie went to the sitting-room, rosy in the light of another wood fire. Every day now she used her sitting-room. Tea was brought to her there, placed at her elbow as she sat in a cosy chair before the fire, and she drank it at leisure—while the maid gave the children their meal in the dining-room. In that chair by the fire, all the spring, Marie had read the new books, for she could afford to pay a library subscription. In that chair, as she rested, the lines had smoothed from her face, her neck had grown plump again, and the stories of modern thought, of modern love and its ways, had stimulated her brain once more to thoughts of its own. She loved the sitting-room better than she had loved it even when it was first furnished; it was now peculiarly her own. When she thought of Osborn's return, as she did now and then with a curious mixture of feelings, she knew, half-guiltily, that somehow she would grudge him a share in those pleasant evenings by the fire.

Marie sat down to wait for Julia and Desmond, and, taking up her half-finished novel, put her silk-stockinged feet on the fender, leaned back, and opened the book at the place where she had left the story. It was a love story, and as she read she thought: "How well I know this phase! and that phase!... but we will just see what happens after they're married." Her thought was not bitter, only interested and curious, because her own hurt was over, and a wisdom, a contentment, had come.

Julia and Desmond arrived together, much against Julia's will; and they all sat down in the pretty pale room, while the maid drew the curtains upon the gathering dusk and switched on the light.

They sat and talked of trivial things, waiting for the serving of dinner to be announced; and Marie remembered how often, in the past years, she had longed to sit there comfortably, thus till a well-trained servant should open the door noiselessly and say: "Dinner is served, ma'am."

Now it happened every night.

They went in to a well-ordered dinner; there was a pleasant peace and harmony in the flat; and as Rokeby looked at Marie's face, which had won back all its old prettiness, as well as attaining the strength of the woman who has suffered, he did not marvel, but he was a little sad. And he wondered slightly just what was going to happen to Osborn when he came home. But Julia, as she looked at Marie, was triumphant; she did not wonder what was going to happen to Osborn; she thought she knew. And all dinner she tried to hurl tiny defiances into Rokeby's teeth, asking with sparkling malice:

"Isn't Marie looking her own self again? Isn't it lovely to see her? Doesn't grass-widowhood suit her? Isn't it a screaming success?"

Rokeby knew what Julia meant, but his patience was invincible.

There was a piano in the flat now; it had been Grannie Amber's, and was old, but still it fulfilled its purpose of a musical instrument. It stood in the sitting-room, across one of the corners by the fire, and after dinner Marie played and Julia sang; and when she refused to sing more, it was Desmond's turn. He looked through Marie's pile of music, selected a song, and sat down to play his own accompaniment with a light and beautiful touch which came as a surprise to the listening women, who knew nothing of his drawing-room talents. He went from song to song, and all at once Marie, transferring her gaze from contemplative dreams, saw Julia's face. Julia leaned forward with her elbows on her knees, her chin in her palms, looking at the man at the piano, and in her eyes ran the old tale, and her red lips smiled and her breast heaved. But she became conscious of Marie's look, and sitting up sharply, drew, as it were, a blind down over the light.

"Julia?" Marie said to herself, all wonder, *"Julia!"*

She looked at Rokeby's creaseless back, at his fingers wandering over the keys, and for the first time she noticed how sensitive, how caressing the fingers were. Yet that two people in her intimate circle could contemplate that through which she herself had passed painfully, as through ordeal by fire....

It made her very kind to them both, though a small stir of queer jealousy was in her. Before hell they would know heaven. Love and marriage began with the celestial tour....

When they came out into the hall presently, to put on their outdoor wraps, she beckoned them to the door of the children's room. The baby had joined the two elder ones, and three small cots now stood in a row, closely packed. A night-light gave enough glimmer to see the warm faces lying peacefully on the three pillows. The women crept in and looked down upon a scene which will always make women's hearts sing, or ache; and Rokeby followed. To his lover's mind, never had Julia Winter appeared so adorable as when she bent low over the fat baby, and murmured to it the small feckless loving things that all women always have murmured to all the babies in the world. She touched its outflung hand delicately with a finger, and lingered there, filled with woman's world-old want. And out of the twilight Marie sent a whisper which reached them both.

"Of course, you're never going to marry, either of you. But if you ever want to, and you're hanging back, wondering, just don't wonder. Remember that the children are worth— everything."

"Thank you," Rokeby whispered fervently in her ear.

Julia said nothing, but straightened herself and passed out.

Rokeby was after her in a second to hold her coat. The way in which she turned her back on him so that he might lift it on was peculiarly ungracious.

Marie was in the background, wanting a lover again. When they had gone she drew back the curtains, threw up the windows, and leaned out into the sweet, chill spring night. She drank it and loved it, and all her being cried out for love.

But she did not want love grown old, which came in and put on its slippers, and grumped: "Can't those kids keep quiet?" if it heard the voice of the children of love, and which hid itself behind a hedge of daily paper, or flung out again from home, in the ill-tempered senility of its second childhood.

She wanted love new-grown; with a bloom upon it, fresh and young; love at its beginning, before it was ripe and over-ripe, and spoiling and falling from its tree; such a love as she imagined Julia and Desmond even then to be driving towards.

In a taxicab—for where else in all London could he be alone with her?—Rokeby was taking Julia home. She allowed it in spite of herself; yet was angry with them both for the circumstance which brought them together close, which enclosed them in a privacy which made her remember, with a vividness which disturbed her, the sensations of that first and only kiss. He was asking her again:

"Haven't you changed your mind, Julia? Can't you relent?"

"You know what I think about marrying."

"I thought I did. But to-night when I looked at you looking at those kids, I knew differently. You want to be married and have children of your own. I don't know as much about me— don't know," he said in a slight break of despair, "that I come into the picture much."

It was dark enough to hide her flush.

"When I ask 'Can't you relent'?" said Rokeby, "I ought to say instead 'Can't you confess?' That's what you don't want to do."

"If—" she began.

"Yes, dear. If?"

"If I married you—"

She paused a long while and he declared passionately: "You're afraid to risk marriage and yet you want to. You don't know what to do. You like being loved; you pretend you don't, but you do. You're feeling how sweet it all is. But you will not own it even to yourself."

And she answered: "I am afraid."

"I know you are," said Rokeby; "and so am I. Haven't you thought of that?"

"What do you mean?"

"Why, look around and see the muddle and mess most people make of the contract."

"That's what I mean."

"So do I. Why shouldn't I be afraid as much as you are? If we got married and muddled and messed things up, wouldn't it hurt me as much as you?"

"Not according to what I've seen. Most men—"

"I'm not most men. I'm just me. You're you. We're different. Besides, we've seen and thought and argued it out to ourselves as well as together. Couldn't you risk it?"

"You know what I want; complete freedom."

"Well, you should have it. And you know what I want?"

"Yes?"

"Complete freedom, too."

"Oh?" she said uncertainly, with a jealous note in her voice.

He laughed. "Couldn't I have it, then? Well, to tell you a secret, you couldn't either. But another secret is that, probably, neither of us would really want it."

"That's true. It's dreadful the way married people learn to cling to each other."

"Well, what else would you cling to?"

"I don't know."

"Well; won't you risk it?"

"I think, perhaps, I dare if you dare."

The biggest moment of Rokeby's life was when he took her, for the second time, into his arms, and felt her lips respond to his. She shut her eyes and saw again the vision of the three cots side by side in a dim room; and his eyes, on her face, saw the mother-ecstasy there. "You wonder!" he exclaimed.

"Why?"

"To give me such a fright when all the while you've been feeling this!"

It was a long drive from Hampstead, and all the time she was within his arms, and all the time he told her of all they would be to each other; of how he loved her. And at last she stood alone in her flat, with her bedroom lights switched on, looking at a radiant creature in the glass, and crying within herself:

"Is this really Julia Winter?"

Already the homelike quality of her home had vanished; the dear possession of her things had become less dear. She could think of another home, a bigger one, and a hearthplace with her husband's face opposite her own. She sat down by the dressing-table, and laid her hands idly in her lap, and thought all the rosy things that women in love do think.

She lunched the next day with Desmond as a matter of course. He called for her at her office, and drove her away possessively. There was no more solitude for her, no more proud loneliness, no more boastful independence. Already she clung and already she enjoyed it. When, over the table, he asked: "Isn't it nice being engaged?" she nodded, smiling, and answered: "I'm wondering why I haven't done it before."

CHAPTER XX

SEPARATION

In November Marie had the letter which announced Osborn's imminent return.

"... In another week," he wrote, "I shall be with you all again. It will be good to see you. Of course, this has been rather a rag, and I think I shall hold down the job for ever and evermore; but a year is a long time, isn't it? I look forward to coming home. I shall have a lot to tell you, but I expect I shall want to hear your news first, and how George has got on at school, and so on."

The letter had an unwonted postscript: "I wonder if you've missed me, old girl."

It was waiting for Marie on a grey afternoon when she returned from a lecture, for which, a year ago, she would have needed a dictionary, but which now entered her brain glibly and was at home there. All that afternoon she had been listening to an exotic discourse on "Woman and her Current Philosophy"; and now—here was Osborn's letter, suggesting calmly, proprietorially almost, his re-entry into her life. Was it possible that he had been away for a whole year? Or possible that he had been away for only a year? Rapid as the stride of Time had been, he was already a stranger, someone dimly perceived, arriving from another life, and hardly making his presence felt.

She stood reading the letter attentively, noting its points and phrases with even detachment; its arrival arrested her thoughts, although she had known it must come soon. Its sender was already on his way to her, expecting the eager welcome of home; and home had nothing but stereotyped compliments to offer. Who was he, anyway?

Just the man who had made the domestic laws in No. 30, had made them disagreeably and could make them no longer, whose power was broken. The keeper of the purse; the winder of the clocks of life; the hostile element in a peaceful day; the shade of a dead lover long since trampled under the domestic battle-ground.

It was almost curious that he had ever existed.

She came for the second time to the postscript and smiled vaguely and faintly. He wondered if she had missed him.

Yes. She had certainly missed him.

As Marie Kerr stood by the fire in her sitting-room with Osborn's letter in her hand, she awoke fully, as from a dream, to the understanding of what was about to befall her.

She was once more, after this year of miraculous growth and power and recovery, to take unto herself her husband.

The door opened and the maid came in quietly, a teacloth over her arm, the tray in her hand. She arranged all to please the taste of the mistress who stood watching as if she watched something unusual.

For a whole year, in that flat, she had been the person whose will was government, who had to be pleased and obeyed. She had made the laws, kept the purse, and set the clock.

It had been a wonderful year.

She laid aside her furs, sat down and poured out her tea. Presently she heard George come in—he now went to school for the whole, instead of the half day—and the happy clatter of the children in the dining-room. There was no one to cry testily: "For God's sake keep those children quiet!" as if the children were aliens—crimes of the mother.

When she had finished her tea, and had heard the maid come out of the dining-room, she went in, to romp with her children. It was an hour she loved and for which she now had zest; she could enjoy it to the full. They played Blind Man's Buff, in which even the baby joined staggeringly, and Hunt the Slipper—the baby's little one, which she wanted to keep whenever it was smuggled under the edge of her little flannel petticoat; and for the last ten minutes Marie went back to the sitting-room to tinkle on the piano, while the maid was requisitioned once more to make a fourth to play Musical Chairs. Then the children came into the sitting-room, hand in hand, and stood by the piano and sang the lullaby their mother had taught them. She joined her voice to theirs with all its old strength and sweetness. And she heard their prayers and tucked them up in their beds.

Then she went into the room which for a year had been hers and, while she changed into her soft black frock, the realisation came that she was again to share it. Her lips curled.

"I won't!" she said to herself.

Why couldn't they go on for ever in this flat as they were now, sufficient unto themselves, she and the children?

She returned to her book by the fire. And while she read on deeper into the love-story, absorbed and credulous in spite of herself, the front door bell rang.

Julia and Desmond Rokeby came in with a great air of mystery and jubilation. They walked with the rich expectancy of people treading golden streets, and though they came up to Marie, captured and embraced her, laughed, and began relevant explanations both together, their eyes looked through her, away and beyond her, and she had a sense of being right outside their scheme for ever and evermore.

Loneliness assailed her rather bleakly as she stood with a smiling mouth, gazing from one to the other and trying to gather the gist of their news.

"We know you'll be awfully surprised," Julia cried, treating her to squeezes of nervous rapture, "but—"

"Now, darling," said Rokeby, "let me. You see, Marie, we've gone and done for ourselves. May we sit down with you just a moment while I tell you? I knew that Julia—"

"He was so stupid about it," said Julia, glowing.

"Don't cut in and spoil the story, dearest," he urged. "I knew she'd never make up her mind really to get married, you know, Marie, so this afternoon I met her coming out of the office, drove her to a church where all arrangements had been made, took one of those handy permits out of my pocket—a special licence, you know—and—"

"You're married," said Marie Kerr in rather a dull way which disappointed them both.

"We are."

"After all, Marie," said Julia breathlessly, "don't you think it's the nicest way; without any fuss and premeditation, and bridesmaids, and cake and things? Just our two selves."

"It was splendid," said Rokeby. "I'm the first man I know who ever really enjoyed his wedding."

Marie sat between them and held a hand of each; after a while she answered:

"I do congratulate you both; it's all so exciting and romantic. Oh! I do hope you'll always be very happy."

"Thank you, dear," Julia beamed.

"We know we shall always be very happy," said Rokeby.

"And now?" Marie asked with an effort.

"We're going honeymooning," said the bridegroom.

Again she sat silent, keeping the smile upon her lips.

"Where are you going?" she asked by and by. "We went to Bournemouth. We had such a delightful time..."

"Our plans are uncertain," said Rokeby.

"That means you are going to hide."

"For a while we are; no letters; no telegrams; no intrusions of any kind. Just us. See how marriage takes a hardened bachelor!"

"And a hardened spinster!" Julia chimed.

"I do hope," Marie repeated, "that you'll be very happy. When will you come back?"

"Early next month," said Julia.

"Perhaps," Rokeby qualified.

"And the first thing we do," said Julia affectionately, "will be to come and see how our Marie is, left all alone without us."

"Don't!" Marie begged. "You're making me gulpy. For two pins I'd cry. You two—you've just been everything to me this year, after the children. You don't know how lonely you're making me feel."

"But soon Osborn—"

"Osborn's coming home next week."

"Oh, great!" Rokeby cried; and Mrs. Rokeby added: "I *am* glad. Now you won't be lonely any more."

"I don't know," Marie said quietly.

She took Julia's bare left hand from her muff and looked at the rings and stroked it.

"I love a new wedding ring," she said.

"Our train, darling," Rokeby reminded his wife.

"We must fly," said Julia, rising. "Our taxi's outside, with all the clothes I've had time to pack, upon it. Desmond had packed in anticipation, the wretch! And we've only got an hour—but we just had to come in and tell you before we went."

"I hope you and Osborn will have another honeymoon like ours is going to be," Rokeby cried as they hurried through the hall.

She shook her head, vaguely smiling, but her lips would frame nothing. She was glad to shut the door upon their happiness. It seemed as if everything young and fierce in her were pulling at her heart. How she wanted it again, that amazing rapture and discovery! As she sat down again by her fire in the quiet flat, she would have bartered half the remaining years of her life for just that first year over again.

She went across to the window, pulled aside a curtain, and beheld rows and darts of lights like stars; street lights and house lights beckoned to her; she opened the window slightly and the distant sound of traffic, the drums of London rolling, excited and affrayed her.

She felt too young for the sedateness into which her life was settling.

Restless as she was, she had trained herself too well in the ruthless habits of method and industry not to begin automatically to set all in order against the coming of the master of the home. Feeling the need of doing rather than of thinking, she went to the bureau, and picked her account-books from their pigeonholes. Accurate and businesslike, they should be presented. They were ruled with neat margins, the columns headed precisely; each quarter of the year showing a favourable balance in hand. There was no doubt but that she was a creditable housekeeper. She opened them one by one memorising with a certain pleasure their tributes to her capacity. One big item had been wiped off altogether last spring, after her mother's death: the rest of the furniture instalments, which, on the extended system for which Osborn had been obliged to arrange after George's birth, would have dragged on for two years more. Grannie Amber's sale had more than paid for all.

"He can't say I haven't been careful," she thought. Besides, she was now a woman with an income of her own; with two hundred and twenty pounds a year in her pocket, the right to which no man could question. If he demurred at the maid, and at George's school bills, she could point to her ability to pay.

She knew how greatly she had changed during their separation; to the change that might have been wrought in Osborn she gave little, thought, not caring much. She supposed that he would come home much as he left it, refreshed doubtless, better-tempered, and full of his holiday, to the stories of which she would give a dutifully interested hearing. But that he could ever rouse again in her the passion and pain which had prostrated her on the night when she knew he was to leave her was ironically impossible. As she sat over her account-books, her memory cast back to that evening, how she had stood, in silent agony, beside the table, sorting over his stock of clothes; how feverishly and blindly she had sewed, trying to hide from him all that to-morrow meant to her; how, when he had gone to bed, she had kneeled by his chair and sobbed, and prayed that no other woman should ever wean him from her....

What an extraordinary exhibition! What weakness of temper and nerve!

She knew it was more. It had been the terribleness of love.

"And now?" she mused.

It made her smile a little, lazily and serenely.

But now and again she sighed with a sharp envy, thinking of Julia and Desmond.

She waked often in the solitude of the night, imaging the bride and bridegroom on the track of rapture, following the unwaning star.

In the morning there was a cablegram for her, reading: "Home on Thursday.—OSBORN."

To-day was Monday. She stood with tight lips for a moment wondering just how to set this scene of reunion; the flat was not large, comprising as it did the tiny slip of a room in which the maid slept, the children's room, her own, and the two sitting-rooms and kitchen. All the day she arranged and rearranged the accommodation in her head.

She was not only reluctant for Osborn, but almost shy of him; he had left her thoughts so that it seemed impossible that he had ever had the right to intrude, at all hours, on her privacy; impossible that it should ever be so again. After all, there were many husbands and wives who went their own way, led their own lives, and the outside world never knew. To such a confraternity would she and Osborn now belong, living under one roof, but separated, separated not only by walls, but will.

For she did not want him any more; she could not contemplate his assumption of the husbandly role. It sounded strange as she uttered it aloud to herself, but there it was.

May Edginton

"I do not want him any more."

She thought: "Had he never gone away, had we gone on living as we lived then, year in, year out, this would never have happened. People don't get out of a deep rut like that unless they're helped out. But now I've had a year to get my looks back; to sit down and think, and I know things that I should never have guessed before."

After she had taken the baby for her morning airing on the Heath, she left the two younger children with the maid, and went into town to lunch. She chose again the Royal Red, but not the table behind the pillar from which she had peered, glad of its shelter for her shabbiness, a year ago. She took a table at the side of the room where she could see and be seen, and she looked at the other women without envy or hatred, with no more than a level sense of rivalry which was almost pleasant. If she had not known how well she looked, the glances of men would have told her. She lingered long over her coffee, enjoying her opportunity and her freedom, and telling herself—resolved as she was that it should not be so—"Well, it's probably my last time like this."

She was in Regent Street after lunch, looking into a blouse shop, when she saw close at hand the Beauty Parlour sign which brought to her memory at once the sleek pale girl with the emerald earrings. Something made her curious to see the girl again, and she went in, to find her still there, the emeralds still in her beautiful close ears, but sharper set, a year wearier.

She uttered charming things of madame's white hands. And, surely, she had never had the pleasure of seeing madame there before?

Madame replied: "No; you have never seen me here before."

She reflected: "It's very true, that. No one had ever seen me, this me, a year ago."

Just as she had felt no hate for the women in the Royal Red, so her sense of hostility to the girl bending over her hand had vanished. She was a friendly rival, not to be feared. And she was not so peerless, after all; there were flaws under the powder with which she coated her pale skin.

"I have never seen prettier nails, madame," said the manicurist, as she smeared on cream.

After she left the Beauty Parlour Marie had nowhere to go. There was no Rokeby to give her tea in his comfortable office while he offered her business advice; he had been very good with his advice over the question of Marie's inheritance. Neither was there a Julia to ring up and invite to tea at one of the numberless cosy teashops of the West End. Marie turned in, at three o'clock, to a matinee and bought an upper circle seat, a few minutes late for the rise of the curtain on the first act of an ultra-modern play.

The play was all about marriage. It dissected marriage into a thousand pieces, and held every piece which was not turned into tragedy up to ridicule. It fostered all the nonsense which fretted in idle women's hearts, and touched many sore spots in others; and made men smile cynically as if saying, "That's got it to the life." This play kept Marie Kerr enchained; it set her wondering why the Marriage Service had ever been written and consecrated; it blew to and fro the winds of the storm in her soul until a tempest rocked her mind; she drew a black comparison between the tragedy of the hero and heroine, and the situation between Osborn and herself. But at last, when the playwright had ridiculed and denounced what he called the oldest and tiredest convention in the world for long enough, the play seemed to turn on a pivot, and the pivot was the cradle. The playwright gave the playgoers the happy ending for which the world craves and sent them home relieved.

He sent Marie Kerr home relieved, too; but the day had not changed her mind. She was fixed and, she felt, irrevocably. Over her solitary dinner she thought of the play; and she thought of the fight to be fought in her own home, and she slept upon it, to awake unmoved in the morning.

She did not want Osborn.

CHAPTER XXI

HOME-COMING

Osborn Kerr was coming home with the happy sense of expectancy which is common to the wanderer. He had prepared for departure with a high heart and a holiday feeling running through everything, like champagne, but he packed for his return with a very warm pleasure in looking forward to the welcome waiting for him, right across all that space, in the flat an which he had established home.

Looking back as well as forward, only the pleasant and sweet things of his marriage remained impressed on his mind. The cosiness of the home and not the worry of paying for it instalment by instalment; the good dinners Marie cooked, not the grudge of giving out that housekeeping allowance which paid for them; the prettiness and sunniness of his wife rather than the faded looks and uncertain temper of the last few years; the three fine kids he'd got, not the nuisance and noise and expense which he had so often declared them.

The rosy cloud of time and distance had rolled between Osborn and all that was his at No. 30 Welham Mansions. Before his year of adventure was up he found himself thinking of them sentimentally; he found that they were embedded pretty deep in his heart. They were real; other

May Edginton

things were—

Looking about for a definition, he stigmatised other things: "They're trash."

He added therefore a postscript to his letter to his wife, an addition written in a sudden thrust of pathos, a want of her almost like the old want:

"I wonder if you've missed me, old girl."

In the trash he felt, though he had not given the idea the form of a thought, that Roselle Dates was included. She had never bored, being too clever in her stupid, instinctive way for that; but sometimes she had sickened him. She had wanted so much. She seemed always wanting something. At first her pallid and raven beauty and her clever silliness had been sheer stimulation, but when you grew used to her....

She had nothing behind. And she was mean with the sex meanness, the cold prudence of the sex-trafficker. She would never have given; she would only have sold, and that at a price far beyond Osborn Kerr's pocket-book even at its recent splendour. But she did not want to sell either; she wanted to take and take, to squeeze and squeeze. Once—that was in San Francisco, where she had beaten together a concert party and shone as its brightest star—when he had been disappointed of a big deal and had come to her with the story....

She had refused to listen.

She had said: "Look here, boy! What do you mean by asking me out to lunch and moping? I don't want to hear your troubles. There are plenty of people here who'll amuse me without pulling long faces over dropping a little cash."

She looked at him very coldly. In that moment he had suddenly thought of another woman, a young bride, who, with tears of consternation and sympathy in her eyes, had brought out an account-book and pencil and said: "I'll get the gas out of the thirty shillings, too."

That was the kind of reception a man expected for his troubles. But after Roselle had let him pay for their expensive lunch, she had needed other things—perfume and candy. And she "borrowed" the rent of her rooms from him for several weeks.

She went back to London two months ahead of him, having written for and secured a moderately good engagement.

During the two months he missed her a little in the Runaway, where her presence had secured for him an extra mark of distinction; but he had rather the feeling of a man surfeited. He put it to himself in modern slang: "I was fed up," he said. "She only wanted me to get the tickets and look after her luggage, and turn up when I was wanted, and be a kind of unpaid courier, while she travelled about getting experiences and hunting for bigger fools than me. I'm about fed up."

Osborn was to stop in Paris for a week on his way back; it was a week to which he had looked forward throughout the year. Paris and expenses practically unlimited! How gay it sounded! What visions it conjured up! But the week was a failure as far as pleasure went, though business was brisk. For Osborn over all the pleasures of Paris there was a frost. It was restless and light and bright, and all this living in hotels and cafes wasn't worth while. He wanted at last, very badly, to be at home again.

He half thought of wiring to Marie to join him. How surprised and delighted and excited she'd be! But how would she arrange about the kids? She couldn't come, of course.

Besides, there was an inimitable pleasure in picturing oneself entering the flat and finding her there just the same as ever.

Home was essentially the place to look for one's wife.

Osborn did not know Paris with any intimacy. A week-end had been his limit hitherto. So he went to the Bon Marche to look for a gift for Marie, not knowing where else to look, and he bought her any trifle that he could imagine—Roselle's teaching was useful here,—little chiffon collars, and a glittering hair-band ornament that he thought looked very French, and handkerchiefs, and a pair of silk stockings, and garters with great big fluffy pompoms on them. She had had to be rather a mouse during her married life, after the trousseau was worn out and since her children came, anyway. How pleased she would be to have these pretty things!

The evening he arrived, after dinner, they would sit down by the fire and he would tell her all his business news—how well he'd done; all about his hopes and prospects, and he would give her some of his firm's letters to him to read. He would be sure of her sympathy and appreciation.

He had made more than a thousand pounds in commissions that year, and it was waiting for him, in a lump. He drew a long breath at the thought of it.

A thousand pounds! And there would be more to follow, for poor Woodall had died, and he was holding down the job.

He crossed to Dover on a still, cold day; it was an excellent crossing for the time of year. He stood on deck, smoking, watching the white cliffs approach, looking back over the last year and forward to those that lay before him. The last year—how mad and jolly it had been for the greater part! It had been a great piece of folly and a great piece of fun, travelling about with a lovely woman like Roselle Dates; it was a situation which half the men he knew would have envied him. Coming as it did after a humdrum period of domesticity, where a man could not afford either folly or fun, the danger signals had been flying all the time.

He could recall fifty occasions on which he could, or would, gladly have lost his head; but now, retrospecting, he was inclined to give himself the credit rather than Roselle, that their relations had been so innocuous. And at the moment, although every second the boat brought him nearer to her, he felt strangely indifferent as to whether they met again or not. He supposed that he might, perhaps, go to see her in this new play, and perhaps take her out to supper.

At four o'clock in the afternoon he was home.

He ran up the grey stone stairs like a boy and attained that dear old door, the portal of home. Having mislaid his latchkey, he had listened eagerly, anticipating the sound of Marie's feet flying down the hall. Feet came with a sort of drilled haste, but no eagerness.

A smart maid-servant of superior type opened his door to him.

He stepped past her, staring somewhat, and the hall porter followed into the hall with the luggage. The sitting-room door opened and Marie came out.

As she came towards her husband she motioned the hall porter to put the bags in the dressing-room. There was about her an assurance and authority, very quiet, but undeniable.

May Edginton

"Here you are, Osborn," she said.

"Hallo, dear!" he answered, rather stammeringly. "How are you? How are the—"

The maid took from him the overcoat which he was shedding, and his wife retreated into the sitting-room, he following.

When the door was shut, she turned, lifted her face, and murmured: "How are you, Osborn?"

He kissed her and, loth to relinquish her, kept his arm about her waist; she was unresponsive, but he did not notice that; they went together to the chesterfield drawn up before the fire and sat down. She took a corner, turning herself to face him a little, so that he had to withdraw his arm from her, and she pushed a billowing cushion which he did not remember into a comfortable position for her back.

She spoke very kindly and sympathetically, but it was with the kindness and sympathy which someone who was a stranger might show. "How well you look! I'm longing to hear all about your doings; your letters did not say very much. I should have met you at Victoria, only there's always a crush, and it's easy to miss people, so I thought I'd stay here."

"I didn't suppose you could leave the children to meet me."

"Oh, I can leave them quite well with Ann."

One of those silences which fall between people who have been estranged fell between them, during which he looked from her to the room, and all about him, and back to her, while she regarded him with that disinterested kindness.

"How nice everything looks!" he said, breaking the silence in a voice which sounded crude to himself. "What a lot of flowers you have, and all these cushions! I don't remember things, as a woman would do, but surely there's something new."

"Only the cushions. I stuffed a lot with one of mother's feather beds. She left me everything, you know."

"Yes. You didn't say much about it."

"No. The flowers *are* nice, aren't they? I love flowers."

"So you do," he exclaimed suddenly. "I wish I'd brought you some; there are such lovely ones at Victoria."

His wife smiled.

"But I've brought you something I hope you'll like as well."

"Have you, you dear kind person?"

He took her hand and drew nearer. "Marie, darling, it's awf'ly good to see you again. This last week in Paris seemed such waste of time, with you so near."

She looked at him with her eyes widening, a trick he found vivid in his memory. A little more colour rose into her cheeks.

"Don't you want to see the children?" she asked, "or do you want tea first?"

"I have an idea I want you. But—where are they?"

"In the dining-room. George will be back from school directly."

"School?"

"Yes, school."

"Things have been happening!" he exclaimed, getting up. He pulled caressingly at the hand he held. "You're coming, too?"

"Go in and see them by yourself. See if they remember you. Dispense with my introductions."

She laughed, pulling her hand from his, and he moved away. At the door he looked back, puzzled. An element which he was unprepared for, could not understand, seemed with them in the room. She leaned back among the fat cushions, pretty and leisured as he had been used to seeing her before their marriage, only now she had something else about her which he could not define. She was not looking at him, but down at her hands lying in her lap, and the curling sweep of her eyelashes, the bend of her head, the white nape of her neck, the colour and contour of her cheek—all these he found newly adorable. He almost came back, with a rush of tenderness, longing for a real embrace, but something, that element which he only sensed, restrained him.

He went into the dining-room, where a four-year-old girl nursed a doll and played with a robust baby by turns. They were merry, healthy children, and their chubby prettiness swelled his heart with pride. These were his; he had fathered them. And just through that partitioning wall was a woman who was all his, too; one of the prettiest of women, and his wife.

"Hallo, kids!" he smiled at them from the door-way, "here's

Daddy come back. Come and see if you remember him. What a great girl Minna's grown, and is that the baby Dadda left behind him?"

He picked up the baby and danced and dandled her, but the four-year-old Minna came more sagely, more slowly; she had to be won over by bribe and strategy, and her aloofness made him a trifle sore. In a moment or two he heard the maid go down the corridor and let in a boisterous boy, who ran into the dining-room swinging a satchel of books and pulled up short at seeing the stranger among them.

But his memory, older and longer than Minna's, served him.

"Daddy!" said George, shy and very nervous.

Osborn wondered why this boy was nervous of him. Forgetting his previous sharpness and irritation with the children, he now suddenly wanted George's confidence.

"Daddy's back!" he said, "with lots of stories to tell you about great big ships and trains and wonderful birds which *you* never saw."

"How splendid!" said the boy, still very shy. He had a guilty feeling about his boisterous entry.

"I was afraid you would be cross with me for making a noise when I came in," he explained.

"Like you used to be," Minna added.

"I'm not cross, old son," Osborn said slowly.

"We're going to have tea now, Daddy," Minna continued, as the maid entered with a cloth and a tray.

Osborn stayed talking to the children while the tea things were set upon the table. He supposed that they would all have tea together in the way which he had once so heartily deplored, and which at this moment seemed so dear and homely, until he saw the maid standing respectfully behind her chair waiting for his departure.

He spoke genially, but ill at ease.

"You give them their tea, do you?"

"Yes, sir," she answered, "and I have taken tea into the sitting-room."

The baby was now sitting in a high chair, bland and fat and greedy, a bib about her neck. George and Minna, after a propitiatory smile at him, had climbed into their places.

"You don't mind if we begin, Daddy, do you?" George asked.

"Go on, old son," said Osborn hastily.

There was no more use there for the father who had been cross, so he returned to his wife.

She was still sitting in the corner of the chesterfield, but she had picked up some knitting, with which her hands were busy. As he entered she looked up and gave him a contemplative regard such as he had given her as he went out, only that it was colder, more detached. She saw him big and splendid, handsome and virile, and the eagerness in his eyes fell into her heart like a cold weight. Her hands became cold and trembled.

She did not want him.

Beside her the tea table was drawn up. Its equipment seemed to him very dainty. It was a picture he liked, this pretty woman by the fire, with the environment suited to her charms.

Through the wall came faintly the jolly sound of their children's voices.

He hurried forward, sat down close to her, and laid a hand over hers which held the knitting.

"What's that?" he asked.

"George's winter stockings; they're to have turn-down tops like grown-up ones."

He took the knitting and pretended to examine the pattern, though he was not thinking of anything save her.

The year's parting had been a miracle. Love had slyly redecorated his house throughout.

"Jolly nice," he commented on the stockings, "but, please, give me my tea now."

He smiled at her a lazy, autocratic smile. All this flat and the people in it were his, and he would not have changed it for a throne. He thought again, though in a more mature fashion, much as he used to do in the first married year, how good it was to come in and shut your own door upon a snubbed world.

She answered the smile by one faint and chilly and reposeful. Leaning forward she began to busy herself with the tea things. The sugar tongs poised: "Let's see," she cogitated, "it *was* two lumps, wasn't it?"

He assented, surprised. "Time I came home," he said, affecting to grumble lightly.

"What do you think of the children?" she asked. "I suppose you find them grown? Did they remember you?"

"Yes, of course. I should think they did!"

"Muffin, Osborn?"

"Thank you, darling. I say," he smiled with gratification, "you look as though you'd all done yourselves pretty well while I've been away. This is cosy."

He indicated the tea table.

"Of course, after mother's death—"

"I was awf'ly sorry, Marie. I'm afraid I wrote rather a brief letter about it; life was rather a rush, you know."

"It didn't matter. I was going to say, that after her death, I found myself quite well off, comparatively."

"You didn't tell me much."

"No. Well, you didn't ask much. Surely, I answered all your questions?"

He remembered uncomfortably the many months of his abstraction with Roselle; she had occupied his thoughts for a while almost to the exclusion of everything else.

"I expect you did, dearest."

"However, I'm going into accounts with you presently, and

then you'll know everything."

"Overspent yourself?" he smiled complacently, with the knowledge of that thousand pounds backing him. "Want money to go on with?"

She shook her head.

"I don't want anything, thanks."

The thought was to her like a bulwark; it was a thought which thousands of wives would have loved to possess. It somehow completed her sense of detachment from him. She puzzled him.

"How long have you had a maid?" he asked. "I must say I was awf'ly surprised when what's—her—name—Ann—opened the door to me."

"Let's see," she considered, wrinkling her brows, "I've had her for six months. Before that I had a woman in to do the rough work."

"Well, if you could manage it—"

"I managed it, and kept quite within our income, thank you, Osborn."

"I must say it's very jolly to have you all to myself like this. We always used to talk of what we'd do when my ship came home, and now here she is!"

"Poor Osborn! You *must* be glad."

"Aren't *you*?"

"Of course I am."

"We'll have a bigger flat; it's rather a crowd here, isn't it?"

"Yes, I'd like another room."

"You shall have what you like, darling."

He put an arm round her shoulders, drawing her face to his. "You know I'd like to give you the world!"

She was silent.

He kissed her cheek, holding her against him. "I must show you what I've brought as soon as I unpack. I got you some things in the Bon Marche—I think you'll like them."

"I'm sure to."

"Tell me what you've been doing. I want to hear all about you," he said persistently.

"There's very little to tell. I've been able to go out a great deal more lately; and I've been resting and reading while I had the opportunity. I took the children to the sea in the summer. Ann went with us, so I was very free and had long walks and swims. It was delightful."

"And you've missed me?" he asked quickly. "I don't hear anything about that."

"We have all missed you."

Her assurance left him vaguely unsatisfied. She drew away from him with a sidelong glance, half sad, half ribald, as if she knew and was regretfully amused at what he was thinking. She leaned over the table, cake knife in hand.

"Have some of this iced cake, Osborn? Bought specially for you."

For a while that pleased and appeased him. He asked more casually for news, and she told him of Rokeby's and Julia's surprise wedding.

He sat back, astonished, exclaiming:

"Good heavens! How unsuitably people marry!"

"They do, don't they?"

The noise in the next room had subsided; and presently the handle of the sitting-room door turned quietly, and three inquiring faces looked in, Minna holding the baby steady.

Over Marie's face there came a change. From its half-cold inconsequence and restraint, it warmed and lighted, as her hands went out eagerly.

"Come along, chicks," she said; and then, turning to her husband, she added quickly: "If you don't mind? I always read to them before bedtime. Do you mind?"

"Why should I, darling?" he said, surprised.

The three children, encouraged, came forward. George had the chosen book under his arm and, opening it at a favourite story, he laid it on his mother's knee. Nursing the baby and with Minna snuggled into her other arm, she prepared to read.

"Come and sit on my knee, old chap," Osborn whispered

to George.

The child came dutifully, but his attention was for his mother. She began to read in her light, clear voice, and for some while that was the only sound in the room; the man and the three children listened, as if entranced. During the progress of the reading Ann came in without interrupting and took the baby away to bed.

A quarter of an hour later it was Minna's turn, and only George remained; he was eager to tell his mother of the day's experiences at school; clambering down from his father's lap he went to her, and, with an arm flung about her neck, began an involved account.

She listened with interest and comprehension. And Osborn looked at George's rapt face and her loving one, and drew a sharp comparison between what mattered and trash.

At last George went, and the husband and wife were alone again.

He started to the door on a sudden impulse.

"I'll unpack and get those things," he said over his shoulder.

"Yes, do," she nodded, "before George goes to sleep. Your things are in the dressing-room, and he will be there."

"We've simply got to have another flat," he replied, with a pleasant sensation of the power to pay for it.

For a few minutes Marie Kerr sat quiet, staring at the fire. The home-coming, so stimulating to Osborn, had for her been inexpressibly stale. She was not thrilled; she was left cold as the November night outside. The new and pretty habits of her life were in peril of being broken, and her reluctance that it should be so was keen. She got up and mended the fire and patted the cushions absently. She could hear Osborn talking to his son, and Ann busy in the kitchen.

A man in the house was once more going to set the clock of life.

Before Osborn had found what he sought she went to her bedroom. The baby and Minna were sleeping side by side in their cots, a screen drawn round them to shade them from the light. Deep in the perfect slumber of childhood, they did not awake at her careful entry. She switched up the electric light over her dressing-table, and began to change her blouse and skirt for the black frock in which she dined. While she was standing thus, half dressed, Osborn came in.

She swung round upon him, hands raised in the act of smoothing her hair, and there was something in her face which made him halt. He looked at her uncertainly.

She could not have helped saying if she would:

"You startled me. I didn't hear you knock."

He had not knocked. The puzzle in his head increased. Why should he knock? His mouth opened and shut again. He came forward hesitatingly.

"I—I—what do you mean, darling?" he began. "I wanted to bring you these."

His coming thus was to her symbolic of legal intrusion upon all her future privacy. In that year, privacy had been one of the things she enjoyed most, after the edge was off the first loneliness. She found it hard to relinquish her right to it. She stepped into the frock quickly, and drew it upwards before he reached her. His hands were full of little things, which he cast in a hurry upon the dressing-table. She knew that he wanted to touch, to fondle her. She slipped her arms swiftly into the sleeves and fastened the first hook across her breast; in her eyes a shrinking antagonism unveiled itself.

She uttered hurriedly: "We have to be very quiet; the children are asleep."

He cast a cursory glance towards the screened corner.

"They're all right; they can't see or hear or anything else. Come here and let me put this hair-band thing on."

She stood a dressing-table length away, fumbling with the hooks, her eyes fixed on him.

"I have lots of things to say to you," she began suddenly.

"Say them to-morrow," he replied in his old way.

"No," she said, "they have to be said to-night—not this minute, perhaps, but presently."

She was in Osborn's arms again, and he was touching her throat, her hair, and the velvet texture of her cheek.

"You've got fatter again," he was saying delightedly; "you look just like the little girl I married, only there's something bigger about you; firmer. There's no doubt marriage stiffens a woman up. That's it, isn't it? You're sure of yourself."

She gazed full into his eyes. "Yes. I'm sure of myself; absolutely sure."

"You always had ripping hair; but I think it's got thicker, hasn't it? It's springy, sort of electric."

"It used to be thick; and then it was thin; and now it's thick again, I think."

"You do it differently."

"One changes with the styles."

"*You* would, you up-to-date thing. Now, you're going to look at these souvenirs of Paris, aren't you?"

He held her close to his side, while he showed her what he had chosen; the pale-pink collars—"You were always gone on pink, weren't you?" he asked—the silk stockings and the vanity garters. With clumsy fingers he tried to adjust the hair-band.

"Let me do it," she protested, "if you really want me to wear it."

"Well, don't *you* want to?" he asked, a little hurt.

"I'd love to, if I may put it on properly. It's sweet."

"It makes you look awf'ly French!"

"Does that improve me?"

"You don't want improving."

He sat down by the dressing-table, while she stood, fixing the glittering circle round her hair with clever fingers. He kept his hand on her waist and, leaning forward, looked at her in the glass. She had a lithe naturalness, a slim strength, which newly arrested his admiration. Struck by the charm of his own wife, he missed no detail of her appearance. She had dressed to please herself with a true woman's delight in *dessous*; and he was quick to notice the mauve gleam of ribbon shoulder straps under the filmy black of her bodice, which gave the sombre gown a charming colour-note; her sleeves, transparent, long, and braceleted round the wrists with black velvet bands, showed the whole length of her white arms; in her ears amethyst earrings repeated the note of the mauve ribbons. Her stockings were silk and her slippers of velvet.

She was as amazing to him as a beautiful stranger.

"It doesn't go with my earrings," she said carelessly when she had fixed the band, "but it's so pretty, and thank you ever so much."

She turned and showed him; and she showed him, too, the interest she took in herself, which had caused her to pull out those waves of fluffy hair over the tops of her ears, from under the hair-band, and the curls she had pulled from beneath to dance on her forehead.

"Give me a kiss for it," he said, drawing her down.

She kissed him lightly.

"Fancy you the mother of a family!" he remarked, with a look at the screened corner.

She smiled to herself, and began fingering the other things. "How nice they are! And silk stockings! They're always welcome."

"But you're wearing them already," he said, with rather a

disappointed glance at her ankles.

"That doesn't matter. If there's one thing you can't glut a woman with, it's silk stockings."

"Thanks, Mrs. Kerr! I'll remember that when I come home in the small hours and have to provide a peace offering."

"Come home any time you like," she said goodhumouredly, "there will always be peace as far as I am concerned."

When he had entered the room, he had missed something in it; and now it occurred to him what it was.

"Where's my bed?" he demanded.

"In the dressing-room. I had it moved there, when you went; I thought I might as well give myself more space."

"Of course! I noticed something unusual about the dressing-room. You waited for me to move it back here, I suppose? It's rather a tough job for women."

"The hall-porter would have done it, you know."

"Never mind, pet. I'll do it ever so quietly after dinner."

She did not reply.

"Are you ready?" he asked. "Come back to the fire, and sit down. There's so much to tell each other about, isn't there?"

She moved to the door acquiescently and switched out the light, he following. A savoury smell crept through the chinks of the kitchen door, with the all-pervasiveness of cookery in flats. He sniffed it.

"How familiar! But you don't do the cooking now?"

"No; I only help, sometimes. Ann's a treasure."

"What do we pay her?"

"Thirty pounds a year."

"Whew!"

She cast a sidelong glance at him. "A domestic drudge is worth it, I assure you; women have been consistently underrated."

"But fool work like cleaning saucepans and helping with the kids—"

"Shutting oneself up with the sink; working early; working late; breathing ashes and dust and grease; keeping tolerably civil and cheerful over it ... that's the job we're speaking of. I ought to know all about it," she said in a low voice, as if to herself.

She sat in her corner of the chesterfield and took up her knitting. He sat down, too, by her, all at once alert, surveying the flying movements of her dear hands; hands as tender and white as ever he remembered them.

"Oh come!" he said in affectionate but uneasy remonstrance, "you don't look much as if you'd been shut up with the sink, working early and working late."

"You forget I've had a whole year's holiday." She kept her eyes on her work, as if re-casting that first year upon her busy needles. "At least," she reflected, almost as if to herself, "part of the time was only half-holiday; but the last six months have been wonderful."

Jealousy rose in Osborn; jealousy of he knew not what. Something or someone had brought colour and smiles to her, and it was not himself. As he began to suggest that fact to himself, before he could do more than begin: "How, do you mean—?" the door opened, and the maid announced: "Dinner is served, ma'am."

Marie sprang up and put her hand kindly in his arm.

"Come along," she said. "We have all your favourite things, so I hope you're hungry."

May Edginton

CHAPTER XXII

PLAIN DEALING

Re-entering the dining-room Osborn was struck by its comfort and charm. It was a room humanised by the hand of a kind and clever woman. And how well-ordered his table was! How nice his silver looked! How well his wife looked! What good cooking he could command! And in what attractively comfortable circumstances he now found himself after that year which had ended by palling; that year in which he had done as other men—free men!

There was no place like home, for permanence; no woman like the wife of one's choice, for permanence. These were the things which mattered.

He was moved to speak to her in some measure of this thought during dinner. They were not separated from one another by the whole breadth of the table. He sat on his wife's right hand, and the maid served them from the sideboard, an arrangement which pleased him because it saved him the trouble of carving, and also because it was rather smart, he thought, for home, where things generally tended to be dowdy.

"I've had an awf'ly good time, this last year," he confided, "but I'm glad to be back. There's nothing like one's own home and one's own girl." The maid having gone to the kitchen, he reached for and squeezed his wife's hand. "I'm going to be an awf'ly good boy now you've got me again," he assured her.

"Don't bore yourself," she said with gentle politeness.

"What—what queer things women say!" he observed, after a pause, in which he had regarded her with some surprise.

"Not so queer as the things men do," she replied thoughtfully.

He started and felt a flush creeping from his collar to the roots of his hair. She spoke almost as if she knew of the folly and fun—but even as the idea came to him he knew it to be impossible. It was just one of the half-bitter remarks which wives made. Bitterness in a woman was horrible. The flush on his face had been imperceptible to her in the roseate light of the pink candle-shades, he was glad to think; but he waited until it had subsided before he spoke with a hint of reproof.

"I say, don't try sarcasm. Sarcasm in a woman jars, somehow."

"I wasn't sarcastic, really." Her tone was of raillery and somehow he didn't like that she should speak so lightly.

"Besides," he said, with an inconsequent effort, "as to the queer things men do, men are natural animals all the world over."

"And you don't suppose we forget it?"

She had a pretty laugh; but what made for laughter in her question?

"Men are men," he stated, rather at a loss, "and women are women."

She laughed more.

"It's been said before" she replied.

Osborn was relieved to find the maid at his elbow with a sweet.

"Alexandra cream, sir?" she was asking confidentially.

"I hope you'll like this, Osborn," said Marie; "I prepared it myself this morning."

When the maid had gone, he switched off to a less troublous track.

"My socks are all in a shocking condition; I don't know how long it'll take to mend 'em, dear."

"I'll spend to-morrow looking over your things. I daresay you want repairs throughout."

"You're a darling. I believe I've wanted you to look after me. But don't stew in over my mending all day. Run into town and lunch with me."

"I'll be delighted, Osborn."

"We must have a beano one evening, quite soon. You'd like it?"

"I'd love it."

He smiled affectionately, pressing her hand. It was nice to give a woman such pleasure.

After dinner they were to make their own coffee in their old way, in the sitting-room; and after Marie had made it and brought his cup to him, Osborn leaned back in his corner of the couch to smoke and dream and talk happily, as a well-fed man does. His gaze, wandering round the room, found the piano, which he recognised with respect.

"I say, you said the cushions were the only different things. There's that!" He nodded towards the instrument.

"Yes," she said, her eyes following his, "there's mother's piano. I must tell you all about her will, Osborn; about everything. She left all she had to me."

"The furniture and money?"

"Yes. I sold most of the furniture; Mr. Rokeby helped me to arrange it and saw the dealers for me."

"Good old Desmond! I must thank him for that."

"He's been extremely kind." She looked into the fire. "*Extremely*," she repeated. "He advised me and told me exactly what to do."

"Did the furniture make much?" Osborn asked with masculine interest in things financial.

"A hundred and fifty pounds, odd."

"Good!" he exclaimed.

"I paid off all the rest of our own furniture instalments with it."

"Oh, splendid!" he exclaimed in approval.

"I hoped you'd think so. A hundred cleared it, as you would know."

"So little Marie had fifty pounds odd for her own banking account!"

"Not at all," she said, smiling into the fire as if she saw a very pleasant vision there; "I spent it."

Osborn took his pipe from his mouth and sat forward. "Whatever on?" he ejaculated.

His motion was surprise rather than disapproval. The money was hers, of course. But that a woman should have the temerity to spend fifty pounds odd in a few months when she was already supplied with enough to ensure comfort for herself and her family....

She lifted her head and looked at him. She dared him. The curls on her forehead danced and the amethyst eardrops twinkled; the shrug of her shoulders brought the mauve ribbons again under his notice.

"As I told you, I'm going into accounts with you this evening."

"Oh, well ... it's your own affair."

"But husbands like to make wives' affairs their own, don't they?"

She rose to find her account-books in a pigeon-hole of the bureau. Her colour had faded; her eyes were bright. Like all women she feared the hour of battle, while she did not flinch from it. So pretty she looked, standing there, that Osborn sprang up after her. He was just man—not husband, not master, nor judge, nor timekeeper of the home; but man, admiring and passionate.

"I say, hang the accounts! Come to me!"

There was again that about her which checked him. It was an almost virginal aloofness, though he would not have known how so to define it. When she sat down once more by his side he reached for his pipe again calmly and put it between his teeth, clenching them hard on the stem.

"Well, pretty cat?" he asked in a strained voice.

The old love-name fell upon cold ears. Opening the first book, she mused busily:

"This is the housekeeping; the other's odd expenses. But I'd better finish telling you about mother's will first. She left me two hundred and twenty pounds a year."

This time he made no sign at the news, except by raising his eyebrows and directing towards her a steady look of interest and inquiry.

"So," she continued, "we have been quite well off. Directly you left I reckoned up our expenses and found we were better off than before, on two hundred a year, and I got a charwoman. I told you the first part of the year was like a half-holiday. After my dear mother died and I had the money, I engaged Ann."

"Quite right," he said rather gruffly.

"I am like you, Osborn, I have had a great year. If it hadn't meant losing mother it would have been a perfect year."

After a long pause, he dropped out, incredulously:

"Without me?"

She felt her hands grow suddenly cold with fear of the battle.

"Yes," she nodded, "without you."

As he looked at her she was again as dazzling to him as a beautiful stranger; and as strange.

He said somewhat stiffly: "That's not exactly what a man expects to hear when he comes back after a long time."

"I'm sorry."

"You've changed somehow. What's the matter?"

"I've grown young again. That's all, isn't it?"

"I don't know if that's all."

"Let's talk of something else," she said gaily; "tell me more about yourself. I've had no details yet, and I'm longing for them. You're keeping the job, are you? And just what good things does keeping it mean?"

"A fur coat for Marie," he said with a hint of reproachful pathos.

"How lovely! But what will it mean to you was what

I'm asking?"

"The salary is five hundred, as you know." And guardedly, for he knew many men who deemed it well to be careful over telling their wives these things, he added: "With any luck the commission's more than the salary."

He left it vague, like that, for safety.

"I do congratulate you, Osborn."

"Our ship's really in, at last, you see, old girl."

"My poor income fades into the background behind yours!"

"Well, yours isn't so bad for a woman!"

"So I've found. I've had clothes, and gone about, and begun to think and read and see good plays again, all on the strength of it."

She opened a bank-book. "This is all the accounting for the two hundred you arranged to be paid in to me. You'll see I've used it legitimately—none of it's gone on frippery. And I've paid George's schooling myself this last six months, and Ann's wages, as I hadn't your permission for either. So you'll see there's even a balance left to your credit."

"Why make a song about my 'permission'? You've always been a free agent, haven't you?"

"Won't you just run your eye over this, now you're taking hold of the family bank account again?"

To satisfy her he took the book and skimmed over figures rapidly.

"You've been a good girl."

"So glad you think so."

Osborn smoked on quietly, but his thoughts were turbulent. She was giving him strange qualms, and he could not quite understand her direction. That something worked in her head he guessed, but, unwilling to hear of it, he asked no questions. It was very comfortable by the fire, and when he pitched the account-books away from her and took her hand again, she let it lie in his.

He pressed it.

"Well?" he whispered with a meaning look, wanting response.

It seemed as if she had none to give, kind and sweet as she was to him.

"I'm forgetting," he said in a few minutes, leaning forward to knock out his pipe, "that I've a job to do for you. I'll see to that bedstead now, shall I?"

"Why?" she said coldly. "It is all ready made up for you in the dressing-room. What do you want to do?"

He stared, bewildered.

"I'm not going to sleep there."

"Aren't you? Then I will."

He began to see dimly the meaning of her mood; but he was stumbling about in darkness to find her reasons for it. What reasons could she have for so extraordinary a reply?

"My dear good girl," he cried sharply, "explain yourself."

"I don't know how to, exactly. But I have liked having my room to myself. I wish to keep it."

"You've got some nonsense into your head—"

"It isn't nonsense. It's just fact. I've been without a husband for a year and I've found it wonderfully restful. I can be without him some more."

"Have you any idea of the rubbish you're talking?"

She looked at him curiously, unaffected by his authoritative tone, and, seeing her disaffection, he felt uncomfortably at a loss, since his authority had failed him. He was dumb-founded; angry and stricken at once; he had not the least idea now what tone to take.

He dropped suddenly to persuasion.

"Look here, my dear girl, tell me what you're thinking of. You know I'm only too anxious to respect your feelings and wishes; I don't think I've ever violated them to the least extent, have I? If I have, it was unknowingly. You women have such queer moods. What is it? Perhaps you're unwell and nervy, though you look all right. Anyway, come here and tell me all about it."

To avoid his encircling arm she rose. She laid one arm along the mantelpiece, and put one foot on the fender as if to be warmed; the attitude struck him as exceedingly negligent, and when she began to speak it was in no sense as an argument, but as a statement of facts long ago cut-and-dried for storage in her mind.

"I'm sorry. I'm really sorry. But I don't want you. I couldn't bear you in my room."

She had got it out, and he was saying nothing, only sitting forward, hands on knees, looking up at her, horror, anger and disbelief in his face.

She went on: "It'll be no good arguing. I've suffered and suffered, and had it all out with myself, and it's over. But I'll tell you everything, putting it plainly, because I'd like you to understand—if men ever do trouble to understand. Look at me!"

"I'm looking."

"Then you see I've changed. You thought so when you came in. I'm young again; I've rested and got my complexion back. My hair's nice; I get time for regular shampoos now. I spend a lot of my time on myself. It's lovely. And my teeth, have you noticed them?"

She set them together and opened her lips to show him all the gleamy whiteness between.

"I spent ten pounds on them, having them filled and cleaned and polished; I go regularly to the dentist now. And my hands, have you noticed them?"

Osborn met her question by a dead silence.

"They're as they used to be again. And I've done it all in this year you've been away. And there's another thing—it occurred to me the other day when I was wondering what really made all the difference—there's not been a cross word or a grumble in this flat for twelve months. That's happiness. Heavens! That keeps women young!"

She stopped and thought, and continued slowly:

"Marriage is funny. It's a thing men can't bear unless it's gilded. And they vent their intolerance. Do you know that before you went away—for four years—I scarcely ever expected you to say loving or civil things. Before you went out in the mornings you shouted for the breakfast, and I was hurrying all I could; and you grumbled if the children made a noise. And when you came in, if dinner wasn't ready or right, you grumbled at that again. And in the week-ends the kids dared hardly play, and I was buffer all the time between you and them. It's just what happens in thousands of homes, of course."

"This exaggeration—"

"Ah, it isn't. It sounds bad, but it isn't so very. It's rather ordinary. And, Osborn, do you remember when I had to ask you for money—?"

She looked at him freezingly. "Do you think a woman who's been begged and cajoled and petted into marrying a man enjoys creeping and crawling to him for odd shillings for household expenses? Do men think we enjoy it or do it wilfully, that they grudge it so? We can't help it."

"Where's all this harangue—"

"There's more to it yet. Do you know when you told me you were going away at once for a year, I thought I was broken? I loved you so. It seemed awful to see the gladness and relief in your face at leaving us, getting rid of us for a whole year! I'd been watching you for so long, and seeing you change, and get irritated with it all, and trying to keep young for you when I was tired out. And that night, when I saw how I'd failed, how dead your love was—"

May Edginton

"No; it was never dead, Marie."

"Wasn't it? Was it sleeping, then? Where was it? What was it doing?"

"You see—"

"Oh, yes, I see. I saw, then, how joyfully you shelved us all. You were like a boy let out of school. And I'd worked so hard to keep home happy for you, but you just thought of it as a place of bills and worry and children, presided over by a perpetual asker. That night before you went, do you remember leaving me to mend your things?"

"Yes."

"When you had gone, I cried, and prayed; it didn't do any good. I didn't know women could suffer so—even when the children were born—"

Osborn sprang up. "Don't," he said hurriedly, with visions of anguish in his mind.

"Very well. I don't want to harrow you. I'm only just giving the explanation you asked. A year ago you left me, glad to go, and I thought my heart would break. But it didn't. And it's changed. You've come back—to exact again all the things that husbands do exact. But I don't want you."

She had appalled him.

He stammered hoarsely: "I don't understand—I can't see what you want us to do."

"Well; to live—apart."

"You can't mean it."

"But I do. How often am I to say, I don't want you? The last part of this year, after the pain was over, I've been as glad to be without you as during the first part of the year you were glad to be without me. Isn't that plain?"

"You're making it horribly plain. And now I'm going to ask you, could I help being poor and short of cash?"

She shook her head. "No! But I couldn't either, and you were awfully down on me."

"'Down' on you! *I!*"

"You grumbled persistently every day. The kiddies and I just waited upon your moods. And if I had to ask for anything, you weren't kind about it; you just flung out of the place, leaving me all the worries. You never helped nor shared. I've come to this conclusion lately; that it simply isn't worth while living with a person who grumbles persistently and has to be propitiated every day."

He reflected deeply, his hands in his trousers pockets.

"I think I'm taking all this sermon peaceably enough," he barked savagely.

Again he had that disaffected look from her; she seemed to analyse him coldly.

"It isn't a sermon. Go on grumbling and nagging and grudging every day, if you want to. I haven't asked you to refrain. I've merely explained that, as a result of your husbandly behaviour, you've ceased to attract me, and I don't want to live with you—intimately—again."

He caught her arm. "Look here! I know. You've been to some of these beastly Suffragette meetings."

She laughed scornfully.

"Suffragette! Don't be an ass, dear!"

"No," he said under his breath, regarding her, "you haven't. Hanged if I know what you have been doing."

"I told you. Getting my youth back. Do you know what a very pretty young girl feels like? Did you know what I used to feel like when you were engaged to me? Like a queen with a crowd of courtiers at her orders and you the most courtier-like of them all! You used to hang on every word I said and promise me heaven and earth, and my every look was law. Oh! the power a pretty young girl feels in herself!"

Standing on tiptoe she looked into the glass, touched her fluffs of hair and the purple earrings with tender finger-tips.

"I've got it back," she said with a thrill. "I feel it flowing back; the power one has through being pretty and magnetic. If a woman's tired out she can't be magnetic. But I've got it all again—and more. I wonder if a man can ever understand the pleasure of having it? It's coming to me again just as I had it fresh and unconquered in those dear old days when you were at my feet."

He spoke in a sort of beaten amazement. "If you want me again at your feet—"

"Thank you, I don't. I'll never pay the price again. Never! Never!"

"Then whom do you want? Do you mean there's anyone

else? By God! if there is—"

As she saw his fury she could laugh. "There isn't."

"Let's sit down again," he said more quietly; "this isn't threshed out yet."

"If more discussion gives you any pleasure I'll discuss. But what I said I meant. I'm not glad to see you; I'm sorry. You mean the breaking-up of household peace for me again. Men would be surprised, if they knew how many wives are glad to see their husbands go."

"Take care you don't drive me into going for good. Your way of treating a man is pretty dangerous."

"I'm sorry," she replied with a convincing gentleness, "that I shouldn't care if you did go. I'd have the children."

"Do you mean they've been more to you than I have?"

"What haven't they been to me?" Her face was soft. "You can't think—you've never troubled to know—how kind children are."

"Once I was first with you."

She quoted with irreverent glee: "'And they that were first shall be last.'"

"You can laugh?"

"Thank God I can, at last."

"Supposing I did go—right now?"

She shrugged her shoulders slightly and the mauve shoulder straps again arrested him. She did not speak; but without her answer, whatever it would have been, he knew that he could not leave her; that he must always come back at last, longing for her arms.

Ten o'clock struck, and she looked up thoughtfully at the wedding-gift timepiece.

"I'm going to bed," she said. "Good night."

A dark rush of colour flooded his face. "You really mean—"

She nodded.

"Then," he almost whispered, "exactly how do we stand?"

"I'll keep house for you very capably and look after our children. You can leave me if you like, you know."

"God!" he groaned. "What are women made of?"

"Ordinary flesh and blood that gets tired and wants loving. Have you only just remembered to inquire?"

He ran after her along the corridor as she went swiftly to her room.

"Marie!" he prayed. "Relent! Marie, it'll be all so different now. I've all this money; you could have what you wanted."

"I know it'll be different. But, you see, you've done something to me; you've killed all the love I had for you, drained it dry somehow. There's none left. I just—I just—don't want you."

She left his hands and gained her door, leaving him standing; he could have followed her forcibly, but it would have been violation. He felt it and was frightened. Through his anger there broke this fear, the fear of further offending her. When she turned to ask naturally, "You'll turn out the lights?" he just nodded. His mouth was very dry. He wheeled round abruptly, returning to the warm room they had just left.

The whole room seemed to bear her impress; the faintest perfume, almost too delicate to be definite scent, hung there; on the bureau the little stocking she was knitting adhered to the ball of wool, pierced thereto by the long needles. It looked homely, but it was not home. Something had happened, devastating home. He sat for awhile in a sunk posture of dejection, his head in his hands and his elbows on his knees.

"She'll come round," he assured himself presently.

Sentences isolated themselves from her burning speech and struck in his brain ... "if I had to ask for anything, you weren't kind about it; you just flung out of the place, leaving me all the worries. You never helped nor shared." ... "A year ago you left me, glad to go, and I thought my heart would break." ... "But I don't want you." ...

"If she knew," he thought restlessly, with Roselle in his mind, "it'd be different. I'd understand what's piqued her. But, as far as she knows, she's been no worse off than other men's wives."

Her joy over her restored teeth and hands surprised him; it seemed so freshly childish. "I'll own it's hard on women," he thought, "but what could I have done? What did she expect me to do?"

He was quivering, soft, vulnerable.

"Did I really mean—just that—to her and the kids? Just somebody coming in to grump and grumble...."

The fire died down while he sat there, but what matter? She was not lying awake for him. When the desire came to him to make one last appeal, he checked it.

"No," he told himself cautiously, "give her time—lots of it. She'll come round."

He began to rake out the ashes suddenly and methodically, to switch out the lights. And very soberly he went to the room where his small son lay asleep.

His entrance roused George.

"Are you going to sleep with me, Daddy?" he asked nervously.

"Yes, old son," Osborn replied as nervously as the child had spoken.

"I'll be very quiet in the morning, Daddy," said George.

"You needn't be, old boy," Osborn replied.

He sat down on the edge of George's bed, with a wish that someone of all his household, this child at least, should be glad to see him.

"We're going to be great pals," he stated, "aren't we?"

"Yes, Daddy," the child answered.

"Give me a kiss and say good night, then."

George obeyed dutifully. Osborn tucked him up and turned away. As he undressed he thought of the toys he would buy the children to-morrow.

CHAPTER XXIII

INDIFFERENCE

Marie met her husband serenely at the breakfast-table next morning. She looked fair and fresh and had other things to do than to give him undivided attention. George and Minna were at table, behaving charmingly, though the baby, being yet at a sloppy stage, was taking her breakfast in the kitchen in deference to her father's return. Osborn paid his family some attention and his newspaper none; and he appeared to be in no hurry to be off.

"My first morning back," he remarked; "I need hardly turn up punctually."

"I suppose," said Marie, with interest, from behind her coffee-pot, "that your work will be rather different."

"It will, rather. I believe I'm to put in some days in town, and then run down to our various agents in the Midlands. There's quite a busy programme mapped out, I believe."

"You'll enjoy that."

"Shall you go away again, Daddy?" asked Minna.

"Don't talk at breakfast, dear," said her mother.

Osborn looked across at his wife.

"I shall be off your hands a good deal."

Bitterness savoured his voice. She smiled at him sympathetically, but he smarted under the knowledge that her sympathy did not go very deep. Yet he was strangely reluctant to hurry away. He remained until George had started for school; until Minna had begged to be allowed to get down and go to see baby finish her breakfast. Then he rose, and went rather heavily round the table to his wife, and laid a hand on her shoulder.

"I couldn't sleep. I was thinking of you and all the things you said last night."

"I'm sorry you didn't sleep. I expect you were rather tired with travelling; over-tired, perhaps."

"I was as fresh as paint when I got here yesterday and you know I was. *You* took it out of me."

"We shan't be able to argue about this every day; I couldn't stand it, Osborn."

"I'm ready to say that I daresay we men are thoughtless sort of brutes; but you didn't marry one of the worst by a long chalk, you know."

A smile twitched her lips, goading him to desperation.

"No," she owned. "There was nothing lurid about you. But, heavens! it was dull!"

He took his hand off her shoulder and went to search for matches and pipe on the mantelpiece. He noticed many little things acutely in his unhappiness; how nicely the silver vases were cleaned, and that the piperack was kept on the righthand side now instead of the left.

"You'll come round."

"If you knew how impossible it seems to me you wouldn't say that."

"I suppose I shall be worrying over this business all day as well as all night?"

"I hope not. I'm lunching with you, at one, at the Royal Red."

"What! You'll come to lunch?"

"You asked me."

Pleasure, almost triumph, lit his face. "I'll give you a good time. Sure you wouldn't like some other place better than the Royal Red?"

"I've got, somehow, a special ache for it."

"Then you must have what you want, of course. I'll get away punctually, so as not to keep you waiting."

Marie accompanied him into the hall to help him on with his coat, and to remark that his muffler needed washing. But she did not kiss him on parting; before he could ask mutely for the salute she was on her way back to the breakfast-table.

She sat there some while after he had gone, comfortably finishing her own meal, which had been interrupted by attendance on the children, as if deliberately determining that Osborn's return should interfere in no whit with her recent ease. Only when she was quite ready, with no hurry and at her own pleasure, did she start out to the Heath to give the children their morning airing.

"Mummie," said Minna, "George said Daddy has promised to bring us some toys."

"That's very kind of Daddy, isn't it?"

She walked thoughtfully. "Things have changed," she said to herself, "I suppose money has changed them. It always can." She thought this with a certain enjoyment, yet down underneath, where that stony organ which used to be her heart lay, she knew that she wanted, more than thousands and thousands of pounds, the light and life of that first year over again. What joy was like the birth of such love? Or what regret like the death of it?

Their walk on the Heath lasted till eleven o'clock, when she returned to put the children under the charge of the maid. She was meticulous in her instructions for their care and requirements, almost passionate in her loving good-byes to them. Truly no one, she thought again, as their arms clung about her neck, could know all that they had been to her, how heavenly kind they were.

Minna, admiring her mother's clothes, walked with her to the door and waved her down the bleak staircase.

It was precisely one o'clock when Marie Kerr entered the lounge of the big restaurant, where she had waited some while for Osborn on a birthday evening which she remembered keenly this morning. But this time he was there before her, waiting anxious and alert, like a lover for the lady of his affections. He had booked a table and upon it, as she sat down, she saw, laid beside her cover, a big bunch of her favourite violets, blue and dewy.

"You still like them best?" he asked.

"Still faithful," she smiled back lightly and, when she had thrown open her coat, she pinned them at her breast.

She looked around her unafraid.

Her clothes were good; her hair was burnished; her hands were white; her man worshipped like the other women's men.

She was once more, after that long, that humble and tearful abdication, at the zenith of her power.

*   *   *   *   *

They did not rise from their table until nearly three o'clock. Twice she had asked: "How about the firm?" and twice he had answered irreverently: "Let them be hanged!" He looked into her eyes wondering and hoping, but in their clearness read no promise. He tried to lead their talk round to the one subject which pervaded and appalled him, but each time that he drove in his wedge of reference she shook her head at him, smiled and closed her lips, as a woman saying: "You don't talk me over in this world or the next."

But when he reminded her "It was here, to this very table, that I took you, on your birthday before last," she joined him in reminiscence.

"And I was miserable, envying every woman I saw, ashamed of my frock and my hands and my old shoes; ashamed of everything. I knew I couldn't compete."

"You could compete with any woman in the world." He cast a deprecating look around them.

"I couldn't then. There was a woman I specially envied, I remember, an actress whose name you knew. How long ago it seems."

"Only a year and a half," he replied quickly, plunging into a side issue.

"You admired her," she said curiously, "didn't you?"

He lied: "I don't remember."

"I do," she said. "I used to pray about you—that woman was in my mind when I prayed, and asked God to make you admire me for the children I'd borne, and not to let you see how old and ugly I should grow. Doesn't it seem funny?"

"It's not at all funny," he said, his eyes on the tablecloth. "I'm sorry you—if you'd told me—talked to me—"

"You'd have thought me more of a whining wife than ever."

"Well, it's over, anyway. Won't you forget it?"

"I'm just delighted to forget it. But there's a kind of joy in remembering all the same, such as a man feels in thinking of his starvation early days after he's made himself rich."

"And now I'm to be starved instead?"

Then she collected her muff and gloves, closed her coat, pinning the violets outside, thanked him for a nice lunch and left him. He paid the bill in a hurry and hastened after her, catching up with her upon the kerb.

"Well," he said in her ear, "I shall keep on asking. What do you think?"

She signalled a passing omnibus to stop and boarding it left him with a smile and wave of the hand. For a few seconds, he stood on the kerb, at grips with a feeling of humiliation and defeat, then he began to walk back to his work. He was not yet accustomed to the setting of this new act he was playing with his wife—he thought of it thus—though it was making him smart badly. As he went forward, threading his way among the hurrying after-lunch throngs, he was thinking hard. He attracted some attention from women's eyes as he swung along, oblivious, big, straight-shouldered and masculine. All the afternoon, while his mind was ostensibly upon his business, he fumed and fretted.

In taking up his job in London, he found a good deal to do and to book that first day. He had to pay rushing visits to two agents, talk over his tour with the head of the firm, and drive about the Park, in a Runaway, a rich undecided peer who couldn't make up his mind to buy her. But he bought the car *de luxe* before they parted, and his cheque lay in Osborn's pocket.

Another twenty-pounds commission, and what for? To spend on a woman who coolly didn't want it. Osborn Kerr started for home, chafing sorely.

On his way to the Piccadilly Tube he passed the Piccadilly Theatre. Outside the doors hung a big frame of photographs of the entire cast of Sautree's new production, and he paused to look, absent-minded as he was, with male interest in that galaxy of charm. In the second row of faces he met Roselle's.

She photographed well, her big, smooth shoulders bare, her hair smooth and smart, her chin uptilted so that she looked out, foreshortened. She smiled inscrutably. He knew the smile well, although he had never translated it so far as to guess that it covered stupidity in a sphinx's mask that baffled and piqued. That smile was of sterling value to Roselle; it was like so many pounds paid regularly into her pocket; it set men wondering what her meaning was when all the while she meant nothing. As Osborn Kerr paused before the rows of portraits, he wondered, a little yet, what Roselle meant when, so inscrutably, she smiled.

She was beautiful, there was no doubt of it. He remembered with some self-gratulation those hours spent with her in the blue Runaway with its silver fittings; Roselle in her fur coat and the purple velvet hat crushed close, in a cheeky fashion, over her night-black hair; and people turning to look at them both. He had seen in men's faces as they passed that they thought him a lucky fellow. They would have liked to be in his shoes, or rather, in his seat beside her, in the Runaway.

He passed on, the trouble in his heart a shade lighter for the intrusion of something else, something pleasant. It was like diluting a nasty draught, or soothing pain by partly anaesthetising it.

He reached home at his old time; it seemed so familiar to fit the key into the lock and step into the hall, redolent, even through the closed kitchen door, of the savoury preparations for dinner. But no little woman ran out, smiling and anxious, to ascertain his mood.

He had to go in search of her; he opened the sitting-room door and found her ensconced on the chesterfield, knitting those socks. This evening she had on a purply thing, a wrap, a tea-gown—he did not know what to call it—very graceful.

It made her look slimmer than ever; and stranger. All these strange clothes had the effect of increasing the gulf between them. In the old days she had to ask him, and she did not do it very often, for what she wanted, and it was his to withhold or to give. Everything about her then had seemed familiar because, in a way, it was his. But now she had a horrible independence, a mastery of life, even to spending her own money upon her own clothes. He did not mind that, of course; he liked her to be able to buy what she wanted; but it made a difference.

She wore her amethyst earrings, but not the hair ornament from Paris.

Coming up behind her quickly, he bent over and kissed her cheek, it being all that she offered. He laid a box of sweets on a table near, and it reminded her of that evening before he went away, when he had brought home a packet of chocolates to sugar his news.

"Not lost your sweet tooth I hope," he smiled.

"It's sweeter than ever."

He untied the ribbons. "Do you still thread these in your cammies?"

"If they're pretty. That'll do for Minna—I'm wearing mauve now."

"I'd noticed."

"Because of poor mother, you know."

"Oh, of course." He put a bonbon in her mouth.

"What a nice baby it is!" he said softly, stroking her silk knee.

He knew himself to be a fool, but all that evening he let himself remain on the rack, wondering; wondering if she'd relent; if her stoniness wasn't just a mood, and if it hadn't passed away; wondering if he couldn't break down that unnatural opposition in her. And when at ten o'clock she rose and nodded "Good night," he detained her, asking again urgently:

"Can't we—can't we—be as we were before?"

"Thank heaven, no!" she replied, with a tiny shudder.

Osborn looked at her narrowly and spoke crudely:

"Do you know, if I were like some men, I should tell you that I wouldn't stand such fool nonsense; and there'd be an end of it?"

She went a trifle paler, but displayed no fear. "Don't you dare!" she said between her teeth. "I'd leave you next day."

Again he went a little way up the corridor, but stopped before the aloof reserve of her look.

"Believe me," she said gravely, "I couldn't stand you."

He bit his lip sharply. "It's dangerous, you know, what you're doing. I told you last night men are natural animals all the world over. I shan't stand being turned down like this for ever; it's absurd, unnatural; it's preposterous after we've been married all these years. I tell you what you're doing is not safe. You'll drive me elsewhere."

"Make your own life," she said, with a cheerful indifference; "I have all I want in mine."

Osborn turned away with a sharp exclamation; and heard her door click behind her while he still stood in the corridor.

"That's that!" he breathed hard.

The next morning he took a bag with him and in the afternoon he wired home: "Shall not be back for dinner."

She read the telegram, uncaring. Two years ago it would have made her fear. She would have trembled over it; her heart would have leapt as at a thunderbolt; she would have run to her glass and reckoned with the sallowness of her face, the little lines about her eyes, each representing little anxieties about little things; her chapped hands and her dull wits. She would have thought of the other women, the hundreds of them, the younger, freer and fresher women who passed him by every day in the streets. But now she smiled; she felt awfully old, experienced in reading under and between the brief message.

She mused: "Tactics! How funny men are! Can he think I'll mind?"

It occurred to her, too, that perhaps it was not tactics; perhaps he genuinely quested in other directions; perhaps, already, she had driven him elsewhere. And still she was unmoved; she could not care. She longed to care very deeply, tragically, to thrill to the pulse of life again, but she could not. She even told herself that she was a little glad on his behalf and her own, if such was the solution. As she went in to dinner, and seated herself at the solitary table, she liked it; privacy had returned to her. This was almost like the year of her grass-widowhood.

CHAPTER XXIV

FOOL'S CAP

Osborn visited a smart flower shop when he went out to lunch and ordered carnations, a generous sheaf of them, to be sent to Miss Roselle Dates at the Piccadilly Theatre at half-past seven. He rang up and booked a stall for himself and, later, sent the wire to his wife.

"She's cut me loose," he said to himself, "and that's that."

He lunched as he liked now, with a memory that could afford to be humorous of the five-shilling weekly limit to which he had cut himself down in the bad old days only just over a year ago. But they were dear old days, too, when this extraordinary complication between his wife and him wasn't even thought of....

His luck was wonderful. He sold another car that afternoon. Two three-hundred-pound cars in two days, meaning forty pounds in his pocket! People liked him; he was big, good-looking and plausible, and he had a way with him which absolutely prevented any possible purchaser from ever giving another thought to any two-seater but the Runaway. When he turned out of the establishment that winter afternoon, on his way to an hotel to dress for his early and lonely dinner somewhere or other, he was pleased. Brisk business did a little towards lightening his trouble, just as less innocuous excitements might do.

"Stick to business and stick to fun," he told himself grimly, as he strode along, "and you'll worry through."

He thought of his children more than of anyone else throughout the courses of his dinner in a light, bright, well-served restaurant. George was a fine little boy, and should be done well, thoroughly well, with no expense spared; he must get to know the little chap, take him about a bit and make him interested in things worth knowing. Minna was going to be pretty, a facsimile of her mother; and the baby was a splendid little female animal. There was no doubt that he possessed three beautiful kids of whom any man might be proud.

Surely, if only for their sakes, some day she'd soften and return to him? Some evening he'd come home and find her as she used to be during the first year, sweet and eager, and shining; loving and passionate....

Osborn smoked several cigarettes over his coffee thinking of these things; he was in no hurry to see the show at the Piccadilly, and there would be plenty of time for Roselle afterwards. But he was rather lonely here by himself, and looked around somewhat wistfully at gay couples, laughing parties, all about him. There was not a woman there who could equal Marie, he said to himself; if she were only here with him, with her fresh, soft face, and her springing hair, and her round and slender figure, she'd put all this paint and powder right out of court.

But she was sitting afar off in a quiet flat, softly lighted, ineffably cosy, in the place called home, where husbands were not wanted.

He confessed to himself: "It used to be pretty beastly for her; a little delicate thing—three babies and no nurse; no help with anything. I suppose I could have done a lot, but how's one to think of these things? I suppose I've failed as a husband, but what am I to do about it now? It's all over and can't be helped."

He went to his stall at the Piccadilly, and, looking about him at other men's clothes, decided that he must have new ones. The price of an evening suit need not trouble him now. He settled down and began to enjoy the play.

Roselle was on the stage, in the beauty chorus, looking magnificent, and her eyes were sweeping the stalls. They paused here and there in their saucy habit, lingering upon more than one man with one of her tiny inscrutable smiles winging a message, but their search continued until at last she had found Osborn Kerr sitting on the lefthand side in the third row. He had scribbled on the card which accompanied his flowers, "Look for me to-night," and when her look met his, he had a sudden thrill of pleasure. Watching her eyes sweeping here and there, it had been exciting to wait for the moment when they should fall on him. After he had signalled back a discreet smile in answer, he put up his glasses and looked at her eagerly.

Her beauty returned to his senses like a familiar thing; he had admired the way her hair grew from her temples, and to-night it was dressed to show the unusual charm; her ankles had always been wonderfully slim, and to-night they looked finer than ever atop of twinkly little Court shoes in a vivid green hue; her eyes had that deep, still look which expressed her inanity, while having the result of concealing it.

During the first interval he scribbled a note to her, and sent it round with an imperative request for an answer. The note asked:

"My dear Roselle, come out to supper? And shall I wait for you at the stage door?—O.K."

And her reply, in her big, silly back-hand writing, said laconically:

"Right. I'll be out at eleven.—R.D."

Eleven found him waiting by the stage-door entrance, and she did not keep him long. Soon she came, big and brilliant, out from the gloomy gully, in the inevitable fur-coat which he remembered so well, but which had begun now to look battered, and the velvet hat shoved on cheekily, like a man's wideawake. Her eyes and her teeth acclaimed him in a kindred smile, for which he felt the warmer.

"Hallo, dear old thing!" she greeted him. "I thought you were lost."

He held her hand, smiling. "This is fine!" he said. "Where shall we go?"

"Romano's."

"Romano's let it be. I've a cab here, waiting." He handed her in, jumped in after her, and slammed the door, with a feeling that for an hour at least he had left his troubles outside.

"How are you?" he asked. "What have you been doing since I saw you last? And didn't you ever expect to see me again?"

Her eyes, in the dimness, looked very deep.

"I knew I should," she answered murmurously.

The inimitable atmosphere of Romano's loosened his tongue. After she had ordered supper, with every whit of the appetite and extravagance which he remembered as her chief characteristic, next to her beauty, and after each had been stimulated by a cocktail, he was conscious that he wanted to confide in her, not so much because she was Roselle, but because she was a woman, would look soft and listen prettily. He wanted stroking gently, patting on the back, and reassuring about himself.

The slight moodiness of his expression set her suggesting confidences. "You've got a pretty bad hump," she said caressingly. "What is it? Has the car slumped? Won't they have it? Or is it indigestion? You're not what you were when—"

She gave a quick sigh and smile, very inviting.

"When we were touring about Canada and the States together," he finished. "Well, you see; when a man has come back to all he left behind him—"

"Did you leave much behind you?"

"Why do you ask?"

"You never told *me* anything," she pouted. "But I'm not *asking*. I've no curiosity. The knots men tie themselves into—"

"You can laugh."

"You make me. Aren't men silly? Tell me about—to whom you came back."

"What does it matter?"

"It doesn't. *I* don't care." She drummed her fingers on the table. "All men are like cats, home by day, and tiles by night. But if you'd told me you were likely to get scolded for saying how d'you do to me, I'd have been more careful of you."

Her smile derided him. "Has someone scolded you?" she asked.

Consomme was set before them and she began to drink it with appetite, not repeating her question till it was finished.

"Well?" she said then, tilting her head inquiringly to one side.

"The fact is," he answered abruptly, "I—I've had a bad let-down."

"Financial?"

"No."

"Oh! Really!" she said pettishly.

"It doesn't matter," he remarked, rousing himself, "the thing is to make the best of life, and by Jove! I'm going to!"

"So you come and look for me?"

"Precisely," said Osborn. "You've been awf'ly decent to me, Roselle. Knowing you has meant a lot to me. I don't believe you'd let a fellow down very badly, would you?" He began to feel tender towards her, and the stupidity and avarice, which he had awhile ago begun faintly to see in her, now receded under the spell of the lights and the hour. "If no one else has cut in since I last saw you," he said, leaning towards her, "you might be kind to me again. Will you? I'm lonely. I'm simply too dreadfully lonely for anything. What are you doing this week-end?"

"Nothing," she said after a careful pause.

"Come out into the country on Saturday."

"I've a matinee."

"Of course. Sunday then? I'd bring the car round for you early, and we'd have a jolly day, get down to the sea somewhere. You'd like Brighton?"

"That's a nice run," she agreed. "Yes!"

"We could get back for dinner. Where shall we dine—Pagani's?"

She suggested, also, a supper club to which she belonged. "You'll have to belong, too," she said with enthusiasm. "It's the brightest thing in town. Will you, if I get someone to propose you?"

"Rather!"

He had felt dreadfully at a loose end before that evening, but now, this old intimacy again established, he was, in a restless sort of way, happier. As they drove home, she slid her hand into his pocket like a cunning child and said: "Osborn, I want a fiver awf'ly badly; lend me one." And it was pleasure to him to pull out a handful of money and let her pick out the gold.

"I'll pay you back quite soon," she said, lying; and he replied:

"You know you won't, you naughty girl; and you know I don't want you to, either."

She kissed him good night with the facility of her type, in the taxicab as they crossed a dark corner.

"Less lonely now?" she queried.

"I don't care who denies it," said Osborn, "a man's got to have a woman in his life; he's just got to. If one drives him...."

"Poor boy!" she said in her murmurous way.

He left her at her door and kept the cab to drive him to the nearest Tube station. A strange excitement filled him as he looked ahead to the direction in which he was drifting. What did it matter, anyway? He was almost in the position of a man without ties.

"'Make your own life,'" his wife had said, "'I have all I want in mine.'"

"Well, I'll make it," said Osborn as he journeyed homewards.

The flat was alight, expecting his coming, though everyone was in bed. The fire had been made up, and his whisky decanter and soda siphon stood by a plate of sandwiches on the dining-room table. Marie was looking after him infernally, defiantly well, he thought, as he splashed whisky irritably into a tumbler. It was almost as though she were making all she did utter for her: "See how perfectly I fulfil my duties! See how comfortable you are! You've nothing whatever to grumble about. Make your own life and I'll make mine."

He drank his whisky, thinking of Roselle. "Here's to Sunday!" was his silent toast. Yet it was not she who tugged tormentingly at his heart.

But he was like a child who has been put into the corner, revengefully tearing the wallpaper.

He wanted someone to be sorry; very, very sorry.

There was dead silence in the flat. What a lonely place!

How queer life was!

He went sullenly to his room, where his son was sleeping peacefully.

CHAPTER XXV

RECOMPENSE

Osborn did not tell his wife that he was going to be away from home all Sunday. What did it matter to her? How could his plans, in any degree, be her plans, which he understood were, for the future, to be made independently of him? But though he asked himself this, he was wishing violently that she should care; he was hoarding up the announcement of his Sunday absence to spring upon her and make her blench. He hardly understood his purpose himself, so vague and racked, so resentful and remorseful were his thoughts. But that was in his heart—to surprise, alarm and worry her. If only, when he observed casually: "I shall not be in at all to-day," he could see her colour quicken and the jealous curiosity in her eyes! If only he could set her longing to cry:

"Why?"

And then he could reply: "I'm motoring," and she might ask further: "Where?"

And then he could drop out casually: "I'm running down to Brighton."

Would she inquire: "With whom?"

He rehearsed these things in spite of himself.

On Saturday he returned to lunch. It was his old way on Saturdays, and the afternoon was free. A soft November day breathed beneficently over London. In the morning, he hardly knew why, he asked the senior partner whether he could take out a car to-day as well as Sunday. He drove home to Hampstead in the blue Runaway, with its silver fittings winking in the sun, and garaged it near by.

He came in rather morosely, and was thoughtful over lunch, saying little, till at the end of the meal he lifted his eyes to his wife's tranquil face and said suddenly:

"I brought a car home. I want to take you for a run."

"And me, Daddy!" George shouted, but his father shook his head.

"No," he said doggedly, "not to-day. I just want mother."

"I'd love to come," said Marie readily.

Osborn was in a strange humour, like a fractious child, and she did more than bear with it. She ignored it altogether. As they drove out of London, the business of threading the maze of traffic kept him from talking even if he would, but when they had run into silence and the peace of the country, he was still quiet, gazing straight in front of him, his hat jammed down over his eyes and his jaw set rigid. At last he heard her voice saying:

"Isn't it lovely? I wish we had a car."

"We can have one if you like."

He drove on fast. Sometime this afternoon, when she had tasted the joy of the day and the comfort of the car, he would tell her about Sunday—no details, only the bleak blank fact:

"I shall be away all to-morrow; I'm motoring down to Brighton."

They went through Epsom and Leatherhead to more rustic villages beyond, and he pulled up at last on the summit of a great hill, fringed on either side with trees.

"This is a jolly place to stop for tea," he said, breaking his long silence. "I've got everything here."

As he pulled out a tea basket from the back of the car she watched him calmly. She still thought him excessively good-looking. In their engaged days they had often escaped into the country—but on foot—and picnicked together; each had known the other to be the most wonderful person in the world. Now that love had passed the memory was well worth keeping, and she enjoyed it quietly as she sat in the car, looking down upon the back of his head bent over his task. He sat down again, opening the basket between them, and set up the spirit stove and lighted it for her to boil the minute kettle upon it. While she did this, it was his turn to watch her; and presently from his moroseness he said in a very soft voice:

"It's like old days, isn't it?"

"Only we're more gorgeous."

"You're enjoying it?"

"Immensely. Why wouldn't you take George?"

"I didn't want him. Did you?"

"I always want him."

"We're going to stay out till long past his bedtime."

"Are we?"

"There's a moon. It's tophole for motoring. I'm—taking this car out again to-morrow."

"Are you?"

He shot a glance at her and postponed the matter. They drove on fast and far, only turning when the moon was up and stars were in the sky. They arrived again upon the summit of the great hill, the fringing trees now black in the light of fairy whiteness, before he spoke again of what filled his brain.

He drew up the car and, turning a look of inquiry upon him, she saw him bending towards her, his eyes fixed upon her face. He flung out an arm along the back of the seat, behind her.

"Marie," he said, "I want to ask you something which you can't answer."

"Why ask it, then?"

"Because I'm going to. It's this: where are we two going?"

"You're right," she said slowly, "I can't answer that."

"What's the meaning of this dreadful indifference? This extraordinary indifference?"

"It's not extraordinary; if you'd only believe me it's the indifference thousands of women feel for their husbands; only in our case special circumstances—your absence, mother's money—have made me able to realise it."

"Well, if thousands of women have this indifference, which you say isn't so very extraordinary, for their husbands, what—what's the way all these chaps win these thousands of wives back?"

"They don't."

"But I want to win you back. Here and now, humiliating as it sounds, I declare I'd follow you around on my knees if—if it meant getting you."

"It wouldn't. I'm very sorry. Do you think you love me?"

His hand dropped down heavily on her shoulder.

"Yes!"

"I wish I loved you, but I don't. You—you've tired me out. I suppose that's it."

"Very well, I'll take what you say. But I've another question. Don't you guess where all this is driving me?"

"Don't hold me like that, Osborn."

"I'll only do it a few minutes. Answer my question. What do you expect of me?"

"Absolutely nothing," she owned.

"And you don't care what I do; where I go; what happens?"

"It's curious; I don't. Once if I thought you met, looked at, spoke to, any other woman prettier or better dressed than I could be, I suffered torture. But now, I'm through with it. I'm sorry it should be so."

"But that's that," said Osborn roughly, with a brief laugh.

He pulled her to him strongly, kissing her.

"I love you, you know. But if you've no more use for me—"

"Well?"

"Don't expect too much of me, that's all."

"I have told you that I expect nothing."

"Then you ought to!" he broke out angrily.

"I thought men appreciated complaisant wives."

"Complaisant? It's callousness; don't-careness. You mean me to understand, then, that you've reckoned with everything?"

"No, I don't. I mean you to understand that I don't trouble to do any reckoning about you at all."

As she uttered the words she was conscious of the brutality of them; but she was speaking truth, representing those feelings which had taken the place of love-emotions in her heart; and what else was there to say?

"I must say," he said, "you're candid."

"I want to be. If we once thoroughly understood each other we'd shake down better and go our ways in peace. I don't want formal separation, for the children's sake."

"Formal separation? If we had that, because you refused to live with me, desertion would be constituted and *I'd* get the children, you know."

"I wonder," she said, starting. "I should fight."

He saw the set meditation on her face under the moonlight.

"Would there be nothing I could say?" she asked, lifting her eyes to his. "I wonder if there'd be no countercharge ingenuity could bring?"

She did not mean what occurred to him; the things in her mind were of too untechnical a nature to find a hearing in the divorce courts; but as she asked her question suddenly his heart seemed to rock and to stand still for a space, while he shifted his eyes rapidly from hers and gazed straight out over the steering-wheel, down the hill, into the blue-white moonlit distance.

Roselle!

Who would believe his innocent tale if he stood up in that sad court which recorded the most human of all frailties, and said: "We travelled together here and we travelled together there; and I defrayed these expenses and those expenses; and I've kissed her; and yes, we've certainly been alone in very compromising circumstances, but I ask you to believe that technically my marital honour is intact, and that I've been true and faithful to my wife"?

The fun and the folly which had been so worth while, so like a draught of wine on the cold journey through middle-class pauperism, now appeared stripped of their carnival trappings.

It was only folly which stared back at him now, and she had become ugly; sickening and wholly undesirable. Folly was utter trash. He replied to Marie in a voice so studied as to rivet her attention, asking:

"What do you mean?"

She looked at him, and knowledge came to her, born of a swift intuition raised by his obvious difficulties. In a flash she knew; but even while she knew, she didn't care; it was lamentable, how dead she was.

"Oh," she hesitated, a faint smile crossing her lips, "I mean nothing. Please don't suppose I wish to make your private affairs mine."

So great was his want that she should feel, should ask and demand him to give up his secrets, that he was impelled to declare:

"Marie, if you were to ask me, I'd tell you everything about this last year. Every little thing. There should be nothing kept back from you."

"I don't ask, Osborn," she replied very gently.

Silence settled down upon them. They remained at the top of the great hill, each staring down it into the long space of unearthly clearness and light. Automatically he withdrew his arm from her shoulders where it had been resting heavily and dropped his hand on the steering-wheel. After awhile he said:

"By the way, I'm going out with this car to-morrow."

"So you told me," she answered.

"Had I mentioned it before?" he said thickly. "Well ... I shall be out all day."

"Thank you for telling me. It's considerate of you. We make a little difference in the catering if you're out."

He clenched his hand round the wheel.

"I'm running down to Brighton; but I shall get back to town for dinner; late motoring's pretty cold in November. I shall be dining at Pagani's—where we used to go so much, you remember."

"I remember. I hope you'll have a fine day."

He gave a savage twitch to the hand-brake, let in his clutch, and in a moment or two the car ran forward.

"It beats me," he whispered to himself. "It—just—beats—me."

His whisper was lost in the rush of the car down the hill. His wife had leaned back snugly under the fur rug and her profile in the moonlight was serene, neither happy nor unhappy, but absolutely complacent. He seemed to get a glimpse of their future, with her figure travelling away into a far distance, divergent from his.

That was marriage.

Two strangers met each other; fused, became of one flesh and one spirit, kindled a big hearth fire called home; travelled away from each other; and two strangers died. Marriage!

The next day, Sunday, he took the Runaway out of her

garage early, and drove, earlier than the hour Roselle had mentioned, to the flat which she shared with another woman swimming down the same stream as herself and catching at the same straws.

She was not dressed; when a charwoman let him in upon the Sunday morning debris of the place, Roselle's voice rang shrill and ill-tempered down the corridor.

"Osborn, that you already? I'm not dressed; I've not breakfasted; I'm not even awake. Just put your head in here and see."

Following the direction of the voice, he opened a door a few inches, and put his head round. An array of women's litter confronted him strewn on every available chair, on dressing-table and floor. The windows must have been closed, or nearly so; the blinds were down; there was a faint reek of perfume and spirits and stale cigarette smoke in the room; and in two narrow tumbled beds were two women, one whose head was still drowsy on her pillow, and Roselle, who sat up in a pale blue nightgown with a black ribbon girdled high about the waist, and her raven hair in a mop over her eyes.

"What a fug!" said Osborn.

"All right," said Roselle, "go away, then! I shall be an hour dressing. You'd better wait in the sitting-room; there's a Sunday paper there, and a fire if the woman's lighted it."

The woman was kindling the fire hastily and grumbling when he went into the sitting-room, still in its state of early morning frowsiness. The curtains had been pulled aside to let in the morning, but the windows were not yet open, and empty liqueur glasses had not been removed from the table.

May Edginton

"It's early for visitors," grumbled the charwoman. "I don't reckon to come till nine on a Sunday morning, and I start with the washing-up, and none of the rooms ain't done."

"I don't care a straw," said Osborn irritably, walking to a window. He flung it up and heard the drab creature behind him shudder resentfully at the inrush of raw air. He put his hands in his pockets, staring out and emitting a tuneless whistle. All was awry, unprofitable and stale as the cigarette smoke of which the place reeked.

Roselle was not an hour dressing, in spite of her threat. By eleven they were away.

*　*　*　*　*

It happened that the only woman Osborn had taken down to Brighton for the day, before he took Roselle, was Marie; and harmless as the proceeding was, it affected him for a while as any first plunge affects a man. It was like taking a first step which signified something. As they sat at lunch, he looked around him and recognised easily the types which he saw. Everybody was doing what he was doing; everybody was out for pleasure with a flavouring of risk in it. Powder and rouge and fur coats were like a uniform, so universal they were; and as he looked around and saw the army of pleasure-women whose company men purchased upon the basis on which you could purchase things at the Stores, his would-be gaiety failed him somewhat and he was a little weary.

Roselle found him dull.

They lunched, and talked, and the talk had to have a silly meretricious flavour in it which tired him further; in the afternoon they walked on the front; and they went to another hotel for tea. There was a blaring band and much noise and laughter from all the pleasure-people. The air was the air of a hothouse where strange, forced and unnatural exotics bloom to please strange, forced and unnatural tastes.

Osborn did not know why he found himself so sick, and so soon, of what, to the woman at his side, was the breath of her life; he was vexed and disappointed that to him the day was so stupid and so savourless.

If the pleasures of men failed him, what was left?

He was thinking definitely while they drove on the much-trafficked road back to more gaudy lights and noise, the lights and noise of town; and he wondered how to fill the emptiness of his heart, how to appease the restless burning of his brain, and stifle before they could cry out all the dear things his soul wanted. He looked at the woman by his side, insatiable, greedy, stupid, nothing to all appearances but a beautiful body, and he asked himself if she could do it, or if she could not. And while he knew, right down in him, that she could not fulfil a fraction of his needs, he desired so much to believe that she could, that, in spite of his weariness with this miscalled business of pleasure, he made hot love to her all the way back.

Over the dinner-table at Pagani's he advanced a farther step upon the road which he was resolved to walk with her, failing other companionship.

"Roselle," he said, deliberately, "this isn't enough. How long are you going to play about with me like a beautiful pussy cat? I've been very good, haven't I? When I think of what a good boy I've been I could laugh." He laughed deeply. "You know, I could love you a lot. Why don't you give me a trial? There isn't anyone else, is there?"

He was amazed at himself to feel jealousy hot in him as he put the question.

There was no one else at the moment; but she sat thinking and playing with the stem of her wineglass, and keeping a half-cynical, half-simpering silence. It was the veil with which she shrouded her stupidity while she debated the *pros* and *cons* with herself as deliberately as she had spoken.

"No," she said at last, with a long, meaning look which meant nothing. "No, there is no one else, Osborn." Her sigh ruffled the chiffons on her breast.

"I'm going to Paris for the firm next month; it'll only be a week-end. Come, too? I'll give you a good time."

"I'll see," she murmured, her stupidity not dense enough to give a promise thus early. A month? A long, long while, an age, in which other things might turn up.

"So'll I," he said, looking into her eyes. "I'll see that you come."

"I haven't a rag to wear."

"You'll have all Paris to choose from."

"I do want a couple of hats," she said, with the worldly yet childish *naivete* of her class; "I'm going to Bristol in panto—at Christmas, you know."

"I'll come down."

She was conscienceless, like the rest of her type. She knew, her observation had told her long ago, that this man had ties, domestic relations, duties; all of which mattered nothing to her. Before her wants and desires, momentary though they might be, all considerations flew like thistledown before strong wind.

A Nero among women, like the rest of her pleasure-sisters, she was planned for destruction and she went upon her way destroying. The loudest cry could not reach her, nor the greatest sorrow touch her; nor could broken hearts block the path to the most fleeting of her desires.

She cared not who wept; as she had no faith, nor power for pity, so she had no tears.

She took Osborn Kerr into her hands.

She said idly, to pass the time, but softly, just as if there was some meaning behind the question: "What made you think there was anyone else, dear?"

He looked at her and spoke rather hoarsely, under the influence of the matter in hand: "Oh well; there might have been. Roselle, do you think you can love me?"

"I could," she answered. She assimilated the details of a near-by toilette. "But—"

"Don't let's have any 'buts.'"

She had no subtlety, only the power of making what she said subtle; and she said:

"I don't know that loving is wise."

Osborn was in her hands; thrown upon her mercy; a beggar for just so much as she cared to give. He answered:

"Who cares about wisdom? It's the only thing worth doing, anyway."

Roselle began pulling her fur coat up over her arms; it was past ten o'clock; and on Sundays she went to bed early, to counteract as far as might be the results of all the late nights during the week.

"Take me home," she demanded.

In the taxicab Osborn took her into his arms and began whispering to her things to which she did not listen; had he only known it, she was extremely sleepy from the effects of all the fresh air during the day, but triumphantly he took her inertia for the surrender for which he had, so suddenly, craved.

He was begging for that promise about Paris, but she would not give it. A month? What an age it was—any good thing might happen.

She would not let him come into the flat. "I'm too sleepy," she declared. She stood before him on the inner side of her threshold, with a faint smile on her face that was as pale as magnolia flowers, and her eyelids drooping heavily; she put out a lazy hand against his chest and warded off his entry. When she sent him away, he felt on fire, from the last look of her, thus.

CHAPTER XXVI

COMPREHENSION

When Marie had waved to her husband a stereotyped good-bye, and had kissed schoolboy George a warm one, on Monday morning, when leisurely quiet had come again to the flat, and as she still lingered over her newspaper, the door bell rang and Mrs. Desmond Rokeby was admitted.

Julia—fresh, heavenly, without a frown, without a care, without a regret—blew into Number Thirty like a Christmas rose and clasped Marie in a glad embrace.

"It's early; it's shockingly early, but I came up with Desmond this morning and knowing your habits—you *do* still wheel your own perambulator on the Heath, don't you, at eleven-thirty?—I rushed here first."

"How splendid you look!"

"I feel splendid!" The two women stood at arm's length, eyeing each other inquisitively and frankly, and Julia's ingenuous blush was the reflection of a divine dawn.

She sat down, put her feet on the fender, loosened her furs.

"I may stay and talk?"

"May you *not*! Oh! I'm glad to see you—it seemed as if your honeymoon was going to last for ever."

"It's not over."

"That's what we all say."

"Don't be cynical, dear," said the new Julia.

Marie waved this away with a brief laugh. "I want all your news," she demanded. "Where are you living? What are your plans? What's the house like, and where did you get your furniture?"

"We've got a wee house, the dearest thing, near Onslow Gardens, and we've not finished furnishing yet; we're proceeding with it this afternoon. I'm lunching with Desmond, and then we're going furnishing together. Desmond loves it."

"And you—you're happy?"

"Oh, Marie! I was never so happy in my life."

The baby rose from its play at the other side of the dining-room, and, tottering to her mother, begged to be lifted upon her lap.

"I only want one of *those*," said Julia, regarding the mite.

"That will come," Marie replied with a forced gaiety.

"Desmond took me for a motoring honeymoon," said Julia. "As you know, we had made no plans. There wasn't time. At least, *I* hadn't, but it seemed he'd got them all mapped out in his head, the wicked thing! We had a simply lovely time, and coming home is lovelier. I adore pottering round a house, arranging this and that, and ordering the dinner."

"*You* enjoy it?"

"Why shouldn't I?"

"But you hated the domestic life; you were always up in arms at the thought of marriage; you loathed even hearing of a wedding. You used to talk of slavery ... don't you remember?"

"Ah, but—that was before I married."

"Then, what do you think now?"

"It's the only life," Julia stated with final conviction. "It's meant for us all; we were made for it; and we're never truly happy otherwise. Desmond and I have talked over all these things, and I understand a lot which I didn't understand before."

Marie stroked the baby's curly head without replying; she held its feet in her hand, and caressed them, and patted its small fat legs, and coaxed a gurgle from it. But even while the baby ravished her heart, the heart was busy with the bride before her and the bridal raptures which she had known, only to lose upon the wayside where so many bridal raptures lie dead and dying; outworn and weary. Tears to which she had long been a stranger rose in her eyes, and formed one of those big hurtful lumps in her throat, so that she would not trust her voice to Julia's ears.

That dreadful softness of longing—she had thought she would never know it again, never more be covered with it like a shore beneath the inward flow of the sea.

"Desmond wants to meet Osborn," said Julia. "He rang him up on Saturday morning, but he was engaged. Won't you and your husband come to dinner with me and my husband one evening at Onslow Gardens?"

Julia uttered the words "my husband" with a pleasure which she could not secrete from the eyes of Marie. Had she not known it, too? Had she not once delighted in saying, "My husband thinks." ... "My husband says." ... "My husband does...." simply for the crass joy of hearing the sound?

Julia went on:

"When can it be? Let's fix a date early. Do, there's a dear! There'll be a peculiar joy to Desmond and me in having in our own house Osborn and you, the very two people who always told us the truth about marriage, and urged us to go and do likewise!"

"The truth?" Marie echoed.

"How wonderful it was!" Julia said sublimely.

As Julia sat there, glowing and content, Marie recognised that she had forgotten all the sad things she had been told and that only the glory remained. Julia had harked back to that first year in which the young Kerrs had chanted together:

"Marriage is the only life."

And separately:

"A woman can be an angel."

"A man a brute? A man's a god."

Julia continued: "To-day's Monday. We're still furnishing, of course, as I told you, but that won't matter, will it? Can you both come to dinner on Thursday and see the two happiest people in the world?"

"Edifying as the sight must be—" Marie began with smiling lips. But then she put the baby down and, covering her face with her hands, cried bitterly: "Would the two happiest people in the world like to see the two miserablest people in it?"

While her face was still covered, she felt Julia's arms about her, heard her disconcerted voice begging to be told. But when at last Marie looked up, with tears salt and bitter on her cheeks, it was to reply sombrely:

"There's nothing to tell."

"What has happened?" Julia begged.

Marie said slowly, twisting her hands: "I felt, when I came home, after a joy-year which he didn't want to give me the remotest chance of sharing, that—that I could never forgive him for all those years of losing my health and looks, those years of work and worry and child-bearing; those years of quarrelling and grudging; those dead, drab, ugly, ordinary married years. And so...."

"And so, my dear?"

"And so I have not forgiven him. He killed the love in me. There is no more for him."

"If there is no more," said Julia, with a sudden instinct, "why do you cry, my dear? And why does this hurt you so?"

"To—to see you so happy," Marie whispered up to her, "to see you and Desmond as Osborn and I once were."

"And as you want to be again, my dear, if you only knew it."

"It's too late for that."

"Marie, what do you mean?"

"I told him to make his own life. I'm not a dog-in-the-manger woman, anyway. What I don't want I'll give away freely."

"What can you mean?"

"I've given him away." The knowledge that had come upon her in the car that Saturday afternoon made her voice grim. "He's gone elsewhere," she said; "I feel it; I know it. A wife can sense these things as a barometer senses rain."

"Oh, Marie!" Julia whispered, and for a while there was silence in the room, broken only by the chuckles of the baby-girl. Both women looked down, at the sound, upon the fluffy head and Julia asked, still in a bated whisper:

"What do you think you'll do?"

"Nothing," said Marie, "above all, nothing. The children will keep us under the same roof. We shall be like thousands of other married people, privately free; publicly tied up tight together in the same dear old knot."

Her brief laugh trembled.

"Marie, you know you think it *is* a dear old knot."

Marie did not reply. After awhile she said:

"We're not coming to dinner with you for a very long while. This morning I've come nearer hating you, Julia, than I've ever done in our lives. I want to hate you because you're so happy; because you've got the love which I want but can never have again."

"Are you sure of that?"

"Sure, my dear? Sure as the world. You can't have that kind of love without giving a return, and I've none to give. It's dead; gone; dried up. I don't know where it is. But perhaps there's a root of it left somewhere—enough to make me envy you."

Ann the maid entered to fetch the baby to be dressed for outdoors, and Julia received the hint sorrowfully.

"Isn't there anything Desmond and I could do?" she asked, as she stood up and muffled her furs about her throat.

"There's nothing anyone can do."

"I wanted to talk about a lot of things—ask you about your fortunes, and everything, darling; but this has driven it all clean out of my head."

"Our fortunes are on the upgrade, thanks, Julia. Never again will I spoil my hands and let my teeth and hair go; it's all over—that part of it."

Julia kissed Marie very tenderly, as she used to do. "I shall come again soon," she called with an anxious vivacity, as she waved her muff in a good-bye signal from a bend in the cold grey stairs.

But Marie went in again very quickly and shut the door. She stood with her hands clenched and her breast heaving, tears running unchecked down her cheeks.

She stood on tiptoe to peer into the glass over the mantel, and the storm in her face quickened the storm in her heart. Raging jealousy entered and possessed her. It whirled about like a tornado, scattering before it all that was orderly, that was lesser and weaker than itself. Marie Kerr was taken up in the grip of it, and driven along upon a headlong course which she could not pause to consider.

As she looked at herself in the glass, she cried aloud furiously: "No one shall ever take what is mine!"

Little pulses began to hammer in her, which had not so hammered since Osborn started upon his joy-year. No more could she bear contemplation of Julia and her delight. She ran along the corridor to her room, calling to the maid:

"You'll have to take baby out this morning; and do the shopping; and, oh! *everything*. I've got to go out, and I don't know when I'll be back."

With the door of the pink bedroom shut upon her, she dressed herself with trembling speed. Her new black velvet suit, her furs, her violets, her amethyst earrings, her silk stockings, and suede shoes and white gloves! Thank God for clothes when a woman was out upon the chase!

She whispered with an anger that was fiendish; that rose from its dust right back from the age of barbarism, and came at her call:

"No one shall take what is mine!"

She swept money lavishly into her bag; no expenses of locomotion were going to stand in her way. She flew down the cold grey stairs and out into the street. Because the Tube would be quicker than a cab, she travelled upon it; and people looked at her fevered cheeks, her shining eyes, wondering what drove this lovely woman, and upon what errand. Excitement beautified her and gave to her a transcendent quality which drew all eyes.

Uplifted as she was, yet she noticed this homage, and her woman's soul leapt, exulting. It was like applause; like a great voice encouraging, cheering her on. It gave her pride and the supreme vanity to pursue her way.

She left the Tube at Charing Cross, and drove in a taxicab to her husband's place of business. One or two urbane men, strangers to her, hurried forward as she alighted from the cab, inquiring her pleasure, and she said, smiling: "I want my husband; I'm Mrs. Kerr."

As she said "My husband," delight took her, absurdly like Julia's. She checked a laugh at it.

Osborn had gone out to lunch.

"Did they know where?"

"I heard him telephone, booking a table for two at the Royal Red," one of the men said, and bit off his words suddenly as he caught the humorous warning look of the other. The look said: "We're all the same; don't get the poor fellow into trouble."

She understood it and again checked a laugh. She thanked them, jumped into the taxicab, and as the two men hurried after her, vying with each other as to which should do her the service of closing the door, she leaned forward and said buoyantly:

"Yes, you've given my husband away badly! The table *wasn't* for me! Tell the driver to go to the Royal Red."

She could joke about the matter, so complete she felt her power to be. She had in her, strong and vital, an irresistible feeling of achievements to come, as if nothing in the world could defeat her purpose, nor gainsay her will; it was like an inspiration which cannot be wrong. And as she entered the restaurant, and swept her eyes over the ground floor, she found at once those whom she looked for—her husband and the other woman.

As she went forward slowly, calm now, confident and at ease, she remembered, with a rising and fierce sense of satisfaction, the raven hair, the high shoulders and white face, the attractive insolence of her rival. They had been before upon the same battle-ground; but now the battle was level; nay, it was more than level; it waxed in favour of the wife, who, with every weapon to her hand, advanced leisurely to employ them against the woman who had none save that of her stupid beauty, allied to the strategy of her greed.

Marie came right up and stood by their table before Osborn perceived her; then she smiled.

She stepped into the breach of silence promptly, with sweet speech.

"I hope," she said, "I'm not intruding? But I'm shopping, and I was told you had come here, and I wanted lunch, so I followed. Do introduce me to this lady and give me some."

He stammered, somehow:

"Miss Dates, my wife."

Marie sat down.

"Where are you?" she said, glancing at the menu. "The roast—I'll join you there. Do tell me I'm not intruding, both of you. I am conscious of this being a horrible thing to do and I want to be reassured."

"Delighted to see you," Roselle chimed glibly, sweeping the wife with a look of comprehending fury to which even her slug nature could rouse itself upon such an occasion.

"If you'd rung me up, dear," said Osborn to his wife, "I should have been charmed to take you anywhere you liked."

"And broken your appointment with me!" Roselle supplied suddenly, and the gage was down between the two women.

Roselle Dates eyed the wife warily and feared her. And the measure of her hate matched that of her fear. Leaning forward, her white chin on her white hands, she cooed across the table:

"But I'd have forgiven him, Mrs. Kerr, if it was only for the sake of the jolly time he gave me yesterday."

"At Brighton?" Marie smiled across at Osborn.

He nodded. "I told you I was going."

"Do you like the car?" Marie asked Roselle sweetly.

"She's a duck," said the other woman, her eyes snapping,

May Edginton

"but of course yesterday wasn't my first acquaintance with her. I know her every trick well. When we were in New York people were so struck by her neatness in traffic."

Osborn started involuntarily, exclaiming as involuntarily:

"Roselle!"

"What?" she asked, turning a stare upon him.

He fidgeted uncomfortably. "Don't be an ass," he said. "Marie—"

"What, dear?" asked his wife.

Again he fidgeted. "When Miss Dates mentions being in New York—" he began.

"And Chicago and all through Canada from Montreal to the West," said Roselle, continuing upon the breakneck course she seemed to have chosen in a moment.

"She means to tell you," said Osborn doggedly, "that she was doing a concert tour which coincided almost, though not quite, with my movements, and that having met her on board, we—we did some motoring together."

Breathless, he awaited the working of the most amazing situation in which he had ever found himself, and he had not long to wait. He did not know how much his wife knew nor what might be her summing up; he did not know that during the night Roselle had slept upon the problem of himself and had concluded he was too good to lose; he did not understand in the least what motives were actuating these two women; the flaming and insolent resentment of Roselle at the other's mere presence; the calm and pretty pose of his wife.

He gazed at each in embarrassed bewilderment, and Roselle, her chin still on her palms, and her eyes bright and stony, commented on his explanation. She drawled:

"Osborn, you're a liar. Your wife knows as well as I do that she could divorce you to-morrow."

"But Miss Dates would be a fool, which I am sure she is not," said the wife's pretty voice, "if she imagines I would do it."

Husband and wife looked at each other across the table, and the question in the eyes of one, the answer in the eyes of the other, were naked and unashamed. They could be read by the woman between them. And regardless of her presence, they asked and answered each other in eager words.

"Marie, do you want me?"

"Yes; I want you."

Osborn turned to Roselle Dates. He turned to her as to something tiresome, hindering the true business of the hour. "Roselle," he said crisply, "my wife wishes to lunch with me alone. Will you go; or shall we?"

"I'll go," she replied very slowly, "but I shall expect some sort of explanation."

He stood up and put on her coat and their eyes were almost level, looking right into each other's.

"An explanation? You won't get it," he whispered back.

"It's due to me. You're a rotter."

"There's nothing due to you," he replied with a sudden air of relief at the discovery.

An abounding idea of happiness to come filled him as he moved beside Roselle down the crowded restaurant. As they went he said: "It's all over; I'm a fool no longer. You understand there's only one woman in the world for me and that's my wife. And since she has some use for me again ... Goodbye!"

He held out his hand, but she refused it angrily. She stood, biting her lip, tapping her foot, her head averted, upon the kerb; her attitude of pique was amusingly familiar to him; often it had gained for her the gratification of some petulant desire; but now all that he wanted was to hurry back to the table they had left.

There were real things; and trash; well defined.

"Taxi!" he said in a ringing voice to the commissionaire.

"Where are you going, Roselle?"

"Home," she answered venomously.

He put her in, paid the driver and gave the direction. "I'm sorry you had not quite finished your lunch," he said perfunctorily, looking in.

She bit her lip and averted her head; but she was aware, in spite of her refusal to see, or hear, or speak to him, that before her cab had started he was returning back with a swift step into the restaurant.

There sat the wife who held all the cards—as wives do if they will only play them aright. She was not smiling, nor exultant, nor blatant over it, but triumph was in every line of her as she waited there, slender, lovely, and sartorially exquisite. From the tip of her shoe to the crown of her hat she was conquest.

He sat down, thinking over words to say, and she looked at him critically, yet eagerly, and waited for him to speak.

He cleared his throat.

"Marie," he said, "hang lunch—until you understand me. This has been an extraordinary quarter of an hour. I didn't know you had it in you. You women—you have me fairly beat. I just want—I hope—I long for you to believe me, when I tell you that rot she talked about divorce ... that is to say, I swear to you, that, except on circumstantial evidence, you wouldn't have the ghost of a case. But, Marie, on circumstantial evidence, I—I don't know that a judge and jury wouldn't convict me."

His wife was still looking at him critically, eagerly; and he met her eyes full, and saw, down in the depths wherein had been his delight, a great faith.

She believed him.

He tingled with joy. "I've been a fool," he weighed out slowly. "We are; and we—we want looking after, you know. We can't stand our wives forsaking us. We ask a lot of you, I suppose. Yes, it's a lot."

"Well," she murmured, "we've always got it to give. We're made that way."

"Not all of you," he denied, with a fleeting thought of Roselle.

"Tell me," Marie asked, "what were you and she talking of so earnestly when I came in? It won't matter anyway—but I'm just curious to know."

"Shall I tell you?"

"I've asked."

He answered very slowly, as if still weighing his words: "We were talking of a coming trip I have to make to Paris; I was asking her if she wouldn't come, too."

A little colour rose in his wife's face.

"I'll come instead," she said clearly.

*　*　*　*　*

Osborn Kerr let himself into No. 30, Welham Mansions, laden with packages. He knew not what thank-offerings to make to heaven, so he made them to his family. Flowers and chocolate boxes hung about him.

He whistled gaily.

Only three hours ago he had parted from her after that memorable lunch and, now, here he was again with her in the place called home.

At the sound of his key she came out of her bedroom, dressed for dinner. The flat was quiet save for homely sounds from the kitchen. Osborn took his wife in his arms and kissed her. He stated exuberantly: "I came home early; I just had to."

They went into the sitting-room hand in hand, and she sat

down on the chesterfield before the fire. He did not want to sit down; he was too happy and restless and urgent. Now and again he hung over the back of the couch, to caress her, or whisper love words in her ear, and now and again he walked about touching this or that familiar object and finding new attractions in each. It was like the first coming to that flat when the very taps over the sink had been superior to all other taps under the rosy flicker of the new-kindled fire of love.

What an evening it was! He kept saying, breaking away from some other thing, to say it: "I can't think this is all true. I can't think that you are just you, and I am just I, all over again. And that we're really going to be the two happiest souls on earth!"

He came to Grannie Amber's old rosewood piano and stood touching it reverently. "There's a little thing I heard," he exclaimed suddenly, "that I'd like to sing to you. It's called 'Please,' and it's just what I'm saying to you all the time."

He sat down to vamp an odd accompaniment indifferently, but Marie was not listening for the accompaniment. It was his voice which she wanted, and gave her ears to hear; and he sang:

"Oh, Heart-of-all-the-World to me,
I love you more than best;
Then lie so gently in my arms
And droop your head and rest.
My kisses on your dark, dark hair
Nor Time nor tears shall grey;
But the little wandering, laughing loves
They flower beside the way.

"Slender and straight you came to me,

And straight the path you trod;
Your faithfulness was more than faith,
Like the faithfulness of God.
I cannot pay you all I owe,
Though what I owe I pay:
But the little wandering, laughing loves
They flower beside the way.

"So take my life, who gave me all,
Between your so small hands,
With the blind, untaught, unfaltering touch
A woman understands;
And save me, since I would be saved,
And do not let me stray
With the little wandering, laughing loves
That flower beside the way."

"That is the husband's 'Please,'" said Osborn, humbly.

She stood up erect, and cried out: "No one shall take what is mine!"

The door opened, and the maid stood there, saying quietly: "Dinner is served, ma'am."

They went in hand in hand, regardless of her. They sat down and looked at each other under pink candle-shades. The golden-brown curtains were drawn evenly down the whole length of the much-windowed wall, and splashed rich colour against the prevailing cream. The wedding-present silver glittered upon the white cloth. What a dear room it was! How happily appointed and magically ordered!

He adored, across the space, the most darling woman that heaven ever spared to make joy for a mortal man. And she, returning his look with the same verdant wonder at the beauty of all things, saw before her husband and lover; he whom she had chosen to mate with; he who had taught her the beginning of joy; the finest man in the world.

　　　　　May Edginton

Choose from Thousands of 1stWorldLibrary Classics By

A. M. Barnard
Ada Leverson
Adolphus William Ward
Aesop
Agatha Christie
Alexander Aaronsohn
Alexander Kielland
Alexandre Dumas
Alfred Gatty
Alfred Ollivant
Alice Duer Miller
Alice Turner Curtis
Alice Dunbar
Allen Chapman
Alleyne Ireland
Ambrose Bierce
Amelia E. Barr
Amory H. Bradford
Andrew Lang
Andrew McFarland Davis
Andy Adams
Angela Brazil
Anna Alice Chapin
Anna Sewell
Annie Besant
Annie Hamilton Donnell
Annie Payson Call
Annie Roe Carr
Annonaymous
Anton Chekhov
Archibald Lee Fletcher
Arnold Bennett
Arthur C. Benson
Arthur Conan Doyle
Arthur M. Winfield
Arthur Ransome
Arthur Schnitzler
Arthur Train
Atticus
B.H. Baden-Powell
B. M. Bower
B. C. Chatterjee
Baroness Emmuska Orczy
Baroness Orczy
Basil King
Bayard Taylor
Ben Macomber
Bertha Muzzy Bower
Bjornstjerne Bjornson

Booth Tarkington
Boyd Cable
Bram Stoker
C. Collodi
C. E. Orr
C. M. Ingleby
Carolyn Wells
Catherine Parr Traill
Charles A. Eastman
Charles Amory Beach
Charles Dickens
Charles Dudley Warner
Charles Farrar Browne
Charles Ives
Charles Kingsley
Charles Klein
Charles Hanson Towne
Charles Lathrop Pack
Charles Romyn Dake
Charles Whibley
Charles Willing Beale
Charlotte M. Braeme
Charlotte M. Yonge
Charlotte Perkins Stetson
Clair W. Hayes
Clarence Day Jr.
Clarence E. Mulford
Clemence Housman
Confucius
Coningsby Dawson
Cornelis DeWitt Wilcox
Cyril Burleigh
D. H. Lawrence
Daniel Defoe
David Garnett
Dinah Craik
Don Carlos Janes
Donald Keyhoe
Dorothy Kilner
Dougan Clark
Douglas Fairbanks
E. Nesbit
E. P. Roe
E. Phillips Oppenheim
E. S. Brooks
Earl Barnes
Edgar Rice Burroughs
Edith Van Dyne
Edith Wharton

Edward Everett Hale
Edward J. O'Biren
Edward S. Ellis
Edwin L. Arnold
Eleanor Atkins
Eleanor Hallowell Abbott
Eliot Gregory
Elizabeth Gaskell
Elizabeth McCracken
Elizabeth Von Arnim
Ellem Key
Emerson Hough
Emilie F. Carlen
Emily Bronte
Emily Dickinson
Enid Bagnold
Enilor Macartney Lane
Erasmus W. Jones
Ernie Howard Pie
Ethel May Dell
Ethel Turner
Ethel Watts Mumford
Eugene Sue
Eugenie Foa
Eugene Wood
Eustace Hale Ball
Evelyn Everett-green
Everard Cotes
F. H. Cheley
F. J. Cross
F. Marion Crawford
Fannie E. Newberry
Federick Austin Ogg
Ferdinand Ossendowski
Fergus Hume
Florence A. Kilpatrick
Fremont B. Deering
Francis Bacon
Francis Darwin
Frances Hodgson Burnett
Frances Parkinson Keyes
Frank Gee Patchin
Frank Harris
Frank Jewett Mather
Frank L. Packard
Frank V. Webster
Frederic Stewart Isham
Frederick Trevor Hill
Frederick Winslow Taylor

Friedrich Kerst
Friedrich Nietzsche
Fyodor Dostoyevsky
G.A. Henty
G.K. Chesterton
Gabrielle E. Jackson
Garrett P. Serviss
Gaston Leroux
George A. Warren
George Ade
Geroge Bernard Shaw
George Cary Eggleston
George Durston
George Ebers
George Eliot
George Gissing
George MacDonald
George Meredith
George Orwell
George Sylvester Viereck
George Tucker
George W. Cable
George Wharton James
Gertrude Atherton
Gordon Casserly
Grace E. King
Grace Gallatin
Grace Greenwood
Grant Allen
Guillermo A. Sherwell
Gulielma Zollinger
Gustav Flaubert
H. A. Cody
H. B. Irving
H.C. Bailey
H. G. Wells
H. H. Munro
H. Irving Hancock
H. R. Naylor
H. Rider Haggard
H. W. C. Davis
Haldeman Julius
Hall Caine
Hamilton Wright Mabie
Hans Christian Andersen
Harold Avery
Harold McGrath
Harriet Beecher Stowe
Harry Castlemon
Harry Coghill
Harry Houidini

Hayden Carruth
Helent Hunt Jackson
Helen Nicolay
Hendrik Conscience
Hendy David Thoreau
Henri Barbusse
Henrik Ibsen
Henry Adams
Henry Ford
Henry Frost
Henry James
Henry Jones Ford
Henry Seton Merriman
Henry W Longfellow
Herbert A. Giles
Herbert Carter
Herbert N. Casson
Herman Hesse
Hildegard G. Frey
Homer
Honore De Balzac
Horace B. Day
Horace Walpole
Horatio Alger Jr.
Howard Pyle
Howard R. Garis
Hugh Lofting
Hugh Walpole
Humphry Ward
Ian Maclaren
Inez Haynes Gillmore
Irving Bacheller
Isabel Cecilia Williams
Isabel Hornibrook
Israel Abrahams
Ivan Turgenev
J.G.Austin
J. Henri Fabre
J. M. Barrie
J. M. Walsh
J. Macdonald Oxley
J. R. Miller
J. S. Fletcher
J. S. Knowles
J. Storer Clouston
J. W. Duffield
Jack London
Jacob Abbott
James Allen
James Andrews
James Baldwin

James Branch Cabell
James DeMille
James Joyce
James Lane Allen
James Lane Allen
James Oliver Curwood
James Oppenheim
James Otis
James R. Driscoll
Jane Abbott
Jane Austen
Jane L. Stewart
Janet Aldridge
Jens Peter Jacobsen
Jerome K. Jerome
Jessie Graham Flower
John Buchan
John Burroughs
John Cournos
John F. Kennedy
John Gay
John Glasworthy
John Habberton
John Joy Bell
John Kendrick Bangs
John Milton
John Philip Sousa
John Taintor Foote
Jonas Lauritz Idemil Lie
Jonathan Swift
Joseph A. Altsheler
Joseph Carey
Joseph Conrad
Joseph E. Badger Jr
Joseph Hergesheimer
Joseph Jacobs
Jules Vernes
Julian Hawthrone
Julie A Lippmann
Justin Huntly McCarthy
Kakuzo Okakura
Karle Wilson Baker
Kate Chopin
Kenneth Grahame
Kenneth McGaffey
Kate Langley Bosher
Kate Langley Bosher
Katherine Cecil Thurston
Katherine Stokes
L. A. Abbot
L. T. Meade

L. Frank Baum
Latta Griswold
Laura Dent Crane
Laura Lee Hope
Laurence Housman
Lawrence Beasley
Leo Tolstoy
Leonid Andreyev
Lewis Carroll
Lewis Sperry Chafer
Lilian Bell
Lloyd Osbourne
Louis Hughes
Louis Joseph Vance
Louis Tracy
Louisa May Alcott
Lucy Fitch Perkins
Lucy Maud Montgomery
Luther Benson
Lydia Miller Middleton
Lyndon Orr
M. Corvus
M. H. Adams
Margaret E. Sangster
Margret Howth
Margaret Vandercook
Margaret W. Hungerford
Margret Penrose
Maria Edgeworth
Maria Thompson Daviess
Mariano Azuela
Marion Polk Angellotti
Mark Overton
Mark Twain
Mary Austin
Mary Catherine Crowley
Mary Cole
Mary Hastings Bradley
Mary Roberts Rinehart
Mary Rowlandson
M. Wollstonecraft Shelley
Maud Lindsay
Max Beerbohm
Myra Kelly
Nathaniel Hawthrone
Nicolo Machiavelli
O. F. Walton
Oscar Wilde

Owen Johnson
P.G. Wodehouse
Paul and Mabel Thorne
Paul G. Tomlinson
Paul Severing
Percy Brebner
Percy Keese Fitzhugh
Peter B. Kyne
Plato
Quincy Allen
R. Derby Holmes
R. L. Stevenson
R. S. Ball
Rabindranath Tagore
Rahul Alvares
Ralph Bonehill
Ralph Henry Barbour
Ralph Victor
Ralph Waldo Emmerson
Rene Descartes
Ray Cummings
Rex Beach
Rex E. Beach
Richard Harding Davis
Richard Jefferies
Richard Le Gallienne
Robert Barr
Robert Frost
Robert Gordon Anderson
Robert L. Drake
Robert Lansing
Robert Lynd
Robert Michael Ballantyne
Robert W. Chambers
Rosa Nouchette Carey
Rudyard Kipling
Saint Augustine
Samuel B. Allison
Samuel Hopkins Adams
Sarah Bernhardt
Sarah C. Hallowell
Selma Lagerlof
Sherwood Anderson
Sigmund Freud
Standish O'Grady
Stanley Weyman
Stella Benson
Stella M. Francis

Stephen Crane
Stewart Edward White
Stijn Streuvels
Swami Abhedananda
Swami Parmananda
T. S. Ackland
T. S. Arthur
The Princess Der Ling
Thomas A. Janvier
Thomas A Kempis
Thomas Anderton
Thomas Bailey Aldrich
Thomas Bulfinch
Thomas De Quincey
Thomas Dixon
Thomas H. Huxley
Thomas Hardy
Thomas More
Thornton W. Burgess
U. S. Grant
Upton Sinclair
Valentine Williams
Various Authors
Vaughan Kester
Victor Appleton
Victor G. Durham
Victoria Cross
Virginia Woolf
Wadsworth Camp
Walter Camp
Walter Scott
Washington Irving
Wilbur Lawton
Wilkie Collins
Willa Cather
Willard F. Baker
William Dean Howells
William le Queux
W. Makepeace Thackeray
William W. Walter
William Shakespeare
Winston Churchill
Yei Theodora Ozaki
Yogi Ramacharaka
Young E. Allison
Zane Grey